I0695448

The Follower of Flowers

TITLE: The Follower of Flowers

AUTHOR: Natalia Hernandez

ON-SALE DATE: JUNE 27, 2023

Print ISBN: 9798986598352

Digital ISBN: 9798986598338

Book Cover Design by ebooklaunch.com

Map Art by: Chaim Holtjer

For more information, including content warnings, please visit:

www.NataliaHernandezAuthor.com

NATALIA
HERNANDEZ

THE FOLLOWER OF FLOWERS

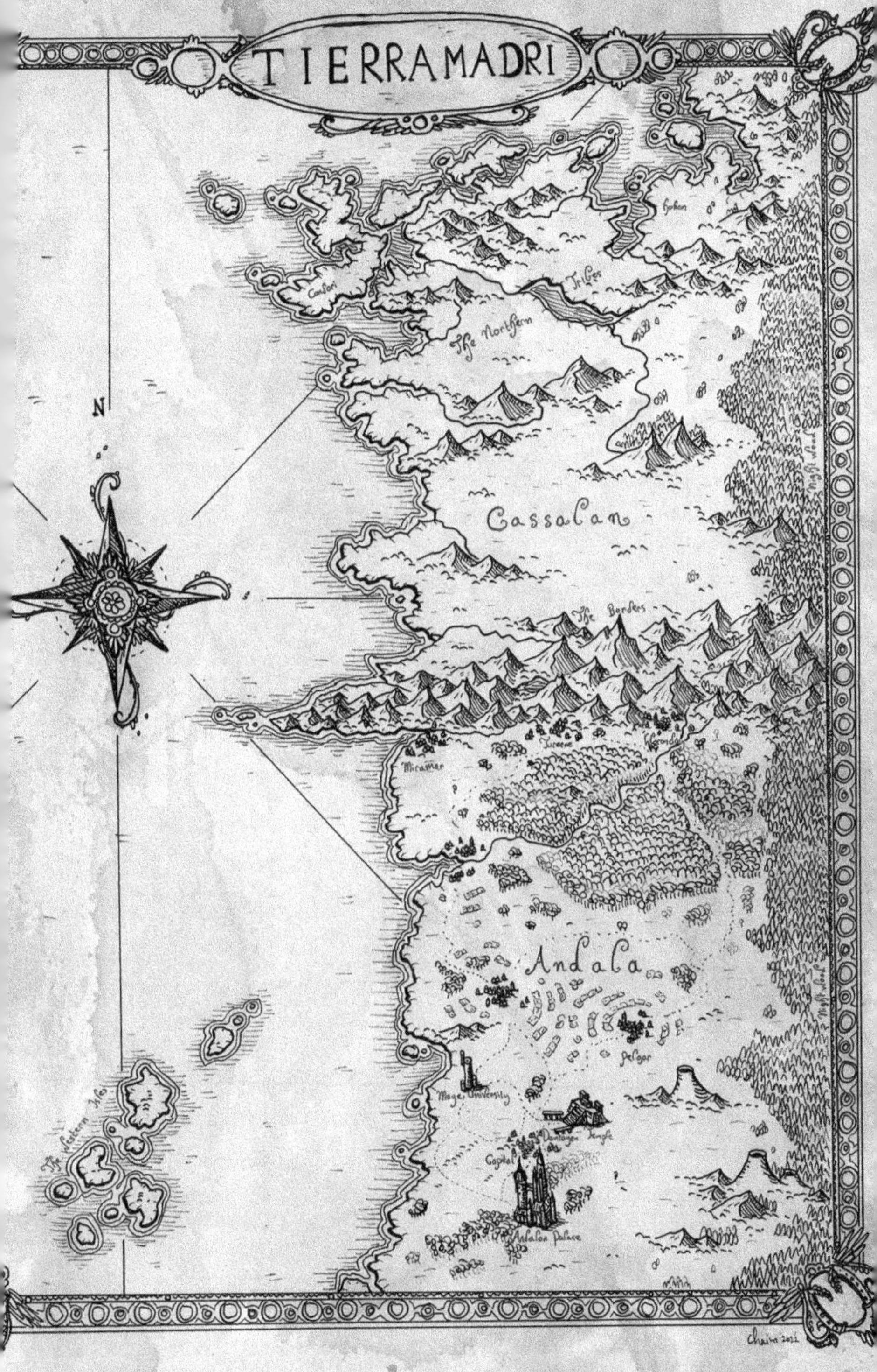

TIERRAMADRI
N
Cortari
Tribes
Gohan
The Northern
Cassalan
The Borders
Serena
Hrondo
Miramar
Andala
Pelgar
Magic University
Capital
Dowager Temple
Andalan Palace
The Western Isles
Magii Wood
Machi Wood

To anyone who has struggled with their identity,
this is a reminder that only you get to decide who you are.

You are enough.

CONTENTS

Fullpage Image   XIII

1. Chapter 1   1

2. Chapter 2   11

3. Chaper 3   24

4. Chapter 4   35

5. Chapter 5   46

6. Chapter 6   59

7. Chapter 7   75

8. Chapter 8   85

9. Chapter 9   97

10. Chapter 10   110

11. Chapter 11   118

12. Chapter 12   129

13. Chapter 13   137

14. Chapter 14   152

15. Chapter 15   166

16. Chapter 16   177

17. Chapter 17   186

18. Chapter 18   200

19. Chapter 19   213

20. Chapter 20   227

21. Chapter 21   238

22. Chapter 22   249

23. Chapter 23   266

24. Chapter 24   279

25. Chapter 25   291

26. Chapter 26   302

27. Chapter 27   311

28. Chapter 28   322

29. Chapter 29   333

30. Chapter 30   344

Acknowledgments   358

CHAPTER 1

JESADIRANY

Jesadirany hadn't even been born yet when a bruja, and a prophecy, ruined her life.

Her mother was no one of any real importance, just a dark-eyed beauty whose husband, like so many others, had been lost to the war. She had grown up in the city of Miramar, at the Andalan coast near the Borders, and the battles.

At the time of her mother's marriage, Miramar was led by Alonzo Guerro, the thirty-year-old lord of Miramar Keep, who kept his subjects in line more from fear than out of respect.

When word came that Jesadirany's father had been killed in battle, Lord Guerro wasted no time before asking the young widow to wed him instead, despite the fact that she was already far along with the girl in her belly.

There was no way that her mother could have refused had she wanted to, not if she intended on having any sort of life in Miramar that was free from poverty or harassment. The lord was a powerful man and could have made life very difficult for her had she thought to deny him.

So she agreed.

She would marry Lord Guerro, and her daughter would be raised in the keep. It might have proved to be a difficult life for her mother, forced to marry a man who she did not care for, let alone love. But such was the fate of so many women in their realm, and her mother was strong. She might have been able to bear it.

But as fate would have it, she would never get the chance. Before her child's birth, the keep's bruja, an old crone-looking woman who resembled the old brujas of storybooks—static white hair in a puffed cloud around her head, hands gnarled and bony with fingernails long and curved like talons—had a prophecy about the unborn child.

"Any babe born of this child will have the blessing of the dioses, and wield the most powerful affinity the realm has ever known."

Lord Guerro, upon hearing the prophecy, was no longer set on marrying the beautiful young widow, but decided to wait for her daughter to come of age, when he would marry her instead. He reasoned that, if he were to bear a child with an impressive affinity, he too would possess the power that he so coveted.

And so her mother was left to bear Jesadirany alone, and raised her in the village with a monthly stipend from the Miramar lord. When the girl was old enough, he also employed tutors to ensure she received proper schooling, and with those came monthly visits from the lord's steward to check on her progress.

When Jesadirany was seven, the steward mentioned the prophecy for the first time in front of her.

"You should try harder in your studies," the steward had sniffed. "You may prove useful to the lord because of the prophecy, but you will not be able to neglect your duties to the keep just because you bear him powerful progeny. So no slacking."

After he left, she had asked her mother about it.

"What does it mean, Mami?"

Her mother was still a beautiful woman, but worry and anxiety had lined her face in the years since the prophecy had been foretold. When she knelt by her daughter, getting eye-level with her, the girl had traced the deep grooves on her forehead absently.

"If you grow up and have a baby, that baby will be a powerful child with a great gift from the dioses," she explained.

At the time, the girl had thought that the prophecy had sounded rather wonderful and would have gotten excited about the prospect of growing up, getting married, and having a baby. But something in her mother's face chilled her to her core.

"You must be careful who you choose to love, little Jesa. For if they know the prophecy, they may choose to use you and your child instead of simply loving you back."

Her face drew together, her eyes so full of pain.

"I loved your father," she told her, cupping her cheek in her hand, "And you are my entire world. I want the same love for you, mi amor."

Jesa frowned. "Will Lord Guerro not love me?"

She had known about her betrothal to the lord for as long as she could remember. Her mother glanced at the door, then dropped her voice low.

"You will not marry the lord, mi sol. I will not see that happen. We will find a way to leave, to go where he cannot find us."

"Not marry the lord? But, I am his future wife!" Jesa responded in shock. She had never met the lord, but she knew about him, the mysterious, powerful man who ran the city and sent her presents on her birthday. Last year it had been a dolly; this year it was sweet treats. She imagined that he was fun, handsome, and kind, and that they would have a wonderful life together like the princes and princesses in her storybooks.

"We will be married, and then you and I will live in the keep, Mamá," she reminded her mother proudly. "He is just waiting for me to grow up a little—"

"No, mija," her mother whispered to her. "You will not have to marry him, because you and I are going to run away and live by ourselves."

Jesa felt her eyes widen with shock. She didn't mind getting married; it was what grown-ups did. But running away and having an adventure with her mother sounded like a lot more fun.

"Today?" she asked her mother, concerned. She had to pack her clothes, her books, and her dolly!

Her mother shook her head. "He is too powerful. I must find a way where he can never track us down, never steal you away."

Suddenly, the adventure that Jesa had imagined did not seem as fun as she had thought. Her mother's words frightened her, as did her serious tone. But she liked that her mother was speaking to her like an adult, and not like a little girl.

"You cannot say anything to anyone," her mother told her, gripping her upper arms tightly in her hands. "Promise me, Jesa."

"Te lo prometo, Mami," Jesa whispered.

"I will find a way," her mother promised her in return.

Not three months later, her mother found that way.

In the late summer of Jesa's seventh year, a Danrayen priestess came to assess the little girls in the village. Anyone who believed that their daughters might benefit from following the path of Danray were welcome to bring their children before the priestess. Some girls even snuck out on their own, excited and ready to join the realm's most elite sect of warrior women.

Jesa had no knowledge of the Danrayens, or the path of their goddess Danray, but her mother smuggled Jesa to the priestess in the dead of night, the day before they were set to leave back to their temple.

The priestess was only a little taller than her mamá, but where her mother was all fleshy, rounded curves and soft pillowy warmth, the priestess was lean, harsh angles, and solid muscles. When her mother had knocked on the door of the guest house, the priestess had opened it with a sword in her hand and a frown etched on her brow. Jesa marveled at the ease in which she had held and moved the heavy-looking blade.

In whispered words and furtive glances her mother explained their predicament, that Jesa was promised to a man thirty years her senior. Jesa noticed that her mother left out the part about the prophecy.

"He is powerful," her mother told the priestess. "If I take her, he will never stop hunting us. Not ever," she stressed. "But if she was a Danrayen trainee, she is protected by the realm and by the dioses. No one could steal her from that protection, and more, she can learn to protect herself."

Her mother's voice sounded a little wild.

"Por favor," she begged. "Please, you *must* take her."

The priestess looked down at Jesa, who drew herself up straight and tall, trying not to look afraid, even though she was. Not of the priestess, but of the urgency in her mother's tone and the secrecy of their meeting.

In a solemn voice, the priestess began explaining the path of Danray. She spared no detail on how difficult it could be, about how worn and beaten her body would become, how stretched and tired her mind would feel. She explained the training, the fighting, the weapons, the expectations.

"It is a difficult life, child," she told her. "But if you succeed, you will become a walking weapon of the goddess Danray. You will be able to protect yourself and others. You will be the champion of the weak, a protector of the people. You will be a warrior."

The longer the priestess spoke, the less that Jesa imagined herself as a pretty wife and mother, or lady of Miramar Keep. Instead, she imagined herself a fearsome warrior, with strong muscles like the priestess and a sword just as big. She pictured herself riding a beautiful, golden horse and slaying enemies like her father had in the war.

She found she liked those new dreams very much.

"Yes," Jesa whispered reverently, suddenly not wanting anything as much as she wanted what the priestess promised. "Yes, I will pledge myself to the goddess."

When the priestess gave her mother a nod of ascension, she collapsed to her knees and pulled her daughter into a bone-crushing hug. It hurt, but Jesa let her.

"You must be strong," she whispered, and suddenly Jesa began to cry without really knowing why.

"Mami?" she asked, tentatively.

"I can't go with you," her mother explained.

Jesa tried to push out of her embrace, but her mother held on tighter.

"I'm sorry mi amor, but I cannot. I need to lead them away from you, so that by the time they realize where you are, there is nothing that they can do."

Her mother pulled back, her own tears running freely down her face.

"Te quiero," her mother whispered, pressing her forehead to Jesa's. "I love you so much."

Jesa was sobbing now, and her mother rocked her in her arms for a few moments before standing up.

"No, no," Jesa cried, reaching for her, but the priestess held her as her mother began backing away.

"Keep her safe," she said to the priestess.

"We will teach her how to keep herself safe," the warrior responded.

With one last look at her daughter, Jesa's mother fled into the night.

She did not resent her mother for it, for she knew that she had provided her daughter the best opportunity that she could. And as it was love that led her to abandon her, she could not begrudge her.

Still, Jesa cried long and hard that night.

The next morning, Jesa met Sofia. She, too, was a child from Miramar, though they had never had reason to cross paths before. She was also seven, but her birthday had been in the winter, while Jesa's was in the spring. She was the only other girl deemed worthy enough to join the Danrayens that year.

Sofia was short for children her age, and plump where Jesa was lithe. Her black hair fell in two fat plaits on the side of her head, tied with ribbons that had looked like they had seen better days. Her skin was a few shade lighter than Jesa's rich umber, her nose wide and flat, her lips full.

Her eyes were as dark as her hair, and locked in on Jesa. She could feel Sofia staring at her, and that awareness was sharp and prickly, like a sunburn. Unnerved, she met the other girl's gaze, then quickly looked away. But when her open scrutiny did not cease, she forced herself to stare back.

"You're the girl from the prophecy," Sofia finally whispered to her, wide-eyed.

It wasn't shocking that the other girl would know of her; there were few people in Miramar who *didn't* know of the bruja's mysterious prediction, or of the lord's intentions with the girl from that prophecy.

"Shhhh," Jesa hushed her, bringing a finger up to her lips.

She quickly looked over at the priestess, who was readying their supplies for their journey to the temple. Luckily, they had spoken low enough that the woman did not seem to hear. Jesa wasn't sure why it was important that others didn't know about the prophecy, but if her mother hadn't mentioned it to the priestess, it must have been important.

"That is a secret," she informed Sofia quietly.

The other girl was silent for a long moment, a tiny frown on her delicate brows.

"Then we should be best friends," she finally decided, to Jesa's surprise. "Best friends keep one another's secrets."

"I've never had a best friend," Jesa confessed, then desperately wished she could take the words back, true as they might be.

She had never been allowed to attend the public schools, Lord Guerro sending her tutors since she was old enough for lessons. She had always wanted a friend, but now worried that her confession of never having had one would make Sofia change her mind. Instead, the girl gave her a large grin, and Jesa noticed she was missing a few teeth. Hers had started falling out sometime last year too. It made her seem less imposing.

"Neither have I!" Sofia admitted, much to Jesa's relief.

From that day on, they were inseparable.

The Danrayen priestess secured them two horses, one for herself, and one that she and Sofia shared. On the long journey south to the temple, the girls spoke of everything and anything. They spoke of their lives in Miramar, Jesa crying into Sofia's shoulder the nights when the pain of missing her mother overtook her. Sofia explained how she was an orphan and had been raised by a cruel aunt, dreaming of ways to escape before the priestess had arrived.

"I presented myself to them when they arrived last year too," the girl confessed. Jesa was surprised, she hadn't even known about the Danrayens before her mother had taken her before them.

"What happened?" she asked Sofia, awed by her friend's courage.

"They told me I wasn't ready," she admitted. "But this year I went straight up to the priestess and said she was taking me with her no matter what. And that if she didn't, I would follow anyway, and sleep on the temple steps like a dog until they let me in!"

Jesa's mouth fell open. Sofia was wonderful, so brave and self-assured. She wanted to be just like her.

The priestess, who had overheard, called down from her mount. "As it happens, sleeping on the temple steps was not necessary, as she is ready for the training."

Her eyes flickered to Jesa.

"You both are, but only if you commit to the path. Without conviction, there will only be failure," she warned.

Jesa thought long and hard about that. She wasn't sure she believed the priestess when she said that Jesa, too, was ready for the temple training and the path of Danray. What if she had only been allowed to join because the warrior pitied her? Because it was a favor to her mother? What if she was, in fact, not warrior material?

But then, Sofia yawned, opening her mouth so wide that a faint pop in her jaw was heard. She leaned back into Jesa, who supported her weight and snuggled in to take a nap. They had been alternating who sat in front and who in the back throughout the journey, trusting in one another to keep them from toppling.

Jesa couldn't help but smile. She had a friend, her first proper friend. She was traveling to a temple full of warrior women, where she would not be forced to marry an old man. She would have a place to stay, with people to care for. And while she missed her mother—and likely always would—the Temple of Danray could be a home to her.

She resolved to do everything in her power to earn her place there.

Once they reached the temple, their lives changed very quickly. They trained hard, throwing themselves into their new lives with vigor. While Jesa had her own reasons to become well skilled and assure her success, Sofia, too, dedicated herself completely to their lessons. She had already been accustomed to a life of hardship, but this was one with purpose. She knew that being selected as a Danrayen initiate was both an honor and an opportunity. If she did well, she would never need to return to the life of misery she had left behind in Miramar.

The girls fit in with the other trainees and made more friends over the years but loved none so well as each other. It felt like nothing could ever come between them.

But then, little girls grow up, and friendships change.

CHAPTER 2

NOVA

On a particularly icy mountain path somewhere between Andala and Cassalan, but high above both, Nova cursed under her breath for the fourth time in the last hour. The piercing wind batted away her voice too quickly and too violently for either Rawl or Alric to hear her, but neither would have been offended or surprised, given that they too had been muttering increasingly foul language as the day progressed.

It had been several weeks since the three of them had been in the presence of a true Seer, a young girl with the gift of Unveiled Sight. Alric and Nova had been seeking information about the Unnamed Prince, a child that the Flowers of Prophecy claimed would bring peace to their land.

The Seer's vision had revealed far more than they could have anticipated. It showed that King Enrique, once thought lost to the war, was in fact still alive. He had defected to Cassalan, their northern neighbors and sworn enemies. The vision had shown them all that he lived there with a bruja, and a young son.

The Unnamed Prince.

Together they had all set out to cross into enemy lands to find the child and had been traveling for nearly a month since the unexpected revelation. At first they had spent time gathering both supplies and information in their own realm of Andala, in preparation for their journey. Then they made their way to the Borders, the extremely dangerous wall of precipitous mountain ranges that divided their land from their enemies in Cassalan.

Once they were there, they had to bribe several Andalan soldiers for the location of the Snow Goat Pass, a narrow and treacherous path that weaved its way from one side of the mountain range to the other—a path well-guarded by Andalan guards on one end, and presumably equally secured by Cassalain soldiers on the other. Nova had thought that infiltrating the path was going to be one of their most difficult challenges. Instead, it had been one of the smoothest parts of their plan. A simple misdirection spell by Alric on the Andalan side had their group slipping past the guards unnoticed.

Unfortunately, the same maneuver would be useless on their enemy's soil.

"There is no way to know where the soldiers are lying in wait, or what traps or precautions they have taken to ensure their safety. They would want to protect themselves from Andalan trespassers," Alric had explained.

A full week into crossing the mountains, however, it was made clear that the Cassalains need not have worried. There was surely no way for Andalan soldiers to sneak into their lands undiscovered. The path was far too dangerous, the terrain far too unpredictable, and the temperature far too cold for it to be a viable point of entry for a large unit of Andalan soldiers.

As it was, Alric was exhausted from his efforts in keeping just the three of them from freezing or plummeting to their deaths. The spells, one for sure-footing, and the other to conserve warmth, would have otherwise been small amounts of magia, but were reinforced on all three of them multiple times a day *every* day. The mage was wasting away from the strain. It left him quiet, irritable, and short, which hurt Nova's heart, and even Rawl's normally cheerful demeanor had dimmed. Their overall morale was likely not improved by the fact that Nova herself had been in the foulest of moods since they had left the second Padir encampment.

The source of her anger was obvious, and entirely justifiable, to her mind.

She was expected to ask a *Cassalain soldier* for help.

Every time she thought of demeaning herself by asking for the aid of an enemy, of a Cassalain *monstro*, she grew enraged. The very idea boiled her blood so violently that she was surprised she still needed Alric's heat-conserving spell to keep her warm. It didn't matter that the Cassalain, Axchel, was the one who had informed them all of Snow Goat Pass, that he had helped her when they were both captured by flesh peddlers, or that he owed her and her friends for liberating him from them. He was still the enemy, and the last time she had been in his presence she had promised that if she ever saw him again, it would be too soon.

Needless to say, their travels had not been pleasant as of late.

The only times when their quest did not seem insurmountable was at the end of their long days, after building a warm fire and filling their stomachs with hearty food and vino. In those moments, color would return to Alric's cheeks, Rawl's worried shoulders would relax, and the scowl would slowly slip off Nova's face. Sometimes they ate and fell asleep wordlessly, but more often than not they would chat around the fire, tell stories, play games, or sing songs. The cold air made the stars in the night sky shine brighter and more clearly than she had ever seen them, and they would trace the constellations with their fingertips, sharing the legends and myths of each one.

It was in those moments that Nova remembered just what they were fighting for, what they were all risking their lives for. Small moments of happiness with loved ones. The end of fighting, bloodshed, war. Peace in their realms.

But they were at least a few hours away from stopping.

Inside her heavy winter gear Nova's body trembled, both from the numbing cold that seemed to seep within her very bones, and from the exertion of the never-ending hike. The path (if what they were on could even truly be called a path) was a winding spiral of loose rock and ice that circled to the top of one mountain, only to descend it on the other side and start its ascension all over again on the next one in the range. Several times a day Nova's heart would lift, she would see what was surely the peak of their mount, and pick up her steps just to be done with it, only to find it was not the end, just a sharp turn that continued to climb.

The entire process was terribly disheartening.

Nova was approaching one of those deceptive peaks, her body tilted forward to offset the weight of her heavy pack that seemed to want nothing else but to drag her backward to her death. Every few steps up a bit of icy slush would slide her back down, making progress very, very slow. Her ankles burned with the strain of keeping her footing, and although she couldn't feel her feet from the cold, she was sure that the blisters that had formed over the last weeks had split open once again inside her thick boots. They had not been able to find suitable trekking shoes small enough to fit her and had had to settle for the largest child's boot they could find, which were a touch too small. She had hoped the leather would stretch to accommodate her, and it had, but not before causing serious injury. No doubt her socks would be filled with blood by the time they stopped.

If they *ever* stopped.

Finally she reached the "top" of their current summit, ready to circle around the mount and continue climbing, when she halted abruptly.

There was no other mountain. No next slope. There was, instead, only precipice.

"Dioses, did we make it?" a muffled voice sounded next to her. She turned carefully, so as not to disrupt her balance, to look at a very rough-looking Alric. Her friend's skin was a sickening combination of sallow and gaunt from the usage of his magia, and pink and chapped from the barbed wind. There were purple-gray bags underneath his eyes, and his lips were cracking. He was certainly not at his best, and her concern for him resurfaced. She opened her mouth to suggest they stop for a while, and then Rawl was there.

He sucked in a breath between his teeth, then immediately sputtered as the cold air pierced the back of his throat. When he stopped coughing, he looked back out at the descent before them.

"We're almost there," he huffed, his voice filled with disbelief.

"Technically, we must be in Cassalan," Alric said.

They all shared a wary look. It was their goal, of course, but the prospect of standing on enemy soil was a sobering one.

Rawl pointed down the slope a ways, at a flat bend with a curved rock formation. "We should camp there, the rock wall is high enough that no one below would be able to see the smoke of a fire, if we keep it low enough."

The thought of being able to stop for the day, to warm and feed themselves, gave them all a renewed sense of vigor, and they made it down in record time.

Once their tents were set up and the weary group huddled around their modest fire, the mood was once again somber. They had made it this far, but what would happen next?

Leaning against the tall rock formation, Nova pulled off her boots, and as predicted, her socks stuck to the backs of her heels with dried blood. Peeling them off revealed raw and ravaged flesh. What had started as small blisters had turned into open, gaping wounds that oozed in a way Nova would rather not think about. The nail of her right pinky toe, which had been black with bruises the night prior, had fallen off entirely. She grimaced.

From the corner of her eye, she could see Alric leaning toward her, fingers outstretched and flickering with weak red sparks, the tell-tale sign of his magia. She knocked his hand away and vigorously shook her head at him. She knew his instinct was to help heal her, but healing magia was not natural to him and would drain too much energy.

Energy he clearly could not squander.

The mage's eyes were pained, but he nodded, pulling back. Nova knew he wished he could do more, but she wished he could see just how much he was already helping. He was keeping them all alive.

She made quick work of cleaning and bandaging her feet, stuffing them into new socks as gently as she could. Then she cleaned the two blood-soaked ones with snow and a small piece of rough soap, hanging them near the fire to hopefully dry by morning.

The three then sat quietly near each other, conserving both heat and energy.

"What should we do tonight? Rawl, will you sing us a song?" Alric asked the archer suddenly, attempting to liven the mood.

"I fear the cold air has been less than kind to my voice," Rawl confessed ruefully. "Why don't you give us another history lesson, mago?"

Nova perked at that. She loved Rawl's songs, but lately Alric had begun teaching them about important moments in Andala's history, and some small bits of information about the Northern Tribes, the Western Isles, and other places in Tierramadri. He told stories Nova had never heard in her studies, or if she had learned of them, Alric's versions were more detailed and far more interesting. He had a way of making history real, and enjoyable.

Alric smiled, resigned, "What would you like to hear about tonight?"

"You were telling us about why neither Andala nor Cassalan can win any ground while fighting. Why we are constantly evenly matched," Nova reminded him.

The Danrayen instructors had discussed some of it at the temple, but the focus had always been on how to be the best fighters, the best soldiers, the best warriors. Some of the girls who had excelled in tactical strategies and warfare must have learned the history in their advanced classes, but Nova had not chosen that path. Mostly because it had bored her, she was embarrassed to admit. But she had come to realize that it was her instructor who had been dull and uninteresting, as Alric's explanations always managed to find a way to pull her in.

"Yes," Alric remembered, sitting up straighter. "It mostly has to do with our advantage of the mage university and their enormous armada. If one side gains any ground it is immediately lost, repeating in an endless cycle that has continued for centuries."

Nova pressed herself against Rawl's side, leaning her weight against him and settling in to hear the mage's explanation. Alric's eyes were pulled to where their bodies connected, but he looked away just as quickly before continuing.

"Both Andala and Cassalan are at a disadvantage with the Borders," he continued, gesturing to the jagged, icy mountains they had spent more than a week scaling.

"It makes little sense to battle in between these peaks, on terrain that has more chance of killing you than your enemy has. Small units cross between Andala and Cassalan through the bigger and 'safer' paths all the time, of course. But we cannot send enough soldiers to make any headway over there, and they have the same problem."

He dropped his hand, indicating below them.

"The same issue arises in the excavated tunnels under the mountains. Cave-ins are not uncommon, some chambers flood with snow from avalanches, and the roofs of some of the caves are covered in giant ice spikes, ready to come crashing down at the smallest changes in temperature or vibration."

Nova shivered at the image, and Rawl leaned more heavily into her.

"Most of our time and efforts go into finding ways to sneak our soldiers across or under the Borders. It takes a lot of research, surveillance, and supplies—and of course, a never-ending stream of new recruits."

Alric delivered the last part bitterly, and Nova wondered if he was thinking of his younger brother, Lionel. When Alric had first mentioned him in her presence, she had thought his story was a fabrication in order to keep their true quest a secret, but the truth was much more sad. Alric had not heard from Lionel in years, and he was presumed lost in the war.

"The only true way to gain any ground in this war would be to attack from the western sea."

"And Cassalan has a much larger armada than we do," Nova interjected. That was where they had left off the last time the mage had tried explaining the dilemma.

Alric nodded. "Yes, they could invade us easily with the size of their fleets," Alric admitted.

"But?" Rawl prompted him.

"But, *we* have the Mage University," Alric declared, pride ringing from his voice.

"Should the Cassalains attempt to mount an attack from the sea, we have mages trained to attack with raining fire magia, some who can shift the tides themselves, or even boil the water under the fleets."

"They are that powerful?" Rawl asked, his voice filled with awe.

"Not alone," Alric clarified, "But joined, sharing their power, they can weave their magia together to reinforce their efforts."

"So if two mages share their power, the magia is twice as strong? And if three, it's three times as strong, and so forth?" Nova asked, intrigued.

Alric pursed his lips, then swore when the motion split the skin at the corner of his mouth. "Yes and no," he mumbled as he fished through his pack for a small pot of salve.

Alric paused to rub some of the balm on his lips before passing the pot to Nova, who smoothed some across her cracked knuckles.

"The power of the magia increases," he continued, "but not because it is blended together."

Nova and Rawl shared a confused look, and Alric chuckled.

"I'm not sure I understand," Rawl said, accepting the salve from Nova and using some on his own chapped lips and hands.

Alric thought for a small moment before answering. "It's not like a stew," he finally said. "If I added a cup of water to the pot, then you added one, and then you, Rawl, we would get more stew, right?"

They nodded.

"But, it would actually be watered-down stew. You would have more, technically, but it wouldn't make it any stronger. This magia is more like..." He paused again to think.

"More like a trenza," he continued, flicking the thin braid that Fernanda, a Padir woman, had woven into the nape of Nova's neck for protection.

"If we view an individual's magia as a thread, then threads can be easily snapped. Some threads are thicker and more durable than others.

But if they are braided together, even a thinner thread with a thicker one, *all* of them become stronger. Reinforced, together."

Nova grasped her braid on two ends and pulled, snapping it taught. It *did* feel stronger.

"Is this 'sharing of power' something all mages can do with one another?" Rawl asked.

Alric shook his head. "Not at all. Learning to weave our energies with the energies of our peers is a large portion of our studies at the university. It takes tremendous practice, and each joint spell requires different steps and intentions; like dances with different music, no two are the same."

"And so, because we have so many mages, and the Mage University, our side can stop attacks from their armada," Nova finished.

Alric nodded again.

"But why do we have more mages than Cassalan?"

"Now that is an excellent question," Alric replied, and Nova felt herself flush with pride. She felt like she was back in her classrooms and had pleased one of her instructors.

"That we cannot answer. The theory is that magia may be passed down through familias, but we aren't sure why some people are born with magia and some aren't. Some families with no history of magia can sometimes produce a mage, or child with a particularly strong affinity. From what we understand, they have plenty of brujos and brujas, and people with affinities, just not as many mages. Perhaps it is simply the will of the dioses, bestowing their gifts on whom they see fit. And perhaps Andalans are just more loved by the dioses than Cassalains are."

"Your bias is showing," Rawl teased lightly.

"You don't think that Andalans are better than Cassalains?" Nova pulled back from Rawl, shocked. He shrugged.

"I have traveled more of this realm than you two have," he said. "I have seen more towns, spent time with all types of people, and you know what I have found?"

Neither she nor Alric answered him.

"There are good people, there are bad people, and there are people just trying to get by. They are everywhere. Yo no creo que any person is born intrinsically good or intrinsically evil, but that their choices makes them so."

Again, she and Alric remained quiet, but Nova was reminded of the conversation she and her friends had had with Taruka many years before. She hadn't believed all Cassalains bad either. At the time, it was an outrageous suggestion. But now …

"I suppose we will find out soon enough," she said, looking out into the darkness. If all went well, they would be walking amongst their enemies soon.

"Perhaps you are right, Rawl, perhaps the war has made me biased," Alric confessed, a small frown drawing his heavy brows together above his nose.

"Why *are* we at war with Cassalan anyway?" Nova asked Alric. In all her years at the palace and in the temple, no one had been able to answer that question. Alric looked surprised that she asked.

"No one knows," he replied, looking at her in confusion, the "you know this" heavily implied in his tone.

Nova was taken aback. "Not even you?" she asked him.

Alric's eyebrows raised sharply. "Why do you think *I* would know something?"

"Because you are university educated!"

"And you are palace and temple educated."

"Well, yes, but I'm a -" Nova swallowed the word "warrior."

"I was *trained* as a warrior. A fighter, if not a soldier," she said instead. "They may not want to tell people like me the same things that scholars are able to learn."

"I promise you that I don't know," Alric replied. "I don't know that *anyone* knows. If there was a true history of the beginning of the war, it has been lost centuries ago."

"Well, if our know-it-all, self-important scholar friend here doesn't know, then surely no one in the realm does!" Rawl joked.

Alric laughed good-naturedly and placed a companionable hand on Rawl's forearm.

"Coño mago!" Rawl yelped, placing his own hand on top of the mage's. "Estas frío! I can feel how cold you are through my clothes," he said, rubbing his palm against Alric's fingers, squishing Nova between them in the process. She laughed and nudged at him with her shoulder.

"We're all cold," Alric said, his voice suddenly sullen. He pulled away quickly. "It's a miracle that none of us have lost anything to frostbite yet."

Rawl's chuckle sounded nervous and forced to Nova's ears, and she shot him a curious glance. He ignored her look and moved toward his sleep mat, which had been placed as close to the fire as they dared.

"Well," Rawl said, clearing his throat. "We should get some rest. We don't know what tomorrow will bring."

Nova wasn't sure what had caused the newfound tension among their little group, but knew better than to try to talk to either man about their feelings. Individually, they confided in her, and she in them. But when they were together, it was as if their pride interfered with their honesty.

"I'll take first shift," Nova said, referring to their night-watch duties. Neither of the men argued with her but snuggled into their bedrolls, turning their backs toward one another across the fire.

In the dark, Nova shook her head.

Idiotas, she thought.

CHAPER 3
NOVA

T he next morning they rose with dawn, Tz'ola's sunrays doing little to ward off the chill that seemed to seep within the very bones of the mountain. The jagged cliffs loomed behind them, their sparkling ice-capped peaks glistening in the light. Ahead of them, the plant foliage was sparse, and in muted tones of browns and grays. But in the distance they could see glimpses of a much more familiar green, which would have felt hopeful if the group wasn't so anxious.

They broke down the camp quietly, each apprehensive about the next part of their journey. Nova knew that no one wanted to admit it out loud, but the closer that they came to their destination, the more it seemed like folly.

At least, that is how it was beginning to feel to her.

What were we thinking? They had propelled themselves forward into their intention with very little consideration. The misdirection spell that gave them a chance to slip by the Andalan guards unnoticed in their realm had seemed, at the time, a sign that their quest was true, that they were on the right path.

But what if it had merely been pure luck, the dioses granting them a small favor? How far would that favor stretch? How deep into enemy territory could they get before it ran out?

She worried, and knew that Rawl and Alric worried too. Too much of their plan relied on unknown variables, and they were placing much of their faith in the fact that Axchel had made it back to his station in Cassalan, that he remained there to this day, and, most importantly, that he would still be willing to help them. Even then he might not be able to offer any assistance at all, and they would have to blindly continue in a strange land. There were a million obstacles between them and finding Axchel, let alone the Unnamed Prince. They could be discovered and captured at any moment.

If not worse.

Knowing it was their last trek down the mountains made the journey feel much easier than the climb, but still not effortless. Their bodies had been ravaged by the harsh conditions of the ascension and now ached and complained at the new muscles activated in order to descend. Before long, the fronts of their thighs were burning.

Worse still, Alric still needed to use bits of magia to keep them warm and their balance steady as the icy stones and slick foliage made slipping and tumbling down the rocky precipice an all-too-likely scenario. In certain areas, melted snow had refrozen into large patches of ice, disguised by the dark stone beneath. If not for Alric's spell, each of them would have fallen and risked serious injury several times over.

Nova wondered how on earth they would make the return journey—especially with a child!—but quickly abandoned those thoughts. They had problems enough in the present; there was no need to borrow more from the future.

The group traveled in an anxious quiet for the remainder of the long day, only exchanging a few words during their breaks for food, water, or rest. It was as if they believed that giving voice to their apprehensions would somehow manifest them into reality.

Eventually they had traveled far enough that speech was inevitable; they needed to discuss and devise at least some semblance of a plan.

By then, each of their somber moods had been swallowed down for too long, the apprehension and anxiety mixing with their aching muscles and exhausted bodies. When you added the fact that they all knew they were moving further into enemy territory with every step, their mutual unease began fermenting into something more volatile.

Quietly they slowed their pace and chatted, voices low, a dampening spell by Alric muffling their conversation.

"I could scout ahead," Rawl suggested. "I've lived my entire life sneaking about in forests, I could sneak—"

"Forests you *knew*," Alric interrupted, his voice tinged with condescension.

Nova glanced at him in surprise. She had never heard him use that tone with anyone before.

"And *rainforests. Ceiba* forests," the mage continued. "Not icy, snow-covered terrain on the other side of the world!"

Rawl didn't try to correct him but blew air from his nose in exasperation.

"I could go," Alric suggested. "Use a blurring spell to cloak myself, muffle my movements, and find out just what we're up against."

"And how much magia would that use?" Rawl asked him, a small frown knitting his brow.

Nova understood his concern. She, too, hated Alric's flippant attitude toward his health. He barely had enough energy to keep them warm, so what if the spell faltered right in front of Cassalain soldiers?

"No," Rawl continued, shaking his head. "If one of us is scouting—and we haven't decided on that course of action yet—but if we *are* scouting ahead, it should be me and Nova. She is the only one of this group with actual training in this sort of thing, and we fight well together, even without magia."

"Oh, lovely to hear you think I'm useless in comparison," Alric said bitterly.

Nova knew it was the cold and fatigue talking, not to mention their nerves, but before she could answer him, Rawl's body snapped around, his body all but vibrating with tension.

"Eres sordo?" Rawl spat at him. "Or just acting dumb? That's not what I—"

"And just how many times have you two had a chance to use this training? In the real world? Since you're such experts? So good together?" Alric challenged.

Rawl visibly bristled. "More than *you*, living your pampered palace life," he hissed.

"*Nova* grew up in the palace!" Alric retorted.

"If you think that is anything at all similar to your—"

But before he could finish his sentence, all three of them were swept off of their feet and hauled up, fast, as if a giant had tied ropes to their ankles and swung them upward like freshly caught game. A shriek erupted from Nova's throat, and she could hear the muffled curses from Alric mixing with Rawl's indignant growl. She attempted to grab her daggers but found she could not move her arms. After a heart-halting moment that stretched for far too long, she realized that the reason she couldn't move her arms—or her legs or her torso for that matter—was because the three of them had been caught in a net trap.

It was the stupidest, most embarrassing trap to walk into. *Children* at the Danrayen Temple had better sense than to fall for such nonsense. Nova felt a wave of mortification flood her entire being. Hadn't Rawl just boasted about her being the only one of their group with proper training?

She tried twisting left, and then right, then struggled to wedge her right arm down to her hips for her blades.

It was no use. Her torso was twisted in on itself, her legs much higher than the rest of her body. She tried leaning forward and up to see if she could reach the dagger in her boot instead, but the nature and material of the rope proved that to be impossible too. She could see, and hear, her companions conducting similar attempts.

After a few moments of futile struggling, the three fell into a sullen silence.

"Now what?" Alric grunted.

"I can't reach my blades," Nova admitted begrudgingly.

Rawl twisted around furiously once again, then finally seemed to give up. "Alric, can you use your magia to get us free?" he asked.

"Oh *now* I'm useful to the group, am I?" the mage countered, sarcastically.

Irritation burned in Nova's chest. Their bickering was getting out of hand! But, once again, before she could come between the two of them, Rawl jumped in.

"Oh no empieces! You're the reason we're in this infernal contraption to begin with!"

"*I'm* the reason?" Alric shouted indignantly.

"If you hadn't been arguing with me over stupid—"

"Oh *I* was the one arguing?" the mage scoffed.

"Tell him, Rojya," Rawl directed toward Nova, using his nickname for her. She only rolled her eyes.

When she did so, however, her gaze was drawn to her right, and her heart clenched in her chest.

"Cabeza de burro!" she heard Rawl yell.

Calling someone a donkey-head was a bit juvenile, but, in any other moment, the childish insult would have made her laugh. Instead, fear gripped her tighter.

"Amigos," she said sternly, trying to get their attention.

"If you weren't so frivolous," Alric was saying to Rawl.

"*Frivolous!*" Rawl started thrashing in the net like a child throwing a tantrum. "I'm frivolous? You are the most stuffy, uptight—"

"*Callanse!*" Nova yelled, loud enough that both twisted their necks to stare at her, Alric beside her and Rawl on his left. Nova never yelled at them, not really. She had little cause to, unless giving orders in the heat of battle. The fact that she had not only raised her voice but told them to *shut up* seemed to shock them both. When she saw that she had their attention, she jutted her chin forward.

"We have company."

The men snapped their heads around at a speed that would have been comical had their situation not been so dire.

Beneath them, and more or less to their right, five people were approaching them with weapons drawn.

They all wore the signature red uniforms of the Cassalain army.

One was a stringy, wiry-looking man, who appeared to be around forty. A patchy, scraggly beard peppered his pockmarked face in little tuffs, like grass that had been pecked over by sheep.

He led the rest of the group, which included a tall, burly woman with a cap of black hair and eyes that bulged out just a little too much, and a stocky, short fellow with a hanging belly that folded over his uniform. There was a second woman, smaller than the first but with a more muscular physique and long chestnut hair. Finally, a young boy, who looked no older than seventeen, still too gangly to fill out his clothing properly.

It was clear at that moment that these were not Cassalan's finest fighters, which made sense for a post as remote as this one. Despite its position near the Borders, the weather was too cold, and the path too perilous to warrant wasting their best soldiers for the assignment.

Likely, this was a place where the Cassalain army dispatched their novices, as an initiation of sorts, or where they sent the more recalcitrant soldiers, the ones who needed punishment or discipline.

Or, Nova thought, *where they would hide away a half-Cassalain, half-Condori soldier that they couldn't afford to get rid of.*

She shook off the thought. She didn't want to feel sorry for the Cassalain, but a twisting sourness lingered in her stomach at the thought.

When the enemy soldiers reached them, Nova's party remained dangling from the sky, rendered speechless with uncertainty. The Cassalain soldiers looked up at them in wonder, and the first man that Nova had noticed swore under his breath.

"I can't believe we actually caught someone!" he said incredulously.

"I didn't think anyone was dumb enough to get caught in a net trap!" the woman with the chestnut hair responded.

Nova could feel Alric bristling to her left, their own argument about the same thing still too fresh in their minds.

"Amiges, we can explain—" Rawl began, but before he could continue, they were hurtling through the air again, this time in the opposite direction, gravity working against them. They landed in a tangled heap of bruised bones and already sore muscles. Before they could leap up and grab their weapons, each of them was restrained by rough hands.

The familiar tinge of red electricity prickled from Alric's skin, but in a much more subdued, muted tone. It looked like the color of a fading bruise, mottled and dull. He opened his mouth, but before he could cast any sort of spell, the leader knocked him over the side of the head with the hilt of his blade. Nova screamed and struggled against her captor as he fell to the ground, the man placing a heavy boot against his neck.

"Looks like we caught Andalan spies!" he cackled as Alric struggled.

"We're not spies!" Nova yelled, then immediately changed her mind. "Well, I mean we *are*, but we've been in Andala, infiltrating them to learn what we can about the enemy. We're on your side!" she lied.

The taller woman had trapped both of her arms behind her back, holding her wrists together and immobile. Nova still struggled.

"Take us to Axchel of the Snow Goat Pass," Alric panted, his voice strained as he attempted to alleviate the pressure of the boot on his neck with both of his hands.

Nova prayed that Axchel had made it back to his land and regiment, and, most importantly, that he still served in this post. Their mission and their lives depended on it.

"Lying Andalan scum!" the soldier that held Nova spat.

"Wait," the young, dark-haired soldier called out, "how do they know Axchel?"

Nova's heart lifted, just a fraction, with hope. The boy knew the name Axchel!

"Callate niñito," their leader growled, but the kid straightened, drawing himself up just a little bit taller.

"How would they know the name Axchel if they were lying?" the young soldier asked.

"We could take them to the boss, ask him if he knows anything about this," the paunchy one holding Rawl ventured, his voice timid and nasal.

There was a pregnant pause, and then the foot was relieved from Alric's neck.

"Fine," he said. "We'll let the captain deal with you."

Alric was hauled up, his hands also caught behind him, hindering his ability to perform magia. The blade held against his neck was another convincing deterrent. The remaining female soldier meticulously searched each of the prisoners for weapons, collecting them as she found each undisguised and concealed item. As she did so, the young boy bent to scoop up their fallen belongings, the packs, water skins, and bedrolls. Nova imagined that receiving fresh supplies all the way out here was a difficult endeavor, and the soldiers were hoping they would find something worthwhile among Nova and her friend's belongings.

They would be disappointed. Their supplies had been steadily dwindling during their travels, and there wasn't much of interest left.

Nova was more concerned with her Espada, a deadly Danrayen sword with an impossibly sharp blade and butterfly-shaped hilt. Danrayens were an elite sect of warrior women in Andala, whose members became the walking weapons of Danray, the goddess of battle and transition. After the disastrous Naming Ceremony, Nova had hidden amongst their ranks, training as one of them for ten long years. It was there that she had received the blade, and it was an enormous honor to be permitted to wield it.

Only true, trial-passed Danrayen Warriors were permitted use of an Espada, but hers had been a gift from the Danrayen's High Priestess, Adira, despite the fact that Nova was not a real Danrayen, nor had she taken the Trial. It was the best gift that she had ever received, and this was the second time it was in enemy hands.

Nova narrowed her eyes at the Cassalain soldier's back as they were rudely shuffled forward.

She *would* be getting it back.

As they marched, the terrain changed from frigid, ice-covered rock and slippery slopes to a somewhat more even ground. They were still descending, but it was at a much less extreme angle, and one where they didn't have to worry about taking one wrong step and plummeting to their deaths. Over time, the ice-over-stone turned into snow-over-vegetation, and finally slush-over-dirt. About an hour after their capture they found themselves on a well-trodden path, their wet, muddy footprints squelching with every hesitant step forward.

The temperature began changing as well, warming the farther down the mountains they got. Nova was just thinking that she wouldn't mind taking off her outermost layer when they rounded a corner and a battle encampment came into view.

It was small, as encampments go, but it was clear that her team was outnumbered, about ten to their one. Nova knew they had defeated worse odds before, but never without weapons, or the element of surprise, and definitely not with such low reserves of energy.

Soldiers began noticing them, springing up from their seats around intermittent fires, others popping their heads out of their tents at the commotion. Some yelled, others stared dumbfounded. A few bounded over to question their captors, grinning broadly at the idea of capturing Andalan enemies, others eyeing each of them menacingly.

A trickle of fear creeped its way from her spine to prick at the back of her neck. It was clear that Nova, Alric, and Rawl were the most exciting thing to happen to the Cassalain troop in a long while, and bored soldiers were dangerous soldiers. Nova recoiled as a man with a pockmarked face leaned over to touch her hair, before a female soldier pushed him aside to pluck at the sleeve of her robe.

"If the captain decides to kill them, I claim her clothing!" she called out, which resulted in an eruption of bickering and swearing. Nova could smell the stale stench of dried sweat and body odor, mixed with the aroma of a roasting hare over the nearby fire. The combination of scents made her stomach roil, intensifying the panic that was building within her chest.

If Axchel was not at the camp, if he did not honor his debt to them, they were going to die.

"We're taking them to the boss," the man leading Alric called out gruffly. Through the new Cassalain additions, Nova was able to gather that his name was Vago. The woman holding her, with the short dark hair was known as Perdita. Nova hadn't been able to catch the names of the rest.

Together they were jostled and shoved to the center of the camp, and then further, seemingly heading to a tent on its outskirts. The tent was made from the same hide and fur materials of the others and wouldn't have looked too different from them, except for being significantly larger. While the other tents could each house perhaps two men lying down, the tent that they were walking toward could easily accommodate a small group standing up. It wasn't a wild guess that they were being herded to the captain's living quarters.

As they reached their destination, the thick pelts that made up the doorway were pushed aside, and the three of them were unceremoniously shoved into the tent. They were pushed hard enough that Rawl and Alric landed hard on their knees, while Nova sprawled onto her side, her bound hands making it difficult for her to right herself. Indignant, she managed to maneuver her way up to a seated position, ready to convince anyone who would listen to summon Axchel to confirm their story. But when her eyes met the captain's, she gasped.

It was Axchel.

CHAPTER 4
DAMIKA

D amika was dreaming.

Damika knew she was dreaming because she had had the dream at least once a year for almost as long as she could remember. The dream was always the same, and she could never wake from it, no matter how hard she tried.

In her dream, she was young, around five years old, and she was hiding. It wasn't the first time she had been told to hide, told to *shhhh, be quiet* by two worried voices, a man and a woman whose faces she could not remember, their features blurred in the dreaming world. *Mami y Papi*, her dream told her, even if her memory did not.

They would tell her to stay still, stay hidden, calladita, like a mouse, ok?

At first she giggled, it was a game, but after hiding again and again she grew to realize that it was no game, and even in the dream she could feel the fear and apprehension clawing at her as she clutched her toy llama to her chest. In the dream her nose itched, the dust from beneath the floorboards kicking up with every stomp of angry, heavy footfalls above her head, but she didn't scratch. She just kept petting her llama, quietly.

"Are you sure you're housing no children here?" a man's angry voice rose from above.

"No! Ya te hemos dicho, we have no children!" the kind man with the worried voice replied.

"Please, let us be!" the woman begged.

"Call out. Say, 'Come out now! It's all right," the domineering man growled.

"Que?" A sharp noise, flesh against flesh, and a pained cry rang out. Damika clenched her toy tighter.

"How dare you strike my wife!" Another sound, a deeper thud and a painful exhale before a body collapsed on the ground, making the wooden boards above her head shake. Then a woman's scream. Damika peeked through the cracks and saw two men dressed in black were in their home, one of them had her mami's hair gripped in his fist.

"Call. Out," he snarled in her ear.

"There's no one else here!" her mamá pleaded.

"Call. *Out!*" She could see his grip tighten, the other man pointing his sword at her papa.

"Come out," her mamá's voice trembled. Damika didn't move. She scarcely breathed.

"Louder," the man prompted her. "Tell her that everything is all right."

"It's all right." Tears poured freely from her mother's eyes. "Come out."

Damika wasn't supposed to. She was supposed to stay quiet, stay hidden until everyone left. Until her parents lifted her from her hiding spot. She trembled, unsure of what to do. Before she could make a decision, she saw her papi spring up from the ground toward the man.

"*Let my wife go!*" he roared.

"No mi amor, no!" her mother cried, before a boot crushed her father's nose. The man shoved her mother by the hair he had been pulling, and her face hit the floor hard. Damika wasn't supposed to be heard; she wasn't supposed to be seen. But the bad men were hurting her mami y papi. They were hurting people she cared about. They were looking for a child, they were looking for *her*, so maybe if they found her…maybe they would stop.

It was against the rules, but at that moment, Damika made a choice. "Mami?" she choked out, her voice quiet.

But not quiet enough.

A look of pure satisfaction crossed the man's face as he marched to her hiding spot, the other pointing a long sword at her parents, now clutching each other on the ground. Her mother was sobbing.

"No, *please*, leave her be!"

As the man got closer, Damika began shrieking and crying, terrified of what the bad man would do to her and her familia. Quickly he pried up the boards and hauled her out by the back of her shirt. She screamed and wriggled, her hands pushing against the scratchy roughness of his beard, trying to force him away, but his hold was too strong.

"Te encontramos," he chuckled. Then he turned to his partner, snapping his head toward her mami y papi on the floor. The motion was so abrupt that Damika heard his neck pop with the force of it. "We don't need them anymore," he told him.

Damika shut her eyes tight and wailed as the second man swept forward with his blade. Suddenly, with a reverberating crash, the front door burst open, the wood flinging inward and splintering as it struck the wall with incredible force. A small woman bounded in, swinging a sword nearly the full length of her body. With a practiced sweep she struck the foe closest to the cottage door, the one who had advanced on Damika's parents. He had been crouched searching their motionless bodies, so the small woman had the rare advantage of height. Her blade landed between the man's shoulder and neck in a quick but brutal downward motion, and he collapsed with hardly a sound. The criminal holding Damika dropped her roughly on the ground where she lay in a dazed heap, watching as he and the woman approached one another in the small room. Her gaze drifted to her parents, who weren't moving.

The home that Damika shared with her family was small and sparse, the insides consisting of a fireplace and kitchen in the far-right corner, and a bundle of sleep mats directly across from it on the left. In between was a brightly colored rug, which had been swept aside to unearth Damika's hiding spot. In the middle of the room was a small table with three chairs, all of which the man thrust aside as he barreled toward his partner's killer.

The strange woman and bearded man locked blades, the warrior's head barely reaching the man's chest. He shoved her away roughly and she stumbled, but quickly used her momentum to dive into a side roll. Leaping back up she swung her sword hard against his, disarming him. Without hesitation she continued the motion, swinging her body around fully before lunging forward to plunge her sword deep into his stomach. The man dropped with a forcible exhale and groan near his fallen partner. Panting, the woman turned to Damika, who scurried backward on her hands and heels.

"Amor, it's ok. Estas bien. You're safe now."

The woman from her dream always looked familiar, but Damika could never remember her face well enough upon waking. But her younger, dream-self inexplicably trusted her, almost immediately. She looked again toward her parents.

"Mami? Papi?" The small woman crossed to her and scooped her up, Damika throwing her arms around her neck and burying her face underneath her chin.

"Don't look, mijita. Don't look."

The next part of the dream had no images, only sounds. There was only darkness, and the musky scent of horse sweat and dung. Her body, heavy with grief and exhaustion, was jostled, as if she was in a carriage. But more than anything was the sensation of strong arms around her, the knowledge that she was held, and the feeling of safety. In that moment, she trusted enough to succumb to her weariness, and the journey passed with her barely feeling it. The next thing she knew, she could hear the woman talking to someone new.

"Her hair?" Another strong, feminine voice asked the warrior holding her.

"Trauma? Shock? No se, it started turning white during our travels." She felt gentle hands lightly smoothing her tightly wound curls. In the waking world, Damika had never known her hair another color. She hadn't ever considered that it wasn't naturally light, until the dreams had started.

"Que paso?" the other woman's voice asked in the darkness.

"They were killed, both of them."

A sharp gasp. "Como? How were they found?"

"They are relentless. They will never stop searching for her."

"Well? Now what?"

"She has to stay in the temple. It's too dangerous out there for her."

"Amiga…"

"No. She can't. And I can't protect her by myself; she needs warriors around her! You know that."

A rustle, and then a sigh. Warm fingers trailing down her cheek.

"She can never know who she is. Or who I am."

"Entendido."

Damika woke up silently, as she always did, eyes burning with unshed tears. It wasn't yet dawn, but she could tell by the feel of the air that the sun goddess Tz'ola would raise her head soon to announce the start of day. She sat up, knowing from experience that she would not be able to go back to sleep after the dream. Not with the heavy clay stone that sat in the pit of her stomach, which would remain there for days to come. Damika felt it every time she woke up from the dream, her body clenched, wracked with three very specific emotions:

Guilt.

Shame.

Remorse.

She had broken the rules …

and people had died.

Grabbing her outerwear, she exited the small tent that had been her home for several long years. The white, fur-lined hood tickled her cheek until she batted it away irritably. The entire cloak was a glistening white that would otherwise allow her to blend in seamlessly with the rough terrain around her. It was a gift from the leader of their quest, Capitan Balam, a great warrior in the Andalan army and the man her regiment reported to.

Not that there had been much to report as of late.

Damika resented the gift, no matter how warm and luxurious it might be. El Capitan had insisted she wear it, to show her and her group's status to anyone who might oppose them. Her issue was not the impeccable craftsmanship, or the thick, buttery-soft material that lined the interior, capable of protecting her from even the worst of the long winter night's chill. And it of course fit her perfectly, was comfortable, practical, and didn't inhibit her range of motion if (and when) she needed to fight.

It would have been a wonderful gift, one she would have appreciated and taken as a sign of his faith in her despite her limited progress to her task. She would have accepted it proudly, were it not for one glaringly obvious problem.

The cloak boasted a large, red butterfly embroidered on its back.

The butterfly was an obvious symbol of her Danrayen status, which, on its own, wouldn't have displeased her. The issue began with its wings, which were less wide than the traditional butterfly, and its red and orange body that cascaded down the center of her back, elongating its form. From a distance, it gave the illusion of a phoenix, which was a clear mark of the Danrayen Riders, and she resented the implication of wearing it. Before she had left the Danrayen Temple, the priestesses had been trying to get her to commit to a position as a Rider, and accept all the responsibilities of the service.

Damika knew it was an honor to be considered, let alone pursued so aggressively, but she hadn't liked the strings attached to such an honor. Danrayen Warriors were free to roam the lands as they pleased, to accept posts and positions of their choosing. Sometimes, the priestesses would request their help or services with specific tasks, like supporting the soldiers at the border of Andala and Cassalan during particularly difficult seasons of their centuries-long war, or suppressing the slow incursion of monstros that trickled in from the Night Wood to the small farming towns in the east. But Danrayen Warriors could forge their own paths and make their own decisions.

Danrayen Riders, on the other hand, were soldiers of Danray. They *had* to follow every order given to them by the priestesses. They were sent to the Andalan Palace to advise on war efforts, they were stationed at the Mage University to keep an eye on the progress of war magia and those who wielded it, and were often assigned as commanders of entire regiments of Andalan soldiers, leading them into battle with Cassalan.

But worse, if Danrayen Riders survived into midlife, they were expected to return to the Danrayen Temple, ascend to priestesshood, and train the next generation of initiates. The best warriors could only be forged by the best instructors, after all.

Damika had spent her entire life at the Danrayen Temple. At least, all of her life that she could remember in her waking moments. She trained and pushed herself to be the best warrior she could possibly be to protect the people of Andala—protect the people of her realm. She had no desire to sit comfortably in a palace, or to lead young boys and girls to slaughter, and certainly not to return to the temple to simply become an instructor. She couldn't save anyone within the temple grounds.

Damika didn't know how many people she would need to save to atone for the lives of the two innocents she had killed in her youth, but she was going to find out. And she wasn't going to be able to do that as a Danrayen Rider, which is why the butterfly–phoenix hybrid on her cloak infuriated her every time she thought about it.

Besides, what good was it to have the rest of the fabric blend in with the surroundings if it was ruined by the large red target on her back?

"Ridiculous *and* impractical," Damika muttered to herself as she squatted to light the fire that would heat their morning wash water, then meal.

"Still complaining about the cloak?" a voice called out from behind her. "It's been weeks!" Petra pointed out.

Damika ignored her, irritated. Petra used to be insufferable in the mornings at the temple, but ever since she and Taruka had set out on their own, she was practically cheerful. Waking up every day next to the love of her life seemed to have changed her outlook on mornings. She had also claimed, on one slightly inebriated evening, that she "never slept better than with Taruka in her arms."

Damika had just rolled her eyes at the sentiment and teased her friend mercilessly about it the next morning, secretly pleased for, and a little jealous of, her companions. But this morning, after a horrible night, that tiny seed of jealousy burned into hot resentment. The fact that Petra, the most surly of their group, could wake up rested and content seemed terribly unfair. Damika tamped out the feeling as best she could, ashamed that she could begrudge her friend's happiness, but it remained smoldering in her belly.

There was a quiet rustling from the tent Petra shared with Taruka. Damika turned in time to see her exit the tent after Petra, and give her a nod.

"Buenos dias, Dami," Taruka greeted her. "How did you sleep?"

Damika turned away before replying, pretending to be preoccupied with the fire. Taruka was too perceptive. If she saw her face when she answered, she would suspect the truth. She had never told anyone of her dreams.

Not even ... well. Not anyone.

"Bien, gracias," she lied. "You?"

"Slept like a baby!" Petra claimed, raising up on her tiptoes to kiss Taruka's cheek. "That snow really muffles sounds, I like it."

Taruka wrinkled her nose. Though she seldom complained, it was no secret that she was not a fan of the cold. Petra, on the other hand, had lived on her family's farm near the Borders before joining the Danrayens. Though it never quite snowed there, she told them that the temperature did drop enough during the winters for her to feel nostalgia with the current climate.

The girls melted some snow over the fire, cleaned their faces and teeth, and then set about cooking their morning meal. The sun was just creeping up the horizon when they sat to eat and discuss their plans.

It was, more or less, the same thing that they did every morning.

"We still have a few towns to visit in this area," Damika said, unrolling a piece of parchment with one hand while blowing on the pan stuffed with frijol y queso she held in her other.

"But if we can't find anything ..." Damika suppressed a sigh, not wanting her friends to see her concern. "If we still don't find anything, we've been instructed to continue north."

Taruka and Petra shared a worried glance. They were already so far north, and because of the war, the North was dangerous.

Damika stuffed the last piece of pan in her mouth, burning her tongue. Quickly, she swallowed.

"It might not come to that."

"In any case, if we have a few more pueblitos to visit, you know what that means." Petra nudged Taruka, who burst into a wide grin, worry momentarily forgotten.

"Sleeping inside!" she squealed happily.

"Y cerveza," Petra added.

Damika smiled at her friends; they never failed to find the bright side to any situation. Despite the fact that they had been traveling Tierramadri for years and seemed no closer to an answer than when they started, Taruka and Petra never faltered, never complained, and never questioned her leadership.

Damika wished she shared their faith in her.

She had been young and naive when she had taken on this assignment. She believed that the quest would be a worthy adventure, and that when she completed it, she would have proven that she didn't need to be a Danrayen Rider to make a lasting impact in Andala. But the longer the years crept by the more her faith faltered. She could have been on other quests, protecting other people, making a difference in a thousand small ways during that time. Instead, sometimes she feared she was leading her friends on a fool's errand. But she had quickly brushed those fears aside each time.

They *would* be successful. They would change the fate of their land. The time, the failures, the shortcomings, it would all have been worth it, and it would be clear to everyone, especially to herself, that she was on the right path.

Damika asked Taruka and Petra to break down the camp under the guise of having to send a communication to the captain of their quest, who was equally as busy searching with his own team many miles away. It had taken a little while to get used to the special parchment she was given that would absorb the ink on her end and deliver it to the matching paper he kept on his. Eventually, she got used to the strange magia and even enjoyed watching her brushstrokes fade into its surface, but she had no letter to write. She had only wanted a few moments to herself, the lingering remnants of the dream making her feel achy and raw.

Damika had vowed long ago not to dwell on her life before the Temple of Danray. As far as she was concerned, she was a Daughter of Danray and nothing else mattered as much as that fact. She didn't even remember the strangers in her dream, her mami y papi, just the fading echoes that was once love, so what good would it do to continue to mourn them? She could leave all else behind, keep her past in the past. Most of the time she was successful, but the dreams were a harsh reminder of the fact that she hadn't always been strong, powerful, and brave. Once she had been very young, and very foolish. Once, she had done the wrong thing, made the wrong choice.

She was never going to do that again.

CHAPTER 5
NOVA

Nova watched the emotions flicker over Axchel's expression.

Confusion. Recognition. Disbelief. Anger.

She imagined her own expressions were not far off from those as well.

The interior of the tent was not as large as it had appeared on the outside. There was a sleeping mat on the right side of the room, which appeared meticulously smoothed down, made in a way that reminded Nova of her time learning under the temple's healers. She had only seen such precision in infirmary beds. On the opposite end of the tent were two uncomfortable-looking chairs with a small table wedged between them, and at the far end of the tent, separating Axchel from the rest of them, was a long wooden desk littered with a jumble of documents, maps, an oil lantern, and an odd-looking gourd cup.

The man himself looked taller than she remembered. Bigger too, more broad chested with thick arms roped with muscle. Not being held captive by bandits had clearly done him good. Like the other soldiers he wore a crimson uniform that made her stomach clench, but just below his left shoulder was a captain's glyph pinned to his cloak. *How had he been made captain*, she thought, *and so quickly?* She risked a glance at Alric and Rawl, who seemed just as stunned as she. Before any of them could say anything, Vago spoke.

"We caught them up by Snow Goat Pass," he told Axchel. "Andalan infiltrators."

"They said they knew you, though," the young soldier piped in, jumping a little when Vago shot him a nasty glare. The boy deflated, his shoulders pulling down and in toward his body, as if to shield himself. As a testament to his bravery, however, he made himself continue. "They mentioned you by name, and said they're Cassalain spies returning from a mission in Andala."

Nova could have kissed the boy. He had delivered their story right at Axchel's feet, which meant they didn't have to find a way to awkwardly explain their situation to him without making it obvious that they were lying. Now all they needed was for the captain to go along with it. Everyone in the room looked expectantly at him.

Axchel stared back, blinking in stunned silence.

There was the sound of rustling fabric as the soldiers shifted awkwardly, one coughing lightly. But still Axchel did not move.

Nova glared daggers at him, her mouth pinched tight, narrowing her gaze menacingly. *If he doesn't speak soon …*

And then Rawl took matters into his own hands. Still on his knees, he straightened his torso and sat back on his feet, flipping his long hair over his eyes as he did so. Nova noticed the chestnut-haired soldier blush slightly as she watched him and resisted the urge to roll her eyes. Pushing his shoulders back, Rawl ducked his chin in a quick, nodding bow.

"Captain," he spoke loudly, making sure all could hear him. Axchel's gaze flicked over to him.

"I am sure that you are surprised to see us alive. When we had to stop sending our correspondence…you must have thought the worst."

Dioses bless Rawl, Nova thought. She had forgotten that his youth was spent conning the people of Andala out of their moneda. He was a proficient liar, effortlessly slipping into the "spies of Cassalan" story that she had created.

"I commend you on the strength and cunning of your soldiers," he went on. "You know we are not so easily captured, though I suppose it happens to the best of us, does it not?" Rawl asked Axchel pointedly. A small frown tugged down his eyebrows, no doubt remembering his own imprisonment. If it weren't for Rawl and Alric, both he and Nova would have been sold off or killed in that bandit camp. He owed them his life, which was clearly what Rawl was attempting to remind him of.

"But," Rawl continued, "if you could ask them to release us now?"

The soldiers looked at Axchel expectantly, and he finally snapped out of his stupor.

"Release them, and then leave them here with me," he ordered.

"Pero, Capitan!" Vago began, but Axchel held up a hand to stop him.

"Release them, and then leave us. We have much to discuss."

His face was set in stone, and for a moment Nova felt as cold as she had on the mountain.

He is the enemy, a little voice whispered inside her head. A voice that sounded like every tutor, every instructor, every person of power that she had ever known. *He is not to be trusted.*

The leather straps that had been used to bind their arms were cut, and the soldiers quickly exited the tent. As Nova and her friends struggled to their feet, Axchel rounded the desk to stand in front of them.

"What in dioses name are you three doing here?" he hissed quietly. Nova opened her mouth, but before she could say anything he held a finger up in the air.

"Wait," he muttered, and crossed to the tent's opening. He pushed the cloth aside gingerly, peeking out the narrow opening it created. When he checked both sides, he strode back in.

"Speak," he growled, towering over Nova, who had to crane her neck all the way back to meet his glaring look with her own.

Alric strode forward, placing a hand on the Cassalain's chest. "A step back, if you please."

The words were polite, his tone was not. Axchel's nostrils flared, but he stepped back, glowering at Nova the entire time.

"You passed the Borders?" Axchel asked, ignoring him. "You all, los tres, you crossed the Borders?" his voice was skeptical. "Como? How did you, and why would you..." he trailed off, dragging a hand over his shortly cropped hair. The motion drew her attention. It was such a contrast to Alric's long, waving locks and Rawl's mop of perpetually tussled tawny curls.

"*Why?*" he repeated.

"We're looking for someone," Alric answered for all of them.

Axchel finally tore his gaze away from Nova to look at the mage, and the vice that had been squeezing her lungs released.

"Looking for someone, in Cassalan?" he asked dumbly.

Rawl brazenly strolled over to the chairs, flopping down on the one closest to the desk and wincing at the stiff surface against his bruised flesh.

"No, in the Western Isles," he replied cheerily. "*Of course* in Cassalan!"

"Where?" Axchel asked, and the three of them looked at each other sheepishly. Axchel frowned.

"Where in Cassalan do you need to go? I know that I am—" He ground his teeth, then swallowed hard. "I know that I am *indebted* to you, so I will release you from our camp, refill your supplies, and send you on your way. The sooner the better."

He glanced around the room at them. Alric seemed to have found something particularly interesting on the tent's ceiling, while Rawl had pulled a small blade—where had he been hiding that?—and was cleaning his fingernails with it. Nova was nonchalantly tracing a pattern on the tent's floor with her foot. She peeked up at him.

Slowly, the Cassalain began to smile.

It would have been a nice smile. A very nice smile, in fact, had it not been so derisive.

And not solely aimed in her direction.

"You need my help," he said, smugly.

Nova bristled, but didn't correct him.

"You have come to me for help," he repeated.

Nova clenched her jaw and tilted up her chin at him defiantly.

She wished she could deny it. Oh, how she *wished* she could deny it!

"We would never seek help from a Cassalain, and least of all from you," he said to her, deliberately.

Nova flushed. He was parroting the last words she had said to him before they had parted ways. Dioses-damn him, did he have to have such a good memory?

"I hope to live the rest of my days and never see you again," he continued bitterly. *"Even in death, it would be too soon."*

Axchel cocked his head to the side to examine her. "You seem flesh and blood enough."

"You're not lucky enough to see me dead, Cassalain," she spat out, inwardly lamenting their final conversation. It was going to make things even more difficult than they had to be.

Rawl lifted both his palms in a peaceful gesture. "Let's all just relax for a moment, bueno?"

"Is that any way to speak to someone whose aid you require?" Axchel shot back at Nova, ignoring Rawl.

Before Nova could open her mouth, and likely only exacerbate the situation further, Alric was right in front of Axchel's face. The man jumped backward in surprise.

"If we seek your aid it is only because *you* offered it, because you are in *our* debt, *her* debt," he clarified, indicating toward Nova. "It was her decision to release you. We could have provided you a quick end, or left you to starve."

Axchel looked back at Nova.

"We?" Alric motioned to himself and Rawl. "We would have let you die. *She* is the one who saved you."

Nova felt a warm flush creep across her cheeks. It was true, of course, but Alric didn't have to make it sound so *sentimental. Or perhaps he did*, she thought, as she caught Axchel's eye once more. The Cassalain looked sheepish, all earlier antagonism snuffed out.

"So," Alric continued when it was clear they had stopped fighting, "are you going to help us, Capitan?"

"How did you end up as captain anyway?" Rawl asked, bending a leg under him in the seat. "Did you return and kill the last one?"

Axchel looked deeply uncomfortable.

"Relajate, Capitan," Rawl said quickly. "I was only kidding!" He looked into Axchel's grave face, and his lips twitched. "Unless..."

"No! It's, I—" Axchel groaned, and then began to pace. Nova exchanged a bewildered look with her friends. The large man continued to stalk restlessly around the tent, making it feel even smaller.

"Did you report what had happened to you?" Nova asked tentatively.

During their journey across the Borders, Nova had filled Alric and Rawl in on the unfortunate circumstances that led Axchel to the bandit camp. His fellow soldiers had turned on him, providing temporary amnesty to a traveling pack of flesh-peddling bandits in exchange for them taking Axchel with them as their prisoner. All because Axchel's mother was a member of the Condori tribe in the North.

Axchel had confided in Nova that the Northern Tribes had become an increasingly worrying problem to Cassalan, attacking their people in the North while the country battled against Andala in the South. Apparently, Axchel's mixed lineage was enough to breed contempt amongst his own people.

Her question made Axchel stop in his tracks. He did not turn to look at her, but Nova could see a muscle in his jaw tick. His hands were clenched fists at his sides. After a moment, he responded.

"Yes," he said. "Yes, I reported what happened to me."

When he didn't continue, Nova bit her lips together and let out a resigned sigh.

"*And?*" she prompted.

With a large sigh of his own, Axchel moved back behind the desk and slumped into his chair.

"As I suspected, my captain knew nothing about it. When the soldiers, Fernando, Paolo, and Carlos returned, they claimed I had been taken by a salta-sombras."

Nova shivered. Shadow jumpers were a particularly dangerous creature from the Night Wood, capable of hiding in shadows and pulling people into their obsidian embraces, never to be seen again.

"It must have been a shock when you returned, alive," Rawl remarked.

Axchel let out a snort.

"That is putting it mildly. When my captain found out the truth, he had the three imprisoned and held for a military trial. High-ranking officers came all the way from the Cassalain capital to impart their judgment."

His eyes unfocused, as if remembering. Then he shook his head and slammed his hands on the desk, a little too hard.

"By the end of the week my captain was back in el capital, along with Fernando. Paolo and Carlos were reassigned to the docks on our coastlands, and I was made captain here."

"Que?" Nova asked, confused. "No entiendo. Fernando went back to the capital for punishment? And the other two were reassigned to the armada? To begin service to their realm anew, their ranks stripped?"

Axchel shook his head.

"No. They went to serve as guards for the Armada, a particularly easy and coveted position, as it requires far fewer hours and incurs far less risk. There is also the fact that the docks are within close proximity to the city, so they have actual living quarters rather than having to sleep among the elements. Fernando went back to the city to take a break and spend time with his family, before beginning his new diplomatic position in politics."

Alric and Nova's mouths dropped open.

"But, why—" Alric started.

"Because they were important," Rawl interrupted. "Or, related to someone important?" he guessed.

Axchel grimaced.

"Each of their fathers is a high-ranking member of the Cassalain army. They were only stationed here, at the Borders, so as not to seem like they were receiving any favoritism."

"You mean, until they blatantly were?" Nova cried out, her outrage at Axchel's situation making her forget that she didn't actually like the man.

"But that doesn't explain why you were made captain?" Alric asked, his voice confused.

"It was a bribe," Rawl guessed again, and Axchel nodded.

"Give him a promotion so he'll ignore the fragrant disrespect to his human rights," Rawl explained.

"Not that I could have changed anything anyway," Axchel muttered. "If I had wanted to protest, I would have been killed quicker than I could whine, 'It's not fair.' If I agreed to not contest, but refused the promotion on principle, and pride, it would have led to the same result."

His face twisted with contempt.

"So I complied. I shut my mouth and took the promotion, like a good little soldier."

Silence descended in the cramped tent, tasting like bitterness and resentment. Nova swallowed hard at the knot that had formed in her throat. She had no love for the Cassalain, but that didn't mean she condoned the actions of his army.

Finally, after a moment, Axchel sighed. "Well, you lot are lucky that I did," he told them. "I don't know that I would have been able to protect you had I not been made captain."

The tension broken, Nova and Alric exchanged a quick look, wordlessly communicating. They nodded toward one another and approached the desk.

"We need to find a bruja," Alric confessed.

They had decided, Nova, Alric, and Rawl, that finding a bruja would be a little easier than searching for *"a man who lives with a bruja who, oh yes, is actually the former king of Andala, presumed dead"* or *"their illegitimate love child who we believe to be the Unnamed Prince, child of the Flowers' prophecy, heir to the throne of Andala."*

That might not go over so well.

"We don't know her name, or where in Cassalan she dwells," Alric continued. "Only that she is raven-haired, lives in a forest with a man and a child, and possesses a magia that is light green in color."

Axchel frowned. "That is not a lot of information."

"We know," Alric admitted, "but we have to try."

Axchel shifted some papers on his desk, pulling out a detailed map painted over thick parchment paper. He set his gourd down on one corner and a dagger on the other to keep the paper straight.

"I only know of one bruja in Cassalan. In Condori there are shamanes, but never mind. The one I know has dark hair as well, as do many Cassalains, but her magia is peach in color."

Nova's shoulders sagged, and even the ever-cheerful Rawl was beginning to look defeated.

"But," Axchel continued, "I know that forest brujas tend to have a network, consorts that they can turn to when they need aid, or supplies, or require help with a spell or ritual. Perhaps Ana, the bruja I know, would have some knowledge of where to find who you seek."

"Gracias, Capitan, it's at least a start!" Rawl said, leaning forward in his chair to look at the map.

"You would travel here—" Axchel started, before a commotion could be heard around the camp. Suddenly, the tent's opening was flung wide open and Perdita stood panting at the entrance.

"Andalans! A band of Andalan—" but before she could finish, her body jerked forward and toppled face-first onto the floor. Nova suppressed a shriek as the woman landed before her feet, two thick arrows sticking out of her back.

"Grab your weapons!" Axchel yelled, tossing Rawl his bow while Nova scrambled for her Espada. Axchel boasted a heavy-looking blade of his own while Alric found his staff. More arrows pierced the tent, barely missing each of them.

Axchel peeked outside the tent once more, much like he had when they had first arrived, and Nova watched as his face drained of color.

"Dioses," he murmured. "We have to go, all of us. There are too many of them. If we can make it to that tree line there," he said, pointing to the northwest, "we can lose them. The forest is thick there, and they don't know the terrain like we do."

Nova wanted to yell that they were not "we"; in fact, they were part of the very "them" the Cassalains were currently fighting! But she knew better and held her tongue. They all crowded toward the exit, bodies tense and alert.

"Now!" Axchel yelled, bounding out of the tent. Nova followed, and then Rawl and Alric. Together they began running toward the tree line, Rawl immediately taking out the assailants with his exacting aim.

An Andalan soldier, dressed in the deep purple uniform of their people came after Nova, an axe held high in her hands. Nova's body moved on instinct and years of training, and she swung her Espada fast and low, cutting the soldier's belly from end-to-end. Her blade pierced through another soldier's neck before the first's body had even hit the floor.

Bile rushed up and threatened to choke her, but she swallowed it down.

"I can't believe we're fighting against our own people!" Nova cried out, horrified and sickened by the thought.

"We're fighting to stay alive!" Rawl corrected her, firing out more arrows from his pack.

Nova could see flickers of Alric's magia, still dull and muted but whipping out to strike soldier after soldier. They followed Axchel deeper into the battle.

"There are too many, al bosque!" he yelled, urging his own people into the woods. A few listened, but most were lost too deep in bloodlust and self-preservation to heed him. Axchel attempted to carve himself deeper into the fray, but Rawl hauled him back. Axchel was much stronger than the archer, but the surprise caught him off guard. Still, when he recovered, he began to struggle.

"I need to get in there," Axchel panted, pulling against both Rawl and Alric now, who had come to help him.

"There are too many of them. You can't fight them all!" the mago yelled at him.

"Those are my people," he roared, jumping back as Nova killed another Andalan that was about to gut him.

"And these are ours," she spat, pointing her blade at the now dead Andalan soldier at her feet. "But they will kill us all, *we need to go!*" she yelled, lending her strength to drag Axchel from the battle. With a desperate, defeated sound, Axchel let himself be hauled away, and after a moment, began leading them anew.

"Come on," Rawl grunted, an arrow whizzing just behind his head. Rawl twisted and shot the rival archer right between the eyes. They were almost at the forest's edge.

When they were almost free, an earth-rattling roar erupted in the distance, shocking them all so thoroughly that the four of them stumbled, swaying as they came to an abrupt halt. Shocked, they stared at one another. An avalanche? They were not uncommon in either of their lands, this close to the Borders, but it would be unlikely for one to reach this far down the mountainside.

But then, on the opposite side of the encampment, trees were suddenly ripped from their roots and tossed aside, as if carried away by a gigantic gust of wind. From the empty space left, the most hideous creature that Nova had ever seen stepped out of the canopy's shade.

An Orcuyo.

It stood as tall as three grown men, but its mottled gray body was as round and thick as a kapok tree. Its face was a grotesque approximation of human features, with sagging bags under its yellow-tinged eyes and a protruding bulbous nose. But its mouth was the worst, as two heavy tusk-like canines jutted up and out from its lower lip, causing spittle to dangle in long strings from their positions.

"No," Nova whispered, stunned. "No!" she repeated, louder, grabbing Axchel on her left and Alric on her right, dragging them toward the forest. She knew that Rawl would follow.

"We can't just," Axchel grunted desperately.

She understood what he was feeling. They couldn't just leave them all to die like that, *not like that*. But Nova knew an impossible enemy when she saw one.

"I know," she replied, but continued dragging him further into the forest. Behind them, screams pierced the air, begging, pleading, hopeless screams.

From where they were, they could not tell which were Andalan and which were Cassalain.

Chapter 6

Nova

Together they moved through the trees, their panting gasps, the rustling of leaves, and the crunching of vegetation on the forest floor, the only sound that Nova could hear above her racing heart. They ran, afraid that soldiers would follow them into the heart of the forest to find them, but more afraid that something worse would.

Axchel led the way, his strides steady, his strong legs easily setting their pace. As tall as he was, Nova, Alric, and Rawl would have had no chance of keeping up with him had his physique, made heavy with the abundance of muscle, not slowed him down. As it was, they matched well in pace, managing to continue for nearly an hour before stopping, adrenaline finally fading from their bodies.

Axchel led them quietly to a rushing stream, so clear and pristine that they could see each individual pebble at the bottom. The water was sweet, and cold! So very cold. Axchel explained that the stream flowed from glacier water high in the Border Mountains, before making its long journey down to their location.

After drinking their fill they sat, battered.

Alric had managed to purge most of the poisonous magia from his system into his Phoenixeye while they ran, but it was a hasty job, so he now sat in quiet meditation as he channeled the toxic remnants out of his system and into the stone.

Rawl dug through the packs they had managed to grab before leaving Axchel's tent, rummaging through the remains of their supplies for food to replenish their strength.

Both Axchel and Nova sat near the stream, cleaning their blades of blood with bits of moss and river water.

Finally, Axchel broke the silence.

"I'm sorry," he said to Nova, who looked up in surprise.

"I know they were your people," he told her.

Nova studied Axchel's face for any signs of mockery or deception, but when she found none she simply sighed in ragged exhaustion; she simply didn't have it in her to keep fighting. "I'm sorry too," she said softly. He nodded but didn't try to continue the conversation.

Nova was glad for it. She meant the apology. She had learned that there were no winners in war. It seemed that everyone lost something.

Rawl approached them, dried meat and fruit in his hands. The only things that had survived the long trek across the Borders had been dried. *Though*, Nova thought, *had we reached the snowy tops sooner, we could have kept anything good for a long time.* But they had eaten all of their fresh rations before then, and there was no use in wishing for them now.

Rawl handed out the food, leaving a larger portion for Alric, who would need to replenish the strength his magia had drained him of.

The four of them sat in an awkward circle round the stream.

"Well," Rawl said, breaking the silence. "Y ahora que?"

They stared at each other blankly. Nova didn't know. She had no idea what they should do next.

"We don't have the map," Alric said to Axchel. "But, if you could direct us..."

"I'll take you," Axchel said, shoving his last piece of dried meat into his mouth and chewing hard.

"Que?" Nova asked, disbelieving.

"I'll take you. I have nothing to go back to anyway, and Ana is a friend; I could use a friend about now." He looked so dejected that Nova almost felt sorry for him. She convinced herself that she didn't, of course. He was helping them, but he was still the enemy.

Except, that was getting harder and harder to believe, especially having just fought against her own people. She hadn't felt any more heartbroken at taking an Andalan life, an ally's life, than that of a bandits. She could now imagine that she would even feel the same sort of remorse in taking the life of a Cassalain soldier. In the heat of battle they were all just people, and no matter where they were from, if they meant to harm her or her friends, in that moment, they were the enemy.

And if an Andalan soldier could be an enemy, did that mean that a Cassalain could be an ally? Or even a friend?

Maybe Taruka had been right all those years ago. Maybe Cassalains weren't the monstrous counterpart to Andala's civilized and peaceful people. Maybe people *were* just people.

She didn't know. She was tired and her head hurt.

"We can set up camp near here," Axchel told them, wincing as he stood back up. "I know a place. We can settle for the night and get started on our trek in the morning."

Nova, Alric, and Rawl turned to look back the way they came.

"Do you think it's..." Rawl hesitated, but Nova understood what he was asking. *Do you think it's safe?*

"I don't know," she admitted, "But something that big? We'd hear it coming."

She was pretty sure they would, at least.

"And we'll set up watch, like always. Alric, best not to use your magia to ward our camp. We may need it later."

No one protested, so together they moved locations and set up their camp. Rawl offered to switch off watch with Axchel, so that when he was awake, the Cassalain could use his sleeping mat.

"Gracias," Axchel had said, looking surprised. "I'll take first watch," he offered.

"I'll join you," Alric said, wearily. "The magia is still buzzing, and I won't be able to sleep for a while anyway. You get some rest, Nova."

She moved to set up her mat and heard Rawl quietly clearing his throat.

"Mago," he said softly, no doubt trying to keep the rest of them from hearing.

"About before. Before the net—"

She peeked from the corner of her eye to see that Rawl had seated himself next to Alric. The mage gave the archer a small nudge with his knee.

"We're good," he said, a tired smile pulling at his lips. "We're always good, right?" he asked him, and she could see Rawl grinning back at him.

"Always," he said.

And with her heart just a tiny bit lighter, Nova fell asleep.

***

When they awoke the next morning the mood was still somber, but Nova felt relieved that they at least had a plan.

They ate quietly, their rations depleting faster now that they had four people. After a few moments they began to break down their camp.

Rawl turned to Axchel, who was helping roll up his sleeping mat. "So, Ax, what's the plan?"

Axchel's eyebrows furrowed at the nickname. "My name is Axchel," he told Rawl primly.

"Of course, Ax," Rawl replied, his eyes crinkling with mischief. Axchel's mouth tightened into a thin line, but he made no further mention of it. Rawl shot Nova a wink, and she coughed delicately behind her hand, hiding a smile.

"I need to know where we are," the Cassalain finally responded. "We left so quickly yesterday, I didn't exactly plan a route. I was just..." He paused.

"Running," Rawl filled in for him. "Yeah, we all were," he continued, his tone understanding. Axchel gave a stilted nod.

"I'll hike that hill," Axchel told them, pointing to a small mount not far in the distance, tall enough to get a better view of their surroundings. "Once I know where we are, I'll know where we're headed."

Rawl nodded. "I'll go with you," he said, reaching for his bow. Axchel shook his head.

"We'll need supplies, provisions. Here," he said, leading them to a small patch of scraggly looking flowers by a tree. "These are called friojas; they grow in frigid climates. Every part of the plant is edible, from root to leaf," he told them, plucking a flower and popping the entire thing in his mouth, stem and all. Chewing, he grimaced.

"They don't taste like much, but it's better than nothing."

He dusted off his hands and motioned toward the stream. "We should do some fishing now, as well."

They had all noticed the occasional school of fatty fish in the stream the day prior but had been too shaken by the emergence of the Orcuyo to attempt catching any then.

"Search for what you can, dig up some friojas, and catch some fish," he said, pulling out his cloak. "Prepare. I'll return in a few hours, and we can set out."

The three watched as Axchel strode off into the forest in the direction of the mount, unease settling over them like a scratchy blanket.

Alric finally asked the question in each of their minds, "Do we think he will actually return?"

Nova bit her bottom lip and pulled her shoulders up into a stiff shrug. "Maybe we shouldn't have let him leave alone."

"I think he'll return," Rawl ventured, turning and making his way back to the friojas. He pulled out a blade and a cloth and began digging the flowers up by their roots before placing them in a bundle. "I don't think he has anyplace else to go."

Alric and Nova glanced at each other, and after a moment the mage moved toward his packs, removing their fishing rod. Nova nodded, resigned. Either way, Axchel was correct; they would need supplies. She set off to walk the forest around them, searching for other edible plants, berries, and anything else that could sustain them for the next stage of their journey.

After a while, their moods lifted. There was something incredibly satisfying about having a purpose, a task that needed to be completed. It helped to ease Nova's mind, at least for the time being. Soon she was back sitting with Rawl, sorting out their finds and cleaning the plants and seeds of dirt.

Rawl had created a makeshift whistle out of a long, flat leaf and was blowing out a rough but recognizable tune when Alric joined them, a few fat pink fish dangling from his hand. He laughed as Rawl hit a particularly ragged note.

"How did you learn to do that?" he asked Rawl as he sat down to prepare the fish for their travels.

"Mi mamá! She could make music with anything, truly," Rawl grinned. "Someday you'll meet her."

He turned to include Nova. "Both of you."

Nova began to smile, but then faltered. The conversation had brought up a point that she had been meaning to discuss but hadn't quite found the courage to do so. She supposed that this was as good a time as any.

"Speaking of mothers..." Nova started, unsure. A wary look crossed Alric's face, but Nova kept her gaze focused on a cut on the back of her left hand. She must have gotten it at some point during the chaos of the day; a wound she hadn't felt until she had a moment to breathe. "I was thinking, after the quest, if we find the Unnamed Prince, and manage to bring him back to the palace, if we restore peace... I can't exactly go back to being the Name-Bearer, can I?"

From her periphery she caught Rawl's eyes flickering over to Alric and noticed the worry in his gaze, but she made herself continue. "I thought, well, maybe after, I could find my parents. *My* family."

Quiet. That was all Nova heard after her confession. When she finally gathered the courage to lift her eyes from her razed skin, her belly clenched in fear at the looks on her friends' faces.

"Nova," Alric sputtered.

"I know it's been a long time," she interrupted him quickly, "But they'd want to see me, right? Wouldn't they want to know who I grew up to be?"

"Rojya," Rawl's voice was laden with pity.

"I mean, they must have heard about what happened. That I wasn't at the palace. They'd want to know that I am all right, wouldn't they?" Her voice was pleading now, begging them to agree with her, to tell her that *of course* her parents would still be thinking about her, that they were out there waiting for her to find them.

Alric abandoned the fish and cleaned his hands before crossing to her side to slip one under hers, interlacing their fingers. He sat there quietly until she lifted her head to meet his gaze. Her eyes were full of tears, his were full of sorrow.

"They're dead, aren't they?" she asked him bitterly. "They kill the families of Name-Bearers, so no one can try to get their children back?"

His hand tightened around hers.

"Nothing so violent. Or, perhaps, just as violent, but not as direct."

His voice grew thick.

"Their memories are erased. It's not easy magia, but the families are moved to a new town, and everyone in their old one believes that they are living their new lives with all the gold and gifts bestowed upon the families of Name-Bearers. Instead, they are taken, their memories wiped clean of their child, and they set up in a new location without the knowledge of ever having had them."

"Magia?" Nova choked, crying freely now.

"Yes. It's complicated magia, not many are able to perform it, but once the memories are erased they can never be restored."

"How can you be so sure? Maybe there's something—"

"I'm sorry, Nova," Alric interrupted her softly, but firmly. "No. The memories are gone. The magia doesn't just suppress them, it *erases* them. There is nothing to restore because there is nothing left. It is permanent magia. Lo siento."

Nova nodded, crying softly. Rawl sat on her other side and placed his arm around her back, leaning into her.

Neither man said anything more, they just sat with her quietly, allowing her to mourn the family she had never met.

By the time Nova had stopped crying and splashed her splotchy face with ice water, she and Alric were beginning to worry that Axchel would not return. Only Rawl remained optimistic, seemingly certain that the man would not abandon them.

"He'll be back any moment now," he claimed.

"Shhh," Alric said to him, lifting a hand in front of his face. Rawl took an affronted step back.

"Don't shush me, mago!" he sputtered, but the mage merely waved his hand more frantically in front of him.

The three quieted, straining to listen, when… There. A faint rustling in the bushes. Someone, or something, was headed toward them. As softly as she could, Nova unsheathed her blade. Around her, Alric picked up his staff, and Rawl drew his bow. They noiselessly spread out in a defensive position and waited. Nova could feel the pounding of her heart in her throat, and she sucked in a deep breath through her nose to try to slow it down.

The rustling became louder and definitely headed in their direction. Nova crouched, Rawl pulled back his bowstring, and Alric tensed…

Just as Axchel emerged from behind a cluster of thick trees. He stopped short, his eyes growing wide at their drawn weapons. Instantly they dropped their guard, Nova resheathing her blade clumsily.

"Apologies, Ax!" Rawl told him cheerily, and Nova caught the quick roll of Axchel's eyes at the nickname before he crossed to the stream to refill his water skin.

Nova was shocked to find that his reappearance had triggered an overwhelming sense of relief within her. It unnerved her.

"I was beginning to think you had run away," she joked, but immediately regretted her words as Axchel's expression hardened. Abruptly he straightened, his body tense and rigid.

"Of course you would believe that," he replied, lip curled up in derision. "Lucky for you, I have more honor than that," he finished, before stalking away toward Rawl and Alric.

Nova wanted to scoff and yell at his back that *Cassalains had no honor*, but something within her hesitated before she could utter the words. As much as it pained her, she had witnessed firsthand on more than one occasion that the Cassalain was, in fact, honorable.

Worse than that, that he might actually be a good person.

When they had both been prisoners of bandits, he had tried to offer her comfort and then had used his body to physically shield her from the bandit's blows. He had done his best to take care of her head injury and tried to protect her from being assaulted.

When she and the others had shown up, here in Cassalan, he had protected them again, and had been intending to help them on their quest. If Nova was being honest with herself, she had secretly agreed with Rawl all along. She had believed that he would return to them.

When she reached the three men, Axchel was finishing explaining that he now knew where they were and, more importantly, that he knew which way they needed to go.

"It's about a three-day journey in that direction," he explained, motioning almost due north. "There aren't likely to be enemy—I mean Anda—" he broke off, visibly flustered. "There shouldn't be any *people* between here and there," he corrected himself. "But Night Wood creature attacks have become increasingly more common here."

Alric nodded. "In our land as well."

They all shared an uneasy look.

Nova shook her head. They didn't have time to concern themselves over why the creatures were attacking more frequently, or so much further than their lands in the east. They had a child to find, and a prophecy to fulfill.

"We should move before we lose any more daylight," she said.

If Nova had imagined an awkward, quiet journey, she should have known better. Seemingly emboldened by the fact that there were no other people nearby, Rawl did what he usually did when things were tense.

He began to sing.

True to his nature, he chose the rowdiest, most inappropriate songs that he could think of, which had Alric flushed from underneath his shirt collar to the very tips of his ears. Interestingly enough, Axchel seemed embarrassed by the lyrics as well, though he seemed more bashful than uncomfortable. Nova suspected that had his skin tone allowed it, they would have witnessed him blushing as well.

Infuriatingly charmed by his reaction, Nova began to sing along, if only to watch him squirm.

The first day passed quickly, as they had set out late. By the time that the group found a space to stop for the night, the mood had been notably lightened, and the four appeared to have come to a certain truce. A tangible, if temporary, alliance.

As they sat around the campfire eating a stew of fish and frioja roots, Axchel finally asked the question they all knew had been coming.

"Why are you searching for this bruja, anyway? She must be important for you to come all this way."

Nova shoved a spoonful of stew into her mouth to delay her response, burning her tongue in the process. She swallowed quickly and wheezed, coughing violently. Rawl leaned over to smack her across the back a few times, a bit harder than was necessary. She shoved him aside and grabbed for the waterskin Alric was offering her.

Except it wasn't Alric, it was Axchel. Her fingers brushed his larger, tan ones, and she inhaled quickly, setting off yet another coughing fit. She drank deeply from the water skin, waving the men off as they moved toward her to help.

When she could finally breathe again without choking, she wiped her streaming eyes and sighed. "Lo siento," she said hoarsely, and turned to meet Axchel's eyes. He shook his head.

"No, I'm sorry," he replied. "Your business is your own. I need not know." He stood, moving away from the fire.

"I'll take first watch," he told them, stalking away.

Nova, Alric, and Rawl shared a relieved look. They had not prepared a convincing lie as to why they were searching for the bruja. They certainly couldn't tell him the truth.

They would sound mad at best. At worst, Axchel would realize that either Nova or the Unnamed Prince would be valuable bargaining chips that could sway the tide of the war in his country's favor. No matter the extent that they were beginning to trust the man—even enough to allow him to guard their camp alone—he couldn't find out the truth. Uneasily, the three of them settled down to sleep.

The next day they all woke up early, and Nova noticed that the goddess Tz'ola's sun crown beamed down on them a little brighter and with a bit more warmth than the day prior. She knew the weather would continue to warm up the farther away from the Borders they traveled, and she was glad. She found she wasn't a great admirer of colder climates and missed the lush, wet rainforests of Andala.

Nova and Axchel were assigned clean-up duty that morning, while Alric and Rawl packed up their camp. But instead, Alric had been looking up at the sky for several minutes.

"I believe it might be Peruda's Day," Alric mentioned, referring to the great goddess of love.

"Ah," Rawl commented, and Nova noticed that for some reason, he flushed. "I noticed that in the stars a few nights past, I thought it might be one of these days."

Nova watched curiously as a still-red Rawl rooted around in his bag for a moment to pull out an item. He made his way over to Alric and presented it to him shyly.

Alric's face filled with wonder.

In his palm he held an intricately carved lion, etched on a piece of golden-bronze bark. Even at a distance Nova could see that it was a thing of beauty. It appeared to be in motion, running, with legs bunched with muscle and mane blown back in the wind. It was a work of art, exquisitely done. Nova wondered how long it had taken Rawl to carve it.

"For your brother," she heard him say to Alric, voice low.

Lionel; little lion, she thought. The younger brother who was lost to the war.

Alric turned the sculpture over in his long hands, brushing the fine detail with his fingertips. He broke into a wide grin, and then clapped Rawl on the shoulder.

"Gracias amigo!" he said, his voice delighted. Then he laughed.

"You know, in the capital we have this tradition, too, to give gifts on Peruda's Day," he said. Then he laughed harder. "Except, we only give them to the people we are sweet on!"

At his words, Rawl turned an even deeper shade of red, one that even Alric couldn't help but notice. He lifted the hand still on his shoulder and patted him on the back with it.

"Don't worry," he told Rawl, still grinning. "I assume they do things a bit different amongst the Padir, hm?" he asked. "You give them to your friends as well?" He swung around to look at Nova.

"Does Nova get one too?" he asked, and she saw the panic and mortification flood Rawl's face.

"He already gave it to me!" she lied, plastering on a grin. "This morning."

"Let's see it then!" Alric said, reaching his hand out to her.

"Oh," she faltered, stumbling back. "Um, no. It's already wrapped up, and at the bottom of my pack," she lied again. "For safekeeping."

"Que pena," Alric mumbled, still admiring his wooden lion. "What was it?"

"Que?" she stalled, anxiously.

Alric looked up. "What did he carve for you?"

"Uh—"

"A butterfly," Rawl blurted.

Alric nodded.

"Claro, of course!" He finally looked up from his gift. "You are truly talented, amigo!" he said, before moving away to finish packing.

Rawl turned his back fully to the mage and shot Nova a grateful grin.

"Gracias," he mouthed at her, before he slunk off into the forest.

Nova sighed before realizing that Axchel had watched the entire exchange, his face betraying his amusement at the interaction.

"Que?" she asked him, and he threw up his hands in mock surrender.

"Nada," he said, a small smile pulling at his lips. "But I've been with you all morning, and I didn't see any wooden butterfly."

"Callate," she hissed at him, darting a look at Alric, who was too far away to hear their quiet exchange anyway.

"It's none of your business!" she told him, and rose to follow Rawl.

She found him not far from their camp, sitting on a dry patch of ground with his knees drawn up to his chest and back against a tree. His arms were crossed over his legs, his head ducked to lay against them. As Nova approached she saw him stiffen and look up, only to let out a low groan dropping his head back down into his hands when he saw it was her.

Nova made her way over to the tree and sat beside him, fidgeting just a little. She didn't say anything because she had no idea what to say, or if she should speak at all. Her friends would know just what to do though, she knew. Taruka would've spoken some kind, soothing words of encouragement that would melt the tension from his shoulders. Raidea would have teased him so mercilessly that his shy blush would quickly turn into heatstroke red. Damika would have beaten it out of him, made him confess his worries and secrets, and he would have felt all the better for it after. And Petra? Petra would have beat Alric instead for being so blind, and for hurting her friend.

But Nova had none of those skills. She had spent so long staying quiet and hidden. She had never been allowed to give voice to her true feelings, her true purpose, her true self. Who was she to offer any council? Especially in the matters of love. So she simply sat next to him in a disappointed silence, wishing she was someone else, someone more. Someone who could be a better friend than she was.

After a few moments, his body relaxed and he leaned into her, nestling his head in the crook of her neck instead of his hands. She could feel his sigh against her collarbone.

"Gracias," he whispered, almost too low to hear.

"No hay de que," she responded.

"No, really," he said, lifting his head and looking directly at her. They were so close that she could see the gold flecks within his green eyes.

She smiled with as much love and reassurance as she could muster, and he pulled her tightly into his arms. The two shared a peaceful moment of affection, until a deliberate and annoyed-sounding cough sprung them apart.

Alric stood in front of them, a frown crinkling his forehead. He looked disgruntled.

"Am I interrupting something?" he asked, his voice testy.

"No," Nova replied, springing up.

Alric's eyes darted between Nova and Rawl. Nova was confused by his sudden mood swing. Had something happened? Before she could ask, Alric turned around abruptly and headed back toward their camp.

"Well, if you two are finished doing *whatever* it is that you were doing, we should head out," he tossed behind his shoulder as he quickened his pace.

The two were left dumbstruck. Finally, Rawl pushed himself to his feet, and he and Nova shared a confused shrug before following him back the way they had come.

CHAPTER 7

JESADIRANY

When both Jesa and Sofia turned fifteen they were allowed to visit the small city of Pelgar, which was the closest neighboring community to the Temple of Danray. It was a rite of passage of sorts for Danrayen girls, and the two were very much looking forward to it. So much so, that when Sofia had turned fifteen in the spring, she promised to wait until winter when Jesa caught up so that they could go together.

Jesa had insisted it wasn't important, that Sofia was free to explore with the other girls rather than wait the many months for them to go together, but Sofia refused.

"It is what best friends do," she said simply.

And so, the day after Jesa's birth day, the two girls ventured outside the temple grounds.

So much of their lives had been spent in the confines of the temple, and the first taste of freedom was both sweet and a little frightening. It was their first chance to explore a part of their realm before their Trial. After the Trial, if they passed, they would of course be free to roam about Tierramadri as they wished.

They traveled together with a small group of girls, other Danrayen initiates and a few friends who had already been to Pelgar. The older girls would show them about town.

"We'll stop by the shops and stall vendors," one promised.

"Oh they have lovely feathers and ribbons," another girl interjected.

"Forget the ribbons, the pan dulce is to die for," someone else shouted.

"I could eat three!"

"You just had lunch!"

"What does that have to do with anything?"

"We'll have drinks at the cantina," another girl interrupted.

"And we can talk to boys!"

At the last statement, all the young women burst out in giggles, and the conversation abruptly changed to stories of several boys whose names neither Sofia nor Jesa had heard of before. They glanced at each other with alarm.

Would they be expected to talk to boys?

Neither had ever spoken to a boy in their entire life, except for when Sofia had needed to interact with her mean, ugly cousin back in Miramar. Lord Guerro's steward had stopped by to check on Jesa's schooling and upbringing from time to time, but she had just been a child and he was an old man, and she didn't believe that counted. Boys were as completely mystifying and foreign to her as the far side of the moon, or what lay beyond the Western Isles. It would be unfathomable that anyone would expect them to speak to such creatures!

And yet, they did.

When Jesa and Sofia reached Pelgar they were delighted. The town was much smaller than the bustling coastal city of Miramar, but after so many years of only focusing on their warrior training, it was a welcomed experience. Pelgar was a concentrated center of cobblestone streets, two-story adobe houses, and a vibrant market. As one of the most central towns of Andala they were in a good location for trade, but also deep enough into the forest that they were not constantly overrun. The result was that Pelgar could be a busy, energetic community with plenty of shops, entertainment, and diversions without the poverty, overcrowding, and muck that was common to larger cities. The girls found it to be a charming retreat.

Jesa and Sofia—with the direction of their friends—began by perusing the shops and stall vendors, which was as colorful and delightful as promised. Though none of them needed any of the pretty vases, pieces of art, or fancy dress that they offered, they found it was very fun to admire and imagine.

Afterward they were taken to the "best" village baker, according to the other girls, where they used some of their stipends to purchase several rolls of pan dulce, conchas with pink sugar, flat, hard cookies known as champuradas, and chocolate caliente. They sat together, trading their sweet breads and dunking them into their hot chocolate and moaning in pleasure at the delicious treats. When Sofia mentioned that the pan dulce was even better than the bread that was baked in the temple for their morning meal, the others agreed, but all promised never to say so on temple grounds, lest they offend the cook.

After a walk around the rest of the village, Sofia and Jesa found themselves inside Pelgar's most popular cantina.

"I've never had any alcohol before," Sofia whispered to Jesa.

"You know I haven't either," Jesa replied just as quietly.

"Should we just order cerveza?" Sofia suggested. They had both heard the other girls talking about how nice it was to end their days with a cerveza.

Jesa nodded, and Sofia ordered for the both of them.

Carefully, they balanced their tall glasses and made their way to a table that had been cleared for them. They sat, shared a small cheers with the other young women, and took a sip.

Both girls scrunched up their faces at the bitter, sour taste of the beer and everyone else laughed.

"You get used to it," one of their friends told them.

"Soon you'll love it!" another added.

Jesa and Sofia were just joining in their laughter when a small group of young men approached their table.

In any other town, a group of strong, confident, warrior women in training would have intimidated most men. But in Pelgar they were used to the comings and goings of impressive women, and all the boys wished for a chance to interact with some of them. When they saw that the usual group of warriors-in-training boasted two new young women, they came rushing to make their introductions.

The boys were no less strange up close, so peculiar with their cracking voices and unruly patches of fuzzy whiskers that they so proudly boasted over their upper lips. (It impressed neither Sofia nor Jesa, who had seen more impressive mustaches on some of the Danrayen women who bore them far more regally.)

Still, there was something exhilarating about chatting with anyone other than their Danrayen sisters, and especially to members of the opposite sex. It was an almost-impossible pull to ignore, and both girls found themselves making conversation, trading names and stories, and blushing furiously at the attention.

Eduardo, or "Lalo," worked in the cantina helping the owners sweep, clean, and wash dishes. It did not entitle him to any free drinks or discounts, no matter how many times the group asked him.

And they asked a lot.

Daniel's family owned the maize flour mill at the edge of town, but secretly Daniel longed to be a part of a traveling troupe. He practiced his zampoña pan flute in any free moment and to any audience, willing or otherwise.

Jose was the strong-armed son of the blacksmith and the quietest of their group, never speaking to any of the girls directly. He joined them for drinks or games, and spoke to the other boys when they all convened, but seemed to avoid the attention of the young Danrayens.

Much to the dismay of many. He was quite handsome, after all.

The entire experience was an odd, awkward sort of mating ritual, but fun! Well, fun in an anxiety-inducing sort way. Danrayens, either full warriors or initiates, were free to pursue whatever romantic relationships that they chose, as long as it did not interfere with their path, their calling, or their service to the goddess. Even so, neither Sofia nor Jesa were seriously interested in any courtship, but accepted the tokens, joined the others for the occasional drink at the cantina, and were even passed a poetic note or two.

It was on one such outing to Pelgar when Jesa was first approached by Alcor.

He was a good-looking young man, in a severe sort of way, high cheekbones and dark piercing eyes. He came up to their group one balmy afternoon and introduced himself, letting them all know that he was new to Pelgar and was hoping to meet new friends. If any of them had any hesitation over allowing the new boy into their group it was quickly quieted when he offered to buy them all their next round of drinks.

After that, he was a constant.

Alcor wasted no time in befriending their group, and as he was generous with his coin, Lalo and Daniel were both quickly and thoroughly won over. He was handsome and charismatic, which drew the attention of several of the young Danrayen initiates, at least the ones who preferred the company of men. The only people who did not seem instantly taken by the charming stranger were Sofia—who regarded him with cool but polite indifference—and Jose, who did his best to ignore the boy altogether. No one thought too much of it, as Jose was not very sociable even with those he considered to be his friends.

Despite winning the acceptance and interest of the majority of their group, it was clear from the beginning that Alcor had his sights set on one member in particular.

On the very first day, he claimed the seat next to Jesa right away, despite the fact that there was not much room to squeeze in, and far more accessible seats elsewhere. The others laughed, admiring his boldness, and Jesa found the attention quite flattering. For the following months, Alcor was relentless in his pursuit. He brought Jesa flowers, which was sweet, albeit misguided—what was she to do with a bunch of pretty peonies?—and useless baubles and trinkets. Jesa liked Alcor well enough, and accepted both the gifts and the compliments, but made no promises or advances on the boy, content with the admiration but not particularly interested in anything more. Alcor, though relentless in his pursuits, did not push the topic, for which she was grateful.

On one evening, Jesa decided to head back to the temple early; she had started to become more serious about training for the Trial of Danray and wanted to wake early for extra practice. Sofia, still drinking with their friends in the cantina, waved her on, assuring her that she would be fine to head back with the others later.

As Jesa was veering toward the forest path that would take her home, she heard a noise. Stopping, she strained her ears to listen closer.

Again. She heard it again, unmistakable this time.

Someone was calling for help.

She ran, grabbing the thin blade that she always carried at her waist, and headed in the direction of the yells.

"Ayuda! Is anyone there?" The voice was masculine and deep, and punctuated with splashing. She changed her direction slightly and headed toward Pelgar River.

"Help!" the voice called again.

"Where are you?" Jesa cried out.

"Here! We're here! Ayuda!"

Jesa broke through the tree line to the rushing river and saw Jose, the blacksmith's boy, hanging on to a fallen log, its roots mercifully still anchored to the earth beside the stream. The water was flowing hard and fast, the river made dangerous from the torrential rain they had experienced not one month prior.

"Hold on!" she called out, running out to the fallen tree.

When she got closer, Jesa could see that Jose was holding on with just one arm, and in the other, he was holding a squirming bundle. She sheathed her blade and stepped gingerly onto the branch.

"Cuidado!" Jose called out.

"No, I was thinking I would rather be stupid and reckless!" she called back, nerves making her testy. Slowly she slid one foot in front of the other on the log, the wood made slick with water and moss. Her arms were thrown out at her sides for balance.

When she was finally within distance of him, she crouched down and leaned forward to grab Jose's arm.

"No, her first," he yelled, shoving the bundle at her. Jesa tucked the wrapped cloth, along with whatever was alive inside of it, underneath her left arm and then extended her right out for him once more.

"Grab on!" she told him, yelling to be heard over the water. Jose strained against the current, then reached out to clasp her forearm.

Together, they paddled back to the water's edge where Jesa collapsed as Jose pulled himself the rest of the way out. He splayed himself out on the solid ground, arms flopped to his sides, wet hair plastering his face, and his chest heaving with effort.

Jesa watched him, astounded.

If you had asked her a few days prior how she felt about boys, she would have answered that she liked them well enough. They could be diverting, and decent friends, though nowhere near as good as her Danrayen sisters. She would have admitted to finding Alcor attractive, in a pleasant sort of way.

Nothing would have prepared her for the shock of awareness she felt when looking at Jose then, sprawled out, soaking wet, his white shirt plastered to the hard planes and muscles of his torso. She could see droplets of water sliding over his eyelashes and nose, and his pulse jumping erratically underneath his jaw. His cheeks were flushed pink with exertion, and his lips were parted as he took heavy breaths in and out. She wondered what it would be like to press her own against his, imagining his eyes snapping open in shock, then closing again as he pulled her toward him.

An indignant squeak pulled her from her absurd thoughts, reminding her of the bundle under her arm. She pulled it out and opened the cloth only to find a black-and-copper puppy shaking out her fur.

Jesa's heart melted.

"Hoooola amor!" she cooed in a voice reserved only for adorable animals and very small children.

Jose rolled himself over to his side, propping his body up with his forearm. Jesa tried not to notice how the motion made his shirt tighten against his chest, or how his hair now hung charmingly over his eyes.

"Is she ok?" he asked her, reaching for the puppy. Jesa handed her over reluctantly, shivering a little when their hands brushed. She told herself it was just the chill of the water.

Back in Jose's arms, the puppy nuzzled into the crook of his neck, while he laughed.

Jesa tried desperately not to feel jealous of a dog.

"Que paso?" she asked him. "How did you both end up in the river?"

Jose shook his hair out of his face.

"I was walking, taking a break from the forge," he said, "when I heard some barking coming from the river. When I looked, there was this bundle floating down downstream. I could tell there was something inside."

"So you jumped in?" she guessed. He nodded.

"I didn't realize the current was so strong, or that it would be that hard to swim us back out with just one arm. I was lucky that I managed to grab hold of that tree," he jerked his head toward the fallen log, "and that you came along."

He struggled to his feet, and then offered her a hand to help her up. Once she was standing they stood very close together, neither of them backing away.

"Gracias," he told her, looking into her eyes. She swallowed. "We owe you our lives," he finished.

Jesa licked her lips and watched, fascinated as Jose's eyes dipped to follow the motion. Then he was back to staring at her, intently.

"I'm just glad I was around," she whispered.

He smiled.

"I'm always glad when you're around," he replied, voice soft.

A thrill raced up her body at his words, and butterflies erupted in her belly.

Is this what it's like? she thought. *To want?*

The puppy squirmed in his arms, breaking the intensity of the moment. Jose stepped away, blinking as if in shock.

"I should," he started, then hesitated. "I should bring this one home, get her dry."

"Of course," Jesa answered automatically, though the last thing that she wanted was for him to leave.

"Thank you," Jose said, backing away toward Pelgar. "Again."

And with that he turned and walked away, leaving a very confused Jesa in his absence.

CHAPTER 8

NOVA

On the fourth morning of travel, Axchel informed them that they were very near the bruja's cottage.

After their meager morning meal, while Alric and Axchel were pre-occupied, Rawl quietly slipped Nova a beautifully carved butterfly, made with an almost white-colored wood. Just like Alric's lion, it was exquisitely done.

"Gracias," Nova told him, completely charmed. Even knowing why he had carved it for her couldn't dampen her joy of owning such a beautiful memento. She kissed his cheek. "It's beautiful, but you really didn't have to!"

"Oh no," Rawl chuckled ruefully. "I really did."

They grinned at each other, and Nova quickly slid it into her bag before packing up the rest of her things.

The group walked for about five hours before a curling tendril of smoke could be seen above the tree line, which Axchel claimed was likely from Ana's home. The Cassalain seemed lighter than he had since Nova had known the man, his mood visibly improving with each step toward their destination. Nova wondered if Ana was perhaps his enamorada. Perhaps, when they arrived she would have a gift for him for Peruda's Day. Perhaps once she had helped them, *if* she helped them, Axchel would stay with her in the woods, rather than return to the capital for a new assignment.

Nova had no idea why the idea of it made her stomach feel as if she had been kicked by a horse. She didn't mind the man's company any longer; in fact, over the last few days she had come to almost like him. He was calm, easy-going, and had adapted to their group with surprising ease. He didn't initiate conversation often, but answered Alric's questions thoughtfully and deliberately, and swapped Cassalain tales for Andalan stories in the evenings with Rawl. They were each amazed that there were so many similarities in both their realm's myths and legends.

He was also helpful, always ready to lend a hand. In the mornings she would find her water skin already refilled from the stream, which continued to run nearby. Twice she had stepped away to relieve herself before packing away her things, only to return and find her sleeping mat rolled and tied up, already attached to her pack. And she couldn't be certain, but on the night he was supposed to wake her for the second shift, she was pretty sure that he had allowed her to sleep for an extra hour.

It all made her feel a little uneasy, but she was doing her best to not insult the man again, so she didn't say anything so as not to come off as ungrateful. She *was* grateful, just, confused.

So she didn't know why the thought of him staying with Ana troubled her, as she had come to like him well enough to not begrudge him his happiness. In any case, there was no way that he could join them on their mission, of course.

Even so, the feeling remained.

The group broke out through a cluster of trees and stood at the edge of a clearing. Ana's cottage was made of adobe, like most homes in Tierramadri. The material was easy to make from clay, mud, and other organic materials, and once dry, was very durable. Ana's home was rectangular with two stories, and a small balcony jutting out from the second floor over the front door. On the left side there was a stone and mud chimney, the source of the smoke that they had followed.

But the most interesting part of the cottage was the terrain that encircled it. The land surrounding the cottage had been flattened and laid over with hundreds, if not thousands, of painted stones. As far as Nova could see, these makeshift tiles continued all the way around the building and extended several feet in each direction out from the home. The stones were painted brightly, in reds, yellows, greens, blues, oranges, purples, and pinks. On the sides of the walkway leading to the front door there were long poles embedded into the ground and standing proudly in two long lines framing the path. From each pole hung swinging ropes that crisscrossed the entire way, and equally colorful lanterns and scraps of fabric hung from their lengths.

Nova blinked back tears as a wave of sudden, unbridled emotion took root in her chest. She hadn't seen colors so vibrant since she had had to flee the Andalan capital, and the sight of them now made her feel conflicting but powerful feelings. With effort, she swallowed them down.

Still, it was beautiful.

Axchel had broken into a wide grin when the cottage came into view, and Nova had been right, it *was* a nice smile. He quickened his pace to reach the door.

"Vamonos," he called back to them.

Nova lagged, taking in the brightly painted stones and hanging cloths. She let Rawl and Alric pass her, and hesitated outside for a moment. Then, with a deep breath, she crossed the threshold into the building. The first thing she saw was the form of a woman, facing away from her, a thick mane of wavy black hair cascading down her back like a dark waterfall. Axchel's arms were around her, her head barely reaching his chest. Nova was of fairly average height, for a woman, but Ana—if the woman in Axchel's arms was Ana—made her feel monstrous. She shifted her weight on her feet and pulled off the alpaca shawl that had been wrapped around her neck, trying to relieve the tightness she felt in her chest. Finally, Ana turned around, and Nova dropped her gaze down to stare into the eyes of a woman no less than eighty years old.

A laugh bubbled in Nova's throat, and it escaped her before she managed to swallow it down. Axchel spun around to look at her, his face scrunched with confusion. Nova merely pressed her lips together and shook her head. He shrugged and shook his head a little, as if dismissing her as crazy. The tightness in Nova's chest released, and the sticky feeling she felt in her stomach all morning dissolved into something else.

Relief.

Before Nova could examine the feeling further, Ana frowned, the lines in her face becoming even more pronounced.

"Who have you brought me, Axchel?" she asked, moving closer to his side.

"Tía," he addressed her respectfully, "This is Rawl, Alric, and Nova."

Nova startled. It was the first time that she had heard him use her name. They had continued their tradition of calling each other "Andalan" and "Cassalain," although with admittedly less malice.

"Everyone," Axchel continued, "this is Ana."

Alric bowed to her while, predictably, Rawl bent to kiss her hand. Nova was sure that the scowling woman would hit him over the side of the head for his brazenness, but instead she snorted in amusement.

When her eyes met Nova's again, all she could do was grant her a curt nod.

Luckily, it seemed to be enough.

With a world-weary sigh, Ana turned to pat Axchel on the cheek. Nova pressed her lips together to suppress a grin; he was so tall he actually had to duck down to allow her!

"Ven," she said, shuffling toward the cocina. "We'll have mate and you'll tell me why you're here."

"Oh no," Alric started.

"We don't really have time," Nova said over him.

"We would be honored," Rawl interjected, louder than the other two had been. "Gracias!"

Nova stared at him in confusion, anxious to receive the answers that they were looking for and go. From the look on Alric's face, she could tell he felt the same. Rawl just shrugged, but Nova saw that Axchel was glaring at her.

"If you would excuse us for just a moment," Axchel directed at Ana and Rawl, who was helping the older woman with a heavy-looking kettle. Ana just waved him off with a gnarled hand. He motioned with his head, and Alric and Nova followed him outside once again.

When the door closed behind them, he regarded them with a stern expression. "Do they not teach basic manners in Andala?" he hissed. "One would think you two, of all people, a mago and a Danrayen would be in possession of *some*."

Alric and Nova shared a glance, baffled.

"We just need answers, and to be on our way; it's not late in the day. Once we get directions we could walk a few miles before needing to stop," Alric said, his voice as confused as Nova felt.

"We're not trying to be rude," she added. "We just don't have time to waste drinking mati, whatever that is."

"Mate," Axchel informed them. "You don't drink mate in Andala?"

Nova shrugged while Alric shook his head.

"It's, well, like, a tea, of sorts, from the yerba mate plant," Axchel explained

"Well, we don't have time to drink tea," Nova said, exasperated.

"It's not *just* tea," Axchel corrected her sternly. "It's a practice, a ritual. It *means* something."

Alric and Nova exchanged yet another confused look.

"Bueno," Axchel sighed. "I'll try to explain," he began, and then stopped, looking into the distance with his eyebrows drawing up.

"Axchel?" Alric said tentatively.

Axchel shook his head.

"Sorry, I've just never met anyone who didn't drink mate." He regarded them once again. "The yerba, the plants, are picked, dried, and then ground up. Then it is placed in a special cup made from the husk of a gourd."

Nova remembered the strange gourd that she had seen on Axchel's desk.

"Then that gourd is filled with hot water, to release the flavor of the leaves."

"Yes, yes, you said it was like tea," Alric interrupted anxiously.

"It's more than tea!" Axchel repeated with a growl. "The person who is offering, who is pouring the water, they drink first. Out of a hollow reed with a cloth on the bottom that filters out the small pieces of leaf. Once the water is gone, they refill the cup and hand it to the next person, and then the next."

Nova was starting to understand what Axchel had meant about a ritual.

"The offerer drinks first, to show that it is safe?" she asked him. "As a show of good faith?"

He nodded.

"The first is also the most bitter cup," he told them. "So it is also out of politeness, and respect. And the act of sharing from a single cup encourages unity and connectivity."

Nova glanced at Alric, and he looked as chastised as she felt.

"Lo siento," she mumbled, embarrassed.

"I'm not finished yet," he said. "Everyone drinks mate here. From the poorest commoner, to the soldiers in the army, to the very monarchy themselves. Everyone drinks it; it is a great equalizer, something that we all share. And to share with others is a sign of great respect, inviting you to participate in the joy of communion as an ally, a friend, a member of the family. To deny that offering is considered one of the rudest, ugliest things one can do."

Both Alric and Nova's heads were hanging low now.

"We apologize," Alric said, lifting his gaze to Axchel's. "We would be honored to drink mate with your friend."

Alric turned to walk back inside, and Axchel was quick to follow him. Before he could cross the threshold of the doorway, however, Nova caught his hand. He turned back in surprise and stared at where she was gripping his palm. She realized it was the first time that she had deliberately touched him, and her instinct demanded that she immediately drop his hand and back away. Instead, she made herself meet his gaze.

"I didn't mean to insult you, or your friend," she told him, her voice thick with shame.

"Truly, lo siento," she finished.

Axchel stared at her for a long moment, and she forced herself to meet his gaze for every second. Warmth flooded her body, starting from where their hands met and creeped up her arm, across her chest, and bloomed in her belly and her collarbone. Just when she thought her skin might catch fire, he squeezed her fingers and pulled her back into the cottage. They dropped their hands as soon as they were inside, but the tingling in her fingertips remained for a long time after.

After drinking mate with Ana and exchanging stories (Nova, Alric, and Rawl were careful to not divulge anything that would betray them as Andalans), the old woman finally shifted in her seat to regard them more solemnly.

"So," she said. "What really brings you out here?"

She looked at Axchel and smiled.

"As delighted as I am to see you, mijo, I know you did not come all this way just to drink mate with an old woman."

"They're looking for someone, tía," he responded, placing his hand on her arm. It completely engulfed more than half of her forearm.

"I am indebted to them," he confessed. "I want, I *need,* to help them."

"And what do you think that I can do?" she asked them.

"We are looking for another bruja," Alric told her, leaning forward.

"Y que, all us brujas know each other?" Ana asked, but there was no anger in her voice.

"Tia," Axchel cut in. "I know you have a network; you may know whom they seek."

Ana let out an irritable sigh.

"Ya, bueno," she said. "I might know. Who are you looking for?" she asked.

"We don't know her name," Nova confessed. "But she has long, dark hair like yours. Dark eyes too. She lives with a man, and a child, about eleven years old, and her magia is a light green, like the stalks of a monja blanca flower in spring."

As she spoke, recognition had sparked in the older woman's eyes. Nova felt a thrill rush through her; she knew who they were looking for! But then, to her shock, Ana sprang out of her chair, much faster than any woman her age had a right to, and backed away.

"You're not Cassalains," she accused them. Nova had sprung up when Ana had, and now Rawl and Alric joined her, forming a tight triangle.

"Tia," Axchel approached her, hands raised in submission.

"You brought Andalans into my home?" spat Ana. "You let me share mate with them?"

Melocoton-colored magia began to swirl in front of her. Brujeria was not an offensive magia, and could do little to harm them, but the fact that Ana was calling on it was shocking. Red lightning danced on Alric's fingertips. He had had plenty of time to recover on their journey, and her magia would be laughable compared to his.

"Tia, they were the ones who saved me!" Axchel cried, throwing himself between Ana and the rest of them. The peachy mist stilled in midair.

"They were the ones who freed me," he told her, ducking to look her in the eyes. She blinked, then peeked around him to stare at Nova.

"That's the Danrayen?" she asked him, a look of shock on her weathered face.

Axchel nodded.

"Well," Nova started, about to explain that technically she had only trained with the Danrayens, but had never taken the Trial, and therefore was not a true daughter of Danray, but before she could Ana spoke again.

"You trust them, mijo?" she asked Axchel, turning back to him.

"With my life," he admitted, his voice betraying just a hint of surprise at his own words. Pride burst in Nova's chest, and she saw Alric stand a little taller while Rawl smiled. They all felt it, then. Against all odds, they had made a friend.

Slowly, the bruja's magia dissipated in front of the woman, and she crossed back to her armchair to sit. She stayed there in silence for a long moment, but no one dared to interrupt. Finally, she looked back at Nova.

"What do you want with her?" she asked her.

"I cannot tell you that," Nova answered honestly, sitting in the chair across from her.

"Then I cannot tell you where she is," Ana responded.

"Tia," Axchel began, but Nova raised a hand to stop him.

"I *can* promise you that I mean her no harm," she said.

"And her partner? The Andalan?" A jolt ran down Nova's spine, and she saw Alric and Rawl stiffen. Ana knew about Enrique. It was unclear if she knew he was Andala's lost monarch, or just an Andalan soldier who had switched sides. Nova was certainly not about to ask. She felt Alric approach the back of her chair. Axchel stared at them with a curious expression on his face but didn't move to speak again.

"We mean him no harm either," Nova replied.

Ana was quiet for another moment.

"Swear to me on your goddess. Swear to me on your great goddess Danray that you mean them no harm," she demanded.

Nova's eyebrows shot up. She hadn't expected the request. She opened her mouth to explain that she was not actually a Danrayen, but then felt Alric's long, tapered fingers dig into her shoulder. She snapped her mouth shut.

"I swear," she said instead. "I swear on the goddess Danray that I mean her, and her partner, no harm."

Ana examined her face sternly, and then finally sighed.

"I only tell you because Axchel is like a son to me." She smiled, "Well, more like a nieto. But if you helped him, I will help you."

She stood up once more and crossed to a small writing desk near the window of the main room. Pulling out a piece of parchment and a quill, she began drawing rough shapes on the page.

"The bruja you seek is named Patli," she said, still scrawling. "She lives on the other side of Zipacna Mountain, usually a two-week's journey from here to go around it."

Nova's heart sank. Another two weeks? She supposed it was a small amount of time considering how long they had already been searching.

"But, there is another way. There is a passage behind Zipacna Falls. Usually it would be inaccessible, as most of the year it is rushing water, but in the winter, the water freezes and creates a path to the other side of the mountain," she explained. "It would take less than a day to cut through."

She looked out the window at the sun twinkling over the small patches of snow that remained in clusters around the forest trees.

"The weather has been warming fast, but if you hurry, the path may last for another few days."

Axchel looked uncomfortable.

"Estas segura that the ice will hold?" he asked her. "Maybe it's best if we just go around."

Alric and Rawl turned to look at Nova, and she understood that they would agree with her decision. She wanted to close her eyes and sigh, to slump back into the chair and relax, to just *be*, for just a moment, without the weight of her responsibilities, of her secrets, of her quest, the prophecy, and all the expectations that she had never known a life without.

What would it feel like, she thought, *to just live?*

Was a normal life even possible for her? Who would she be if she didn't have to be the Name-Bearer, traitor to the realm? Or Phanessa, the Danrayen initiate? Or Nova, follower of the Flowers prophecy? She didn't know. All she knew for certain was that she would never have the opportunity to figure it all out if she was unsuccessful in finding the Unnamed Prince.

Nova stood.

"We cross the Zipacna Pass," she decided.

CHAPTER 9

NOVA

A na let them all know that the falls were about an hour's walk on foot, at least for "younger and stronger bodies than hers."

Axchel suggested that they spend the day with the bruja and set out in the morning instead, but Nova dismissed the idea. They were so close, and there was still plenty of daylight left. If they could cross the mountain and reach the other side before nightfall, there was a chance that they could find the Unnamed Prince as soon as tomorrow.

She couldn't stomach the idea of wasting another day, of sitting around doing nothing and waiting until sunrise to continue, not when they were so close.

Ana replenished their supplies, which was both much needed and much appreciated. After three days of frioja stew, frioja salad, and dried frioja roots and leaves, they were delighted and thankful for the fresh produce, meat, beans, and, of course, more mate for the road.

After conferring with Ana, Axchel was certain that he knew how to lead them to the falls. They said their goodbyes to the bruja, Axchel bending almost in half to give the tiny woman another enveloping hug. Alric bowed deeply to her, thanking her again for her hospitality. Rawl held both of her hands within his and kissed them, and then kissed each of her cheeks for good measure. To Nova's shock, the older woman flushed and stammered like a young girl, waving him away and calling him a travieso. Nova also bowed, as Alric had, and genuinely thanked her for her help.

As the group was filing out of the cottage, Ana reached out and grabbed Nova's arm. Her gnarled fingers were wrinkled and browned, her knuckles pushing hard against the thin skin in awkward angles. Yet they gripped Nova's tanned flesh with great force.

"Ten cuidado, niña," she whispered to her. "I don't know why, but the dioses have their eyes on you. The path for those who have stolen their attention is never an easy one."

Her eyes drifted over Nova's form, glazed over, as if she was searching for something just out of sight.

"You have a shroud around you, making it hard for me to see your path. All I know for certain is that it will be much longer and much more perilous than you hope." Then, the woman's eyes shot up to meet Nova's, her gaze startlingly clear.

"You will lose more than you can imagine, by the time it ends."

Shocked and deeply disconcerted, Nova wordlessly wrenched away from the woman's grip and turned to follow the others into the woods. Her heart ached and her skin tingled with pin pricks. Nova dragged her knuckles across her eyelids, determined not to cry in front of the men. It had been a horrible thing for Ana to say to her, and even more terrible for Nova to hear.

But the worst part of all was that somewhere, deep down...

Nova believed her.

True to her word, the thunderous roar of the falls could be heard less than an hour's journey from Ana's cottage. As they drew closer, their voices began to increase in volume in order to be heard over the cacophony of falling water.

"There is a path on the right side of the mountain that leads behind the falls," Axchel shouted over the noise. He checked the rough map that Ana had drawn for them.

"Over there," he called, pointing.

Together the group navigated up the side of the mount, and found a dirt path behind some of overgrown vegetation. It was partially obscured by the twisted roots of trees, and they had to walk carefully to not trip and fall. Soon they made it so close to the falls that a fine spray of mist began soaking their faces and outerwear. They got so close that Nova was sure there was nowhere left to go, that they would hit the mountainside and be stuck, for surely no hidden cavern could lie behind such a powerful force of nature. And if there was, how could any living creature breach its impenetrable wall?

They continued the approach, the water so near that she felt surrounded by it, and she could hear nothing but the roaring of the falls, tumbling from rock over rock and down into the swirling pool below. Soon the mist turned into fat droplets that splashed liberally over herself and her companions. Her hair became plastered to her forehead, over her ears, and on the sides of her neck. She could barely see Rawl and Axchel in front of her. She felt like she was walking directly into a cloud. A very loud, very violent cloud.

And then, Axchel disappeared. She gasped, the sound infinitesimally small compared to the roar around her. Rawl continued walking until, suddenly, he too was gone! Nova scurried to catch up, careful not to slip on the slick, wet stone beneath her feet. When she had almost reached the mountain wall she saw it, a bend, just behind a rivulet of cascading water. She turned into it, and if she wasn't already fully soaked before, that last step between the outer world and the entrance to the cavern certainly finished the job.

Alric followed close behind her, shaking his head like a wet puppy once he was clear of the cascade. Ana had been correct; behind the waterfalls was a long winding path of ice. Nova crouched to look at it more closely and could see running water underneath the thick frozen sheet above it. The sound of the falls was dampened within the cavern, but she still had to raise her voice to be heard.

"Will it hold?" she asked, referring to the cap of ice, the only thing between them and a rushing river below.

No one answered.

"It'll have to hold," she decided.

"We should stick to the outer edges where there's a small rim of earth and stone," Axchel suggested.

"Agreed," she said, shivering. The cavern was freezing, and she was soaked.

Alric noticed, of course, and quickly brought his fingers together, mumbling strange words as red lightning danced over his fingertips. This time, Nova didn't stop him; he was no longer weak and gaunt from their long journey over the Borders. He had finally recovered and had magia to spare. Besides, if he didn't help them to dry off, they would likely freeze to death. Cold and wet were a dangerous combination.

After a moment, Nova felt a warm gust of wind ruffle her clothing and hair, sneaking in between the thick layers of fabric and finding its way into her shoes. It was over almost as quickly as it had begun. When Nova raised her hand to touch her hair she realized that it was completely dry. Turning to look at Rawl and Axchel, she could see that they, too, had received the same treatment.

If Axchel was perturbed by the magia, he surely didn't show it. Nova found Axchel's calmness strange. With Cassalan not having that many mages, she thought that being the recipient of spellwork would come as a shock to him, but he seemed undisturbed. Then again, he had spent time with brujas. Perhaps magia was not as strange to him as it had been to her when she had first been introduced to it.

Slowly, they began walking down the icy tunnel. After a while, the drum-like noise of the falls faded into a pleasant background hum, and then disappeared entirely. The sound of the rushing water was muffled by the layer of ice under their feet. Soon, the light from outside the cavern began fading, promising only darkness ahead.

"Should we light a torch?" Rawl asked, looking down at the ice skeptically.

"Too risky," Nova replied. "We don't know what that added heat could do to our path."

"I can do something," Alric interrupted, lifting his staff in the air and muttering a few words. It crackled with red, and suddenly a disconnected globe of luz balanced above their heads halfway in between the four of them, illuminating them and their path.

He reached into his cloak pocket and purged the remnants of the poisonous magia from his blood into his Phoenixeye stone, before replacing it in his garments.

The lantern spell was useful but eerie, the light casting long, frightening shadows, their forms elongated and deformed against the cavern walls. At first, conversation was sparse as they took care not to step too close to the center of the ice river pass; however, once their bodies began getting accustomed to the awkward shuffling progress (which consisted more of gliding movements than planted steps), conversation began again.

"How did you meet Ana?" Alric asked Axchel.

"Before I was promoted to captain, I was a healer," he answered, his lumbering frame made awkward by the sliding motions that he was attempting to emulate.

"I have an affinity for it, and I'm better suited for it than killing, I think."

Once, Nova might have scoffed at his statement, insisting that all Cassalains were killers. Now, she mentally nodded to herself in agreement; Axchel cared too much about people to make an efficient soldier.

"Ana trained me," he continued.

"The Cassalain army sends people like me to brujas y brujos to hone our abilities. Ana was the closest bruja to my future station, so I stayed with her for six weeks before starting my position at Snow Goat Pass."

"You two seem close," Rawl commented.

Nova couldn't see Axchel's face as he led their party, but she could hear the fondness in his voice when he replied.

"She was very kind to me. Tough, but kind. I learned a lot from her." He paused. "She was the first person who was decent to me since I had joined the army. She didn't treat me any differently, even though I was clearly half Condori. I wish I could say the same for my brothers in arms."

Before Nova could think of a proper response, Axchel froze in his path.

Nova tensed and reached for her daggers, but before she could draw one, he laughed.

"Obsidianas!" he called out, his voice pleased.

The river path had bulged out to form a half circle protrusion along its path, and the cavern wall curved up to accommodate it. On that wall, Nova could see dozens of pitch-black flowers growing in tangled vines over its surface. The petals were so dark that they were iridescent, sliding between endless black and shimmering blue, depending on how you looked at them. Nova was reminded of a small bird that used to live near the temple, its feathers mimicking a similar color pattern, black in one angle, a glittering, midnight blue in another. Axchel was making his way toward the blooms.

"They're incredibly rare," he told them while removing a small dagger from his belt. "They only grow in cold climates and in complete darkness, but once plucked can live for weeks before wilting."

He turned, parts of his features shrouded in darkness due to the meager light. But Nova could see he was smiling. Carefully, stepping closer to her, he reached out with his right hand. Nova looked down in surprise and saw that he was extending a small bouquet of obsidianas to her.

She immediately recoiled.

His action, innocent and simple as it might have been, was entirely too much for her. Her history with the Flowers of Prophecy had left her with a strong aversion to flowers of any kind, and while she could stomach the sight of them, she still preferred not to be near, smell, or touch any of them.

As if that wasn't enough, the person offering her the source of her discomfort, the trigger of her terrible memories, was a Cassalain soldier.

The enemy.

Any progress that Nova had made in not viewing Axchel as an opponent completely evaporated at the sight of the bundle of flowers in his hand. At that moment, she wanted to put as much distance between her, and them, as possible. Unfortunately, when she leapt backward she did it quickly and forcefully, without thinking of where she was going, only that she needed to get away. It landed her directly in the center of the ice path.

There was a breathless moment when the three men stared at her, frozen in place, unsure of what to do, as Nova realized her mistake. She held as still as possible, her body crouched and arms extended out to her sides for balance. For the span of two breaths, it was deathly silent. Nova's heart was pounding in her ears. Two breaths became three, then four, and then Nova lost count. After what seemed like an eternity, she felt secure enough to straighten her spine slowly.

Nothing had happened, the ice had held!

"I think it's ok," Nova started, and then an earth-splintering crack echoed against the tunnel walls and reverberated inside Nova's skull.

She had a quick moment to look down at the ice crumbling beneath her feet, just before she was pulled into the rushing ice water.

Nova could feel nothing but numb.

Even the momentary shock of cold when she was pulled under the water had been erased, and substituted with nothing but numbness. She tried to kick, to move her arms, to push against the pull of the current, but she could barely feel her limbs, let alone get them to work properly. Even so she floundered her arms, trying to grasp something to stop her movement, but there was nothing to hold on to. Finally, her hand slammed against something hard, and she tried to dig her fingers in to grip it but could not find purchase. Belatedly, she realized that what she was touching was the sheet of ice above her, but she had been pulled too far by the current, and it was unyielding and unbroken above her reach.

Nova's lungs burned, but not with fire, with pin pricks of ice, stabbing at her chest, her throat, her tongue. She couldn't stop, she couldn't breathe, and there was no way that she would make it to the other side of the mountain in time for her to save herself. Eventually, her panicked body, desperate, would inhale, trying to suck much-needed oxygen into her system. She would pull in ice water into her lungs, and drown.

Without warning, a violent force slammed into her, and something was wrapped around her torso. She squirmed hard and fought the creature, bubbles expelling through her nose and mouth with her repressed scream. A part of her, however, was relieved. Dying at the hands of a river monstro was a better way to go than drowning from a foolish error. At least in her last moments her body would be preoccupied with fighting, rather than drowning. The pressure on her torso increased, and she felt herself being dragged to what she thought was the side of the cavern. Unable to resist the urge to witness the face of her demise, she squinted her eyes open.

It was not a river monstro.

It was Axchel.

He held her against him as he maneuvered them to the side of the underwater river where the water was more shallow. His feet were planted on the riverbed, heels digging in, body straining against the current. His left arm was wrapped around Nova and his right hand was pressed against the ice above them.

Nova wondered how she could see him at all in the darkness, but then noticed that Alric's light orb had seemed to follow them, and was dangling above their heads on the other side of the ice. Axchel's eyes were open too, his face set in grim determination. He was staring upward at the luz, straining, and then seemed to come to a decision. He made a heavy fist with his right hand. His arm bent at the elbow, drawing his hand back, and then he extended, punching the ice above their heads.

Nothing happened.

He brought his arm down further the next time, and extended it even harder, working against the heaviness of the water. Nova's body jostled against him with the force of the impact. A hairline fracture appeared above them. Air gurgled in the back of Nova's throat, and she felt like she was being squeezed by a python—she needed to breathe, she needed to inhale. Axchel punched the ice again, more fractures appearing with the blow.

Black spots swam in front of Nova's eyes, her body growing limp within Axchel's hold. His gaze jerked to hers, filled with worry.

Her eyelids fluttered.

Axchel began pounding on the ice above them, harder and faster, more and more breaks appearing on the surface.

A small whine escaped from the back of Nova's throat, just as the world shattered above them. She closed her eyes, but before Axchel could pull them up to safety,

Nova inhaled.

The next time Nova's eyes opened she was retching, body turned to the side, and a heavy hand was whacking her across the back.

She vomited, expelling all the contents of her stomach: water, her morning meal, more water, and then water again. She continued to throw up what felt like an endless amount of water, until only bile coated the back of her throat. The pounding on her back eased as her heaves did, and then the hand was drawing soft, soothing circles against her soaked clothing instead. When she twisted to sit up, she realized that she was freezing, her teeth chattering and vibrating within her skull.

"Thank you," she whispered hoarsely to Axchel, then looked around him. When she didn't see anyone else with him, she panicked.

"Alric? Rawl?" She tried to yell, but her voice was too raw, and the sound came out like a croak.

She tried to scramble past Axchel to look down under the ice, as if she would see them swimming underneath.

"Relájate," Axchel said, gripping her tightly.

She looked at him, her eyes desperate and panicked.

"Hey," he said, rubbing the outside of her upper arms.

"They're all right," he said. "Te lo prometo. The ice didn't break everywhere, just under where you were standing. I dived in after you but told them to meet us down the path. I knew that if I were able to rescue you, someone would need to come to rescue *me*."

He delivered it glibly, almost as if he was joking, but it did make sense. There was no need for the four of them to end up soaking wet and half drowned.

"I think that Alric bound the luz to me when I jumped in the water; it helped light the way so that I could find you," Axchel said, looking up at the globe which illuminated their position.

"Why?" Nova asked him, so cold that she could barely force the words from her mouth.

Axchel looked confused.

"Why what?" he asked her.

"Why," her lips trembled, making speech difficult. "Why did you come in after me?" she managed to ask him.

His gaze softened, but before he could answer, Nova swooned. He grabbed her before her head could hit the cavern floor.

"We have to get you warm," Axchel said, his voice laced with worry.

And then, inexplicably, he began peeling off his clothing.

Nova frowned, confused.

"I naturally give off more body heat than most people," he told her, moving to remove her clothing next. Surprisingly, the action did not startle her. She had a vague, far away thought that she should probably object, but couldn't remember why. But in the moment, she wasn't afraid of him or what he might do. She was just confused.

The cold is making me dumb, she thought.

"It's part of the healing affinity," he continued. "Higher body temperatures mean I'm less likely to contract illnesses; I burn them right off."

When both he and she were down to only their under clothing, he pulled her into his arms. Any room she might have had for embarrassment was immediately occupied with an overwhelming sense of relief instead. *He was so warm!*

"It also helps when you're a soldier stationed at the coldest post in Tierramadri," he joked.

Somehow, the close proximity to warmth set her body into overdrive. The shivers turned into full blown, body-wracking shakes, and her teeth chattered so hard against each other that she was sure she was going to chip them.

Axchel was so big that both his arms wrapped around her torso covered most of her upper body, and her face was buried in the crook between his chin and collarbone. Instinctively she twined her legs in between his, trapping them between his muscular thighs and calves. He rubbed the skin on her arms and back with brisk, rapid motions, and slowly the shivering subsided. After a while, her palms found their way to the center of his chest, and she tilted her head so she was lying against his shoulder, rather than buried in his neck. She untangled her legs from his but didn't pull away.

Once her brain was capable of working again, she remembered her Danrayen training. Axchel had acted exactly the way that one was supposed to when someone was at risk for cold sickness.

"Gracias," she repeated to him, quietly.

He felt her nod against her hair, his cheek lying over the top of her head.

"Get some rest," he told her. "I'm sure that Rawl and Alric will be here soon, but the water and the cold drained a lot of your energy, so you should sleep while you have the chance."

Nova knew he was right, and felt herself drifting even before he had finished his statement. Before she gave in to her exhaustion, she asked him once again.

"*Why?*"

Then immediately fell asleep.

CHAPTER 10
DAMIKA

It wasn't the seediest cantina that Damika, Petra, and Taruka had ever been to, but it certainly wasn't the most reputable either.

The establishment was dark, despite the fact that the sun had not yet finished setting, all the windows and doors shut tight to block out the day's lingering light. The long rectangular room was crammed with sticky, splintering tables and chairs, their tops marred with stains in various colors and consistencies that were best not too closely examined. There was a long bar along the left wall, and a raised platform not far from it, presumably for live entertainment. At the moment, it was empty. The room smelled strongly of body odor, dirty hair, tobacco, and beer, a nauseating combination upon first entry, but to Damika's horror, she found that she had gotten used to the stench.

In the shadows of the room's corners were groups of dangerous-looking men and women, dressed in equally dark colors that allowed them to blend into their surroundings like fantasmas. Damika and Taruka had claimed a small round table with three rickety stools near the back wall, Damika angling her chair to get a clear view of both the entire room and the entrance.

Petra joined them after a few moments, balancing three large cervezas between her small hands. Damika eyed the smudged glasses warily, wrinkling up the side of her nose. They didn't seem any cleaner than the tables and floor. Taruka accepted her own glass gingerly, holding it with only three fingers, which she subtly wiped on her pant leg after setting the beer down. She didn't reach for it again.

Petra, on the other hand, brought her own straight to her lips and swallowed down nearly half its contents in one go, sighing loudly and slamming her glass down on the table with a small burp.

"Did you find out anything?" Damika asked them both softly, not wanting her voice to carry. She swirled the liquid in her cup, but didn't drink.

Taruka leaned in and dropped her own voice.

"There is a farmhouse on the outskirts of this town that may have what we are looking for," she answered, using the careful, neutral language they all used when discussing their mission in public. "I am told it might be abandoned now, but perhaps we should pay it a visit, and see if those reports might be mistaken?"

A thrill of anticipation rushed through Damika, making her skin tingle. Her heart kicked in her chest, threatening to climb its way up to her throat, but she stamped it down.

"You're sure that this farm has what we are looking for?" she asked evenly, not allowing her voice to betray how desperately she wanted it to be true.

Taruka nodded. "There are people there who match certain descriptions. Or there were, at least. They might have answers to our questions."

"It was confirmed by several members of the town," Petra added. "They all tell the same story. The farm was bought a few years back, but the people never planted any crops, or housed any livestock. They didn't seem well-trusted in the town, they still call them 'the outside rs.'"

Utterly lost to the hope that blossomed within her, Damika took a sip of her cerveza, not even noticing Taruka's grimace.

Finally, she thought. *Finally, some progress!*

"We should go now," she said, standing from the table so abruptly that she rattled its uneven balance, Petra's beer nearly falling to the floor before she caught it. She shot Damika with an affronted glare.

"Surely we can stay for one drink?" she muttered, pointedly moving her eyes about the room, where several heads had turned at Damika's hasty motion.

"Of course," Damika replied as cooly as she could, lowering herself back down onto her stool.

An ugly heat burned the back of her neck. The last thing that they wanted was to draw attention to themselves. She was acting like a green recruit, not a Danrayen Warrior. Deliberately, she grabbed her cerveza and took another long sip, forcing her body to relax. After a few moments, the curious stares in their direction ceased, the patrons returning to their own business.

As embarrassed as Damika was by her actions, there was still a large part of her that wanted to jump up from their table again, rush out the door, and run to the farmhouse as quickly as possible. It was the first real lead that their group had had in months, and the closest they had come in their quest in years. If there was any possibility that the rumors were true, and that what they sought was as close as the outskirts of town, then Damika wanted to waste no time in getting there.

The truth was that Damika was getting desperate. It had started out as a tiny sliver of doubt that had lodged itself somewhere behind her ribs, twinging every time she got close to an answer, only to have it slip out of reach. Over time the sliver had festered, burrowing itself deeper into her flesh, spreading like infection. It poisoned her from the inside little by little, with every dead end, every failed attempt, every day, month, and year that their quest continued unfulfilled.

"You are a disappointment," it whispered. *"Strong Damika, powerful Damika, pride of the Danrayens. If the others could see you now, they wouldn't be so impressed. What does it matter if you were the youngest initiate to ever pass the Trial, if you have nothing to show for it now? If the priestesses knew of your failures, they wouldn't be so keen to recruit you to the Danrayen Riders. If Nessa knew how far you've fallen, she wouldn't look at you with admiration shining in those big, brown eyes ever again."*

As inconspicuously as she could, Damika took in a deep breath, holding it, then released it slowly. She repeated the action several times, driving down the panic that always accompanied the nasty thoughts that would so often rise to her mind unbidden. She clutched her hands together on her lap, hiding her trembling fingers from her friends.

As Damika was attempting to calm her racing nerves, cheers and lewd whistles erupted in the cantina. From behind the bar walked out a lovely young woman dressed in scraps of fabric that concealed very little. The top was decorated in golden feathers that spanned across her chest and upper arms, but stopped abruptly at her sternum, leaving the rounded expanse of her stomach exposed. The bottom portion of the outfit was fashioned by twisted ropes, with more feathers covering her rear. Her long, tanned legs were also bare.

From behind her, a young man held a small, flat drum in his left hand, which he soon began hitting with the slender long stick in his right. At the music, the woman began to dance. Her hips moved in a rapid tempo to the beat, her stomach rolling and undulating in a way Damika had never thought possible. As she stepped up onto the performance platform, the feathers on her backside twitched and shuffled, her feet never ceasing their relentless rhythm against the hardwood floor. Every single pair of eyes in the room were fixated on her in awe.

Power, Damika thought, impressed. *Not the same sort of power as being a warrior, but its power nonetheless. She commands the room with it.*

Damika noticed that Petra's eyes were wide on her face, almost forming two perfect circles which matched her open mouth. Taruka stared at her partner in amusement, shaking her head. Eventually, when Petra didn't move for several long minutes, she elbowed her in the ribs.

"Que?" Petra sputtered, tearing her gaze away from the beautiful performer to Taruka. "Oh, sorry," she chuckled, grabbing her glass. Almost immediately her eyes flickered back to the dancer, just as she rolled her hips, causing the ropes to swirl in circles against her thighs. Petra's mouth dropped open once again, and she managed to upend most of her beer over the front of her shirt rather than in her mouth. Taruka rolled her eyes and stood, crossing the room to exit the bar.

"Ah, wait, amor!" Petra called after her, following hot on her heels. Along the way patrons grumbled and muttered as she tried to wipe the beer off of her chest, droplets landing from her hands on the people around her. Luckily for her, most were too transfixed with the feathered dancer to make too much of a fuss.

Damika knew that Taruka wasn't really worried about Petra looking at another woman, they were too in love for petty jealousy. But it was one thing for Petra to look, and quite another to act like a fool in front of her girlfriend. They would argue a little or bicker a lot, Petra would apologize, and they'd make up in no time. Damika knew she should probably give them their space, but she was too grateful for an excuse to leave and continue on their mission to let the moment go to waste. Abandoning her still-full glass, she hurried out the bar to join her friends.

When they reached the farmhouse, it did indeed appear to be abandoned, but Damika would not be deterred so easily.

"Maybe they only want to make it *look* like no one lives there," she suggested, as they all crouched behind a patch of long grass a few yards away.

"I don't know, Dami," Petra said skeptically. "It doesn't look like anyone has been in there for a while."

Damika unsheathed her sword. "Let's check."

Taruka looked alarmed. "Maybe we can start by knocking on the door first?" she asked, eying Damika's Espada warily.

Damika dropped her guard, but kept the blade at her side. "Fine," she agreed.

Together they crossed to the entry, but when Petra raised her hand to knock, the door jiggled inwardly, clearly unlocked. Petra pushed it forward cautiously.

There was no one inside. There was barely anything inside at all, just an abandoned kitchen table, a few old blankets, and a lot of broken glass. Ahead of them the hallway looked equally deserted.

"Check all the rooms," Damika said, panic clawing at her throat once more. "It can't be empty," she stressed between clenched teeth. "It can't."

A few moments later they all met back in the main room, confirming that the house was, in fact, empty. Damika shook her head.

"No," she said. They were so close. They couldn't give up now. "No, check everywhere. Check the ceiling, check underneath the floorboards," she insisted, ignoring the flashback to her dream when she mentioned floorboards.

"Dami—" Taruka started gently.

"Check it," Damika interrupted, pulling out a dagger to try to pry up the wood beneath their feet.

"Dami," Taruka repeated, her voice heavy with concern.

"No," Damika grunted, spinning around the glare at her. "No! This was our best lead; we can't abandon it. Someone here knows something."

"Damika, there is no one here," Petra said.

"We'll burn it," Damika decided.

Petra and Taruka shared a shocked look.

"Que?" Petra asked.

"We'll burn the farmhouse down," Damika repeated, loudly. "If there is anyone hiding, they'll have to reveal themselves!"

"Dami, *no one* is here!" Taruka insisted, but Damika just shook her head.

The panic was more acute now, her heart raced with it, her fingertips tingled like she was being stabbed with a thousand tiny splinters. She felt dizzy and out of breath, like she had run a very long way. A ringing started in her ears and she clutched at her head.

"No," she said, then straightened quickly, trying desperately to calm herself. Slowly, deliberately, she sheathed her sword and imagined that with the action, she sheathed all of panic and emotions along with it. The ringing dimmed, and the pressure behind her eyes lessened. "If no one is here, if we cannot get the information that we need here, then we move on. *Now.*"

"Dami, we already have rooms at the inn," Taruka reminded her. "It's late, we can spend the night, and head out in the morning after a proper meal and rest."

"No," she repeated, terrified that if she rested, the feelings of disappointment and regret would catch her. "We leave now."

"Where to next?" Petra asked, resigned.

"We go north."

CHAPTER 11

NOVA

Nova awoke to someone screaming her name. Dazed, she lifted her head off of a warm and comfortable pillow. It took her a second to remember where she was, and what had happened. And, that the pillow was, in fact, a living breathing person.

Awake, alert, and not on the brink of death, Nova found that she finally had room for mortification.

Why did she always end up falling asleep on the man?

Cheeks flaming with embarrassment, she managed to pull herself away from Axchel just as Rawl and Alric rounded a corner of the cave, a second light orb suspended above their heads. Alric rushed at her, kneeling to throw his arms around her. She gripped him gratefully, relieved to see them both well. Axchel stood awkwardly, picking up his wet and partially frozen clothing in a poor attempt to cover himself more fully. It didn't do much good; the man was just so large!

Alric looked between the two of them, and Nova felt the uncomfortable urge to insist, *"This is not what it looks like!"*

Which was absurd. Alric was a grown man, a university-educated mage, and knew as well as she did the correct steps to take to counteract cold sickness. He didn't even hesitate before understanding flickered across his features. The mage repeated the same spell from earlier, when they had first crossed into the cavern, and a rustle of wind blew across each of their frames and discarded clothing. Grateful, Nova scrambled up to pull hers on, and from the corner of her eye she could see that Axchel was doing the same. When she was done, Rawl nudged Alric aside to give Nova a hug of his own.

"You scared us, amiga," he murmured into her hair.

"I scared myself," she admitted, deeply embarrassed.

It had been her own fault that she had fallen into the ice, and because of her folly the rest of her group had been put in danger as well.

Especially Axchel.

As ashamed as she was of her unwarranted response to a simple cluster of flowers, she knew that she couldn't dwell on it. The most important priority was getting them all out of the cave, the sooner the better. At that moment, she couldn't care less if the Unnamed Prince was just ten steps away. She wanted a fire, she wanted food, she wanted to rest, and she wanted to make sure that Axchel had all three as well. He had taken care of her, and she wasn't going to allow him to get sick on her account—no matter how unlikely it might be with his affinity. She owed him that much.

Luckily, it seemed as if the current had taken them farther and faster than they would've gone if by on foot. In their rush to find them, Rawl and Alric had also traveled above ground much quicker than they would have had they continued the same pace as the morning. As soon as Axchel and Nova were ready, they continued their journey, all of them anxious to get out of the cave and off the dangerous ice path. They continued their strange shuffle-sliding as they moved across the outer edge of the ice. Conversation once again died down with all of their attention on keeping themselves upright and safe. Before long, the group was stepping out on the other side of the mountain, the sun just setting beyond the horizon.

Nova let out an enormous sigh of relief.

"Let's stop and rest," she said, pointing to a flat area around the bend of the river where the water had melted enough to flow without an ice cap. There was a cluster of trees in a thick, crescent moon shape framing the area. If Alric hadn't exhausted his energy with the drying and light spells, he could ward their camp easily.

The men quickly agreed and made their way much more confidently down the mountain and toward the clearing, everyone very obviously relieved to have dependable earth beneath their feet once again.

The camp was set up quickly, complete with a crackling fire in its center. They dug out some of the provisions that Ana had gifted them and ate ravenously. Nova and Axchel refueling after their struggles in the water and nearly freezing to death, Alric replenishing his energy and his magia, and Rawl because, well, he was Rawl.

As a group, they agreed to wake early so that they could make it to Enrique and Patli's cabin, and the Unnamed Prince, as soon as they could.

Sleep came easy as they all went to bed with warm bodies, full bellies, and hopeful hearts.

For almost all of them.

That night, lying in her bed mat, the crackling fire made a pleasant background noise, Nova thought of Damika. Which wasn't surprising. Nova often thought of Damika.

What *was* surprising were the emotions that came with thinking of her. At first, she didn't understand the uncomfortable feeling that was wrapped up in the memory of her face, her smile, her kiss. So she lay, frowning in the darkness, a knot of worry forming just below her ribs and just above her stomach. She breathed into that spot, imagining her breath filling that space, and then exhaling the feeling through her mouth. It was a technique they had taught her at the Danrayen Temple to help identify the myriad of emotions that could crop up, not just during battle, but in life. She repeated the motions until the feeling was clear.

Guilt.

She was feeling guilt.

But why? What did she have to feel guilty about? She hadn't seen Damika in years, had done nothing to hurt, or offend, or betray her friend.

Or had she?

Nova forced herself to delve deeper into the feeling of guilt, and surprisingly, Axchel's face came to mind. When she imagined his eyes, like dark expansions of the night sky, his skin, so deep and rich, and his body, so strong and reliable, the pang of guilt intensified so strongly that it almost knocked her breath away.

She was attracted to Axchel.

It was unbelievable. She had never been attracted to a man before. She had never been attracted to *anyone* besides Damika, and to be attracted to the *Cassalain* of all people made no sense. She barely knew him, not the way that she knew the other men in their group. Over the past few months, she had grown to know Alric inside and out. She and Axchel were not friends, not confidants, or companions like she and the mage were.

And he was not beautiful like Rawl was, all honey, tumbled curls, mischievous grins, and piercing green eyes. He didn't make her laugh or feel at ease the way the archer did.

He did, Nova realized with a start, make her feel safe. If she was honest with herself, she had felt safe in his presence from the moment they had met, locked away together in a bandit camp as fellow prisoners. He had helped her, tended to her wounds, and attempted to keep her protected. Now, months later, he had risked his own life to save hers, despite the fact that her peril had been her own fault. But he had not made her feel foolish about it, had not reprimanded her error, had not been angry or chastising. He had merely attempted to help her, again. He dove into the churning, frigid water to find her, smashed an impossibly solid sheet of ice to drag them from the river, revived her, and then held her in his arms to conserve their heat.

In the moment, she hadn't had time to feel anything but the numbing cold, but now, thinking about the way her body had curled into his, she suddenly felt nothing but warmth. She was grateful for the darkness that concealed the furious flush that burned in her cheeks. He had felt so solid, so reliable, so secure. She had let herself drift into sleep within his arms, never hesitating for a moment to wonder whether or not she was safe. She knew that she was, that he would take care of her.

Nova didn't know what any of it meant, or what she wanted. As uncomfortable and embarrassed as she felt, she was just grateful to have finally given voice to her emotions. Maybe, now that she realized them, there was some way that she could navigate them. Even so, she dreaded the break of dawn, when she would have to look him in the eyes with the new knowledge that a part of her was beginning to care for him.

Nova woke with a strong hand shaking her shoulder. Her eyes shot open, landing on Rawl's emerald gaze.

"Today is the day," he greeted her cheerfully.

Nova was instantly filled with a rush of anxious anticipation that left little room to dwell on the previous night's revelation. The emotions that had kept Nova up long into the evening seemed so insignificant in the light of day, especially when they were so close to the culmination of their quest.

"Don't get your hopes up too high," Nova told him as she sat up and stretched, but she knew the warning was as much for herself as anyone else. Even so, she couldn't help but be cautiously optimistic. In a matter of hours, they could be in the presence of the Unnamed Prince. If they found him, they could start their journey back to Andala.

Back home.

Better still, if the Flowers' prophecy was true, finding the boy would be the first step toward peace.

As she rose from her bedroll, Axchel and Alric broke through the tree line, holding a pail of water, their hair still slightly wet and their faces scrubbed clean.

"Buenos dias," Nova said shyly. Alric merely grunted, but Axchel returned her greeting.

After they broke down the camp and ate a quick morning meal, Axchel led the way once again. By then, the mage was finally fit for human company and engaged in conversation with the Cassalain. Nova hung back a little, choosing to walk with Rawl at the rear, rather than risk being pulled into their conversation. She was still feeling uncertain about her feelings toward the soldier, and she couldn't afford to get distracted.

Nova thought that this last leg of their travels would be excruciatingly slow, time drawn out in a seemingly endless pace, but before they knew it, a cottage could be seen through a thick cluster of trees. The four of them glanced at each other, and conversation died down. They quickened their pace and were suddenly in the clearing before the front door.

It was the exact house that Nova, Alric, and Rawl had seen in Seer Sarakshi's vision. Jagged cuts of rock were stacked to form the cottage's walls, held together by dried mud. Like Ana's home, there was a long stone chimney with curling ringlets of smoke. They stopped, unsure of how to proceed.

"I suppose we should just knock on the door?" Nova ventured, but before anyone could answer, the ground in front of them split open with a reverberating *crack*.

The four of them were thrown backward, landing on their rears and spines and skittering on the dirt before coming to a stop. Nova and Alric sprang up first, but Axchel and Rawl were slower, having received the brunt of the blast. Then, a sparkling green energy crackled in the air in front of them. Alric threw up an orange-red shield of magia in front of himself and Nova, but wasn't fast enough to protect the archer and Cassalain. The green electricity surrounded them, freezing them in place like stone statues. Nova was already moving forward, Espada drawn, not sparing a glance to check whether or not her friends were still alive. If they were, then she needed to do everything in her power to protect them and Alric.

And if they weren't?

She couldn't fathom it.

But they would be avenged.

Alric ran forward with her, his magia a deep crimson that Nova had only seen when they were battling. From around the corner of the cottage, a bruja emerged, her own green magia lifting up her hair in static waves.

"How does a bruja know battle magia?" Nova yelled at the mage, but before he could answer, a man ran out of the front door of the house, wielding an impressive-looking sword, and had she not been so well-trained, Nova would have dropped her own.

It was him.

It was Enrique.

The king of Andala.

There was no time to worry about the implications of fighting with her own monarch when he came after her with a practiced and lethal-looking strike. Nova parried on instinct, and then they were dueling. From the corner of her eye she could see Alric and the bruja locked in combat magia, but she made herself tune them out to give her full attention to her own fight.

King Enrique was a renowned swordsman, always had been. He was one of the fiercest fighters that Andala had ever known, and had once been thought to be the one who would bring an end to the war. His attacks and lunges had been innate, and his movements had always seemed as effortless to him as breathing.

But he had been missing for the last twelve years, and it was clear to Nova that, in that time, he had had little need for swordsmanship.

His technique was still masterful, some of his movements as beautiful as works of art, and Nova could not help but be impressed.

But he was slower than he should have been and relied on the same weaponry techniques that were taught to all Andalan soldiers. Nova was not an Andalan soldier; she was Danrayen trained.

She allowed the king to lunge forward, feigning a retreat, but at the last moment spun into his side, jamming a hard elbow into his ribs before landing. He pivoted, too slow, and Nova swung her Espada hard against his sword, forcing him on the defensive. His eyes widened at the attack, and he brought his sword up again and again and again, narrowly managing to deflect each of her blows in time. She could see sweat beading on his forehead, and she knew he was tiring.

Then, on her right saw a flash of red magia and a woman's cry of alarm. Enrique looked to his left, his face betraying his fear. He dropped his guard fractionally, and just for a moment, but it was enough. Nova brought her arm around, hard, and knocked his blade from his grip. He sank to his knees, his hands high, still facing Alric and the bruja.

Nova held the tip of her Espada to her former king's throat.

"Patli!" he called out, his voice desperate.

Nova watched as the bruja sat up from the ground Alric had knocked her down on. The electric green energy of her magia dissipated as she took in the sight of the mage looming above her, and then her partner at the end of Nova's blade.

"Por favor—" she started, before Enrique interrupted her.

"Don't hurt her! You can have anything, please, just don't hurt her," he pleaded.

Nova's head swam at the sight of the last king of Andala, begging at her feet. She felt deeply uncomfortable, ashamed, as if she were committing the most grievous sin, the worst form of treason. In a way, she was. She still didn't drop her guard, however. The two of them were still dangerous.

"Release our friends," Alric demanded of the bruja, who nodded quickly.

"Wait," Nova called out. Alric turned to her with a small frown.

"We can speak more freely if the Cassalain isn't involved," she told him, a bit ruefully. It seemed unfair to leave him in the dark after all of his aid, but they couldn't risk him finding out their true identities, or their mission. Alric gave her a curt nod, and Nova turned her gaze back to Patli.

"Just the archer, the one reaching for his bow. Leave the larger man frozen, for now," she told her.

If the bruja found the request odd, she didn't betray it. Under the watchful eye of Alric, she flicked her wrist and then Rawl was sputtering and scrambling up behind them.

"Que paso?" he asked when he had caught up to them.

"Freeze spell," Alric told him, his eyes scanning him up and down, presumably checking for injury. Nova saw Rawl fluster at the mage's attention.

"Y Ax?" Rawl asked, turning back to look at the Cassalain, one knee and hand on the floor, crouched as if ready to spring up at any moment.

"After," Nova replied simply.

"You called him 'the Cassalain'" Enrique suddenly interjected.

"Dioses, it's really him, isn't it?" Rawl gaped as he finally drew his attention to the kneeling man. "That's King Enrique!"

Enrique ignored him, still staring intently at Nova.

"You called him 'the Cassalain,'" he repeated. "Meaning, you are not Cassalains?" he looked between the three of them, his gaze landing back on Nova.

"You're Andalans."

Nova could see different emotions flickering over the man's face, confusion, suspicion, distrust. She could see when he started piecing things together, because he looked at her in shock, then horror, and disbelief.

Nova waited him out, not breaking her gaze. She had only been a child the last time she had been in his presence, but she had no doubt that he knew of her and suspected who she was. But she wasn't going to save him the effort of acknowledging her. Finally, he dropped his head in resignation.

"You're her, aren't you? You're the Name-Bearer."

Every cell in her body rejected the title, the mantle that she had held for so long and hidden away for even longer. The designation that had been forced upon her and had cost her a normal life, her freedom, her very identity. She swallowed down the wave of panic she felt anytime she heard those words and forced herself to address the king.

"No," she responded curtly. "I haven't been for a very long time. But I once was."

"Que?" a confused voice asked behind them. Everyone turned at once, Nova making sure to keep her blade trained on Enrique.

Behind them, shock carved on his face, was Axchel.

"You're... Que?" he stuttered.

Patli gaped at him, and then looked up at Alric.

"I didn't release him from the spell, te lo prometo!" she said, worry lacing her words. Alric stared at Axchel in disbelief.

"How did you..." he started, before trailing away.

Axchel finally looked away from Nova, and she gasped, realizing that she had frozen under his gaze. He turned toward Alric and Patli.

"It was a capture spell? Or a freeze spell?" he asked the bruja, who nodded. Axchel shrugged.

"Something to do with my healing affinity, I burn hotter, run faster than most people. Spells are effective, but break down over time."

Then he turned back to Nova.

"You're really her, the Name-Bearer? The traitor of Andala?"

At his words, Nova looked at Alric and Rawl, afraid. The safety that she had felt in Axchel's presence evaporated. Rawl quickly lifted his bow and swung his body around to aim it at the Cassalain, who threw his hands up quickly.

For a breathless moment they all stood there, Enrique kneeling with Nova's blade at his neck, Patli seated on the dirt floor, Alric's red-tinged fingers extended toward her, and Rawl, his arrow pointed straight at Axchel, who looked more confused than scared. Before any of them could continue speaking, a small voice called out from the cottage.

"Mamá? Papa?"

They all turned to the front door.

And saw the Unnamed Prince.

CHAPTER 12

JESADIRANY

After their fateful encounter at the river, Jesa had a new awareness of Jose.

And he watched her.

Jesa felt his eyes on her anytime they were together and could glimpse him staring from the corner of her vision. It would have been disconcerting, if Jesa hadn't been staring right back.

She had no name for it, the strange pull, the undeniable attraction. She didn't know why her body responded to his mere presence as if she were anticipating a battle, her heartbeat racing, palms sweating, head rushing. She thought of him constantly, and was often led to distraction. She was thrilled when he had moments to spare for her company, and shattered when she noticed his absence.

It was both confusing and exhilarating.

One fine summer day, Jesa was walking with Sofia and a few other young Danrayen women toward the cantina, hoping to spend a few of their off hours with good drink and even better company. Daniel's music had drastically improved as of late, and he had promised to serenade them with a new tune.

As soon as the girls crossed from the forest and into the city, a dark figure pushed off from a shadowed doorway on which he had been leaning and made his way to them.

"Jesa, if I may, can I have a moment?" Alcor asked when he reached them.

There was a chorus of "oohs" and snickers, but not wanting to be impolite, Jesa agreed. He held out his arm as if they were at a grand ball, and swallowing a groan, Jesa took it gingerly.

He led her to an alleyway, but Jesa stopped him before he could pull her too deep inside of it. She preferred to have a clear view of the main road.

Alcor released her, much to her relief, and pulled out a small rectangular box.

"A gift, for you," he said smoothly.

Jesa hesitated. She had accepted gifts and tokens from him before, but that was because it had all seemed like a silly game. After her encounter with Jose, and the way she felt every time that she saw him after, she wasn't sure it was right to accept the attentions of others—even if it was just a game.

"Alcor," she hesitated, not reaching for the box.

Ignoring—or disregarding—her hesitation, Alcor opened up the box himself. Inside it, nestled in pretty scraps of paper, sat a very beautiful and very ornate necklace. The chain looked to be made of pure gold, and held a large piece of polished jade.

Jesa gaped.

"Is that real?" she asked him.

Alcor smirked, and Jesa had a quick moment to wonder how she could have ever found his smiles charming. Compared to Jose's rare but unguarded grins that made her feel warm from the inside out, Alcor's seemed cold and detached.

"I'm sorry, Alcor," she finally said, when she had recovered from her shock, "but I cannot accept that, it is far too much."

"Nothing is too much for you, querida," he rebuffed, lifting the necklace from the box and moving as if to drape it around her neck.

Jesa took a step back.

"You misunderstand me," she told him, holding up a hand to stop him. "I cannot accept it because it is too grand a gift to give a woman who does not share your affections."

She said it as kindly as possible, but she saw Alcor's eyes flash with anger before composing himself. It was just a moment, but it was enough to frighten her.

Just as quickly as it came, it vanished, leaving Jesa with a churning swell of discomfort in her belly. Then Alcor was back to his usual, charming self.

"It is only because they poison your mind against men at the temple," he said to her smoothly, and Jesa, too stunned to reply, just stared at him in disbelief.

"Do you not want a normal home, a normal life? You all walk into town black and blue from your training, sometimes with broken fingers, open wounds. It cannot be worth it," he insisted.

The more he spoke, the less she knew what to say. It was so ridiculous, so preposterous that he could think to know her wants and dreams better than she did. That he could believe that the path of Danray was anything but a tremendous honor to any deemed worthy to walk it.

"You could have a simpler life, an easier life, Jesa."

Her name in his mouth made her recoil.

"You could have a husband, children, a family."

Finally, Jesa was able to speak.

"I don't want any of that," she declared angrily. "And if I wanted it, I could seek it. But not with anyone who diminished my path or my goddess."

Alcor shook his head, looking at her with pity.

"You don't know what you want," he said.

The audacity.

"If you will not believe that I know what it is that I want, believe that I know what I do not. And I do not want anything to do with you."

With that, she shoved by him and stormed away in search of her friends.

The entire interaction left her shaken, but to her shock, Alcor never wavered in his pursuit of her, no matter how many times she insisted that she was not for him, nor would she ever be for him.

She never admitted that there was another, because in truth it was not the only reason she had turned him down. It was his brazen disregard for her thoughts, feelings, and choices. She didn't believe that Alcor suspected her heart lay elsewhere either, but still, he refused to back down. Eventually, Jesa stopped trying to dissuade him and opted for simply ignoring him, as she had spent enough time considering his feelings. If he would not believe her refusals, then his disappointment would be his own. She had far more important things to worry about.

Her friendship with Sofia.

Her life in the Temple of Danray.

Preparing for her Trial.

And of course, Jose.

And so their slow, tentative romance progressed, exchanging secret, furtive glances and small smiles when no one was looking. Over time, he picked up on her scheduled trips to Pelgar and would schedule his work around them to join the small group that she, Sofia, and some of the other Danrayen girls had formed with some of the local youths. They began sitting nearer to one another, and then closer still, until at the cantina, under the long wooden table, their legs were pressed against one another's.

The first time it had happened, Jesa thought that her leg might catch fire from the heat of it and consume the rest of her in a flaring blaze.

Finally they began speaking, at first, quiet pleasantries, then exchanging longer, more personal stories and beliefs. Eventually they bickered and argued, whatever one would say the other would contradict.

Their mutual friends were sure they hated each other, for they were always at each other's throats. What they didn't understand was that was the only way that they could show passion to one another, without revealing the depth of their emotions.

On the day that Jesa turned twenty years old, Jose slipped her a note.

She was shocked, as their relationship had always been one of distant longing. A written note seemed far too personal, far too intimate. But he was barely out of sight before she tore it open to read it.

Meet me at the forge, it said. *Tonight.*

"You can't think of actually going!" Sofia whispered to her that evening, as they were drying off after their baths. Sofia was of course the only person who knew the true nature of her relationship with Jose.

"We're not allowed out of the temple after dark!"

Jesa laughed.

"So I'll sneak out," she told her friend, her entire body tingling with exhilaration at the very thought.

And the idea of seeing Jose alone.

"You know other girls have done so."

"Other girls have been caught and punished for it!" Sophia insisted.

Jesa shrugged.

"Maybe it was worth it."

So that night, after everyone had retired to their beds, Jesa snuck out of the temple walls, and made her way back to Pelgar. With a cloak brought up over her head, she slunk in the shadows, winding her way to the Blacksmiths' forge. She tried hard to listen for any late-night wanderers or guards, but her heart beat in her ears so intensely that she could barely hear anything over their pulse.

The street leading to her destination was mercifully dark, and few oil lanterns flickered in the windows of the neighboring homes. Jesa easily skirted around their glow, not wanting anyone indoors to see her figure walking alone in the darkness. When she reached the forge she only hesitated for a quick moment, her palm pressed against the cool metal door, before pushing it forward.

It opened. Jose must have been there to unlock it.

"Hola?" Jesa whispered into the dark room.

From around a corner she could see a soft glow, a low burning lantern. Then, a moment later, a figure made its way around the wall, their shape casting ominous shadows over the forge's walls and stone floor. Jesa reached for the dagger on her belt, before she recognized the figure. It was still too dark to see his face, but she would recognize him anywhere.

It was Jose.

They stood awkwardly for a moment, unsure of what to say. Finally, Jose spoke.

"You came," he said softly.

"Did you not think I would?" she asked him, uncertainly.

"I hoped that you would," was his quick reply.

They both lapsed into silence once more.

"I have a present for you," he said finally.

Jesa resisted the urge to sigh. She had no use for pretty picked flowers, like the local boys gave her, or the useless trinkets from the traveling merchants' sons. Least of all the fancy jewelry in jade and gold that Alcor had tried to gift her with. It all made her deeply uncomfortable.

But she liked Jose, so she plastered on what she hoped was a gracious smile and stepped further into the smithy.

Then she stopped, frozen in her stance, mouth hanging straight open as he pulled out the most exquisitely crafted sword that she had ever seen. Jose held the grip in his open right palm, balancing the blade with his left fingertips, presenting it to her.

Jesa couldn't speak, couldn't move. The sword's hilt was molded in the shape of the sun, the blazing circle in the middle with long, piercing rays of its light extending up to the pommel, and horizontal across the guard. The entire thing was overlaid with gold, making it shine even in the dull light of the room.

The blade itself was expertly crafted, the steel looking both delicate and deadly at the same time.

She stepped forward, her eyes finally flicking up from the work of art in Jose's hands to his bronze eyes.

"You made this for me?" she asked him, unbelieving. He broke out into a grin.

"Try it," he insisted, turning the hilt toward her.

It was physically paining her not to touch it, so she all but leapt forward to pick it up from his hold. She gasped as it slid into her palm as if it too had been waiting for her touch. The weight was flawlessly balanced, the size perfectly suited for her size and stature.

"How?" she asked, not offering any more context to her question. Jose understood anyway.

"I watch you, a lot," he confessed, as Jesa raised to point the blade forward. He stepped around her, trailing his hand from the wrist that held the sword, up her bare forearm, over her cloak-covered bicep. She could feel his body heat behind her when that same hand brushed the hair off of her shoulder, grazing her right earlobe.

Jesa shivered.

"Why?" she asked, lowering the sword and daring a glance at him behind her. His lips were so close.

"You know why," he answered, cupping her cheek. She felt his thumb graze over her skin.

She did know. The sword in her hand would have taken countless hours, and it was fitted to her like a dream. It was not a silly token; it was a declaration.

"Tell me anyway," she whispered, her lips gliding over his jawline. She felt him swallow.

"Because I respect your strength and your unwavering determination. I admire your courage and your dedication to your path and to your goddess. Because you are beautiful, in body, spirit, and mind. And because I lo—"

Then Jesa's lips were on his and her left arm—the one without the deadly blade—was thrown around his neck. Gently she eased her present down onto the floor and was then crushed tightly against him.

Jose didn't stop kissing her as he picked her up and crossed the length of the room. He didn't stop kissing her as he lowered her onto a bedroll near the low light of the oil lamp. He didn't stop kissing her as their clothes were discarded, landing in a tangled heap next to them. He didn't stop kissing her until the early light of dawn, when they both fell asleep in each other's arms.

CHAPTER 13
NOVA

Nova stared at the boy.

He was so little, so young. Younger than even she was before her entire life was upended by the Flowers of Prophecy, and now his would be too, because of their prophecy—and because of her.

The boy had a thin frame, his arms and legs too long and gangly. His chubby cheeks were the only parts of him that were rounded, the rest of his body stuck in the awkward change of growth and youth. He stood unsurely, leaning against the doorframe, half obstructed, his right leg bent and his foot rubbing uncertainty over his left.

Of all the emotions Nova expected to feel when finding him—relief, pride, excitement—she had never expected *pity*. The poor boy's life was about to be changed irreparably; he would no longer be the sweet-looking child before them. His life would be forever altered, just as hers had been.

Nova sheathed her Espada.

"I think it's best that you invite us inside."

A few tense moments later, and the adults were all sitting around a long kitchen table inside the cottage.

The boy—Huallpa they found out—had been sent out to the river to check their fish traps. It was, of course, just a reason to get him out and away from the home while the rest of them spoke.

Nova had just finished awkwardly explaining her botched Naming Rite, and the Flowers' prophecy, the reason that had led her, and as a result the others, to this moment.

Enrique looked as if Nova had beat him over the head with the hilt of her Espada.

The bruja looked confused, at first, but then realization traveled across her face, before being replaced by horror.

"No!" she cried out. "No!"

"Mi amor," Enrique reached for her, but she pulled away and sprung up back from the table.

Magia danced across Alric's fingertips in warning, but she didn't move to attack them, just stared at them in desperation.

"You knew about this?" she demanded, staring at the former king. "You knew she was the Name-Bearer, so you knew about this prophecy?" she cried.

Enrique hung his head, and Patli gasped.

"You did! And you said nothing?" her voice was stained with betrayal.

"I didn't know; I couldn't be sure," he tried explaining, looking flustered. "I was dead, they thought me dead, they had no reason to look for me. Especially here. They had no way to know about Huallpa!"

"Why didn't you tell me?" her whisper was horrified.

"We already live so far removed from anyone else, and we already have to hide to keep my identity a secret. I thought we were safe. I saw no reason to worry you further. How could they find us out here?"

His last sentence was delivered dripping with venom and directed at Nova and the others.

"He's my son!" Patli whispered, her voice pleading. "*Our* son! He's not a prince," she insisted.

"But that's not exactly true, is it?" Alric said gently, turning to look at Enrique. "If you're not dead, you still have a claim to the throne."

"That is not who he is!" the bruja snapped. "Or should I say, who he is anymore. None of that matters now. He is my *husband*, and that boy out there is our son. Not a *prince*. Not in line for the throne. Not any dioses-damned child of Prophecy. He is just a little boy!"

"I gave all of that up when I decided to stay in Cassalan," Enrique told them firmly, grabbing his partner's hand and pulling her back to the table. She sat again, reluctantly.

"When Patli found me and spared my life I decided… " He looked at his wife, eyes shining with so much love and devotion that the force of the intimacy caused Nova to look away.

"I couldn't leave," he finally finished.

"How did this happen?" Rawl asked them. "How did you meet? What caused you to stay?"

Enrique sighed and rubbed his love's palm with his thumb.

"I went to the front lines of the battle, of our endless ridiculous war, just as I had intended to. I was so young," he said, his voice rueful. "So young and so naïve. I had half a mind that I would win the war myself, single-handedly, bring peace to Andala, our people, and come home to my queen and family."

"But you didn't," Nova interrupted, hot resentment churning in her belly. "You let us all believe that you were dead. Killed in war. You let your *pregnant wife* believe it."

Nova had been there, in the palace, when the queen had received the news of King Enrique's death. Her despair could be heard even in Nova's room, high in the tower, away from the main body of the palace. The entire kingdom mourned for him, and yet, there he sat, alive and well in front of them.

"I didn't know she was pregnant when I left," Enrique said, having the decency to look ashamed.

"Oh, well, that makes it all right then," Nova seethed, and Enrique winced.

Alric shot her a glance, and she knew him well enough to know that he was quietly telling her to calm down, to not antagonize him. If they wanted to know the truth about what happened, and if they were going to leave that cottage with the Unnamed Price, she would have to tone down her anger.

Nova bit her lip, but stayed quiet.

"So what happened?" Rawl asked again. Enrique nodded.

"My regiment crossed the Borders. I wasn't meant to go with them, as the ruler of Andala I was not to risk the safety and well-being of our kingdom by crossing into enemy territory. But, like I said, I was young and foolish then," he replied.

Then he took a deep breath, and his wife slipped her hand out of his to place it reassuringly on his shoulder. He leaned into her touch, closing his eyes for a moment, and continued.

"The battle was terrible. I had never seen so much blood, so much violence, so much death. It barely mattered who we were fighting against, no one was any more than a wild animal, struggling just to stay alive." He shuddered, clearly in the grip of old, unwanted memories.

"I was injured, badly," he continued. "I fell down a small ravine, half buried in mud, and left to die. And I would have, too, had it not been for Patli."

He kissed the hand on his shoulder and smiled at her.

"She saved my life."

"And he wanted to kill me for it," she confessed.

Nova's brows drew together in confusion, but she did not interrupt.

"How did you come across him?" Rawl prompted, and Axchel leaned in, seemingly interested in the answer as well.

"I am a bruja, which you know, but I also have a gift from the dioses."

"An affinity?" Alric guessed.

She shook her head.

"A larger gift than that. I do not know why I was so blessed, but I can ... *travel*."

The four of them exchanged confused glances across the table.

"Travel?" Axchel asked.

Clearly the bruja meant more to the word than what was usually inferred.

She nodded. "If I have been to a location before, I can *will* myself there again."

Then, faster than a blink of an eye, she disappeared from where she sat.

Nova and Rawl gasped audibly, Nova pushing back from the table to spring up. Axchel was half a beat behind her, reaching for his blade. Before he could, however, a voice sounded from the opposite end of the room. They turned and saw the bruja standing in the living space near the far window.

"Like that," she explained, crossing over to them by walking this time.

Nova did not sit back down, still too rattled by the sight.

"Why didn't you do that when we were battling outside?" Alric asked her, his face full of awe.

She shrugged. "I was using borrowed magia, bottled battle magia from a mage. Far beyond what brujas are capable of, even brujas with gifts such as my own. Even the explosion at our home's border was laid out ahead of time. It was much to maneuver all at once," she confessed. "You were also battling my husband, and I did not want to leave him unprotected. Also, the gift requires a somewhat calm mind. If not, I can travel too far or end up in the wrong location entirely."

"That's quite a gift," Rawl said admiringly.

Nova didn't say it out loud, but she agreed. It would be quite an advantage to be so blessed.

"It is," Patli replied, though her voice sounded sad.

"I didn't see the use in it for many years, until, one day, I was walking back from collecting herbs and stumbled across a fallen soldier. There was a battle nearby, and I traveled with him back to my home, where I was able to heal him before sending him on his way."

Patli sat back down next to Enrique.

"And so I began, walking closer and closer to the Borders, getting near places where I knew battles were fought. Just so I could travel back there at other times and help the wounded Cassalain soldiers."

"But," Axchel started, turning to look at Enrique.

Patli laughed a little.

"You're thinking, '*Then why did you help an Andalan?*'"

Axchel nodded.

"Simple. I did not know he was Andalan. His purple uniform was covered in so much blood that I mistook him for a Cassalain soldier. I did not realize my error until we were both already back in my home, and he tried to kill me."

The last sentence was delivered with a sly smile to her husband, who looked mildly exasperated.

"How long will I have to keep apologizing for that?" he asked her.

"The rest of your life sounds about right," she teased.

"You fell in love," Axchel stated, obviously, and they both nodded.

"Somewhere between him trying to kill me, or escape, and me attempting to heal his wounds, but wondering if I should just let him die, we fell in love."

"I didn't tell her who I was, of course. She just assumed I was an Andalan soldier."

"I knew I had to help him, hide him, and then return him to his people, even though it would break my heart to do so."

"So why didn't you?" Nova asked coldly.

"Trate!" she snapped. "I tried! I even traveled him back to the Borders, at a safe spot for him to cross. As safe as the Borders can be, in any case. I left him there and cried for days."

"I had no idea where I was or how to return to her. But I had spent enough time in and around her home to know the terrain well enough to head back in the right direction," Enrique said. "Eventually, I found her again."

"You could have been killed," the bruja said softly.

"Leaving you would have surely killed me," he replied, equally soft.

"I returned," he continued, "and told her everything. Who I was, what waited for me back home, that I had a wife, a queen, a kingdom. But I told her I would renounce it all, if only she would allow me to stay. With her."

"I wouldn't have let him," Patli confessed. "I don't think I could have lived with myself, thinking he had given up everything for me. But I realized, the day after I had left him at the Borders, that I was pregnant."

She laid a hand on her stomach, as if remembering.

"And if I could not ask him to stay for me, I could ask him to stay for *him*."

"He was born early?" Alric asked her.

Her face hardened, but she nodded grimly.

"We almost lost him," she whispered. "We will not lose him now."

They were all quiet, for a long moment. Then Axchel spoke.

"Living this close to the Borders, you must have been witness to so much fighting, so much death."

The former king and bruja did not respond, they only looked at him.

"Living the way you do," Axchel continued, "traveling to the battle sites, tending to the wounded. You must have seen so much."

He looked at Alric and Rawl, and then turned to face Nova. Her stomach fluttered at his gaze. They had not had time to speak about what he had found out, about her having been the Name-Bearer. She did not know what he made of the situation, but she made herself stare back at him, stubbornly.

"Word of the Flowers' prophecy reached even my ears here in Cassalan," Axchel said. "Though, admittedly, I learned more in my brief stay in Andala. Even still, I'm surprised you had not heard of it," he directed back toward Enrique and Patli.

"We keep mostly to ourselves," Enrique told him.

"I even stopped healing soldiers," Patli confessed. "We couldn't risk anyone recognizing Enrique."

"I only found out myself when I overheard the conversation of a traveling trader," the former king said. "Luck, or fate," he admitted begrudgingly.

Axchel nodded. "But you heard the Andalan," he said, tilting his head toward Nova. "The prophecy promises peace. Not just for their realm, but *for all*. Is peace not worth fighting for?"

"Not at the cost of our son!" Patli exclaimed.

Enrique placed a hand on his wife's shoulder. Nova noticed the trembling of the bruja's shoulders slowly still.

"It is too dangerous," he replied. "If we traveled back to Andala, if the people found out I was still alive, they would be more likely to turn on him than trust him. He's just a boy. How can he bring about peace?"

"The Flowers are the voices of the gods. The dioses speak prophecy through them; they may even be dioses themselves. If they claim the boy will bring peace, how can we not believe?" Nova insisted, her voice laced with desperation. She was shocked that they could even consider doubting the Flowers' prophecy.

"How do you know that he is the child? The Flowers did not name him!" Patli argued.

Nova gaped at her incredulously. From the corner of her eye she could see Rawl and Alric shooting her pitying looks.

"The son of the king, born on the same day as the Andalan prince?" Alric spoke softly. "It does seem fairly clear."

"But Huallpa wasn't born on the same day as my son—I mean, the prince," Enrique said, his voice laced with confusion. "We heard about the birth of the Andalan prince, of course, it was at least a month before Huallpa was born."

Patli nodded, her hand was on her stomach again.

"We had paid for news of his birth to be delivered to us. By then, we knew Queen Issalia had been pregnant. Enrique just wanted to be assured that they would both be all right. But Huallpa was born at least one moon later."

Nova swung around to face Alric, who looked as stunned as she felt.

"The Flowers said 'a future king was born this morn, but not unto the queen,'" she told him. "Those were their exact words. I wouldn't forget; I could never forget it. *Born this morn,*" she insisted.

Alric shook his head.

"Could the message have been delivered wrong?" he asked them.

The bruja stood and crossed to a small cabinet near the back hallway. She opened a drawer and pulled out a piece of parchment.

"This is Huallpa's star chart. He was born under the first blind star of spring. More than a moon after the prince, and another moon earlier than his due."

She passed the birth chart to Alric, who quickly examined it. He shook his head.

"She's right," he murmured. "He had not yet been born when the Flowers spoke their prophecy."

"What does that mean?" Nova demanded, her voice frantic. It couldn't mean what she was thinking.

"It means..." Alric's lips drew down into a thin line. "He is not the Unnamed Prince."

Patli collapsed against Enrique, relief radiating off of them both.

"No," Nova whispered.

Alric shook his head again.

"No," Nova repeated, more fiercely.

"Rojya," Rawl reached for her hand, but she pulled back and whirled on Alric.

"Tu tatuaje," Nova said. "You said that the dye was made from the pollen of the Flowers."

She heard Enrique suck in a shocked breath, but she continued.

"You said it would glow in the presence of the Unnamed Prince. We'll try it."

"Nova," Alric began, but she refused to see the defeat in his eyes.

"When he returns, we will attempt it," she repeated, crossing her arms in front of her.

Silence filled the room once more, but the hopeful looks did not leave the faces of Enrique and Patli. Nor did the resigned ones fade from Rawl and Alric. Axchel was as stoic as ever.

Then, Patli rose.

"It is almost lunchtime. You will stay to eat, at least," she said, moving further into the kitchen.

"How can I help?" Rawl asked, following her.

"You can pick some vegetables in the garden, for sopa. We could also use more wood," she answered, hands already busy hanging a pot of water over the fire.

Axchel stood and began following Rawl outdoors.

"I'll help," he said.

They could hear the two men rounding the house toward the back garden. Patli frowned and swore under her breath. "I forgot to tell them to be careful with the herbs; there are several sensitive ones that I use for potions."

Ever the scholar, Alric perked up at the mention of potions.

"I would love to know what you have planted and see if they differ at all from what we have in Andala," he told her.

Patli smiled her first real smile since they had met her and crossed toward the door, a hand sweeping outward to lead Alric outside.

"What would you say are the most commonly used herbs in your realm?" Nova heard her ask, before their voices faded away.

She gaped at the now empty doorway. "Not an hour ago they were trying to kill one another," she grumbled.

"Magia-users. They're a different sort," Enrique snorted.

It was then that Nova realized that she had been left alone with the King of Andala.

The former King of Andala?

She wasn't sure what the correct title was for the man who was once the ruler of her realm, presumed dead, who now sat before her. She felt a rush of butterflies in her stomach, which annoyed her. She had no reason to be nervous around him. Whatever he might have once been, whatever she might have once been, they were clearly no longer those same people who had been connected by fate. That life was long ago and far away.

Ignoring the ridiculous urge to bow, she chanced a quick look at him. Incredibly, he looked as uncertain as she felt.

"Puedo," he cleared his throat. "Puedo preguntar ..." he said, then trailed off.

Nova clutched her arms to her sides and curled her hands into fists. "Ask what?" she challenged. She was fairly sure she knew what he wanted to ask but didn't help him. He had left his wife, his unborn child, his kingdom. Discomfort was the least he was due.

"How is Issalia? And my—the prince?" he finally blurted.

"You mean *your son?*"

Enrique winced and looked toward the back door, where Huallpa had run out earlier. "Yes, how..."

"You lost the right to ask about their well-being when you abandoned them. You claim you are no longer King of Andala, or Queen Issalia's husband, that means you cannot be Prince Frederico's father. You can't have it both ways."

It was cruel. She knew that it was cruel. He had been so young when he had left for war. Barely nineteen, with the weight of an entire kingdom upon him. Of course a life with Patli, a life full of love, without the weight of the crown, would have been appealing. But it didn't change the fact that he did have responsibilities and that he had abandoned them and his people. Nova would not, could not, easily forgive that.

But when she saw his face crumble, his eyes suspiciously glassy, she couldn't help but feel empathy.

"I haven't heard much in the last year," she confessed, "but they were both well last time there was news. Queen Issalia also has a daughter, Princess Zerlina, though no one is sure of the father."

A small smile curved the right side of Enrique's mouth. "Good for her," he murmured.

Before they could say anything more, the front doorway became crowded with their entire party all at once. Rawl's arms were filled with carrots, potatoes, and another pale-looking root vegetable, along with some green sprouts of something that Nova could not identify. Axchel carried an impossible amount of firewood in his enormous arms, and trailing behind the group came Alric, then Patli.

Who was holding Huallpa's hand.

The child had returned and brought two fat fish in a woven basket.

"We're in luck," Patli said, her voice strained, a bit too cheerful. "Looks like we will have sopa de pescado!"

Huallpa carefully placed the fish on the kitchen counter, his gaze darting about the room curiously. Nova could see him scraping up every bit of his courage, until finally he met Alric's gaze.

"Who are you all?" he asked him, then blushed and ducked his head.

"Son amigos!" Enrique told his son, rising to prepare the fish.

Huallpa looked doubtful.

"You didn't look like friends outside; it looked like you were fighting," he said to his father.

"We had ... forgotten that we were friends," his father replied warily, "but we are not fighting anymore."

"I'm Rawl," the archer said to the boy, crossing to shake his hand. Huallpa did so solemnly, but the pride in his face betrayed his pleasure at being given an adult greeting.

The Cassalain introduced himself next.

"I'm Axchel," he said.

"Alric," the mage bowed to the boy, who then turned expectantly at Nova.

"I am called Nova," she told him awkwardly.

Could he still be the Unnamed Prince, despite his star chart? She needed to know.

"My friend Alric has a tattoo," she blurted, knowing her statement was completely lacking in subtlety. All eyes turned to her, Alric's surprised, Rawl's reproaching, Enrique's and Patli's angry. Axchel just watched her.

Nova knew that it was a strange change in conversation, but they needed to be sure, and she thought she might explode if they didn't find their answer soon.

"Would you like to see it?"

Luckily for her, eleven-year-old boys didn't seem to have much sense of social cues, so her strange and abrupt question did not appear to faze him. Instead, his eyes widened, large, like the moon on a clear night.

"Si!" he replied eagerly, turning to Alric. "I want to see!"

There was nothing to be done but follow it through. Slowly, Alric removed his cloak, and then rolled up the right sleeve of his shirt to reveal the bandage, which concealed the art. With a half second of hesitation, the mage then pushed the cloth away.

On his forearm was an intricately drawn tattoo of a Flower of Prophecy.

Nova inched closer to see more clearly. Alric was sure that by using the pollen of the Flowers mixed into the ink, there would be a reaction when it was in the presence of the Unnamed Prince. Specifically, it would glow.

Nova looked between Huallpa and the tattoo, then back to Huallpa, then the tattoo once more.

Nothing happened.

"Wow," Huallpa said appreciatively, completely unaware that Nova was falling apart, or that his mother had tears of relief in her eyes. He simply admired the art, then smiled politely back up at Alric.

Completely devastated and on the verge of tears, Nova turned abruptly and stormed out of the cottage.

Chapter 14

Nova

Nova ran.

She didn't have a direction, a destination, or a plan. She simply ran.

Eventually, the cold burning within her lungs forced her to slow. Her breath came out in little huffs of mist in front of her face. Then, she was crying, her tears cutting hot trails down her icy cheeks, still stinging from the wind. She wrapped her arms around her stomach and sobbed.

She cried for the life she had never known, the infant she was before taken to the palace. She cried for the child she had been, so excited to serve her realm and fulfill her duties as the Name-Bearer. She cried for the girl she had become, having to hide her identity from her Danrayen sisters. And she cried for the young woman she was now, still serving others, bound to destinies and prophecies and fate that saw her as a pawn, a thing to be used rather than as an individual.

Strong arms encased her from behind, a chin tucked into her neck. Rawl.

She let herself sag against him, letting him rock her slowly until she was finally spent. Then she turned in his arms to hug him.

"What do we do now?" she asked against his chest.

A hand came up to stroke her hair.

"No se, Rojya," he answered. "I don't know. But we'll figure it out. Together."

A twig snapped on their left and they leapt apart, whirling to face the noise.

It was Alric, his face drawn tight as if in pain.

"I was just coming to see if you were all right," he said in a tone Nova didn't recognize. "But I can see you are fine."

His face looked a little sad and a little uncertain. He shuffled his feet.

"Well, maybe not fine. How could you be? But you are, Rawl is here, and I..." he cleared his throat. "I will just, leave the two of you to..." Then he turned around and walked briskly away.

Nova looked at Rawl, puzzled.

"Que le pasa?" she asked him, confused as to her friend's reaction. They were all upset at Huallpa not being the Unnamed Prince, why would they not find solace together? As a team, as friends?

"I'll go," Rawl said grimly. "You head back to the cottage, bueno? We'll figure out our next steps there."

Nova nodded, wiping the last of her tears from her eyes and taking out a cloth to wipe her streaming nose. Then, with a resigned sigh, she turned back the way that she had come.

It didn't take long for Rawl to catch up to Alric, the mage was too tall and awkward to slink off quietly and had left plenty of crushed leaves and bent bushes in his wake that allowed Rawl to track him easily. When he found the mage, standing motionless in a grove, he felt irritation bubble up in his chest.

"Que te pasa, mago?" Rawl asked him curtly.

"What's wrong with me?" Alric asked, his face dumbfounded.

"You heard me. You've been acting strange for a while now!"

Which was true. Perhaps it wasn't obvious, wasn't overt, but Rawl was so in tune with the mage's subtle shifts and mercurial moods that he had noticed. At some point during their travels, Rawl felt like the two of them had grown close. It had delighted him. Nova was so easy to care for, to befriend. She had become as special to him as his younger sister, Filomila, training in magia far away in Andala's Mage University. Alric had been more difficult to win over, but Rawl had liked that. He had enjoyed coaxing tiny smiles from the mage's sullen lips, making him blush from bawdy songs with dirty lyrics. He appreciated Alric's inquisitive mind and seemingly endless supply of questions. He even liked how surly and dour he was in the mornings, making it a game to see how quickly he could make the man snap at him.

At some point, Rawl had realized that he did not like the process of befriending Alric because it was a challenge, but because he simply liked Alric.

Maybe more than liked.

And then, things had changed. At first, Rawl thought that the distance the mage put between the two of them was nothing more than exhaustion and worry. They were all under an enormous amount of stress, but crossing the Borders had been more challenging for Alric, who had to use so much of his magia to keep him safe. Rawl tried to keep his spirits up, but the man kept pulling away from him. Rawl had told himself it wasn't personal, but he would be lying if he claimed his feelings were not hurt.

He began spending more time with Nova, and the two of them had grown even closer than ever. Rawl assumed that eventually Alric's mood would change, and that the three of them would return to their easy comradery, but he continued to pull away.

Rawl was fairly certain he knew why.

Alric must have guessed Rawl's feelings for him. And whether he was pulling away because he was uncomfortable or because he didn't want to give the archer false hope, Rawl was mortified. His heart clenched painfully within his chest, and his stomach twisted with embarrassment. He had never meant to make his friend feel awkward around him and was ready to set the situation right, no matter what it took.

Rawl watched as Alric clenched his jaw, his dark brows pulling downward, and tensed, ready for the inevitable *"I care for you, but not in that way"* speech. Alric took a deep breath.

"Are you in love with her?" the mage finally asked him.

Rawl took half a step back as if he had been physically struck. Of all the things that he had expected, he had never even come close to considering that question. It seemed to come from nowhere. Then—he couldn't help himself—he laughed.

At the sound, Alric's face switched from grim resignation to bristling frustration. He stalked over to the archer, towering over him.

"Are you?" he demanded.

Rawl's laughter died, and something sticky lodged itself in his throat. If Alric hadn't guessed Rawl's feelings for him, then there was only one reason why the mage would be so sad and angry about the situation.

"It seems pretty obvious *you're* the one in love with her," Rawl replied, softly.

To his surprise, Alric reared back, and a look of confusion crossed his face. Rawl frowned. Had he guessed wrong?

"You are, aren't you?" Rawl prompted cautiously.

"I— No, I, que?" the mage sputtered.

Rawl cocked his head, still unsure of why his friend appeared so surprised. Wasn't that the reason he had been acting so strange around them?

"You *are* in love with her, aren't you?"

"With Nova?" Alric asked, his tone bewildered.

"No, with the moon goddess Mama Killa. Of course with Nova!" Rawl shouted, then surprised himself by lifting his hands to Alric's chest and shoving him back.

The mage stumbled, but it seemed to knock him out of his stupor.

"I'm not the one sneaking off with her at every opportunity!" he yelled back.

Rawl bristled.

"Well, if you're not in love with her, then why do you care?" he questioned, both confused and angry. And confused as to why he was angry.

"I-I," Alric stammered again.

"What?" Rawl demanded.

"I don't know!" Alric cried. "I don't know! I love her, but not like that, but every time I see the two of you—" He dragged a rough hand through his hair and turned, pacing away and then back. He stepped up to Rawl again, his face a few inches from his own, so close Rawl had to tilt his head back to look into his eyes. They looked furious.

"It burns me inside. Like someone has plunged a dagger in my stomach. It crawls under my skin, like Mage Madness, and I don't know why."

Rawl was breathing faster, his skin warming from the closeness of their bodies. A thought crossed his mind then, a dangerous thought, a beautiful thought, and with it the tiniest sliver of hope.

Could he let himself believe?

"I'm not in love with her."

Rawl meant to declare it, loud and definitely, so there would be no room for doubt. Instead, it came out in a half whisper. He thought he saw the tiniest traces of relief cross Alric's eyes. But why?

He watched as the mage swallowed, hard, then took a step away. He missed the heat of him immediately.

"Lo siento," he said to Rawl. "I don't know what, why ..." He took a deep breath.

"I'm sorry," he repeated. "The stress of the quest, of the Unnamed Prince, I don't know what came over me." He awkwardly patted the archer on the shoulder, and Rawl felt himself die a little inside at the friendly gesture. The tiny spark of hope fizzled out.

"We should get back," the mage said, then began walking back toward the cottage.

With an aching heart, Rawl followed him.

When Nova returned to the cottage, Huallpa was sent outdoors to play and to leave the adults to "visit among friends." It took some convincing, as it was clear he had not had much opportunity for socializing with others and would have much rather stayed with the rest of them.

Despite the fact that he was not the Unnamed Prince, Nova found that she still felt a bit sorry for him, she remembered her solitary days in the palace, before the Naming Ceremony. She had not had many companions, other than her nurse maid and instructors. And they were simply her guardians, not her friends.

She knew how lonely life could be as a child without friends. By the time he was finally persuaded to leave, Rawl and Alric had returned. Patli had continued cooking and encouraged them all to sit for a meal. They all agreed reluctantly.

In their absence, Patli had made a chupe de pescado. The thick seafood stew had simmering carrots, corn, lima beans, and pieces of yellow potato bobbing happily in the pot. It smelled of freshly caught fish mixed with garlic, onion, and chile. The bruja had taken out rustic clay bowls, painted a happy orange color on the outside. Carefully, she ladled a portion for each of them, adding large chunks of queso fresco over the top, and sprinkling each bowl with cilantro.

It looked and smelled delicious, but Nova could not bring herself to take a single bite.

Nova's training as a warrior made it difficult for her to turn down food, She and the other initiates had been taught at the Temple of Danray to have full and proper meals whenever and wherever they could find them. But after the devastating disappointment of having traveled so far and not finding the Unnamed Prince, Nova didn't think that she would be able to stomach anything. She sat anyway, not wanting to offend the bruja, as did the others.

The room was quiet, save for the scraping of cutlery against wooden bowls and soft chewing. Finally, after pushing her meal around in her bowl for a few minutes Nova put down her spoon.

"I don't know what to do," she admitted, her voice defeated. Alric swallowed the mouthful of sopa that he had just sipped and made a few quick hand motions, his red magia flickering in the wake of his quick fingers.

"Pardon us," he directed toward King Enrique, Patli, and Axchel, and the air shimmered around them.

Nova gasped. It was as if she, Alric, and Rawl were behind the thinnest of veils, with the Cassalains on the other side.

"It's a privacy spell," the mage told her and Rawl. "You've seen me do one before, Nova, although much more refined than this, but in this case, I did not have to conceal what I was doing from anyone."

Nova could see Axchel's lips moving, his face slightly distorted by the spell, but she could hear no sound coming out of his mouth. In fact, she could hear no other sounds beyond their small bubble of space. She gave Axchel what she hoped was a reassuring smile and raised her hand to indicate for him to wait. He looked concerned, Patli seemed annoyed, but Enrique continued to eat unperturbed. Despite having lived in Cassalan for nearly half of his life, he must've seen many strange and interesting spells when he lived at the palace.

"Bit rude though, isn't it?" Rawl asked, a bit sullenly. "We could have at least finished our meal."

Alric looked pointedly at Rawl's nearly untouched bowl, and then at Nova's, which was even more full than Rawl's was.

"It is clear that we will not be able to think of anything else until we come up with a plan," Alric responded. "And I already have one, which is why I put up the privacy spell."

Nova sat up straighter in her chair, twisting to look at the mage, who had sat himself between herself and Rawl.

"You have a plan?" she asked him hopefully.

"We can return to Sarakshi," Alric replied, referring to the Padir Seer.

Nova's heart, which had lifted slightly with the promise of a plan, sank at the prospect. It was definitely not what she wanted to hear. For them to return to where they had been less than a month prior, to cross back over the Borders when they had just made it into Cassalan, seemed so unbelievably cruel. The thought alone was so disheartening she felt like she could weep again.

"We can ask a better question this time," the mage continued. "A more direct question: 'Where is the Unnamed Prince?' Maybe she will have a vision."

"We *could* return," Rawl admitted reluctantly. "You are always welcome among the Padir."

Nova sighed, slumping back into her chair. From beyond the veil of magia, she could see Patli and Enrique getting into a heated discussion, Axchel watching them with interest. But because of the spell, she could not hear what they were arguing over. Nova was about to turn and grudgingly agree with Alric's plan, when the former king began waving his hands in front of their faces. Quickly, Alric dropped the spell.

"My wife has something to tell you," he informed them, once it was clear they could hear each other once again.

Patli looked annoyed again, but Enrique gave her an encouraging nod. She let out a small huff, then turned to face the rest of them.

"There has been talk," she began, "among the brujas of the forest. Our network stretches far across the lands."

She hesitated, but then made herself continue.

"There have been rumors of a child in the North. A child the same age as my Huallpa. A child who is uniting all the leaders of the Northern Tribes. Uniting them to fight as one people against the Cassalains who would try to control them."

"It is true that the Northern Tribes have been battling more fiercely against Cassalain soldiers in the North. And that they are more organized, clearly better led," Axchel said. "But to ally the different tribes, each so deeply individualistic, each so set in their own ways and customs, would be an almost impossible feat for anyone, let alone a child!"

"They say he is no ordinary child," the bruja continued, then turned to look Alric straight in the eyes. "They say he is a sorcerer."

"Imposible!" Alric said, immediately. "There has not been a recorded sorcerer in over a century. I cannot believe that there is one now."

"Times are changing; the world is changing. Don't you feel it?" the bruja asked him. "It's in the night sky, in the wind, the very land feels different. The impossible has been happening with much greater frequency as of late."

"The Naming Ceremony failed," Nova whispered, too in awe to speak louder. That was another extraordinary, unprecedented event.

"There is also Sarakshi," Rawl told them, his voice quiet as well. They would not speak of her gift in front of strangers, but the existence of an individual with the Unveiled Sight was also a miraculous and momentous occurrence.

"Attacks from creatures in the Night Wood have also been increasing," Axchel added, "with monstros venturing out farther than they have ever gone, and lasting longer than ever before."

"And now, a sorcerer?" Alric asked, his voice dubious.

Patli shrugged.

"You seek a child, a special child. One who will bring peace. He is already bringing peace to the Northern Tribes, and he is of the right age."

"So, now you are in favor of a child bringing peace, so long as it's not *your* child?" Nova asked her, perhaps a bit unfairly.

Patli looked her in the eye. "No parent would willingly put their child in harm's way," she told Nova. "Had your parents had a choice, I believe they would've attempted anything to keep you from becoming the Name-Bearer."

It hurt. Oh, how it hurt. She had no way of knowing if that statement was true. If her parents would have been kind, loving, and protective. She had never known them, and never would. The barb dug deep, lodging itself somewhere between her skin and her soul. Nova laughed bitterly.

"None of us ever had a choice," she replied to the bruja, before turning to Alric.

"He's not a prince," she reminded him, and he frowned.

"But the prophecy did not say anything about a prince, did it?" he answered.

She felt like ice water had replaced her veins. He was right. The Flowers had not said anything about a prince. They had all just assumed …

"*A future king was born on this morn,*" she recited.

"Kings are made in many ways," Rawl reminded them.

They all shifted uncomfortably. They were already considered traitors to the crown for aligning themselves with the Unnamed Prince, when they believed that the child in the Flowers' prophecy was actually a prince. But if he wasn't and had no legitimate claim to the throne, then what they were talking about was a different sort of treason entirely. None of them would speak it out loud, but the implication was usurpation.

"What do you think?" Rawl asked her and Alric.

"About the sorcerer child?" the mage clarified.

"Churan," Patli interrupted.

"What?" Nova asked her, startled, her mouth falling open.

"His name is Churan," the bruja clarified.

Nova inhaled swiftly, and Axchel looked at her face with concern clearly apparent on his own.

"What is it, Andalan?" he asked her, sounding worried.

"Savior," she whispered.

"Que?" Alric asked. She turned to face him.

"Churan means 'savior.'"

Realization dawned on the mage's face.

"You think it's a sign?" he asked her seriously.

She didn't answer; she couldn't answer. Did she think it was a sign? It made sense. The Flowers of Prophecy delivered the names of royal children. Important children. Even if this boy had not yet made it to his Naming Ceremony, if he was truly the Unnamed Prince, would his name not already be powerful?

Finally, she nodded.

"A child sorcerer," Alric said, "uniting the Northern Tribes, a feat that no one has ever been able to accomplish before, with a name that means 'savior.'"

He looked at Nova and then Rawl.

"Do we believe we have the next contender for the Unnamed Prince?"

Rawl raised his eyebrows, and Nova gave a small nod. It was their best lead.

"You intend to travel to the Northern Tribes?" Axchel asked them, his tone incredulous. "That is a journey that would take weeks, if not months! And you are Andalans, on enemy territory! You won't last five days."

"What would you have us do?" Nova snapped at him, falling into the easy memory of arguing with him. It felt safer than the other emotions she had been having around him lately. "If there is even a possibility this child is the one of the prophecy, then we must try. What is the alternative? Abandoning the quest? Returning to Andala? To war?"

Resentment burned in her belly.

"How could I? How could any of us, when there is even the slightest chance for peace?"

"You would not have to travel on foot," Patli suddenly interrupted. They all turned to look at her.

"What do you mean?" Rawl asked her tentatively.

"I have never tried it with three people," the bruja admitted, "But I can *travel* with both Enrique and Huallpa. As long as we are connected by touch, I can take more than one person along with me."

"You mean, you would use your gift to take us to the Northern Tribes?" Alric asked her, sounding eager.

"Not *in* them, but I have been near their borders. It would be less than a day's journey once you were there," she answered.

Nova looked at Alric and Rawl, trying to gauge their reactions. Alric, ever the scholar, seemed thrilled at the prospect of experiencing Patli's strange magia up close. Rawl too seemed intrigued, though Nova would guess it was more due to the fact that they would not have to cross the entire span of an enemy's realm on foot.

But she would rather brave all the Cassalain soldiers between them and the Northern Tribes herself rather than be that close to magia.

It was no secret that she did not enjoy magia. Though she had gotten much more used to being around it thanks to her friendship with Alric, it still made her feel uneasy.

Still, she knew that if the bruja was truly able to transport them, they would be very foolish not to take advantage of her offer.

"You really believe you can take the three of us?" she asked her.

"Four."

Nova turned in surprise to Axchel.

"Four? But why would you—"

"I am half Condori, remember? I haven't been to my home in years. Besides, your quest is for peace. Peace is all I have ever wanted."

His face was so pained at the words that Nova couldn't help but believe him. She looked at Rawl, who was smiling, and then Alric, who gave her a small nod.

"We could use all the help we can get, and he knows both Cassalan and the Northern Tribes. He would be an asset," Alric said.

Nova forced herself not to overthink it, or the tiny blossom of relief that blossomed within her chest. Deliberately she turned back to Patli. "Do you think you can *travel* with four?" she asked her.

The bruja looked slightly concerned.

"I have never attempted it," she said hesitantly. "I imagine it would take more power, but as long as we are all connected, I believe it can be done."

"How long do you believe it will take for you to restore your power?" Alric asked her.

The bruja thought for a long moment.

"You know that we brujas y brujos do not drain as you do, mago," she directed toward Alric. Still, she chewed on her lower lip, brows slightly furrowed. "But *traveling* is different, and without disagreement earlier, it would be best to wait a while still."

She locked eyes with her husband, who had looked concerned since she had suggested the *traveling* but hadn't tried to dissuade her.

"We can leave in the morning," she finally replied.

Nova turned back to her friends, and Axchel.

"Looks like we're going to the Northern Tribes."

CHAPTER 15

NOVA

The rest of the day was filled with preparations. Enrique took Huallpa—who had returned from playing—and Rawl out hunting. The former king claimed that "Huallpa was getting even better with a bow than he was," waves of pride radiating from him.

Axchel asked Patli's permission to use some of her herb garden to concoct healing potions and salves, to which the bruja readily agreed. Alric joined them, fascinated to witness Cassalain healing arts and compare how they measured up with Andala's.

Nova was left mostly to herself, which suited her mood just fine. She set up their camp outside, past the bruja's large garden, but still in sight of the cottage. There were too many of them to spend the night indoors with the family, even if they had been invited to do so, which they had not been.

She found a nice, flat area with springy grass and not too many stones. She collected dry wood and set up the campfire, ready to be lit later in the evening. She rolled out their sleeping mats, including a new one that Enrique had gifted Axchel. Though the former king was not as large as the Cassalain soldier, he was still a formidable size, and the mat looked big enough that Axchel could rest comfortably.

She found a nearby spring with Patli's instruction and refilled their water skins. While there, she found a new whetstone that she used to sharpen her Espada, and then Axchel's blade for good measure. When she returned to the camp she carried new wood—of a sturdier, crafting substance rather than kindling—and after rifling through Rawl's pack for materials, sat to make him some new arrows. When she fashioned as many as she could, she even took out a small bottle of oil and polished Alric's wooden staff.

She knew that she was keeping herself busy to avoid thinking about the day's earlier disappointment, as well as the dangers of their upcoming journey.

Nova had always known that her quest would not be an easy one. When the Flowers had imparted their incredible prophecy, they had given her no clue as to where she was supposed to find the Unnamed Prince or how she was to return him to the palace for the Naming Ceremony. When Alric had come to find her at the Danrayen Temple, almost a year prior, he had suggested that perhaps King Enrique had sired an illegitimate heir before perishing in the war. The mage's suggestion was to go to the king's last known location to try to find more information about the potential mystery lover, and any children she might have borne.

That location had been the Borders, and it was how Nova had found herself in the most northern part of Andala. It seemed an insurmountable distance, the farthest Nova had ever traveled within her realm. But then, once they were close, Sarakshi's vision had led them even further still, across the Borders and into enemy territory, into Cassalan. A place Nova had never imagined that she would ever go.

And now, even that was not far enough? They had to journey to the top of Tierramadri, as far north as anyone had ever known, to the unrestful lands of the Northern Tribes?

What would follow, the very moon in the night sky?

Nova was frightened. She was worried. She knew that each person joining her on the quest, Alric, Rawl, and now Axchel, had done so on their own accord, unbidden by her. But she still felt guilty, as if it was her fault that they would be placed in further peril. She felt responsible for them, and it was a heavy burden.

She could admit, at least to herself, that a small, selfish part of her was also glad. She was grateful for their aid and their company, despite the dangers.

In the evening they shared another meal with the family, this time consisting of a small deer that Huallpa had shot down, which Patli cooked with rice and yellow squash. Nova forced herself to eat this time, and was glad of it, as the food was delicious. The meat was spicy and juicy, the rice studded with nuts and dried fruits. The squash was sweet, to offset the spice of the deer. She noticed that Rawl's appetite had returned as well, and they all ate ravenously and gratefully.

During the meal, Huallpa peppered them with questions, many of which they could not answer easily. Who were they? Why were they here? Where were they going? What did they do? How did they know his parents?

Luckily, Axchel did most of the speaking, and he could answer more honestly than the rest of them could. He was a Cassalain soldier. He was there because he was helping his friends find someone. They were going to venture further north, together. He hadn't met their parents before but did know Ana, his mother's friend.

Huallpa had met Ana on a few occasions, when Patli had *traveled* them to her home. He spoke delightedly about the vibrantly colored cobblestone exterior of their home, and there the rest could join in conversation about the beautiful absurdity of her decor.

After dinner, the group retired to the outdoors, to give the family their space. Together they sat around the fire, the dwindling light in the horizon doing nothing to encourage fatigue. Both their bellies and their minds were still too full to attempt sleep yet.

"Tell us of the Northern Tribes, Ax," Rawl prompted him, leaning against a fallen trunk with his legs splayed out before him. His hands were clasped in front of his distended belly. "It would be helpful if you could give us whatever information that you can," he urged the soldier.

Axchel perked up, and Nova noticed that for the first time, he did not react negatively to the nickname. In fact, he didn't even seem to notice. She swallowed a smile.

The Cassalain was sitting near his new sleep mat, which Nova had placed in between the two other men, as far from her as possible. She still wasn't sure how she felt about the man and didn't want his presence to distract her from sleep. They would all need their rest.

Axchel nodded thoughtfully. "It has been many years since I have returned, and even a few months is enough time to completely change the state of the Tribes," he informed them. "But I will tell you what I can."

Nova twisted to see him more clearly, crossing her legs and then wincing when the motion pressed on her overly full stomach.

"The largest difference between the Tribes and Cassalan, or Andala, is their system of rule," Axchel began. "Here in Cassalan we have a monarchy, and our monarchs rule until death or incapacitation."

He leaned toward Alric, inquisitively. "Is it true that in Andala you allow children to rule?" he asked, his voice incredulous.

Alric tilted his head back and forth on his neck, not a yes, but not quite a no. "Our rulers begin their reign when they come of age and marry. Usually between the years of sixteen and nineteen."

"But they are so young! What would they know of ruling a nation?" Axchel asked, shocked.

"All living prior rulers sit on a council that guides them, especially in those first few years," Alric explained. "Enrique's parents both sit on the council still, as does one of his grandmothers."

"But then why give them the rule at all? If they are governed by a council?"

"Because we believe it is the youth and the influx of their new ideas that keeps our realm moving toward the future," Nova responded. She remembered as much from her studies. "Young people are the future of the realm, after all; should we not shape a nation that reflects them?"

Axchel looked simultaneously appalled and impressed. "I will admit it is an interesting thought," he confessed. "But we believe that wisdom comes with experience, and we keep our monarchs on the throne for as long as they are able."

Nova could understand the idea as well, though she did not agree with it.

"The Northern Tribes are completely different," Axchel continued. "They have no monarchy, only tribal leaders. And the tribes change and fluctuate as often as the seasons. My tribe, my mother's tribe, the Condori, are one of the longest lasting tribes in history. The Alcanta tribe and the Hakhan tribe hold similar histories, being large and strong enough not to be overthrown and absorbed by any others."

Nova was frowning and could see similar expressions on both Alric and Rawl's faces.

"The leaders must be the strongest, or most persuasive, individuals in the tribe. If one tribe is conquered by another—which happens often—their people are absorbed into the new tribe. Tribe leaders, members, and even tribe names change quickly and often."

"It sounds," Nova hesitated, not wanting to offend him, "inconvenient?"

Axchel barked out a laugh.

"To say the least. It is violent, volatile, and dangerous. If it is true that someone has managed to unite the people..."—he shook his head, trailing off—"it is almost too impossible to imagine."

"We will have to proceed very carefully when we are in Tribe territory. If we are fortunate enough to land near the Condori lands, we are likely to have more success, though that cannot be assured," he confessed. "We will have to blend in as best as possible and learn what we can to find our way to this mysterious Churan. *If* he exists."

After hearing Axchel's descriptions of the Northern Tribes, she understood better why the soldier would have difficulty believing in the sorcerer child. His stories did not tell of a people easily united, especially not by a mere boy.

Still, they had to try.

"On a more practical note," Axchel added, "we will have to find new clothing. The tribe lands are far hotter than what we've been experiencing here. It is all rainforest, thick with humidity and sticky with heat."

Nova felt a little shiver of anticipation. *Thank the dioses,* she thought. She missed the warmer, more temperate climate of mid-Andala where she had grown up. She would gladly exchange the current cold for a little bit of heat.

The next morning the group met early back inside of Patli and Enrique's home, where the woman had prepared thick fried pieces of tortillas smothered in salsa verde and topped with queso fresco, aguacate, and fried eggs. It was delicious, and once again, Nova could understand why Enrique had chosen to stay, all those years ago.

Not for the food, of course, but the care and comfort that Patli placed in every aspect of her home. The meals were fresh and mouth-watering, her decor homey and inviting. There were brightly covered pillows on the seats and sofas, with thick and cozy knitted blankets and throws. She tended an immaculate and impressive garden, knew the healing arts, and had an ability unlike any Nova had ever seen.

Even more important, however, was how she interacted with the former king and their son. She was warm, Nova realized. Affectionate. Caring. Kind. She touched both of them often, a hand on Enrique's shoulder when handing him a plate, enveloping Huallpa in a large hug when he stumbled, sleep-rumpled and drowsy from his bedroom. She squeezed Enrique's hand before he stood up to collect and then wash their dishes, and he in turn placed a kiss on the top of her head.

Nova had never experienced that kind of familial affection, and her heart ached from watching it unfold before her, as natural to any of them as breathing.

She remembered what the monarchy was like in Andala. She knew what life in the palace was like. She doubted that Enrique had experienced any semblance of this sort of love before meeting Patli.

Yes, she thought reluctantly, *I can see why he stayed.*

Afterward, when they were all well-fed and packed for their journey, they gathered outside in a group.

"How does this work?" Alric asked Patli.

"It should work just fine as long as we all stay connected," Patli answered. "But since I have never traveled such a great distance with more than one person, or with this many people in general, perhaps it is best if you all link with each other and touch me directly."

Alric stepped forward cautiously and placed a hand on Patli's right shoulder.

"Is this all right?" he asked her, and she nodded, smiling.

Rawl stepped forward and placed his hand over Alric's, overlapping his palm over both the mage's fingers and Patli's shoulder, then reached his other arm out toward Axchel. Ax stepped forward and allowed the archer to place his hand on his back, mirroring the action on his. Then, he turned and offered the crook of his arm to Nova.

She hesitated only a second before linking her arm with his, and with their arms entwined they placed their palms against the bruja's back. With her left hand, she reached around the front of Patli, and clasped Alric's free hand.

"Like this?" the mage asked, and Patli nodded.

"I think this will be fine," she answered.

Then, she looked at her husband, who had an arm around Huallpa's shoulders.

"I will be right back," she told them, and Enrique nodded curtly.

"Don't delay," he told her.

Huallpa was the least nervous of the lot, beaming at his mother with a toothy smile.

"Bye!" he said, waving to them all. "It was nice to meet you!"

Before they could answer him, they were gone.

Nova gasped and stumbled, feeling as if the world had shifted under her feet. And indeed, it had, because while a moment ago they were in the forests of Cassalan, they now stood in the midst of the towering jungle of the Northern Tribes.

The first thing that she noticed, other than the massive tree trunks with their thick, gnarled roots and covered in swinging vines, was the heat. Axchel had been right; the temperature was stifling, and the humidity made her feel as if she was breathing in steam. They all detangled themselves from Patli and immediately began shedding their outer layers.

"This is where I leave you," the bruja told them, stepping backward. "I wish you luck in your quest."

"Thank you, for all you have done for us," Axchel said to her, bowing his head.

"You can thank me by never returning to my family," she replied, not unkindly. "I mean no offense, but I truly hope to never see any of you ever again."

And with that, she was gone.

"I could never get used to that," Rawl said, his voice impressed.

Nova turned around in a full circle to take in the luxurious and abundant foliage around them. The region was mountainous and verdant, with thick, wet-looking plants and impressively tall trees. Everything around them was lush and so very green, different shades blending in with one another. There were large, flat-looking leaves the color of ripe limes, stretching wider than even Axchel's chest. The rolling, twisting vines blended from a deep pine to a rich emerald. The moss that grew on the ground and tree trunks were the color of the backs of cocodrilos.

Large, colorful birds could be seen flying above the canopy, their feathers an explosion of reds, blues, greens, and yellows. Nova could hear monkeys grunting and chattering with each other in the trees but couldn't catch a glimpse of them. In the distance, she spotted a thunderous waterfall. Where Zipacna Falls had been a cold cascade, this one looked majestic and refreshing.

"It's beautiful," she murmured to herself. Then, she turned to the group. "Now what do we do?" she asked them.

"Patli drew out more or less where she thinks we are on this map here," Axchel responded, taking out a piece of parchment paper. He was already sweating, his temple glistening by his hairline. Nova snapped her attention away from his face and onto the page, though none of the drawings or words meant anything to her.

"We shouldn't be too far from a small trading village here," Axchel pointed. "If it's still there, it is the best place to start. Trading outposts like these are neutral territories," he explained. "Members of any tribe can go to swap for things their people need, and there is no violence allowed, no matter how bad relationships are between groups. The truce is sacred, so no one would dare breach it. Outside of these borders, however..."

Axchel stopped, and looked around them. "We are not safe. We should make our way there and pray to the dioses that it still exists."

"Lead the way," Rawl said, nodding.

Axchel looked at Nova for confirmation, and she too nodded.

"You know this area far better than we do," she admitted. "We will follow your lead."

Looking pleased, Axchel began leading them. Alric pulled Nova back a little.

"We were lucky that he decided to join us," he told her.

Nova agreed. But how long would their luck continue?

The hike through the Northern Tribe territories was a difficult one. They were at a much higher altitude than any of them were accustomed to, and Nova found herself losing her breath much quicker than normal. Rawl confessed that he had developed a nauseating headache, which Axchel also attributed to the altitude, and the humidity had them drinking from their water skins much more often than usual.

Finally, Axchel checked his map and the position of the sun, nodding.

"We're not far now," he told them.

And then the very foliage around them all shifted, rising up and moving around them. For the span of a heartbeat, Nova had no idea what it was that she was seeing. Then she realized that it wasn't the foliage at all, but that there were people under it, covered in roots and grass and moss and vines. They had blended seamlessly into their environment, and no one of Nova's group had seen or heard them at all.

And they were completely surrounded.

CHAPTER 16
JESADIRANY

Jesa was in so much trouble.

She and Jose had managed to disentangle themselves from each other before Tz'ola lit up the day too much, but her exit was still not as stealthy as she had hoped. Several merchants were out beginning to set up their shops for the day, and other Pelgar citizens were walking about the dimly lit streets, either heading to or returning from work (or perhaps other amorous encounters.)

Luckily, the early hour had most people unwilling to exchange in idle conversation, so most barely spared her a glance. Jesa crept through the city as quickly as she could, her cloak disguising both her face, and her beautiful new sword, which she had tucked close to her body. She had almost made it to the city's edge, where the forest began, along its path back to the temple, when she heard the unmistakable fall of feet behind her. They were being clever, stepping when she did, and attempting to remain concealed, but she was a Danrayen-trained warrior.

Jesa picked up her pace and slipped around the corner of a small warehouse, but instead of running for the tree line, she stopped and waited, carefully laying her sword on the ground and clutching her dagger instead. After a few short moments, a figure rounded the building, their pace faster than before.

Without hesitation, Jesa grabbed the person by the front of their shirt and whirled them around, pressing their back against the wall and her blade against their throat.

Then gasped.

It was Alcor.

"Why are you following me?" she demanded, releasing her grip on him, but keeping her blade extended.

An ugly grimace twisted Alcor's cold but usually handsome face, and Jesa almost staggered back at the anger and disgust in his expression. He had never looked at her that way before; he had always been a man of neutral pleasantries and charming smiles. It was as if he had been wearing a carefully curated mask, one of polite propriety and had now dropped it, revealing something far more sinister underneath.

"Did you enjoy yourself with the blacksmith's son?" he sneered.

"Yes," she replied. Her simple, straightforward response seemed to surprise him. Did he think that she would be embarrassed? Shamed? How little he knew her.

With a bitter curl to his lip, he proceeded to call her a very foul name.

Jesa simply laughed. The fact that Alcor believed he could offend her by insulting her virtue was absurd. She was a warrior, not a maiden. Her body and her decisions were her own.

Her laugh seemed only to enrage him further.

"The fact that you would dirty yourself with common filth like him," he began, but Jesa stepped in closer with her dagger, and he stopped.

"You would have preferred I dirty myself with you, is that it? I have told you time and again that I have no interest—" but he interrupted her.

"You were never for me, you stupid girl," he yelled, spit flying from his mouth and landing on her cheek with the ferocity of his words. She winced and wiped her face with her shoulder, her eyes never leaving his.

"I don't understand," she admitted.

"You were always for Lord Guerro."

At the name, Jesa went cold, and her grip on her dagger nearly faltered. It was a name she had tried so very hard to forget. How could Alcor know of it?

"Did you think yourself safe? Did you think you had escaped? He has known where you were this entire time."

Jesa swayed on her feet.

"No," she whispered, looking around frantically as if the lord might appear from any door, any shadow, at any moment.

"He can't," she gasped, not sure how to finish her statement.

"True, I was meant to enamor you, but only to encourage you away from the temple. Charm you into choosing a life with me instead. But that was only a means of getting you to renounce the Danrayen path, so that no one would come after you when I took you to him."

This wasn't happening. This couldn't be happening!

"You are a silly, stupid girl for denying me. You should have fallen for all my gifts, my promises, my sweet words. But now I see, it wasn't my fault at all that you didn't. You pulled away from me for that common piece of trash."

His face was recognizable. She couldn't believe that the man in front of her had ever been the annoying but sweet boy who had tried so hard to woo her.

"How you would ever choose that soot-covered peasant over me, I will never understand," he snarled.

Anger flared within her, burning away the sickening fear that had clung to her like tar at the mention of the lord's name.

"He will never have me." She tilted her chin up high so he would know she was looking down on him. "I am protected by my Danrayen sisters and the goddess Danray herself. I am a member of her Temple. I will pass my trial and become a full Danrayen Warrior. Untouchable," she vowed.

"He will never have me."

Alcor only continued to sneer at her, his calmness disconcerting.

"No one is untouchable," he responded.

At that moment, they heard footsteps heading in their direction, and a soft voice called out.

"Jesa?"

Jesa felt the blood drain from her face. It was Jose. Her heart pounded faster in her chest. She didn't want him involved in anything that had to do with the Lord Guerro.

She had a quick moment to witness the flash of satisfaction and malice cross Alcor's face before realizing she had dropped both her guard and her arm, her dagger dangling uselessly by her side.

He lunged for her sword.

"No!" she cried out, but it was too late, he had scooped it up and was spinning to point it at Jose, who had just come into view.

Jose dodged just in time, side-stepping the wide arc of the blade. Jesa ran forward with her dagger, but Alcor swung wildly at her too, seeming too far gone to care that Lord Guerro would not want her dead. He spun back around toward Jose, who was holding nothing but a pretty leather scabbard. Jesa's eyes flicked to her sword, she had not even realized that he had crafted one to match her gift.

Jose continued to back up, desperately, deflecting blows with the sheath. Jesa tried to find an opening, but it was hard to get close, her weapon so much shorter than Alcor's.

Then, Jose tripped on a raised tree root, losing his footing and falling backward, the scabbard tumbling in the dirt. Alcor raised the sword high, inelegant but deadly, and began swinging it down over his head toward Jose, who raised his arm up in front of his face in a useless attempt to block it.

Jesa didn't hesitate, but launched herself in the air, clinging to Alcor's back and wrapping her left arm around his shoulders. With her right hand, she plunged her dagger dead into his neck.

Sputtering and gurgling, Alcor dropped the sword, clawing at his neck before collapsing on the ground.

Jesa fell to her knees next to Jose, who pulled her in close.

"Que paso?" he asked her, both his voice and his body shaking. Or perhaps it was her own body, she could not tell. "Why would he?"

In a tumble, Jesa confessed everything. She told Jose of the bruja's prophecy before her birth, of Lord Guerro, first set on marrying her mother and then herself, because he coveted the power of her unborn child. She told him of her mother presenting her before the Danrayens, begging them to help. And she told him of her very recent realization, that Alcor had been working for Guerro the entire time, set to lure her away from the Danrayen Temple to bring her back to the lord.

By the time she had finished pouring out the entire story, a group of townspeople could be heard approaching their location. They had no doubt heard the commotion and were coming to investigate.

Jose looked down the path, where they would soon be in sight.

"Go," he told her, shoving her new sword and sheath in her hands, and taking the bloody dagger from her.

"No," she shook her head furiously, understanding his intent.

"Jesa—" he started, but she interrupted.

"No! I will not leave you to shoulder my blame," she said.

"Listen to me," he yelled, gripping her shoulder with the hand not holding the blade. Then he trailed it up to cup her cheek. Jesa leaned into his touch.

"If this Lord Guerro is as dangerous as you say, this is the perfect opportunity to trap you," he said. "They will lock you up while they investigate, the Danrayen priestesses will not be able to come to your aid until a trial. It will leave you alone, and vulnerable."

"I am not vulnerable!" she insisted. "I am a Danrayen Warrior, or soon to be, I am strong, and I was only defending myself. The law will be on my side!"

"I know, I know," Jose said, pulling her in for a hug. "But powerful men have a way of evading the law, and we cannot take that risk."

The voices of the villagers were closer now.

"What about you?" Jesa asked him, tears streaming down her face. He gave her one of his rare grins.

"I am an upstanding member of the village, the son of a well-respected blacksmith. Alcor was a stranger, with no family and no connections here. I will be fine. They will believe I acted in self-defense."

"But—" Jesa started, but Jose stopped her, his fingertips over her lips.

"Do you love me?" he asked her, his brown eyes searching hers.

"Yes," she said, without hesitation.

"Then please, mi amor, go."

He grasped her face and kissed her hard, and swiftly, before pushing her away. Jesa clutched her sword and ran.

By the time Jesa had made it back to the temple, it had been very apparent that she had not spent the night on Danrayen grounds. The priestesses wasted no time in handing out her punishment—mandatory cleaning duties, mucking out the stables, and assisting with every meal for the next two months.

And no trips outside of the temple during that time.

That night, Sofia and Jesa sat in the gardens, under the statue of Danray, and Jesa told her friend everything. She cried over a prophecy that had altered the course of her entire life, for her mother who had to abandon her to save her from it. She cried over the first life that she had taken, and cried harder when she realized that she couldn't truly be sorry for it. And she cried that she left Jose to deal with the aftermath of her actions alone.

Sofia merely held her and rocked her as she cried. When all of the ugly business was finally spoken, Sofia pulled out a handkerchief and handed it to her friend.

"Jose is right," she assured Jesa. "His family is well-liked and well-respected in Pelgar. No one would believe anything other than Jose defending himself. He will be all right, you'll see."

"I just hate that I left him, I shouldn't have done that," Jesa replied nasally, then blew her nose.

"He was right to tell you to go," Sofia said. "I like him all the better for protecting you. Besides"—she gave Jesa a sly smile—"you will have plenty of time to make it up to him later."

Jesa sputtered, and then laughed. Sofia leaned in.

"So? How was it, before? At the forge?" she asked her, her face full of naked curiosity.

"It was wonderful," Jesa admitted, sighing a little at the memory. "He is wonderful."

Her face clouded with concern once more, which Sofia was quick to notice.

"I have some free time tomorrow," Sofia told her. "I will go into Pelgar and make sure he is all right," she promised.

Relieved, Jesa threw her arms around her friend.

"Gracias, hermana," she said.

"It's what best friends do," Sofia replied.

***

The next day Jesa was a bundle of nervous energy. She woke up early and helped out with the morning meal as promised, then went about her training. She was distracted and ended up with several new bruises, but the pain helped keep her mind off of Jose.

She didn't hear a word that her instructors said during the strategy and history classes, but let her mind wander. In the afternoon, when she should have been mucking out stalls, she sat on a bale of hay and penned Jose a letter instead.

She hoped it didn't end up smelling like sweat and horse dung.

Just before heading to the kitchens to help with dinner, she found Sofia and slipped her the note, making her vow to return with news the moment she could. Her friend promised her, and set out for Pelgar.

A few hours later, Jesa was sweeping the front steps of the temple, keeping an eye out for Sofia's return. The second she saw her, Jesa dropped her broom, which clattered down the long golden steps, but Jesa didn't hear it, nor would have cared if she had. She flew down the stairs herself, and collided with her friend at the bottom.

"Que dijo?" she asked her, pulling back. "Did he ask for me? Is he all right? Did you give him my note?"

It was then that Jesa really looked at Sofia's face. Her friend looked both somber and pained, and her eyes looked as if she had been crying.

"Que paso?" Jesa demanded. "Sofia, tell me what happened!"

"Amiga, I'm so sorry," she said. "They say Alcor was the nephew of a rich lord."

"Guerro?" Jesa asked, swaying. She felt the world drop from underneath her feet and wondered how she was still standing.

Sofia nodded.

"They say he demanded justice," she continued.

"Jose," Jesa whispered, feeling the blood drain from her face. "Where is Jose?"

"He's gone," Sofia said with a sob. "They sent him to the capital, to train. They've assigned him to be a soldier in the war."

Jesa sat down on the bottom step of the temple and wept.

CHAPTER 17

NOVA

Nova stared in a mixture of shock and admiration at the people surrounding her party. They were all holding weapons currently pointed in their direction, bows and machetes and flute-looking things that Nova was sure would release poisoned darts if blown. She knew that they were in trouble, but she also couldn't help being impressed. They had been so quiet, so still, that Nova hadn't sensed them at all. Neither had the men. They were clearly formidable.

Axchel raised his arms outwards, fingers spread wide, and the rest of them followed his example. A man with long black hair, a bare chest streaked with mud, and a hat fashioned from moss stepped out in front of them. He said something to them in a language Nova was unfamiliar with, and she glanced at Axchel.

"Ah, lo siento," he replied to them. "I'm not familiar … Condori?"

At the word "Condori," several other members of the tribe began speaking over each other, fast. The leader turned back to them and answered in the same, unrecognizable language.

Axchel winced. "I shouldn't have mentioned my tribe. There is no way to know who is battling with who right now. Get ready to fight."

Nova shifted her weight and began lowering her arms slowly. Axchel, on the other hand, began raising them slightly, likely to be able to reach his sheathed sword more quickly. Nova could see Alric moving his lips, the pads of his fingers beginning to glow red.

Then, the leader faced them once more.

"You are Condori?" he asked them, in a tongue they all could speak.

Axchel hesitated, then nodded. "My mother is Condori."

There was a tense pause, and then the leader nodded back. In an instance, all the weapons were dropped, and postures were instantly more relaxed.

"We are the Totec. Allies to the Warrior Child, as are the Condori. Our tribes are at peace."

The man bowed to Axchel, and handed him a small cluster of leaves. Axchel accepted them soberly and tucked them into his right cheek. He then reached into a pocket and took out a puma tooth, wrapped in a leather strap, and offered it to the man, who accepted it happily.

"I am Atuq," he told them.

Cunning like the fox, Nova thought. Not a bad name meaning for a leader.

"I am Axchel," the Cassalain responded.

"We are brothers now, Axchel!" Atuq claimed, opening his arms wide. "Do you travel to the Warrior Child's assembly?"

Nova exchanged a quick glance with her group. It looked as if their luck was holding after all!

"Yes," Axchel answered hesitantly. "Churan, the Warrior Child, he will be there?"

"Of course! He calls for us to join. Together, we can end the invasions of the Cassalains and live in our lands in peace," Atuq responded.

"May we travel with you, hermano?" Axchel asked him.

"I would insist. Many of us are allied now, but not all. It is safer in numbers," Atuq said seriously.

With that, Axchel and Atuq made the introductions, and Nova was pleased to see that there were warriors of all genders among the Totec. They spent a few moments in polite discussion, getting to know one another, before they set off once again.

Axchel and Atuq were deep in conversation in the front of the group, too far for Nova to hear. Alric was, of course, asking as many questions as he could in the least amount of time, which was making the Totec people laugh. Rawl had exchanged his bow with the smaller one of a pretty young woman boasting elaborate face paint, and they were examining each weapons differences and ranges.

A few members of the tribe attempted to draw Nova into conversation, but quickly abandoned their efforts when it was clear that she would rather walk in silence. She meant no offense by it, and no one seemed to take it poorly; she was simply nervous and anxious about their mission, not to mention, still out of breath from the altitude.

Luckily, their journey did not last much longer. It seemed that fate was working with them, Patli *traveling* them so close to the area in which the Unnamed Prince would be this very evening. Nova was hesitant to let herself hope; she had felt hopeful right before the disastrous disappointment that finding Huallpa was. But for once, everything seemed to be going their way.

When they arrived at the meeting place, they found that the peacemaking ceremony was to be held in a large cave, carved into an enormous mountain range. At the entrance they were forced to turn in their weapons, with a promise that they would be returned afterward. No one was happy about the arrangement, neither Nova's group nor the Totec tribe, but they all ultimately acquiesced in order to move forward.

Inside, the space was far more than just a cave. The walls had been carved and shaped into ascending ramps and paths, leading to smaller caverns and rooms. The space was lit with hundreds of sconces, jutting out of the rock and illuminating the domed main room, as well as the caverns and tunnels.

Axchel led them all down a series of winding paths, and Nova inwardly thanked the dioses that she was not afraid of enclosed spaces. It would have made their current situation incredibly uncomfortable. Finally, Axchel stopped at two small stone rooms, divided by a stone partition. There was a cot with a mat on either side with space on the ground to roll additional sleeping mats and several basins of water set out along the edges of the rooms.

"I'm told that there are underground passages that remove waste," Axchel told them, pointing down the hall. "We can use them to relieve ourselves. Atuq said that the ceremony will begin at nightfall, so we have a few hours to clean up and rest. He also let me know where I can find the traders, so I will find us all more appropriate clothing."

He grinned at them ruefully. "Apparently, these outfits make us look like Cassalains."

"Well, we certainly wouldn't want that!"

The words slipped out of Nova's mouth before she could think, and they shocked her. Had she just teased him?

Axchel chuckled and rubbed a hand over the back of his neck. "Of course not. Don't worry, I'll find you something nice."

Before Nova could respond, he was gone.

Rawl shot her a look waggling his eyebrows up and down, and she narrowed her eyes at him. Luckily, Alric was too busy setting down his pack on the cot to notice.

"You take the other cot, Nova," the mage told her. "Rawl and Axchel can take this room. I'll set my mat on the floor of yours later," he said.

Nova didn't argue. If the men felt like acting gallantly because she was a woman, she certainly wasn't going to try to dissuade them. Not when she had the opportunity to sleep on an actual bed instead of the ground.

"Well, if we have a few hours, I think I'll take a nap," she said, stretching out. The mattress was thin and warm, but clean. And after the many months spent sleeping outdoors, it felt like a luxury. With a contented sigh, she fell asleep.

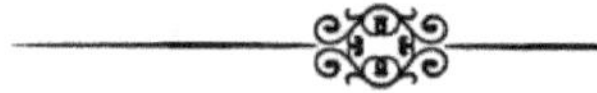

When Nova woke again, she could tell by the feel of her body that she had been asleep for quite some time. She looked around the room, but Alric was nowhere to be seen. She hopped out of bed and indulged in a large stretch before peeking around the stone partition. Rawl and Axchel were not there either. But on their extra cot lay a folded piece of fabric with a piece of parchment paper on top.

"*We decided to let you sleep for a while longer. We have all cleaned up and changed and will meet you in the main chamber. Don't worry, I made Rawl save you some clean water. Axchel found this for you to wear. See you soon, Alric.*"

Nova pushed the note aside and lifted the fabric underneath it.

It was a dress. A beautiful dress, at that. Nova had never had much cause to use dresses, but even she could tell that it was lovely. It was the color of jade and embroidered in a gold as vibrant as the sun itself.

Nova quickly dragged a basin of water behind the dividing rock wall and used an old wash cloth and hard piece of soap to scrub herself clean. She even took a moment to wash her hair, though the amount of time it took to untangle it after made it almost not worthwhile. Once she was clean, and feeling more refreshed than she had in a long time, she slipped the dress over her head.

It was long, the gold-bordered hem just grazing the floor. The sleeves were short, falling just below her shoulders, and the neckline left the top of her chest exposed. The fabric was light and airy, and the layers swished as she walked.

Nova smiled. There was no mirror to see herself in, but it didn't matter. She felt pretty.

Slipping on sandals that had also been left for her, and marveling that Axchel had guessed her size perfectly, she left the rooms and made her way to the main cavern.

It took her several tries, as the tunnels all looked identical. She made several wrong turns before the noise of a large group of people steered her in the right direction. When she reached the open space, she was shocked to see so many people. They were gathered in number, throngs of individuals milling about, sharing food and drink and conversing. Everyone was dressed much like she was, in light, airy clothing that was clearly nice enough for special occasions. Most of the people had long, dark hair, several with intricate braids displayed in various fashions. Their skin tones varied from a warm bronze to a deep brown, but most of their features were similar. There were several members with facial tattoos, and Nova assumed that they all belonged to the same tribe, but she didn't have enough knowledge of the Northern Tribes to guess which. As Nova examined her surroundings, she heard someone calling her name.

She looked down and caught a glimpse of Alric waving his arms above his head to get her attention. Rawl and Axchel were with him. She grinned, and followed the rock path down to meet her friends.

Alric was wearing a long, emerald-colored tunic that belted in the middle and ended at his ankles. It had no sleeves, but it did have a hood, hanging against the mage's upper back. Axchel was also wearing a tunic, but his was a bright, buttery yellow and hit him just below the knees, showcasing his muscular calves. Rawl was wearing all black, loose-fitting pants and a flowy shirt that opened wide on his chest. They were all smiling.

"Well, don't we clean up well," Nova commented when she reached them.

"I told you that I would find you something nice," Axchel said.

"It's very nice," Nova said honestly. "Thank you."

The four of them moved in closer together.

"What's our plan?" Alric asked them softly.

"We have to find the boy, of course," Nova answered. "I assume he will be speaking at some point during this event. Once we know who he is, we can figure out a way to get to him."

"To speak to him, of course," Rawl clarified. "We're not just going to abduct the kid, are we?"

"Que?" Nova gasped. "Of course not! We're going to convince him to come with us."

"And if he refuses?" Axchel asked, frowning. "What if he doesn't want to come?"

Nova shook her head.

"Let's not borrow tomorrow's problems. The first thing we need to do is find the boy." She tried to sound confident, but internally she worried. What if the boy refused? What then? Her quest had been the most important thing in her life for so long, but if the boy did not want to be a part of it, then she didn't think she had it in her to force his hand. He was just a kid, after all. He should get a say in his own destiny.

"All right," Rawl said. "Let's try and figure out what we can. Alric and I will start at that end of the room," he said, pointing to the farthest wall of the cave, "and you and Axchel start here. We'll meet somewhere in the middle."

Nova nodded, and Alric and Rawl began walking away.

"Let's see what these people know about Churan," she said to Axchel.

It didn't take long for them to realize that people knew a lot of rumors about the Warrior Child, but not a lot of fact. By the time a very earnest man insisted that he had heard that the boy could change his shape into that of animals, Nova was getting a headache.

"Come on," Axchel said, grabbing her hand and leading her toward the center of the cave, where people were dancing.

"Where are we going?" Nova asked.

"We are going to dance."

Nova instantly dug in her heels, and Ax stumbled when he met her resistance.

"We have a mission. I'm not going to take a break to dance with you," she hissed under her breath.

"How suspicious do you think we'll look if we keep moving from group to group, asking for information about Churan?" he whispered back. "We need to at least *try* to blend in!"

Nova knew that he had a point, but still.

"I don't know how to dance," she replied churlishly.

"Lucky for you that I do. I'll teach you." Then Axchel grasped her arm and pulled her forward once more.

Nova felt herself tense all over. She very much did not want to dance, but she wanted even less to draw attention to them, so she allowed him to lead her on to the makeshift dance floor.

They squeezed in between happy, moving people, and he wrapped one of his arms around her waist, his strong calloused hand resting just above the base of her spine. With his other hand he held her right lightly.

Nova stumbled over the first few steps, unfamiliar with the music or rhythm, but adapted quickly, and found she was able to keep pace. It helped that Axchel was easy to follow. After a few moments he pulled her a little bit closer to him, which did things to her heart that she rather not examine at the moment.

Axchel dipped his head toward her ear, which was a laughably long distance, and spoke quietly. "You lied to me," he said.

Instantly, Nova tensed in his arms, her face abandoning the relaxed expression that the dancing had coaxed out of her just moments before. Trying to keep her composure, she mentally ran through which lie he could be referring to. She had lied so many times in her life, and to so many people, it was almost second nature at this point. It seemed that most of her life was built around lies. Before she could spiral into panic, she caught his amused smirk from the corner of her eye.

Confused as to why he would be smiling, she tilted her head up to meet his eyes.

His grin grew wider. "You *can* dance," he said.

Oh, that lie.

She *could* dance, as a matter of fact. She had been taught in her youth when she was living in the palace, as Name-Bearers are taught all aspects of palace etiquette. At the temple, she learned the Dance of Danray, but more than that, they also learned court dances. Danrayens, especially Danrayen Riders, often spent time with nobility and members of the court, and they were expected to keep up with all of them. As a result, their training was comprehensive. The only reason that she had lied about not being able to dance was because she wasn't sure how she would feel being held by the Cassalain.

She still wasn't sure how she felt about it.

Instead of answering, she lifted up her right shoulder in a shrug. His smile didn't dim, he just tucked her back close to him and continued leading her. Nova found, to her surprise, that for a while at least, she was happy to be led.

Nova and Axchel only managed a single dance together before the loud blasting of horns reverberated around the cave. The result was instantaneous, everyone stopped what they were doing and turned to the source of the noise. The horn players were stationed on a high and wide ledge, about halfway up the cave's expanse. The musicians moved aside and revealed that on that ledge stood an older man, as well as a middle-aged man and woman. And in between them, a boy of approximately twelve years of age.

A rush of anticipation coursed through Nova, and she shared a pointed look with Axchel. The sea of people were moving like waves toward the area beneath them, and they allowed themselves to be taken by the current, Nova scanning the crowd for Alric and Rawl. She finally spotted them, much closer to the boy than they were, and pointed them out to Ax. They slowly attempted to make their way over to their position, but it was a complicated task, as the bodies of people were so densely packed, it made movement difficult. They were still inching toward their friends when the boy began to speak.

"Amiges," he said, in a loud, commanding voice, using the common tongue of Tierramadri. "Gracias por venir."

There was a jumbled greeting in return, the people's faces eager and curious to what the boy was about to say.

"I have asked you here today, to speak of peace."

The crowd murmured amongst themselves, shifting. Ax and Nova used the opportunity to move closer to Alric and Rawl.

"I understand," the boy addressed them again. "What are talks of peace, when all our people have ever known is war?"

There were many short nods and grunts of confirmation.

"And who am I to speak of war, when I have only known it for twelve years, and some of you, for many decades?"

Louder noises of agreement filled the cave, before someone called out, "You are Churan! Warrior Child!"

Which was met with loud stomping of feet and cheers.

"I am Churan," the boy agreed. "But to many of you, I am not 'Warrior Child,' but simply, a child."

The room became quiet once more.

"I am here before you to tell you that when the truth has been buried so deep, sometimes only new growth can unearth it once more."

At that, he had the attention of the entire crowd. The silence stretched, and even Nova found herself leaning in toward the child, waiting to hear what more he had to say.

"Our people have been battling each other for generations," he continued. "Why? Petty squabbles over land, resources, and territory. It only takes the smallest of slights for us to begin once more. But we are not who we should be fighting."

Churan stepped closer to the edge of the jutting rock and looked down at them all.

"What do we fight over? Why are there not enough resources? Who has laid claim to lands that were always ours and pushed us north to the furthest recesses of Tierramadri?"

The murmurs began again, the energy more strained than before.

"Who has reached out to certain tribes and offered them food, weapons, supplies, if they turn on their brother and sister tribes?"

Nova noticed some people looking down, shame-faced.

"And who has invaded our lands, taken our women, and recruited our warriors to a southern war that has nothing to do with our people?"

"Cassalan!" someone called out.

"Cassalan! Cassalan!" others joined in.

Soon, the room was filled with loud, aggressive discussions and angry shouts. Nova was jostled about, until Axchel planted her in front of him, using his body as a shield. She looked up at his face, and his expression was one of thoughtful consideration.

Churan raised both of his arms in the air, and almost immediately, the room quieted. A steady, powerful energy seemed to radiate from his small form. There was something about the child that made him seem ancient and wise, rather than just a small boy. If Nova had not known he was a sorcerer, she still would have guessed at his power. It was apparent in how his stillness could quiet an entire room of people.

"Alone, we are no match for a nation as large as theirs. But together, united, we stand a chance against the real threat. I know that lifelong, or even generations-long, feuds between our tribes may not be an easy thing to forget. But we have the week here to begin laying them all to rest and getting to know one another not as enemies, but as brothers, sisters, families, friends. We can share our grievances, but also our knowledge, our wisdom, and our beliefs, all the things that define us not as members of different tribes, but as the children of the dioses de la Tierra. And if we all come together, at the end we can become allied against the true enemy."

There was an eruption of cheers and yells, people excited about the prospect of unity and peace. Under the persuasive power of Churan's presence, Nova had found the speech youthful and idealistic, but there was an earnest hopefulness that she couldn't deny. Perhaps a bit of youthful idealism was just what these people needed. Even she was feeling a bit inspired.

Just as Nova and Axchel began squeezing their way toward their friends once again, there was a cry, louder than the others in the room. The noise died down, and an uneasy stillness settled over the crowd like a fog.

There was a lone individual on a ledge opposite to that of Churan, and she was holding a bow pointed straight at the boy.

"Death to the Warrior Child!" she yelled, and there were several terrified shrieks as she released the arrow.

Time seemed to slow for a moment as Nova watched the arrow in horror, heading straight toward Churan, the Warrior Child, uniter of the Northern Tribes, potential child of prophecy, the might-be Unnamed Prince.

Just before the arrow reached its intended target, a bolt of fiery blood red magia crackled in the air, disintegrating it into nothing but splinters that rained down harmlessly over the people beneath it.

There was a shocked pause, and then furious shouts and screams as people ran up to catch the would-be assassin and also apprehend Alric and Rawl.

"No!" Nova called out, shoving her way more forcefully to them. "Stop it, he saved him! Leave him be!"

Axchel was right behind her, calling out "Move! Muevanse!" as he helped her part the violent throng. They reached the two men just as they were being dragged away.

"Nova, no!" Alric called out, as she grabbed the arm of one of the men who held the mage and tried to pry it off of him. In less than a second, she too was grabbed, as was Axchel. They all struggled in vain; there were too many of them.

"Stop, where are you taking us?" she yelled as she squirmed, trying to find a way to release her arms.

"The Warrior Child wants to speak to you," someone finally answered, and the four captives froze, making them much easier to drag along.

"Very well," Alric said, projecting his voice. "We will come."

When it was clear that the group had stopped fighting, the grip of their captors loosened, just a bit, and together they all walked up the pathway toward the boy.

Chapter 18

Nova

They were led to a carved-out stone room, but larger than both of theirs had been combined. It was deep, and they had to walk several feet in to reach the far wall, where there were several seats and chairs fashioned in a half-circle. At the head sat the boy, the tribespeople who had stood with at the platform flanking him.

He was very different from Huallpa, even though they were of almost the same age. Where Enrique's son had been all gangly limbs and chubby cheeks, and the picture of boyish youth, Churan seemed much older than his years. His expression was calm and considering as he looked at them. His face was sharp and angular, his cheekbones high under his golden-bronzed skin. His nose was wide at the bottom, with the tip curving back in toward his face. The eyes that were regarding them impassively were hooded, and so dark that they appeared black, with a thick strip of dark brows over them. His unsmiling mouth was full, with the barest hint of wispy hair over his top lip.

Nova and the others shuffled in and stared at him awkwardly. Alric looked over to her, and she gave him a tiny, one shoulder shrug to indicate that she had no idea how to proceed. Lucky for them, Churan spoke first.

"You stopped the arrow?" he directed toward Alric, his voice lighter and softer than it had been during his speech to the crowd.

"I did," Alric responded.

"Using magia?" the boy asked, and Alric nodded.

Churan glanced at the people who stood behind him, the older man on his right and the two others on his left.

"Leave us," he told them.

"Pero, Churan," the old man began, but the boy held up a hand to stop him.

"I will be fine. Please leave us."

"I must insist," the older man tried again, but Churan shot him a stern look.

Reluctantly, the others shuffled out of the room, and Churan watched them as they disappeared from view. Then, the stoic expression on his face dropped, and he burst into a wide smile. Leaping from his chair, he crossed hurriedly to Alric and beamed up at him, his eyes wide with admiration.

"Are you a mage?" His voice was reverent.

Alric seemed startled, as they all did. In front of them was a very different child than the one they had met upon entering.

"I am," Alric answered.

Churan bounced excitedly on the balls of his feet. "I've never met a mage!" he confessed happily. "Do you think that you'd be able to teach me?"

Those wide eyes looked up at Alric again, imploringly.

"We were led to believe that you were a sorcerer," Alric told him, glancing at Nova in confusion.

"Oh, I am," Churan answered easily, crossing back to his chair and flopping onto it. Instead of the stiff, regal posture he had held when they had first entered the room, the boy was now slouched, with his arms crossed in front of him.

"I don't know how to control my magia though. Things just happen. Sometimes they're good things, other times..." he trailed off. "It would be so wonderful if you could teach me," he repeated, perking up again.

Nova stepped forward.

"Churan," she said hesitantly. "I am called Nova."

The boy sprung up from his chair.

"Oh, lo siento, of course, I am being a terrible host. Kunaq, that's one of my advisors, he was just here, has tried to teach me, but there are so many things to remember and I forget sometimes," the boy rambled. "He is a shaman too, so he also tries to teach me about my magia, but it's very different, and I don't think we've made much progress," he continued, crossing to a tray with a pitcher and an assortment of fruit. He picked it up, wobbling a little with its weight, and the pitcher began tipping precariously. In a flash, Axchel was there to help him.

"Gracias!" the boy said cheerily, craning his neck up to look at his face.

"Wow, you are so big! I don't think I've ever seen anyone as tall as you. Well, maybe one. There was a tribe we visited once, the Bandari, their members were pretty tall, even their women! It was impressive. But I don't think that they were as tall as you. Or maybe they were as tall as you, or taller! But they weren't tall and strong, and you are both tall and strong. What did you have to do to get all of those muscles? I think it would be wonderful to have muscles like that. You know, they call me the Warrior Child, but I'm not much of a warrior. I've never even fought with my hands! Just my magia." The boy seemed to deflate for a moment, but before anyone could interject, he shook himself off and continued.

"Also, why would they call me the Warrior Child? I know I am young now, but I'm bound to grow up, aren't I? What about when I'm not a child anymore? It'll be a silly title then, won't it?"

Nova looked around the room at her friends' faces, who looked as shocked as she felt. Churan was not what they had been expecting at all.

Axchel cleared his throat and motioned to the tray he had been holding while the boy had rambled on.

"Oh!" Churan exclaimed. "I'm so sorry. Please, place it in the middle here, and have a seat." He motioned to the center of the half-circle and selected a floor cushion to sit on rather than returning to his chair. The rest of them followed suit, seating themselves on the various cushions around him.

The same serious expression came over Churan's face that he had had when delivering his speech, and when they had first walked into the room. He sat up straight, and the quiet, still energy Nova had noticed about him in the cavern settled over him like a cloak. Regally, he motioned to the pitcher and food.

"Please, sirvense," he offered. "And tell me a little about yourselves." He nodded to Nova. "You said your name was Nova?"

"Yes, and this is Alric, Rawl, and Axchel," she replied.

He nodded solemnly. "Very nice to meet you all." Then, in a flash, his serious persona dropped again.

"What are you all doing here? You're not from the Tribes, are you? Well," he corrected, "Maybe you are, Axchel is a Condori name, isn't it? But the rest of you aren't from here. Are you Cassalain?" he asked them. Despite his earlier words against the Cassalains, the question didn't seem accusatory.

Rawl seemed to notice too. "And if we were?" he asked the boy.

"Oh, I don't think all Cassalains are bad!" the boy replied. "Not the regular people anyway. It's those in power who keep taking more and more every day. Their people suffer from their greed as much as ours do. Well, almost as much, maybe," he conceded. "So you are Cassalains?"

"Actually," Nova hesitated, then gave in. He had to learn the truth at some point. "We're from Andala."

Churan's eyes grew wide.

"Andala!" he exclaimed. "How did you get all the way here from Andala? Did you cross the Borders? How? And then you made the journey all the way up here? How long did it take you? A really long time, I'll bet. But why would Andalans want to come all the way up to the Northern Tribes?"

When Churan stopped to suck in a breath, Nova jumped in before he could continue.

"We're here because of a prophecy and a promise of peace."

Churan was finally quiet as Nova explained her entire quest. He simply stared at her, in wide-eyed bewilderment, as if she was telling him a particularly riveting bedtime story. When she finished, he looked into the distance thoughtfully for a few moments, his dark eyes glazing over like night fog settling over dark lakes. The solemn power that continued to war with his childish personality claimed him again, and Nova shivered at its intensity. She didn't interrupt his contemplation, however, letting him fully absorb the implications of her tale.

"You think I am the child from the Flowers' prophecy?" he finally asked her.

Nova took a deep breath. "We hope that you might be," she confessed.

"How can you know for sure?" he asked.

Alric shifted forward and held out his arm. Quickly he explained how the ink in his tattoo was fashioned with the pollen of the Flowers of Prophecy, and that they believed it would glow in the presence of the Unnamed Prince. Then, he moved to remove the wrappings that kept it covered.

"Wait," Churan said, raising a hand. "If I am this... 'Unnamed Prince,'" he turned to Nova. "You're saying that I can help to bring peace? Actual peace? Not just to Andala, but to all of Tierramadri?"

"The Flowers said that you would 'bring peace to this realm,'" she repeated. "I do not know if the realm they meant was Andala or the entire territory east of the sea, but there can be no peace in Andala without peace in Cassalan," she reminded him. "And Cassalan cannot have peace without peace in the Northern Tribes. I have to believe it is all connected. Why else would the child of the prophecy be a member of the Tribes?"

Churan sat thoughtfully for a long moment. Then, abruptly, he stood up.

"Please stay here," he told them, giving them a short, choppy bow. "I will return momentarily."

And with that, he rushed out the cavern entrance.

"Well, that went well," Rawl mumbled, grabbing a piece of sliced mango from the tray. After a moment, Axchel followed suit. Nova sighed, and then grabbed the pitcher, pouring them each a glass of what looked to be jugo de melocoton. They might as well get comfortable, who knew what was to come.

"I don't know about this," Alric finally said.

"About what?" Nova asked him. "You don't think he could be the child of prophecy?"

"I'm not even sure he's a sorcerer, as they claim! He certainly doesn't seem serious or formidable enough."

"He's a child," Rawl reminded him. "He's not supposed to be serious or formidable."

Alric looked at him. "You have to admit that he doesn't exactly seem like a wise and powerful sorcerer."

"Who said sorcerers had to be wise and powerful?" Rawl challenged. "Well, maybe powerful, that sort of goes hand in hand with that level of magia. But if he's not all that powerful yet, perhaps he has to grow into it. Perhaps he has to grow into his wisdom as well. After all, isn't wisdom earned?"

Alric continued to look skeptical. "He's not what I was expecting."

"He spoke well," Axchel interrupted, much to everyone's surprise. When they all turned to look at him, he jerked his shoulder up, looking embarrassed by the attention. "Before, when he made the speech. He spoke well. He may just be a child, but he already commands loyalty and attention. There are different types of power."

Nova agreed, but before she could speak, Churan finally returned, along with the three individuals who had been with him before. Nova and her group sprang up to their feet.

"Friends," he greeted them. "This is Kunaq," he motioned to the elderly gentleman, "Kallpa, and Lucia. They are my advisors."

"Hola," Kallpa greeted them, bowing. "Thank you for saving Churan," he said to Alric, who nodded back.

"We are in your debt," Lucia told them, crossing deeper into the room. "There were once more of us, and better able to provide for his safety. But the business of peace is a violent one, and we can never be sure who to trust."

"I told them what you told me," Churan said, and Nova tensed. After all the time that they had spent keeping their mission hidden, and seeking out the Unnamed Prince, the fact that the child could be so casual about their secrets felt unnerving. Still, as it was his future they were discussing, she couldn't fault him for confiding in the people he trusted.

Churan moved deeper into the room and sat back down on the floor. He motioned for the others to do the same. Cautiously, the group took their earlier places, while Kallpa and Lucia joined them.

Kunaq chose a chair instead, easing his older body onto the surface gingerly. "What makes you so certain that Churan is the boy that you seek?" he asked them.

"We're not certain," Nova confessed. "He's just our best option. We're hoping that he is the one, for we have journeyed a very long way to find him."

"And if he is this child of prophecy?" Kunaq demanded. "What then? You intend to take him from his people, his home? Carry him off to a foreign land?"

"No," Nova said, as evenly as she could. "We would never take Churan against his will. But if he is who we seek, then he has the opportunity to bring about the peace you are fighting so hard to achieve."

Kallpa and Lucia were both shaking their heads.

"He has work to do here," Kallpa said. "He is uniting our people, something that has proved impossible until now."

"How is it that your people are so willing to trust him?" Alric asked them.

"My magia," Churan responded, but he didn't sound proud. If anything, his voice was melancholic. "When I was younger, members of the, well, it doesn't matter which tribe. People came and attacked my tribe. They came, ready to raid and steal and kill."

"Churan stopped them," Lucia said. "All of them, with a burst of magia that eliminated them all at once, in one fell swoop."

Alric sucked in a breath. Nova knew that that amount of magia was almost unimaginable.

"But many of my own people were killed in the blast," Churan admitted softly. "Including my grandparents, who had been raising me." His eyes met Alric's. "I couldn't control it; it just burst out of me."

"Word of his power spread, and we have seen him use it several times after. Others have witnessed it as well, and it was enough to begin spreading the word of the powerful Warrior Child throughout our lands," Lucia continued.

"Kunaq, Lucia, and I had been on a part of a larger council who had been trying to speak about peace for years," Kallpa said. "We found Churan and offered to counsel him, to advise him, and help him to unite our people. It is what we have been working toward ever since."

"But with you, I am just a mouthpiece!" Churan argued. "Of course I believe in everything that you have taught me, but I am only making a difference because of your words and your influence. The people may believe in me, but I am just a symbol. I want to do more."

"You are doing more than anyone has ever been able to accomplish!" Kallpa assured him. "You may be a symbol, but it is one that is uniting us. That is important, mijo!"

"But what if there was another way? A way that could assure peace for us all? You believe in the dioses. As do I. If the dioses have spoken through the Flowers of Prophecy, and I have the chance to save not only our people, but Tierramadri, how can I deny them?"

"It has become very dangerous for Churan here in the North," Lucia added thoughtfully. "We cannot hire more guards if we do not know who we can trust. The archer today was just one of many attacks, and who knows how many more there are to come."

"So your suggestion is to let him run off with complete strangers? Alone? Without even his own people to protect him?" Kunaq cried.

"I can take care of myself!" Churan exclaimed, but everyone ignored him.

"Peace, Kunaq. It's all we have ever worked for," Kallpa said slowly. "What if this is real? What if this is true?"

"There is no way for us to know for certain. It is too much of a risk," Kunaq insisted

"What if there was a way to know for certain?" Alric asked as he gestured to his arm once more. "If it glows, we'll know that Churan is the one we seek.

"It could just be a mage's trick," the old man argued stubbornly.

"Please," Churan said softly. "I want to try. I need to know."

When no one else interjected, Alric shifted closer to Churan, extending his arm. Then, swiftly and deliberately, he unwrapped the bandaging that covered his Flower tattoo.

As soon as it was visible, Alric hissed and gripped his arm around his wrist. Rawl jumped up and crossed toward him, but Alric shook his head.

"It burns," he winced.

Then, as they watched, the Flower tattoo began to glow, petal by petal. It was subtle, at first, but then it was like tiny pinpricks of gold were humming inside of Alric's skin. Soon, that humming became a louder purr, and Alric cried out as the tattoo began lifting off his skin. Nova jumped up as well, just as all of the ink burst from his flesh and took the form of dozens of buzzing bees. They swarmed around the baffled Churan, creating a quick, golden halo around him. Then, with a flash, the bees burst, raining a light cloud of yellow pollen over the boy.

"That was no mage's trick," Lucia whispered.

They had found the Unnamed Prince.

After the incredible spectacle, no one attempted to doubt the legitimacy of their claims. Plans were quickly made to get Churan back to Andala for the Naming Rite.

"He cannot go alone," Kunaq insisted. "I am not saying that these people cannot be trusted, but he needs a Tribe member to accompany him as his sworn protector. I cannot, for I am too old."

"I will go," Kallpa offered, bowing to Churan. "I will protect the Warrior Child."

"You cannot," Kunaq said sadly. "You are our only representative of the Alcanta tribe. Without you, these peace talks will stall. And no matter what Churan is able to accomplish in the South, we need our people allied."

"Me, then," Lucia offered. "There is no one outside of us three that can be trusted, so it must be me."

Kallpa shook his head. "No," he said.

"Amor," she answered, placing her hand against his cheek.

"No," he insisted, gripping her wrist. Then he turned to the rest of them. "She is expecting a child, she cannot go."

"There is no one else—" Lucia insisted, but Kallpa cut her off.

"You don't know how long this journey will take. Will you continue with an infant on your breast?"

"I am Condori," Axchel interrupted loudly. When Nova turned to him, he looked as if he had surprised himself. The others turned their gazes at him expectantly.

"My mother was Condori," Axchel clarified. "But I am of the people. I will take the oath."

There was a long moment of quiet that Nova did not dare interrupt. Whatever this was, it had nothing to do with her or Alric or Rawl. They needed to let it play out amongst the others.

"I accept you as my protector," Churan said seriously, then turned back to his advisors. "I know that we don't know them well, but we know their intent. And I believe we can trust them. So please trust me, and my judgment."

Kunaq, Kallpa, and Lucia exchanged a long look. Finally, Kunaq nodded.

"Very well. The Condori will perform the oath and be Churan's sworn protector."

Churan wriggled with apparent excitement, until Kunaq shot him a look. Churan stopped and straightened, projecting the calm, regal presence once again.

"I am a shaman," Kunaq continued. "I will conduct the ritual. We will do it quickly; there is no need for any added ceremony. Come," he motioned to Axchel and Churan. "Kneel here."

Axchel and Churan kneeled in front of one another, Churan's frame looking laughably small compared to Axchel's looming one. But they gazed upon each other solemnly.

Kunaq withdrew a small, intricately decorated knife with a semicircle blade from his belt. He made the two of them clasp hands, and on the lower, fleshy part where their thumbs were pressed together, he made a quick cut, in the shape of an x. Neither of them moved or winced.

"Repeat after me," he told Axchel. "Blood of my people."

"Blood of my people," Axchel repeated.

"Now blood of my blood."

"Now blood of my blood."

"I swear on all the dioses of land, death, and the heavens, to protect your body with my own, until the last drop of my blood is spilled on this earth, and I perish to return to the sky."

Axchel repeated the words, and a chill ran through Nova. The words held weight, and the room was filling up with an ancient power that even she could feel.

Churan took a deep breath.

"I accept your oath, blood of my people, now blood of my blood. And I ask that all the dioses of land, death, and the heavens see your promise fulfilled, without a drop of your blood spilled on this earth, without you perishing in my name, or returning to the sky before your time."

"It is done," Kunaq said, and Axchel and Churan stood up. Lucia offered them both bandages to wrap their hands, and they turned back to the rest of the room.

Churan's eyes immediately found Alric, and he broke out into a large grin.

"Will you teach me magia now?"

CHAPTER 19
NOVA

They left Churan with his advisors shortly after, promising to meet him at the cave entrance in the morning. As they traveled back to their rooms, they were met by several people who wanted to get a better look at the strangers who had saved the Warrior Child's life. Alric received a few distrusting glares and pointed mumbles about mages, but most wanted to thank him. They made their way through the main room, which was still crowded, most people joining in the dancing and celebration. It seemed that an assassination attempt was not enough to dampen their spirits.

Rawl diverted Alric toward the long spread of food that was being offered, encouraging the mage to build his strength back up, despite the fact that Alric insisted he had not spent all that much magia and was fine. Axchel and Nova continued to their rooms.

Once there, they separated on opposite ends of the stone partition, changing out of their nice, new outfits and exchanging them for more travel gear. Then, Nova stretched out on her cot and heard Axchel do the same on the other.

"Cassalain," she called out after a while.

"Andalan?" he replied.

"The language of the ritual just now, it seemed fairly...well, permanent."

"This is because it was."

"But surely that doesn't mean you are tied to the boy for the rest of your life."

"That is exactly what it means."

Nova sat up in bed.

"Que?" she exclaimed. "Did you know, before the ritual? Did you know what it would entail?"

"Yes," he answered simply.

"Then why on earth would you agree to it?"

She heard shifting and imagined that he, too, was sitting up in bed, staring at the stone wall that separated them.

"Because maybe he's right," he spoke thoughtfully. "Maybe he is just a symbol, but symbols hold power. Already he has done what no one living has been able to; he has begun to unite the Tribes. He is a symbol of peace here in the North, and since he is also the Unnamed Prince, he is a symbol of hope in the South too. Someone like that is worth protecting."

"But if we succeed, and he becomes the next king of Andala, you would need to remain in the palace? To protect him?"

"Yes."

"And you are all right with that? With leaving your realm, your people, your family?"

"I don't have much family to speak of. I would love to see my mother again, of course, but that can wait. But as for the rest of it, I was never really accepted by the Condori; they disliked the fact that I had Cassalain blood. And the Cassalains saw my Condori lineage and could never see me as anything but a member of the Northern Tribes. I have never been enough for either side. Maybe, in Andala, I will have a chance to decide who it is I want to be."

Nova was quiet, thinking. When this was all over, she would have to decide who she wanted to be as well. As if reading her mind, Axchel spoke again.

"And you? If we succeed, what will you do?"

"I don't know," she answered honestly. "I haven't let myself think that far."

"Perhaps you will also stay at the palace? The boy will need new advisors, and more importantly, friends."

Nova felt her eyebrows twitch. There was a period in her life where she would have wanted nothing more than to have a life behind palace walls, to attend the royal functions, and be a member at court. But now, after so much time with the Danrayens, and on the road, that life seemed stifling and far out of reach. Still, Axchel was right. She would be naive to think that everything was going to magically change once they got Churan to the Flowers for his Naming Rite. They had promised peace, but they never said how soon that peace would occur.

"Perhaps," she admitted hesitantly. "I have never really felt like I had a choice in all of this. I have been told what to do and who to be since I was three years old. It would be nice to make a choice for once." *Terrifying*, she thought, *but nice*.

"But first, we need to deliver him safely to Andala, and to the Flowers," she said, easing back into bed. "It won't be easy."

"Nothing worth doing ever is," Axchel answered.

***

The next morning they all met outside of the cave, as promised. Axchel's advisors already had all of their weapons at the ready and passed them out to each of them. Then, they also handed them additional packs full of food, water, and supplies.

"Churan knows how to reach the coast where you can find passage on a small trading ship. It cannot take you to Andala, but it will take you to the lowest point in Cassalan, at the Borders. The captain can be trusted, but no one else should be. Be careful, and keep him safe," Kunaq said.

He then turned and pulled Churan into a hug. Churan leaned into his frame and buried his face into the man's robes. "You are the best of us, mijo," Kunaq told him affectionately. "You will deliver us peace. We have always known this."

Lucia stepped forward next, hugging Churan briefly and placing a kiss on the top of his head. "Que los dioses te protegen," she whispered, tears escaping her eyes as she blinked.

Kallpa extended his hand, and Churan shook it. The brave, excited energy that he had greeted them with was beginning to crack. "Stick close to Axchel, and be safe. And we will be here should you want to return."

The councilors watched as the group walked away, Churan turning his head every few feet to look back at them, until they were finally out of sight.

The boy was quiet for almost a mile, which worried Nova. Maybe it had all been too much for him, and at any moment he was going to turn around, decide that he didn't want to go after all, and demand they take him back to his people.

But Alric had also been watching the boy and eventually sped up to walk beside him. "Do you still want to learn magia?" he asked him.

Churan's entire being lit up as if the sun was shining directly down on him. "Yes! Can you teach me? What is magia anyway? Where does it come from? And why do some people have it and other people don't? Is it true that when mages use magia, it poisons their blood, so they have to drain away the excess in things like rocks or crystals or something? That doesn't happen to me when I use magia; it never makes me sick. But I've never been able to control it, it just happens, so maybe if I can start controlling it, it'll start poisoning me? Is that how it works? How does it feel when you're using it? And after, when it's poisoning you? Does it hurt? I don't want it to hurt, but Kallpa says that sometimes pain is necessary for change. I never really understood that. How can pain be a good thing?"

He looked up at Alric expectantly, who looked stunned. When he desperately looked up at the rest of them, Rawl was red-faced from holding in his laughter. Nova couldn't look him in the eye for fear it would set her off too, and even Axchel had a wide grin on his face.

"Ah," Alric said, turning back to the boy. "Let's just start with the basics."

For the rest of the day, Alric tried to teach Churan the fundamentals of magia, while the boy interrupted him any chance he got.

"But why would a clear mind help things? Wouldn't it help to know exactly what you want to happen? Of course, no matter what I try I can't get my magia to do what I want, and I've certainly never had a clear mind, so maybe you have a point, but how does one achieve a clear mind anyway?"

By the time they stopped for the night, Alric looked exhausted, and even Nova felt like she could use a break from the endless chatter. Rawl, who seemed delighted rather than annoyed at Alric's new protege, offered to prepare the camp while the mage attempted to lead the sorcerer on his first meditation. They sat cross-legged together on the floor, and Churan was mercifully quiet, though Nova noticed that the boy would periodically open his eyelids in little slits to gaze at Alric in admiration.

Nova shook her head.

"I'll refill our water skins," she volunteered, gathering them up.

Axchel crossed to her. "I'll join you, and grab some more firewood along the way."

Together they walked away from the camp and deeper into the woods. Water wasn't difficult to find; the jungle was teeming with ponds and rivers and streams. And despite the dampness, Axchel managed to find a decent amount of dry wood. They didn't need much of it, only enough for their dinner. The nights were warm enough in this part of the world that they didn't need to have them burning all night.

"I'm sorry," Axchel said to her suddenly, as they were walking back to camp.

Nova looked at him in confusion.

"For what?" she asked.

"Last night, our conversation. I said a lot of things about my experiences with the Condori and the Cassalains. How I never felt like I was enough for either. I shouldn't have laid that all on your feet. I know we don't know each other that well," he answered.

Nova was surprised. She hadn't thought twice about their talk, but it appeared that Axchel had been feeling vulnerable about it all day. She considered her answer carefully.

"I never felt like I was enough either," she said. "At the temple, when I was raised with the Danrayens. All the other girls, they were meant to be there. They had been chosen and deemed worthy. They were fierce and beautiful and brilliant. And I was just an interloper. A traitor, hiding amongst them, and passing time until I could fulfill the Flowers' prophecy. I was never really one of them, no matter how much I wanted to be."

She looked up at him, and he was staring at her intently. "It was hard," she finished.

"Si," he agreed. "It was hard."

The next few days passed much like the first, with Churan talking all of their ears off and slowly learning magia from Alric. The boy rolled his mat out right next to the mage's every night and clung to him like tree sap during the day. Nova found it extremely adorable.

Because they were traveling west, and away from the Night Wood, they had no run-ins with any monstros, and thanks to Churan's knowledge of the land, they did not come across any human enemies either. They made it to the coast quickly and easily.

When they arrived, Nova was dumbfounded. She stopped and stared at the wild expanse of sand, dancing and swirling in the wind, looking very much like stepping into a different world entirely.

And the ocean.

Nova had always wanted to see the ocean.

She had caught glimpses of it, from afar, up in her palace tower. If she leaned far enough out her window and looked to her left, she could see the seemingly endless stretch of blue, fanning out as far as the eye could see. But in person, it seemed even bigger and more expansive than she could have ever dreamed. It was loud, too, and violent! Waves crashing thunderously on the surf, and then pulling back only to slap against the wet sand once more. It didn't scare her; it thrilled her. That being said, Nova wasn't sure just how they were meant to travel on it, especially not on the small boat that they had identified as Kunaq's captain friend. Surely the thing would be picked up by the turbulent water and be dashed to pieces!

The captain assured them that they would be fine, however, and Nova waited eagerly at the ship's prow for them to advance further into the uninterrupted water. The change was subtle at first, the wind tussling her hair as she watched the waves break foamy and white against the wood of the vessel. Then, the ship quickened, and sharp bursts of salty spray began splashing upward over her arms and face.

She tilted her head up toward the sun, and laughed.

Nova spent the majority of the trip on the ship's deck, watching the rolling ocean tides in wonder. Rawl joined her often, but Alric found that he was not a fan of ocean voyages and spent much of his time below deck, managing his nausea. Axchel, being a healer, stayed below with him to help. Unable to continue with his lessons in magia, Churan spent the time playing table games with some of the ship's crewmembers and listening to Rawl's songs and stories. Nova had to warn the archer several times against some of his material, reminding him that not all his tales were fit for children.

Which, of course, only caused Churan to widen his eyes and insist that he was old enough to hear them.

One evening, as Nova lay on the upper deck enjoying the cool night air and gazing at the night's constellations, she found she was not alone. She didn't speak but shifted over so that a small body could join her on the wooden floor. They were quiet for a long moment.

"I do not know how to bring peace to the realm," Churan finally confessed, so quiet that his voice was almost carried away by the breeze.

Nova considered her words carefully. "But you are willing to try," she finally responded.

"I have been told my entire life that it is my purpose," Churan said. "Since I was very young, it has been all that I am meant for."

A deep pang twisted low in Nova's gut. His words were far too familiar. She, too, knew what it was like to be told, from an early age, who to be.

"Is it what you want to be meant for? Would you have a different life, if you could?" she asked him.

"I do not know. I have never known a different life. I do not know what that would be."

He hesitated, and Nova waited patiently for him to find his words.

"But maybe, if I wasn't the Warrior Child, or the Unnamed Prince, maybe I would have a chance to find out."

Nova watched as he pursed his lips in frustration.

"Why me?" he asked. "Why was I chosen? Why would the dioses gift me with the power of sorcery, put me in the path of the Northern Tribes, and now make me the boy of the Flowers' prophecy? What if I don't want any of it? What if I want to learn to play the pan flute? Or learn the art of the Alcanta hunters? What if I do not want to be important? What if I don't want to leave my lands and my people, or be involved in wars that I am too young to even understand?"

Nova didn't answer him, but her eyes pricked with unshed tears. She of all people knew what it was to have her life decided for her by those with more power. She knew what it was to be trapped within the path of a prophecy. She also did not know who she would be, if she could choose for herself. She reached for his small hand, which felt warm in her palm.

He shifted to look at her, his dark eyes shining in the moonlight. "I do wish for peace though. And if there is something that I can do to help, I will do it. It's just..."

His little voice was so solemn, so determined. Nova was reminded of the young leader who had spoken so confidently in a room full of adults, who had begun uniting warring tribes, and survived multiple assassination attempts, all before the age of thirteen. She thought of her own life at thirteen, the failed Naming Ceremony, her escape from the palace, and her first disastrous months at the temple, and her heart ached for him.

Nova twisted and rested her weight on her elbow, facing him.

"I do not know what the Flowers have planned for you," she told him honestly. "But I do know that you are allowed a life. A *full* life, of your choosing. If you choose to aid in bringing about peace, it could change all of Tierramadri. You would be a hero. However—"

She waited until Churan met her eyes.

"However, you should have the chance to be a child as well. Take those moments, when you can. Train with Alric, but sing with Rawl. Practice your speeches, but find time to play. Ask me questions about palace life, and Andalan politics, but also ask the captain if he'd let you steer the ship."

Churan visibly perked up. "Do you really think he'd let me?"

Nova grinned. "It can't hurt to ask, can it?"

Before long, their boat was getting ready to dock at their destination, in the south of Cassalan. Nova found herself disappointed, their ocean voyage had been a welcome respite, and she was sad to see its end. It was apparent that Alric, on the other hand, felt quite differently. When they finally set foot on land once more, he let out a very audible sigh of relief.

The group thanked the captain and said a quick goodbye. Before they left, he advised them against using the main roads—which they would have avoided anyway—and gave them an updated map with forest paths toward the Borders.

"They shouldn't be very well traveled," he told them, "but be careful, you never know."

They were walking one of those paths the next morning, when the topic of the Borders came up.

"How are we going to cross them again?" Nova asked desperately.

"We only know of one safe path over," Rawl reminded them, and Nova shuddered. The trek from Andala to Cassalan had been one of the most physically draining experiences of her life, and not just for her.

"Alric won't be able to keep us all from slipping or freezing to death," she said. "He barely had enough for the three of us!"

"Maybe I can help?" Churan asked, excitedly. "You can teach me or use my power through me. I can give you energy while you do your spells, maybe I can learn the spells, or we can come up with a new spell, together and—"

"No," Alric interrupted him, but placed his hand over the boy's shoulder to soften the rebuttal. "You're nowhere near ready to weave your magia with anyone else's."

Churan pouted but didn't try to persuade him. He had too much respect for the mage to argue with him.

"Besides, we all know what was in the area of Snow Goat Pass last time we were near," Axchel reminded them.

They all fell silent. There had been the Night Wood attack, and the Orcuyo.

It was in that silence when they heard it. There were other people on the trail. They scrambled, looking for a place to hide, but it was too late, the other party heard them as well.

"Who's there?" a deep voice rang out, and before they could even think about climbing a tree or ducking into a bush, a group of Cassalain soldiers emerged, weapons drawn.

"Who are you? Why are you on an official soldier path?" the first one said.

"We apologize," Axchel called back. "We did not know that this path had been claimed by the army. My name is Axchel, captain of Snow Goat Pass."

"Snow Goat Pass was completely wiped out by Night Wood creatures!" the man yelled. "I don't know who you are, but impersonating an officer is punishable by death. You're coming with us."

In an instant, Axchel had drawn his sword, Rawl his bow, and Nova her blades. She saw Alric shove Churan behind him, his fingers lighting up with magia. Axchel crossed to stand with him, blocking the boy.

More Cassalain soldiers began emerging from the path, darting around trees and circling them, until Nova's group was completely surrounded. There were too many of them; there was no way that they could fight against all of them. She readied her knives, when three arrows flew by her and embedded themselves into three separate soldiers. There was a shocked pause, and then a battle cry.

Petra leaped out of the forest, swinging her morning star and taking down two Cassalain soldiers before they could even register she was there. Taruka came bounding in, loosening arrow after arrow, which Rawl joined her in. Axchel began fighting with the Cassalain captain, swords clashing. Alric's magia crackled through the air, knocking down several soldiers while Churan whooped behind him. Nova threw several of her daggers then unsheathed her own sword, fighting as many soldiers as she could.

And then, Damika was there.

Her white hair was a blurry streak with how fast she was moving, thrusting her Espada into one soldier's belly, then rolling over his falling body to attack another one. She leapt and swung, the clash of steel ringing out again and again like bells. Nova managed to drag her eyes away from her just in time to defend herself from an attacking assailant and threw herself back into the fray, no matter how overjoyed she was feeling at the moment.

What are my friends doing here?

Before long, all the Cassalain soldiers (save for Axchel) were defeated, lying on the ground in bloodied heaps. Churan's eyes were wide with excitement at the same time as his lip curled back in disgust. Alric was bleeding the magia residue that lingered in his system into his Phoenixeye stone, and he nudged Churan so that the boy could examine how he did it.

Nova turned to face Damika.

Beautiful, wonderful, fearsome Damika.

She took a step toward her.

"Don't lower your weapons," Damika yelled at Taruka and Petra. "Keep them on them!"

Nova stopped, confused, looking between the three of them.

Taruka and Petra also hesitated, but after a moment Taru raised her bow to point at Rawl, who lifted his in response. Without warning, Petra attempted to knock Axchel's blade away from him, but he managed to hold on to it, growling in response.

"Wait, stay back," Nova told him, then she swung her head back to face Damika.

"Dami, no, they're friends!" she tried to explain, but Damika was glaring at her with an expression that Nova had never seen on her face before.

Alric's skin crackled with new magia, but Damika yelled out "*Don't!*" bringing her sword closer to Nova's throat. Alric let the magia fizzle out, and raised his hands up, frustration etched on his face. Nova just continued to stare past the tip of Damika's sword at her in confusion.

"Dami, why?" Petra started to ask, but then trailed away.

Damika's eyes never left Nova's.

"It's her. She's the one we've been searching for."

Nova gasped, but Damika continued.

"She's the Name-Bearer."

CHAPTER 20

NOVA

"Deny it," Damika demanded, her face so drawn and cold that Nova barely recognized her.

The overwhelming sense of relief and joy that she had felt upon seeing Damika's face evaporated so fast it left a hollow, empty pain in the center of her chest. Gone was her first childhood friend. Gone was the sweet girl who had recruited Nova into her fold and introduced her to the first family she had ever known. Gone was the tutor who had helped Nova become a better warrior. And gone was the young woman who had shown her the first stirrings of romance and love.

Damika had her sword pointing directly at her, so on instinct she raised her own in defense, though it hurt her heart to do so.

"Dami," she choked out.

Petra was swinging her body, staring at Damika, then Nova, then Damika again. Taruka just stood in the background, watching with horror in her eyes, her bow pointed at Rawl, who was aiming his right back.

Red magia danced on Alric's fingertips, hands, and was snaking his forearms in undulating pulses of power. Churan was standing slightly behind him and to his right, but instead of looking frightened at the situation, he was gazing at Alric in admiration.

Axchel stayed back as Nova had ordered him to do, but his fist was clenched tightly around his sword, and he was glaring at Damika with more animosity than she had ever seen reflected on his face.

"Dami, are you certain?" Petra finally asked, her voice unsure.

"She arrived at the temple right around the time we received word of the prince's birth, and the failed Naming Ceremony," Damika explained. "She was terrible at all of the training, you remember that, Petra, Taru. How much she struggled."

Nova was flooded with shame. She hadn't thought she could feel any worse in that moment, but hearing Damika detail her flaws so coldly had proved her wrong.

"She never talked about taking the Trial, or the adventures we would have after, because she knew she would never get that chance," Damika spat.

"Now, the first time we get real information about the missing Name-Bearer, traveling with the false prince and her company, and it leads us here? To them? To *her*?"

Nova pressed her trembling lips together, not knowing what she could possibly say to make the situation any better.

"I was recruited for this mission right around the time that word and support of the false prince began growing. I was sent out to find the disgraced Name-Bearer, traitor to the crown and realm," Damika told Nova, her voice a combination of anguish and anger.

"If only I had known she had been right in front of me the entire time."

From the corner of her eye Nova could see Petra and Taru staring at her, no doubt putting the pieces together as Damika laid them all out. She could see the exact moment when they accepted the truth, because their bodies stiffened even more than they already had been, and their faces became as cold as Damika's.

"So many years wasted," Dami whispered. "That's why you left before your Trial, because you *couldn't* take it. You were never really one of us. You were never a warrior, never a Danrayen. You lied to us. After everything we did to help you, you betrayed us."

A knot was growing in Nova's throat, and she was finding it hard to swallow, hard to breathe. She didn't know how she was still standing upright when all she wanted was to lie down on the cold ground and have the very earth swallow her up.

"*Deny it,*" Damika repeated, her voice trembling with emotion.

"I can't," Nova finally answered, fighting the urge to duck her head in shame. As mortified as she felt that her secret had been discovered, and that her former friends were looking at her with a mixture of disgust, confusion, and betrayal, she was still trained to be a warrior. She did not drop her guard.

"How?" Damika demanded roughly. "How could you have kept this from everyone for so long?"

Nova couldn't speak; she just shook her head.

"How did you fool everyone? How did I not ..." she broke off and swallowed hard. "How did you trick the priestesses into letting you into the temple?"

"I didn't," Nova responded. "I didn't trick them. High Priestess Adira always knew who I was."

"*Liar,*" Damika accused her, and Nova's heart clenched painfully. "Adira would *never*."

"She would, and she did," Nova retorted.

"I don't believe you."

It was clear that she didn't. Damika's pose was as rigid as ever, her face furious.

"Dami," Nova started, desperate for her to understand. "I promise that I did the Naming Ceremony right. I did everything right. I trained my entire life for that day, but the Flowers would not name the prince."

Damika was shaking her head again, her chin swinging back and forth in small, pointed jerks.

"You are a traitor to the realm. You must have done something wrong. You broke the rules, and we are here to bring you back to the capital for judgment."

Nova's eyes burned with unshed tears, but she refused to let them spill.

"It seems that you have already judged me," she responded.

"What do you mean that Priestess Adira knew?" Taruka called out.

"There was a man in the palace, the Archwizard Auberon. He knew of the Flowers prophecy, so he sent me to the temple, and to Adira. He said that she would hide me and train me. To keep me safe."

She turned her head back to Damika, trembling, the adrenaline shocking her system.

"I was to stay hidden until the day we could find the Unnamed Prince and return him to the Flowers for the Naming. They promised it would bring peace, Dami. The wizard believed in that peace, and so did Adira."

"Archwizard Auberon that is in the palace dungeons for treason against the crown?" Damika demanded.

Nova stifled a groan. She had been hoping that Damika and the others weren't aware of that little detail. She stayed quiet.

"I am that man's apprentice," Alric called out. "Or, I was. He believed in Nova, in the prophecy and the Unnamed Prince. As do I. The Flowers are prophets, and the voice of the dioses. If they believe that this child can bring about peace, who are we to disagree?"

"Nova?" Damika's eyes flickered away from the mage and landed back on her. "Not Phanessa? Are you ever who you claim to be, Name-Bearer?"

"I am trying to save us! I am trying to help!" Nova yelled. "All I have ever wanted in this life is to be of service to my realm and its people. Everything that I have done has been for Andala! You have no idea how difficult it has been, or what I've been through. Or how much I wanted to tell you."

She tore her gaze away from Damika to look at Petra and Taruka. "*All* of you."

Petra's face was scrunched up in confusion.

"Then why didn't you?" she asked.

"I couldn't," Nova answered, feeling defeated. "It wasn't safe, not for me or for you."

There was a small pause, a delicate silence in which Nova prayed with all of her body and soul that the Danrayen Warriors before her would believe her.

Then, Damika broke that silence. "We are taking you back to the capital," she said curtly, raising her sword arm just a fraction.

Axchel took two steps forward with his own sword raised, and Petra stepped in his way to head him off. Both Taruka and Rawl pulled their bow strings taut, glaring at each other. Alric's magia flared, showering off of his limbs like drops of electric rain.

"You are outnumbered," he told Damika evenly, looking like he was engulfed in flames.

"It's never stopped us before, mago," she growled at him, baring her teeth.

Nova was frozen in place, terrified. More terrified than she had ever been in her entire life. She had faced a failed Naming Ceremony, fled the Andalan palace and capital, and lived in secrecy and in hiding as a traitor of the realm. She had battled monstros from the Night Wood, been captured by flesh peddlers, crossed the almost impenetrable Borders into enemy territory, and found the Unnamed Prince. And yet the fear that she had felt in all of those occasions paled in comparison to what she was feeling now. More than anything, she was terrified that her new friends would injure or kill her old ones, or that her Danrayen sisters would hurt her new family. She was afraid that she would not know who to defend and who to attack. She was afraid that if they began to fight, it would only end in heartbreak. Or that Churan would try to prove himself to Alric and overextend, killing them all. She didn't want anyone to get hurt.

"Stop!" Nova yelled, throwing her arms out. "Just stop! We don't need to do this!"

They barely spared her a glance, shifting in preparation for battle.

"I'll go with you," Nova decided, desperately, and everyone turned to stare at her as if she had gone mad.

"No, Nova," Alric yelled at her angrily, most likely believing that she was willing to sacrifice herself for the rest of them.

He was right, of course, she would, in a heartbeat if she thought that it would help. But she knew Damika and knew that she would not be content with only bringing back the missing Name-Bearer, when the Unnamed Prince was within reach as well.

"We will all go with you," Nova clarified, looking toward Alric, whose magia continued to crackle.

"We have to head back into Andala and to the capital anyway," she explained to him, then turned her head back toward Damika. "We can go through the Temple of Danray," she continued, trying to project the confidence that she did not feel. "And you can see that your priestess knew, and believed me. That she still believes in me."

She knew that Damika of all people would respect the opinions of her High Priestess. She was the greatest Danrayen Warrior that the temple had ever seen and was more dedicated to the path than anyone she had ever known. She knew that Adira's word would hold great sway over her.

Hopefully, more than that of her superiors.

"But we will not be your prisoners; this is a mutually beneficial alliance."

When Damika scowled and opened her mouth to speak, Nova threw up her left hand to stop her.

"A *temporary* alliance," she added, knowing Damika was ready to argue.

"It couldn't hurt, Dami," Taruka called from behind her. "I know that we have our orders, and the mission, but it isn't completely out of our way."

Damika was quiet for a long moment. "We don't owe her anything," she finally replied, glaring at Nova.

"No, but they're not wrong' they do outnumber us. We have you, but they have a mage. I still think we could take them," Petra replied, scanning their group impassively. "But if you're right and Adira didn't know about Nessa, I mean, the Name-Bearer, then there will just be more people to help bring them in."

"She only wants to do this to try to escape on the journey," Damika said.

"So we won't let them," Petra responded with a shrug.

"We have no reason to try to escape," Nova told them. "In any case, we will not be your prisoners, remember?"

"Nova," she heard Alric call her softly. "I know they were your friends, but we can't trust them."

She could understand his hesitation.

"Swear that you will not try to hold us captive while we travel to the temple, and we will swear not to try and run. I swear by the goddess Danray."

Damika laughed.

"What use is that promise from your lips? You are not a Danrayen, so the oath means nothing."

It hurt. The hostility, the hatred in her eyes. The weapons pointed at her, in the hands of friends. And the casual dismissal of a vow that meant everything to her, despite the fact that Damika was correct. She was not a Danrayen, she never had been, and she never would be.

"Fine," she replied, trying to hide her hurt feelings. "You swear by the goddess, and I will swear by the Flowers; I am their follower, after all. I swear by the Great Flowers of Prophecy that neither I, nor my people, will attempt to flee and will travel with you to the Temple of Danray, so long as you do not try to take us as prisoners."

There was a long, strained pause, where everyone watched Damika, waiting to see what she would respond.

"Very well," Damika finally answered. "We will travel back to the temple. Adira will sort this all out, once and for all. I swear by the mother of my path, Danray, goddess of battle and transition, that we will not attempt to hold you as prisoners until then."

It wasn't a perfect vow, the ending left much to be desired, but Nova was too relieved to dwell on it. They could figure out the rest when they got to the temple.

Nova turned, nodding at Rawl, Alric, and Axchel. Hesitantly, Rawl lowered his bow, and Axchel dropped his sword, though she noticed he did not sheath it. The red magia began to dissipate over Alric's skin, and he pulled out his stone to leach the last remnants of the magia toxins from his system.

When she turned back around, Taruka had also lowered and stowed her bow, and Petra's morning star had likewise been put away. Damika sheathed her sword slowly.

"The first thing that we need to do is get out of Cassalan," she said. "We know of a safe crossing point to get across the Borders. Then, we will make our way down Andala to the temple."

Nova wanted to resent the fact that she had self-appointed herself as the leader of their new mission, but found she couldn't. Damika had always been the leader of anything they had ever done. In fact, she couldn't help but feel how right it was to have her take charge. Nova was still frightened and anxious about the possibility of any of her friends hurting each other and devastated that her Danrayen sisters now looked at her as if they had no idea who she really was. The only thing that didn't feel out of place was Damika taking charge. That felt natural, which bothered Nova. She needed to stop thinking of her as the friend she had once known. The woman before her was closer to an enemy than she was a friend, and Nova couldn't afford to drop her guard around her.

She moved closer to Churan and Alric, who was just finishing putting his stone away. She nodded at the boy, hoping it looked re-assuring.

"We can't trust them, Nova," Alric said to her, echoing her earlier thoughts.

"I know," she admitted. "But we can trust Damika's oath; she would never betray a vow she made in Danray's name. I think we're safe until we reach the temple."

"It won't hurt to have three more warriors for the journey home," Rawl added, joining them with Axchel by his side. "And if they know an easier way across the Borders, all the better."

Axchel stood next to her.

"Are you all right?" he asked softly.

Nova shook her head. She wasn't, nor was she going to pretend that she was.

"No," she said honestly. "They were my family, and now ..." she trailed off. "You don't have to come with us, you know. I can't guarantee your safety once we reach Andala. No one will fault you if you decide to stay in Cassalan."

She made her words as light as she could, but inside, her heart was twisted in knots. The last thing that she wanted was to lose yet another person that she cared about. She didn't know how she could handle it. But if Axchel decided that their mission was not worth it, or that traveling with a group of Danrayen Warriors who viewed them as enemies was more than he had bargained for, she would accept his decision. No matter how much it pained her.

"Of course not," Axchel responded, and Nova stifled a sigh of relief. "I, too, made a vow, and I intend to see it through."

"We're moving!" Damika called out, making Nova's group move apart to face her. "The passage through the Borders is a few days' walk from here.

Petra looked up at Dami's words. "If we are headed back that way, then can we—" she started, her voice hopeful.

"Yes," Damika cut in before she could finish. "Yes, we should go through Tureene."

Despite the situation, Nova couldn't help but brighten just a little. She had always wanted to see the town where Petra had grown up and meet the rest of her family. Of course, she would have preferred to do so in a less awkward situation, but maybe her friend would be more forgiving surrounded by her family.

"It'll be so lovely to see Raidea again," Taruka said with a smile, putting her arm around Petra's suddenly tense shoulders.

Nova was confused. "Raidea? Why would Raidea be in Tureene?"

Damika and Petra glared at her. Nova internally kicked herself. The truce meant they wouldn't kill each other, not that Nova could ask questions.

Only Taruka seemed less than hostile, a small smile twitching on the side of her face, before she pressed her lips together to repress it. Nothing could hide the amused twinkle in her eyes, however.

"Do you remember mine and Petra's Trial, and our joint ceremony? How Raidea disappeared for most of it with Petra's brother Dante?" she asked Nova.

It was a very Raidea thing to do. Young men had always flocked to her, drawn in by her radiant smiles and flirtatious attitude. She never lacked for attention, and the fact that Petra's brother fell under her spell had been no surprise. The rest of them had found it amusing, even more so when it was apparent how irritating Petra had found the entire situation. They had teased her about it for days.

"Yes," Nova answered. "Of course I remember Raidea and Dante."

Petra looked up with exasperation and threw up her arms.

"Well, they went ahead and *got married*!"

Chapter 21

Damika

Damika felt like she was being torn apart from the core.

Her insides, from belly to chest felt like she had swallowed a volcano, which was a bubbling, rumbling thing underneath her bones. She felt tremors run beneath her skin, making her limbs tremble and her eyelids twitch. It felt like thick smoke clogged her lungs, making it hard to breathe, and sometimes hot, bubbling lava made its way up her esophagus, forcing her to spew up bile.

When she had first seen Nessa again on that Cassalain path, she had thought she was dreaming. Nessa looked so different from that shy, hesitant girl at the temple, and yet at the same time, completely unchanged. She would have known her anywhere. She was so proud in that moment, watching her friend battle her enemies like the fiercest of Danrayen Warriors. Then, like a dream switching into a nightmare, it all fell into place.

She, Petra, and Taruka had been on that path following the description of a group just like Nessa's. A group said to be traveling with the Name-Bearer.

In a blink of an eye, Damika remembered Nessa's late entrance to the Temple of Danray, right around the time of the failed Naming Ceremony. All descriptions that her group had gathered over the years matched her exactly. And if she was in Cassalan, now, traveling with a young boy around the same age as Prince Frederico, there was only one explanation.

Nessa was the Name-Bearer.

Since that staggering revelation, Damika had felt lost. She felt detached from everyone around her, with a numbing regret that felt saturated in every freckle, every pore, every strand of hair.

They had found their target, uncovered their enemy. But how could she rejoice when her enemy was in the form of a woman she once loved? Despite her better judgment—and though she would never admit it—she still cared for her. How was she meant to rectify that with her quest?

Every single step on their return to Andala only served to make Damika's heart ache harder. Every day that passed felt like the most horrible day of Damika's life. She and the mage Alric took an instant dislike of one another, and the two traded nasty quips and barbs throughout the duration. Their archer attempted to liven the mood with jokes and conversation, but only Taruka responded to him consistently, and cordially. Petra seemed to take her cue from Damika and remained mostly quiet, but would sometimes forget herself and laugh at one of his more outrageous antics, before forcing herself back to sullen disapproval.

Then there was the Cassalain giant. For four days, the man hardly said a word, but he watched her with open hostility. Damika also couldn't help but notice that his gaze would soften every time he looked at Nessa, and how he went out of his way to care for her.

Not that it mattered to Damika, of course.

Every night they had twice as many lookouts as needed, one from their group and one from Nessa's. When Damika had assigned herself, Taruka, and Petra their shifts the first night, Alric made it very clear that they wouldn't be trusting the Danrayens alone with their protection. Either he, Rawl, or Axchel would stay awake to ensure their group's protection. As a result, more energy was expended than was officially needed, but neither group would budge.

No one asked Nessa to take a shift, and Damika was grateful for it. The situation was already breaking her soul; she couldn't stand the thought of sitting across the fire from her old friend in strained, guarded silence.

She tried to tell herself that Nessa deserved their treatment, after lying to them all for so long, but trying to keep up her disdain felt like it might actually kill her. Every morning when Damika pointedly ignored her gaze felt like a dagger in her chest.

When they made it to the outskirts of Tureene, Damika was more than ready for some rest, and some space away from Nessa and her group. There, with Raidea, they could figure out their next move.

They began approaching the flatter farmlands, with neat, alternating rows of corn and beans, rectangular green swatches of avocado groves, and the bushy lengths of coffee plant fields. And of course, the empty fallow fields, sitting idly until their turn to bear warmer-weather crops.

They approached a cluster of small farmhouses where Petra's large family lived together, a short walk from the main town center of Tureene. Cutting through fields of maize, the sound of voices began ringing in the distance, along with the sound of chopping wood and children's laughter.

Instead of rocky and mountainous terrain, the dirt under their feet was flat and densely packed, careful paths cut through rows of fresh produce. Tz'ola's crown was raised high above their heads, and the very earth seemed to stretch and expand under her warming rays. Stalks and leaves rustled in the light breeze, the sound barely audible over the clanging of gear and the shuffling steps of their two groups.

Petra, despite having betrayed her annoyance over her brother's choice in wife, grew visibly lighter and more excited with each step. They were a few yards away from the village when a streak of amber and cream burst out of a gated yard and sprinted toward them.

Raidea.

Her tumbling honey hair streamed behind her head as she rushed toward them, her round cheeks even fuller with the broad smile pushing them outward. When she was nearly to them she finally caught a glimpse of Nessa, and shrieked.

"Nessa!" she screamed, launching herself into the girl's arms and nearly toppling them both to the ground.

"Nessa, Nessa, mi amiga linda!" she cried, pulling her back to look into her face. Tears fell from both girls' eyes. Nessa drew her back in again, and Damika had to squeeze her eyes shut. It was too hard to watch Raidea respond to her in the way that Damika wished she could have. She stayed quiet, allowing them to preserve the moment for just a little while longer before Raidea learned the truth and that easy friendship was snuffed out forever.

Through the corner of her eye Damika could see more people approaching their group, men, women, and a gaggle of small children. Raidea pulled back and snatched the hand of a tall, handsome, dark-haired man.

"Amor," she said, wrapping her arm around his waist. "You remember Phanessa?"

He lifted his adoring gaze off of his wife and met Nova's eyes, which she was wiping tears from with a handkerchief.

"Claro!" he replied joyously, then leaned down to capture her in another hug. Nova gave a watery chuckle, and awkwardly patted his back.

"Si claro, Dante, saluda a todos before your sister. I see how it is, hermano. Not like I haven't seen you in years or anything!" Petra belted loudly, removing herself from a tangled heap of children who must have barreled into her with so much force it sent her to the ground. They were all piled atop of her, giggling furiously. Carefully, she shoved herself back up.

Dante let go of Nessa with a friendly pat and then crossed to his sister, leaning down to scoop her up into a bear hug. Petra's feet dangled comically around his shins, which she repeatedly tried to kick.

"Let go of me you oaf!" she shrieked, her voice laced with laughter. "I said saludame, not assault me!" But her arms made it around his neck with a strong squeeze. Raidea took advantage of the moment to hug Taru and Damika, tears gathering in her eyes once again. Damika met Nessa's worried glance over Raidea's shoulder. She knew that she was afraid of what words may pass between them, and how Raidea would react to the truth.

Wordlessly, Alric and Rawl came to flank her, Churan a tiny shadow by Alric as always. Axchel came up behind her and Damika narrowed her eyes at their show of solidarity.

They are all traitors, she reminded herself.

Finally done with her greetings, Raidea turned back to Nessa, staring at her pointedly. When she finally caught her gaze, the girl startled.

"Que?" she asked her nervously.

Raidea sighed and shook her head. Nessa looked worried.

"Aren't you going to introduce us to your friends?" she asked her, then lowered her voice, "I haven't seen you in years and suddenly you show up with not one, not two, but *three* gorgeous men? I'm impressed!" she whispered with a wink.

Nessa flushed.

"It's not like that!" she stressed. Raidea grinned, seemingly unconvinced.

"No, really, Dea!" Raidea's grin only stretched wider. Then, Alric stepped forward, hand outstretched.

"I'm Alric," he introduced himself. "This is Rawl," he continued, motioning to the archer.

Rawl gave Raidea a slow smile, and then bowed to kiss her hand. Raidea's eyes lit with both amusement and interest. Damika rolled her eyes. It seemed that not even marriage could tame Raidea.

"And this is Ax. Axchel." Alric finished. The Cassalain tilted his head at her friend.

Before they could say anything further, an older gentleman joined the group outside. He was short and stocky with arms the size of oak barrels and thick, tree trunk-looking legs. His nose was broad and bulbous at the end, and both his hair and beard had a distinguishing smatter of salt and pepper streaks. His eyes were just like Petra's, a blue/green/brown that could not seem to decide their color.

"Papa!" Petra yelled, dropping her equipment to careen into her father's enormous arms. A large hand came up to cradle the back of her head as he rocked her from side to side.

"Mi niña!" he murmured. "Como te e extrañado!"

"I've missed you too, Papa," she heard Petra say softly.

"Papa," Raidea called out. "Come and meet some new friends!"

Petra twisted in her father's embrace but didn't let go.

"Papa?" she asked Raidea, a small frown pinching between her brows. Raidea shrugged.

"Si mi amor," her father replied, finally stepping back. "Now I have three daughters," he said, crossing to hug Taruka as well. "Except Dea is the only daughter who has stayed with me," he continued, frowning in mock severity at Taru and Petra. "The other two have decided to leave this poor old man alone in his old age, traipsing about the realm!"

Raidea crossed over to him with a laugh and held one of his thick, calloused hands between her own.

"Que old age?" she asked him. "You're healthier than the rest of us combined!"

"And besides, you have more than three daughters!" Petra reminded him. "Adan, Iskay y Chusku are also married, what about their wives?"

Petra's father shrugged dismissively and waved a hand in front of his face, as if brushing something away from him. Raidea burst out laughing, and Taruka chuckled. Petra looked scandalized.

"They're perfectly nice—" but before she could continue, Damika stepped forward.

"Raidea, we need to speak to you."

Damika spared half a glance at Nessa and her friends, then nodded at Petra.

With sad eyes, Petra turned to address her brother.

"Dante, could you bring those five inside? Make sure they don't go anywhere unaccompanied."

"Petra!" Raidea gasped, shocked. Damika didn't blame her. It was an appalling way to treat guests, but Nessa and her group were not guests. At least, they wouldn't be as soon as Raidea learned the truth.

"If they try to leave, do your best to stop them, and call out for us. We won't be far," Damika added.

"Dami!" Raidea shouted again, scandalized.

"We really need to talk, Dea," Taruka said softly.

"Well," Petra's father belted out, snapping them all from their frozen places. "You all look like you could use some food and drink, and I daresay rest." He turned to address Churan, and Damika almost smiled to see that the boy was almost as tall as the older man.

"What do you say we all go in and have some chicha morada?"

Churan instinctively glanced up at Alric, his brows furrowed. "I don't know what that is."

Rawl placed a strong hand on his back, nudging him forward, while Petra's father began ushering them toward the nearest farmhouse.

"Never had chicha? Well, mijo, we are about to change your life."

In a wooden stable across the way, Damika had just finished explaining the truth of Nessa, Nova, the Name-Bearer, to Raidea, who was sitting on a hay bale with a deep frown marring her pretty face.

"La pobre," she murmured. "Poor thing. I can't imagine how difficult that must have been for her."

"'La pobre?'" Damika repeated, her voice breaking from frustration. "She *lied* to us. She lied to us for *years*. She's a traitor to the crown!"

Raidea looked up in surprise. "Well, of course she lied, she didn't know who she could trust. She was being hunted, for dioses sake." She stared at each of them pointedly. "Still is being hunted, apparently."

Taruka lowered her gaze, Petra looked pensive. But Damika remained angry, afraid of what she might feel if she let that anger fizzle away.

"She's a traitor," Damika insisted. "She broke the rules. She ran away instead of facing the crown. It is our duty to bring her back."

Raidea shot up from her seat, pieces of hay tumbling off her skirts onto the barn floor. "You're not serious!" she cried.

"It's our mission, Dee," Petra told her, the tiniest hint of sorrow seeping through her words. "Damika has been searching for the missing Name-Bearer for years. She recruited us to help as soon as Taru and I set out too; it's our assignment from the crown. Bringing her in doesn't just help Andala; it's for the good of all Tierramadri!"

Raidea scoffed. "Is that the mierda they've been feeding you?"

"It's our mission! It's important!" Damika yelled at her.

"She's our friend! *That*'s important!" Raidea yelled back.

"We don't even know who she is!"

At that, Raidea threw up both her arms in exasperation. "Of *course* we know who she is! She's our sister. Our family. Our friend. More than that, to some of us, once." She looked knowingly at Damika, who clenched her jaw.

"It doesn't matter if she goes by a different name now. The Nessa we knew then is the Nova we know now, and the woman I saw out there is every bit as sweet and strong and loyal and loving as the girl we once knew. The only thing that has changed is the way you all are treating her."

Taruka rubbed her forehead. "Dea, she's bringing that boy back to Andala. She's claiming he's the Unnamed Prince from the prophecy. At best, it's dangerous. At worst, it's treason!"

"But why? What if that boy *is* the Unnamed Prince?"

Damika and Petra both clicked their tongues dismissively.

"What? What if the prophecy is true? I'll admit I never paid too much attention to the Name-Bearer scandal, or thought much about whether or not the prophecy could be true, but that was before I knew it was Nessa who heard it. I've always trusted us, trusted in you, and in her. It has always been us five, the Daughters of Danray, remember? Maybe Nessa is telling the truth. Maybe there is an Unnamed Prince, and maybe that boy is it."

There was a moment of heavy silence, the girls lost in their own thoughts. Then Damika shook her head sharply, her white curls bouncing off of her cheeks.

"She's not a Daughter of Danray, though, is she? She's a liar. We can't take her word for it alone."

"And what if you reach the temple and Adira confirms everything? That she knew about her from the beginning, that she believes in the Unnamed Prince? What then?" Raidea challenged.

Damika shrugged dismissively. "Then we'll know she isn't a complete liar."

"And if she isn't? Then how will you feel about the way you've been treating her?"

Damika didn't answer.

Taruka sighed. "We should get back inside. We want to spend some time with the family before leaving tomorrow."

"Tomorrow?" Raidea wailed. "You're leaving *tomorrow* already?"

"You know we can't delay this, Dee," Petra answered.

"Still, to not see you all in so long, to have us all together again, and with the family, it's just so wonderful." Her voice wobbled.

"We'll come back for a visit soon, Dea." Taruka promised, stroking a comforting hand down her back. Raidea leaned into her.

"*All* of you?" Raidea asked, looking at Damika, who sighed.

"Come on, let's get inside."

"What would you have done, Dami? Pretend, for a moment, it's all true. What would you have done if it had been you as the Name-Bearer, if the Flowers had spoken to you, given you a quest, a mission. Perhaps the most important mission there has ever been, one that can bring peace to our realm. What wouldn't you do to see it done?"

Damika stayed motionless for a long moment, back to the rest of them, her shoulders tense up by her shoulders. The rest waited, patiently for her answer. None were surprised when she walked out the barn without one.

CHAPTER 22

JESADIRANY

After Jose was taken away, Jesa threw herself into her training with added vigor.

She refused to return to Pelgar, no matter how much the other girls tried to tempt her back. She couldn't walk those streets without hoping that Jose would round each corner, ready to flash her his rare grin. She didn't want to sit in the Cantina listening to Daniel play his songs or listen to the mindless chatter of her friends without his leg pressed against hers under the table. Worse still, she didn't want to hear the gossip and speculation on why Jose had done what he had done, why he had killed Alcor, when she knew the truth.

Jose was no killer.

She was.

Instead, Jesa spent every extra moment of her spare time in the yards, honing her craft with her new blade, meticulously cleaning and caring for it after each session.

But she did not stop at swordcraft.

Jesa, who had already been skilled with her bow, practiced shooting moving targets, from greater distances, while running, and even from horseback. She ran every day, building up her stamina, and pored over scrolls and parchments at night, memorizing battle strategies, techniques, and history lessons.

Almost two months after the day Jose had been taken from her, Jesa approached the priestesses with her intention of taking the Trial of Danray.

"But we were going to wait another year!" Sofia cried when Jesa told her that the priestesses had deemed her ready.

"I'm sorry, Sofia," Jesa said, wrapping her wrist, which was sore from overuse. "But I cannot stay here any longer. I need to pass the Trial, become a full Danrayen Warrior, and leave."

"Even me?" Sofia asked softly, and Jesa noticed her lower lip quivered. "You would leave me too?"

Jesa wrapped her arms around her friend, pulling her in for a hug. "I don't want to, amiga," she told her. "It's just not safe for anyone to be near me. Mamá was right; Lord Guerro will never stop hunting me."

"So we will fight him! We will defeat him! Together," Sofia claimed, pulling back. But Jesa shook her head.

"I am protected behind these walls," Jesa said. "But I cannot stay behind them forever. And anyone who ventures outside of them with me will be in danger. I will not ask it of you."

When Sofia opened her mouth to speak, Jesa grabbed her hand and squeezed. "I will not allow it."

Jesa swallowed the knot in her throat and fought hard against the pinpricks of tears that were burning behind her eyes. More than anything she wanted Sofia to join her, for the two to become Danrayen Warriors together, to fight injustice and protect the people of their realm. But she could not bear the thought of putting her in danger. She knew that this was the right decision.

"You cannot forbid it," Sofia replied, her voice even and defiant.

Jesa looked up from their clasped hands. "Sofia," she started, but Sofia continued.

"You will never be safe until Guerro is stopped, and you cannot stop him alone."

"It's too dangerous," Jesa insisted.

"It is even more dangerous for you, alone! So you will not be alone. I will ask the priestesses to schedule my Trial as well."

The tears that Jesa had been so valiantly fighting worked themselves free, painting two long tracks down her cheeks.

"Gracias, mi hermana," she said.

"It's what best friends do," Sofia replied.

Jesa took the Trial two days later.

She rose early and made her way to the gardens, where she sat at the feet of Goddess Danray's statue. She let herself tilt her head back and regard the golden sculpture for a few moments, taking in her tightly curled hair, not unlike her own, and the strong lines of her face, her rounded chin the only softness in her features. Even her lips, large and full, seemed to radiate strength.

Jesa closed her eyes and let herself fall into meditation, banishing all other thoughts from her mind, and let herself drift to wherever the dioses wanted to take her.

A firm hand on her shoulder roused her, and when Jesa opened her eyes again she realized that the sun was in a different position in the sky entirely, indicating that many hours had passed. She rose, shakily to her feet, and tried to stretch out her stiff limbs and muscles.

From the corner of her eye she could see that a small audience had formed in the gardens. Other trainees were waiting to see if she would emerge from the Trial defeated, or a true warrior. She knew that Sofia was among them but did not need to seek out her face. She knew what she would find on it. Support. Pride. Love.

Jesa accepted her sword from a priestess, and with a deep breath, stepped from the altar to inside the inner sanctum.

Inside, the long room was fashioned in the shape of a long oval. The walls towered above her head, so high that they gave the illusion of bowing in toward each other.

Like all of the important buildings and structures within the Danrayen Temple, everything was fashioned of pure gold. The floor beneath her feet was a solid gold pour, with geometric glyphs etched into the surface, mirroring the glyphs that adorned the outside of the temple itself.

The air smelled clean and fresh, despite there being no windows, nor any other entrances or exits besides the one that Jesa had stepped through. The priestesses obviously kept the interior immaculate in between the Trials.

There was also light despite the lack of apertures in the form of several golden torch sconces that lined the walls, illuminating most of the space while casting the rest in shadow.

Despite the flickering of the light and the soft crackling of the fire, the room felt still.

Jesa only had time to walk to the center of the sanctum before that changed.

With a deep, liquid gurgling, the very floor beneath her feet began churning, the gold appearing to move under her like water, until it collected like a puddle in front of her. Then, that pool of gold raised, becoming taller and taller, and shaped itself into the form of a soldier, cast completely in gold.

The golden soldier raised its weapon, a large battle axe, and came charging at Jesa, moving very much like a flesh-and-blood enemy and not like a metal illusion.

Jesa swung up her blade and a loud clang vibrated her arm, from fingertips to shoulder. She didn't stop but used her force to force his axe down and away from her body before swinging her sword straight at the thing's neck.

Blood splattered just as the metal form melted back beneath her feet, but before she had even managed to land the blow, another two soldiers were solidifying from the golden floor.

Jesa ran up to the one closest to her, twirling her sword in her hand to find a better grip before striking the figure. It blocked her with its own blade, and they traded blow after blow. By then, the second figure had reached them, and Jesa released a dagger from her belt with her left hand, throwing it into its golden face before stabbing the first soldier through the stomach. It exploded in a burst of liquid gold, as if the stitches had popped in a too-full water skin.

She wasn't able to think about it further, because the second soldier had managed to deflect her dagger with its blade, and was approaching, fast. Another three shapeless blobs were rising off of the floor.

Dioses, how many of these things am I supposed to fight?

Jesa reached her target just as it was raising its weapon to strike, and instead of attempting to block it she used her momentum to slide forward on her knees, slipping through the thing's golden legs and using another dagger to slice through the major artery in its thigh.

When it staggered forward, she severed its spine. As it fell face-first, it melted back into the floor upon impact.

Turning, Jesa saw the other three figures approaching her. Two had the same golden soldier forms as her first attackers, but the third was a creature unlike anything that she had ever seen before.

Its long lithe body resembled that of a serpent, but the size of a small boat. Its golden body was liberally studded with spikes that looked as sharp as blades. Its face was more feline than serpentine, with large fangs glistening from a long, protruding snout.

It must have been a creature from the Night Wood, for no monstro could dwell in Andala.

The two soldiers flanked the creature, and they approached her slowly. Jesa lifted her sword, and was just about to run and attack them head on, when a sound from behind her made her pause.

It sounded like crying.

Angling her body so that she was not completely turning her back on her enemies, Jesa looked toward the back of the sanctum at the wall farthest from the entrance.

There, in the corner, was a little girl, no more than six years old.

She was tucked in against the walls, where the shadows had been concealing her little body. Her legs were pulled up, and she was hugging her knees to her chest with her arms.

The girl was wearing the typical clothing of Danrayen trainees, in the usual colors of bronze, cream, and tan. Her hair was tied back in two braids and secured at the back of her head. Her face was splotchy with crying.

"I'm sorry," the girl sobbed. "I just wanted to see the Trial, I thought it would be exciting."

Jesa swung back around to the soldiers, and the terrifying serpent beast.

"Get behind me, now!" Jesa commanded, and thankfully, the girl scrambled up to comply. Jesa could see other blobs of gold starting to take form around the sanctum; soon they would be overrun.

"Listen to me," she said as calmly as she could, sweeping her left arm behind her and ushering the girl as she moved sideways across the room.

"When I tell you, you run to the entrance, entiendes? You don't stop. You run to the doors and you get out."

The girl whimpered.

"I need you to tell me you understand!"

"I understand!" the girl responded automatically.

Jesa pulled another two throwing daggers and tucked them between the knuckles of her left hand. The first three enemies had almost reached them, and the rest were almost solid.

"Now!" Jesa yelled, and leapt forward.

She cut the first soldier across the chest while spinning and throwing one of the daggers at the second. It hit them in the shoulder, but they barely seemed to register it. Jesa pulled her blade free, intending to keep the serpent monstro between herself and the soldier, both battling it and using it as cover, when she noticed a blur of motion across the room.

The little girl was running, as promised, and was almost halfway to the door.

But Jesa wasn't the only one who had noticed the motion.

The creature lifted its head on its sinuous body, cocking its head to the side. Its muscles bunched up, and Jesa knew immediately that it meant to lunge toward the child.

"No!" she screamed, and threw herself at the serpent cat.

She hurdled over the thing's body, jumping up to wrap her arms around its throat. Luckily, the sharp blade-like spikes on its back did not extend that high on its body. Even so, Jesa's calves were cut by grazing them as she vaulted onto its neck.

She squeezed, under no illusion that it would be enough to kill the creature, just hoping that she could distract it long enough for the girl to reach the door. The creature thrashed back and forth beneath her, straining to chase its fleeing prey, but Jesa held on as tightly as she could.

Then, the second golden soldier was coming for her, two large, curved blades gripped in their hands. Jesa glanced desperately toward the girl. She was still too far away; if she released the creature it would reach her before she could get to safety.

But if she didn't release it, she could not battle the soldier.

They were three steps away, and then two, but the girl was still not close enough.

Just a little further, just a little more.

The soldier lifted their blades high and began bringing them down overhead, and that is when Jesa knew she was going to die.

She couldn't risk releasing the serpent a moment too soon. She needed to give the girl every opportunity to escape. She saw the blades, and her death, falling toward her but still did not release.

She held on tighter, and closed her eyes.

Suddenly, Jesa was falling. The creature beneath her disappeared completely—as did the rest of the golden soldiers in the sanctum—and Jesa hit the ground with a thud.

"Ow," she grumbled, dazed. She looked up to see the little girl, no longer across the room near the entrance, but standing right in front of her.

She grinned at Jesa.

"Very good, my child," a rich voice broke out, seeming to emanate from the very walls themselves.

In a flash, the little girl disappeared, not melting into the golden floor like the others, but in a blink, as if she had never been there at all.

Instead, standing in front of Jesa, was the Goddess Danray.

Not an illusion, not a figure from the gold, but the goddess, standing before her looking very much like flesh and blood.

Jesa scrambled to settle on her knees, bowing her head deeply.

"My lady," she gasped breathlessly. "I am so sorry that I failed you."

"Failed me?"

Jesa risked a peek at her goddess through her lashes, and she did not look disappointed, or upset. Instead, she smiled down at her, showing just a flash of white teeth behind her lips.

"I-I wasn't able to remove the threat," Jesa continued, confused. "I would have died."

"And you think that in that way, you have failed me?" the goddess responded.

Jesa remained silent, not sure what to say. She had no idea of what the correct answer could be. After a moment, the goddess spoke again.

"It is not failure to lose against an impossible force. It is not failure to understand that not all battles can be won. It is not failure to fight your hardest, and still not succeed."

Jesa was so shocked that she forgot herself and looked straight up into the goddess's eyes. They were warm and proud.

"What is important is that you did not give up. You continued fighting for what you believed to be right. You did not surrender."

Jesa was baffled. "I did not even know that was an option," she admitted honestly.

The smile on her goddess's face widened. "And that is exactly why you passed."

Sha had done it! She had passed the Trial! Jesa's heart swelled with more happiness than she had felt in a very long time.

"Thank you, my lady," she said reverently, bowing her head once more.

"Do not thank me yet, child. There is another reason I have come."

Jesa remained kneeling but allowed herself to look up once more.

The smile had vanished from Danray's face, and she regarded Jesa solemnly.

"You stand at the precipice of a time of great change, mija," she told her. "Things are in motion that have the capacity to change the fate of all Tierramadri."

In front of the goddess a large butterfly formed, seemingly made from smoke and magia. It was beautiful and hovered in the sky, larger than each of the women. As if in slow motion, it beat its wings.

Jesa's heart thundered so hard, she could feel it in her throat.

"But the ripples of change are delicate, with every breeze they threaten to change course, and a large enough gust can destroy them entirely."

A wind picked up in the sanctum, swirling around the room before colliding with the fluttering butterfly. With a poof, it disappeared entirely, leaving only wisps of smoke behind.

"You are a part of that change, daughter," Danray explained. "You can help affect the change that will save your realm."

Jesa swelled with pride.

"Or you can destroy it completely."

And with that, her pride dissolved like sugar in water, and a bone-deep fear settled within her body.

"What must I do?" she asked the goddess.

"You are aware of the prophecy?" Danray asked her.

If the situation hadn't been so imposing, Jesa would have laughed. Of course she knew about the prophecy; it had changed the course of her entire life. Instead, she just nodded.

"If I have a child, it will be blessed by the dioses and given the greatest affinity this world has ever seen," she recounted.

"And are you aware that the child already exists?"

At first, Jesa just blinked at her, not understanding. Of course the child didn't exist; she was not a mother. She had never been preg—

Her hand flew to her stomach, while her mind raced backward the past two months.

Jose.

The forge.

Their night together.

"Impossible," she whispered, and Danray laughed.

"Very possible, mija, and true."

Jesa looked down at her flat stomach, hardened with muscle. She couldn't believe that there could be the beginnings of new life somewhere inside of her.

"That is not all I need to say to you, child," the goddess said. "Come."

The golden floor lifted up once again and fashioned itself into a long bench. Regally, the goddess sat on one end, and tentatively, Jesa perched herself on the other.

What more could the goddess have to tell her? Wasn't the fact that she was pregnant with a child of prophecy enough?

"There is much I cannot say, for to put things into words is to put things into action," the goddess explained. "But there is much you must believe, even without the explanation."

Jesa frowned, but nodded.

"You are telling me to be brave."

The goddess's face softened. "I know of your bravery, Jesadirany. I am asking you to have faith."

The goddess looked at her soberly.

"Your child, your daughter, has my blessing. She will be my weapon in the coming battle that I cannot directly fight."

Jesa sucked in a breath. A daughter, she was going to have a daughter.

"And you, my Jesa," Danray continued. "You have your part to play as well. You will become the High Priestess of my temple, one of the best they will ever know."

Her? High Priestess?

Jesa's head swam. It was too much, it was too fast, she couldn't process it.

"And there will come a day when another child of prophecy seeks your aid," she continued. "The child will need guidance, she will need training, and she will need sanctuary. You must give it to her. If you do, you can help usher in a reign of peace for all of Tierramadri."

Jesa nodded. Of course, of course she would help anyone who needed it. And if doing so created a chance for peace? She would do anything to assure it.

"But in order for both you and your daughter to play your parts, you cannot be the one to raise her."

Jesa recoiled. "What?" she cried out, springing up from the bench, her arm wrapped protectively around her middle. "What do you mean I cannot raise her?"

"Faith, mija," the goddess said.

Jesa took a deep breath, and then slowly sat back down.

"I don't understand," Jesa replied, emotion making her voice thick. This morning she had no idea she was carrying a child, but now, she would burn the entire realm down to protect her.

"You will be the youngest High Priestess in the history of the temple," Danray explained. "You must do this, and do it well. You cannot rise among the ranks as quickly as you need to if you are raising a child."

"Then I won't be High Priestess!" Jesa exclaimed. "I can still help. I will help the other child when it is time, I promise!"

The goddess Danray shook her head.

"You know that all of my daughters are allowed to have children, if they so choose. But you know that no children can be raised within the temple unless they are of age, and selected for my path. You would need to raise your daughter outside the safety of the temple walls, and if you are with her, he will find you."

Jesa didn't need to ask the goddess who "he" was. She knew. Lord Guerro. She stood, defiantly.

"I can keep her safe," Jesa replied, lifting her chin up stubbornly.

The goddess nodded, thoughtfully.

"Perhaps," she replied, standing as well. "But you will not be able to keep both her, and the realm safe. It is your decision, but the fate of Tierramadri rests in your hands."

With that, she was gone, the bench vanishing with her.

Jesa collapsed on the floor, feeling numb.

I am going to have a daughter, she thought.

I will not see her grow up.

I can protect her.

Who will protect the realm?

She was not sure how long she stayed in the inner sanctum, but eventually she knew that she needed to move. Stiffly, she stood up, collected her weapon, and made her way out of the sanctum.

As she emerged she was greeted with cheers and applause, the priestesses beaming at her. The temple healer approached her, but she waved her off, searching for Sofia.

She found her, running toward the altar, her long dark braid flailing behind her. Jesa moved toward her friend and collapsed into her open arms, too shocked and tired to even cry.

Sofia had led her to the baths, urging her to clean off the sweat and blood that had accumulated during her battles. Jesa had a moment to wonder how golden enemies could bleed real blood, but there was too much else on her mind to consider it too closely.

Then her friend had insisted that she eat, though all she could stomach was some broth and bread. She wouldn't have even managed that, except for the fact that she knew it was not just her health she needed to look after now. Finally, Jesa collapsed on her bed, and fell into a restless sleep.

That is how Jesa spent the next few days, in bed sleeping, rousing only when Sofia would bring her meals. Her celebration to welcome her as an official Danrayen Warrior was canceled, much to the disappointment of the other girls. They tried to get her to change her mind, but left quickly when it was clear she was not speaking to anyone.

Sofia was the only one who didn't press her, didn't try to get her to speak about her experience, not that she was allowed to anyway. The Trial was for the Danrayen who took it only; it was forbidden to speak of it after.

And yet, almost a week after her Trial, and a day before Sofia was meant to take hers, she made a decision. When Sofia came to bring her friend supper, she found her sitting in bed, more alert than she had been seen exiting the sanctum.

"I need to tell you something," Jesa told her.

The young women found themselves back in the Danrayen Gardens, though not so near the statue of the goddess this time. There, Jesa told Sofia everything. She figured that if she was about to give up everything in faith of Danray, then the goddess would have to forgive her this one transgression.

When she finished the tale, Sofia stayed quiet for a long time.

"What will you do?" she asked Jesa, finally.

Jesa looked around her, at the temple grounds.

"I'm leaving," she confessed, squeezing Sofia's hands. "And no, this time, I cannot allow you to join me."

"Jesa, we've been over this," Sofia started.

"No, Sofia. I will only be gone long enough to have this child,"—she couldn't bring herself to say *my child*—"and return to become a Danrayen Rider. Only then can I become a priestess. It is the goddess's wish."

"And what is your wish?" Sofia demanded. "What do you want?"

"I want to see peace, Sofia! Don't you?" she yelled. "Don't make this harder than it already is, please."

"I don't understand why I can't come with you. Tomorrow is my Trial, and after, I am free to go anywhere I please," Sofia said.

"In service of the goddess! You are meant to spend your first year traveling and training. Exploring the real world as a warrior. Not hiding with a pregnant woman, evading capture from an insane lord."

"Don't you think protecting you would be in service to the goddess?" Sofia demanded. "Especially since she is the one who has set you on this path!"

"The priestesses cannot know I am with child. No one can ever know that I bore the child of the prophecy. You would not be able to claim your service."

"I can lie."

"No," Jesa said firmly. "I will do this. I will have this child and find her a home. A good home. I will return to become a Rider. You will take your Trial tomorrow and become a great warrior, doing wonderfully heroic deeds. And when I am High Priestess I will call you back to my side, whether you want to or not, so we can live our days in the temple, together."

Sofia was crying openly, but Jesa did her best to stay resolute. Finally, she nodded, and the two women embraced.

"When will you go?" Sofia asked.

"At first light," Jesa said.

"If you wait until after my Trial, I can go with you at least part of the way—"

But Jesa was shaking her head.

"That would make things so much harder. Please, Sofia, please let me just say goodbye tonight."

The next morning, Jesa packed up her things and strapped on her blade. She snuck out early, not wanting to distract from Sofia's Trial. She knew that her friend would pass and become a fearsome warrior.

After leaving the temple she walked for many miles, heading south. She intended to find a nice, quiet farming town on the outskirts of the capital, far from both the temple and Miramar, where hopefully Lord Guerro's reach did not extend.

She had just stopped to refill her waterskin and have her midday meal when she heard a noise in the forest behind her. She whirled around, unsheathing her blade in an easy movement. A million threats rushed through her mind. She was too far west to encounter any creatures from the Night Forest, but bandits and thieves were known to hide in the woods. Or worse, it could be one of Lord Guerro's men, maybe they had been monitoring the temple, maybe they had been watching, waiting to see if she would leave, and any second they would leap out, grab her, and drag her to the lord—

And then, from out behind the trees, a familiar figure stepped toward her.

"Sofia!" Jesa yelled, rage burning within her. "Que haces aqui?"

"I am coming with you," Sofia replied easily, crossing toward the stream where Jesa had refilled her water. She took out her own water skin and bent down.

"I told you, it's impossible!" Jesa stopped, in horror. "Wait, what about your Trial?"

Sofia shrugged.

"No, Sofia!" Jesa gasped, shoving her friend so hard she nearly fell into the stream. "No! How could you? How could you do that?" She was crying.

"This is more important," Sofia insisted.

"Maybe if you go back now," Jesa said, tears flowing freely. "Maybe if you go back, and apologize, you can still take the Trial. It's not too late; it can't be too late."

"It is most assuredly too late," Sofia said evenly.

"You can't give up being a Danrayen for me," Jesa cried.

"Someone needs to raise your daughter."

At that, Jesa's head snapped up, her mouth gaping. She was speechless. Sofia waited, her face full of understanding, and love.

"Why?" Jesa asked, finally.

"It's what best friends do."

CHAPTER 23

DAMIKA

As the women walked back into the farmhouse, Damika caught sight of Nessa sitting right next to Axchel. The ridiculously enormous man was pouring some chicha morada into her glass, and saying something that made her smile, shyly. She looked more relaxed than she had been since their reunion on the battlefield.

At their entry, Nessa looked up and caught Damika's eye, and the tension immediately found its way back into her body. She looked away again quickly with a flush. The oversized brute noticed the interaction, and his mouth pressed into a thin line, his eyes glaring daggers at Damika. She wasn't sure what was between the two of them and told herself for the hundredth time that *she didn't care,* but an ugly, hot feeling churned in the pit of her stomach and her fists clenched without her realizing it. She leaned against the wall near the front entrance, unwilling to move any closer to them.

The gaggle of children that had met them outside were sprawled across the wooden floor of the main room. They were Petra's nieces and nephews, the children of four of her six brothers. There were almost too many to count, and Damika wondered absently if Raidea and Dante would be adding to their number soon.

The image startled her, imagining a honey-curled toddler sitting on the floor with their cousins, a happy baby living an easy, uncomplicated life. What would that be like?

Dami noticed that some of the older children were playing a game of messy sticks, and Churan was with them, his tongue sticking out the left corner of his mouth as he focused on extracting a single stick without tumbling the entire pile to the ground. His hair was mussed and tangled, and his right big toe was peeping out of a large hole in his sock.

He looks exactly like a young, silly little boy. Not like someone who is capable of toppling an entire realm.

Damika frowned, but shoved the thought aside. It was wrong. What they were doing, what Nessa, the mage, the archer, and the aggravating giant of a man were trying to accomplish with the boy was treason. It was dangerous, and so were they. Damika wasn't going to make the wrong decision again, and nothing and *no one* could convince her otherwise.

Petra and Taruka crossed the room and settled themselves on some open chairs at the long kitchen table. Raidea followed them, sitting herself in the open space next to Nessa. Damika tensed.

"So," Raidea started. "We both grew up in the Andalan capital? Though I am willing to guess that your place in the palace was slightly better than my home in the slums?"

Nessa glanced at her, then swiveled her head to stare at Damika, who pointedly turned her face away. Something hot and spiky clawed at her chest when she did so, but she refused to meet her eye.

"Did they, do you—" Nessa sputtered, her voice laden with confusion.

"Si," Raidea answered. "They told me everything."

To everyone's shock, she pulled Nessa in for another hug.

"Lo siento amiga, I can't imagine how difficult it was for you to hide that secret for so long. And to have to lie to all of your friends."

Still in her embrace, Nessa broke down, sobbing into Raidea's shoulder. Her arms wrapped around her friend's body tightly, clutching at the fabric of her dress. Axchel looked concerned, but when he turned to Alric and Rawl for guidance, Alric gave a small shake of his head. The children glanced up from the floor, but when it was clear that none of the adults were too concerned they continued their game. Emotion was clearly not taboo in their household.

Damika swallowed down the knot in her throat, along with the ridiculous urge to comfort her old friend. It had sprung up, unbidden but powerful, the moment she had heard Nessa's sobs. But she forced herself to stand there, plastering a neutral look on her face, while shoving the desire back down.

When Nessa finally pulled back. Raidea fished a handkerchief out of a dress pocket and handed it to her, which she used to mop up her splotchy face.

"Lo siento," she told Raidea, eyes desperate and pleading.

"You don't have to apologize to me, hermana," Raidea answered. "I know what it's like to do what you need to in order to survive."

Raidea turned to look at her father-in-law, and her gaze softened. "Should we open the bottle of ron?" she asked him, and his eyes lit up.

"Claro! Excellent idea!" he answered, standing and crossing to drop a kiss in Raidea's hair.

"This is why you're my favorite daughter," he mock whispered.

"*Papa!*" Petra admonished him in shock.

"In law," he finished, then roared with laughter, which Raidea joined. She stood up and linked arms with him, and together they made their way down some stairs off the main room, presumably toward the cellar.

Petra looked after them, dazed.

"She's never had parents," Dante reminded his younger sister softly. "When she came here, they started getting to know each other, and I swear even if she hadn't agreed to marry me, she would have stayed just for him. He's so proud of you, but he's missed having a daughter. And she's found that she loves having a father."

Petra's eyes misted, and she nodded at him with a small smile. Taruka draped a comforting arm over her shoulders.

"It's nice they have each other. That you all have each other." She then looked at Nessa, letting her gaze fall to Axchel, then Alric and Rawl. Nodding, she grasped the hand Taruka had on her left shoulder and gave it a gentle kiss before meeting Nova's eyes once more.

"It's important to have people who make you the best version of yourself. I'm glad you haven't been alone all this time, Nessa."

It was a peace offering, Damika realized. A small one, but more than any of them had given her since they had found each other. Damika wasn't sure how to feel about it. She couldn't have the others doubting the mission. She needed to remain strong, they all did. The fate of the kingdom relied on her doing the right thing.

Resolutely, she attempted to build the wall back up around her heart that had been crumbling since seeing Nessa's face again.

At Petra's words, Nessa had swallowed hard and nodded, looking from Petra to Taruka, then at Damika's torso, clearly not ready to meet her eyes yet either.

Good, Damika thought. She wasn't sure what she'd find there anyway. Would she betray her conflicted feelings? Or would what she saw kill the new, lighter mood entirely?

"I'm glad that you all had each other too," Nessa said quietly.

An awkward silence hung in the air, as delicate as a bubble. Once it popped, would the room be filled with tense animosity once more?

Only the children remained unaffected. Luckily for all of them, it was Raidea and Papa who interrupted the heavy moment, returning holding two fat bottles of rum.

"Ron Rendello!" Raidea showed them. "The sugar cane used to make it is cultivated on the volcanic soil surrounding Andalango," she explained, referencing one of the more prominent volcanoes of their realm.

"If you haven't tried it, you haven't lived!" Petra's father claimed, and by the pink flush in his cheeks and the glassy look in Raidea's eyes, it appeared that they both had tried it themselves before bringing up the bottles.

Just like that, the tension that had strained the group for days dissipated. Everything from glass goblets, to ceramic mugs, and anything in between were passed around. Rawl was caught trying to give Churan a sip from his own glass before being stopped.

"He's old enough to change the fate of not one, not two, but *three* realms, but he can't even have a sip of ron?" he asked, scandalized, to which the rest of the room responded with a resounding, "*No!*"

"I tried my first taste of ron when I was his age," Damika heard him mutter to the mage, Alric.

Alric slid his long-fingered hand around the curve of the archer's neck, his fingers tangling in the curls around the man's nape.

"We're not all forest rats like you," the mage murmured affectionately, the ron already making his words loose. The look of amusement that had shone in Rawl's eyes a moment prior was almost completely overpowered by the naked desire that radiated from them when looking at Alric. She watched as he swallowed hard, leaning ever so slightly into the other man's touch before the mage pulled away. Damika averted her gaze, the intimacy so delicately sweet that it felt wrong to witness.

Eventually the groups began to mingle, Axchel and Petra's father discussing farming in cold weather, Petra, Rawl, and Dante playing a table game involving flat discs that had each of them swearing loudly on occasion, which the children would happily echo from the floor.

Some of Petra's other brothers and their wives had made their way back to the main house to pick up their children, but when they realized there was a reunion, stayed with copas de ron of their own. The women, seeing that the children were well taken care of, had retreated back to their own homes for a rare quiet night, while Petra's brothers remained to spend time with their younger sister, who they so rarely saw.

Shulka, Petra's youngest brother had cornered Alric, peppering him with his many questions about magia and the mage university, and the two were involved in a spirited discussion that became more and more slurred as the night went along.

Raidea and Nessa spoke at the end of the kitchen table, the noise of the room too loud for Damika to pick up on their conversation.

Not that she wanted to, of course.

No, she was perfectly content to sip her ron at the other end of the table and observe.

She could almost convince herself of it.

Eventually, the children were sent off to bed, some picked up off the floor and carried to their own homes, the overexertion of the day having claimed them before they could retire themselves.

Extra blankets, cots, and pillows were pulled out and spare rooms were prepared. Raidea and Dante left for their own home with a promise to return in the early morning, and Petra and Taruka claimed Petra's old room. The rest of them spread out in couches, the floor, and every free corner of space they could find. Wordlessly they all agreed that a night watch was not needed, and for the first time everyone fell into an easy, deep sleep, aided by the help of strong volcanic ron.

Nova slept soundly for the first time in a long time and woke only with the commotion of young children's bare feet slapping the hardwood underneath them as they scampered out to meet the day. Her mouth felt dry and scratchy, and her head pounded at the temples, which was not soothed by the clatter of pots and pans clanging in the kitchen. They were soon joined by the sounds of cabinets and drawers opening and closing, and small voices asking for leche, for pan, and one rather ambitious request for galletas, which was quickly shut down.

Nova rolled over and smiled. She had spent the night on the small, two-seater sofa that had fit her small body almost perfectly when she drew up her knees a little. She had fallen asleep almost as soon as her head hit the pillow, but not before she had seen Churan peacefully snoring in a puppy-like pile with Petra's cousins. How often had he had a chance to just be a child and play with other children his own age?

As Nova lay there she considered the rest of the evening prior. She was unsure what to make of it all. Raidea had surprised her; she hadn't expected her friend to be gentle and understanding of her situation. She felt sorry to have underestimated her, but after Petra and Taruka's reactions, and Damika's anger, how could she have dared to hope for anything different?

And yet, Raidea's treatment of her had shifted something in the rest of the group. Petra had opened the door first, but then Taru had spent most of the evening sitting and chatting with her and Raidea. They had spoken about their travels, where they had been, and what they had seen. They avoided the specifics of both their missions, of course, but Nova explained the wonderful workings of the Padir camps, the ridiculous antics of Rawl, and the magia that Alric could weave.

In turn, Taruka spoke of their wanderings, the different cities and towns they had visited on their journeys, and the differing cultures and practices of each. She gushed excitedly over the incredible seafood dishes that they had sampled at the coast, and Nova was able to share her excitement over some of them, having finally been to the ocean.

Together they remarked at how wondrous and strange it was to live in a realm where the heat and humidity of the rainforests could feel like moisture was finding its way into your very lungs, to have your hair plastered to your head and droplets of sweat trickling down your back, only to travel a few days west and find roaring waves and endless, endless blue seas instead. Then, to travel north and find a cold so crisp and bitter and snow and ice so frigid that they could rob you of your very limbs if not careful.

Raidea seemed content to just sit and listen, a satisfied smile pulling on her full lips. But when prompted, she had gladly shared about her new married life, and what it was like to be living on a farm on the edge of the Borders.

"La verdad es que lo amo," Raidea confessed.

"You love your husband? Or the land? Living here, in a farming town?" Taruka asked.

"All of it. I love all of it." The smile stretched wider, her face beaming with love and affection. Raidea continued, "Amo a Dante. I think I fell in love with him the very night of your ceremony, Taru. I never told any of you this, but nothing happened that night between us. Nothing physical, I mean. We just spent the entire evening talking."

Nova's mouth dropped open in shock, and even Taru's eyebrows shot up in disbelief.

"Truly?" she had asked.

Raidea nodded.

"Truly. I let you all think what you would because, well, Petra's reaction was hilarious," she said, her face full of mischief and mirth. "And because it was what you all expected of me. But the truth is, what happened was so much more intimate than anything I had ever experienced before. I think I fell in love right then and there."

"Did you keep in touch after he left? You never mentioned anything," Nova asked her.

Amazingly, Raidea had blushed. "He wrote to me. A letter almost every month. Adira passed them along to me, but I never wrote back."

"Why not?" Taruka asked softly.

Raidea shrugged. "He seemed too kind. Too pure. Too good to be true, I suppose. You know how well Petra always spoke of her family, how close they all were, how much they all loved each other. What would an orphan-turned-warrior know about that kind of love? Of family?"

She shrugged again.

"So I never wrote him back, despite desperately wanting to. Despite reading his letters every free chance I got. I thought I could be content with that, with the small, stolen glimpse of a future that could never be mine. Until the last letter he wrote me."

At that she had stopped, which of course had made her and Taruka lean forward.

"Well?" Nova demanded. "What did he write?"

Raidea grinned a little sadly, seemingly lost in memory. "He told me that he loved me. That he had fallen in love with me the night of the ceremony. That he could see a future with me. But that he also understood that my lack of response was a lack of interest, a lack of consent, and that he would not disregard that any longer. He wished me well and told me it was the last letter he would ever send me."

A silence descended on the group, Raidea remembering, while Nova and Taruka imagined what that would have felt like.

"I was devastated. I realized that I couldn't be happy with that hidden dream, that stolen moment of time where I was with him and I *could* be with him and I was *worthy* of being with him. I reminded myself that I was no coward, and that only *I* could decide my worth."

She turned to look at Nova ruefully.

"Well, only me and Danray."

"That's why you decided to take the Trial!" Nova realized, shocked. There had been so much her friend hadn't shared with her! Maybe more people kept secrets than she had thought.

Raidea nodded.

"I went to you first, hoping maybe you were ready too, but when you gave me your blessing I went straight to the priestesses and asked for the Trial." Raidea paused and brushed underneath her right eye with her fingertips. She continued, "I often wonder if that is why my Trial was so difficult. Maybe the goddess knew my intentions for leaving the temple weren't entirely pure. I wasn't leaving just to serve the realm as her weapon, but for selfish motives as well."

Taruka shook her head gently. "Goddess Danray is the goddess of battle and *transition*. She would not begrudge you the desire to transition into a new phase of your life, and you still serve her, after all."

Raidea smiled at Taru gratefully, reaching out to squeeze her hand with her own. "Of course I do. When I left the temple, I traveled up to the farmlands of the Borders, protecting each of them as I cut across to Tureene. I was terrified," she confessed. "I wasn't sure if I was too late, if Dante had moved on, found someone else. Or if he would even welcome my presence after not having heard from me for so long."

Raidea stopped to beam at her handsome husband across the room. "Turns out, I needn't have worried. As fate would have it, his was the first face I saw when I stepped into Tureene. Well, face and chest, actually. You see, he was out in the fields, and it was a rather hot day, and Tz'ola's crown shown onto his brown skin, muscles rippling in the light and dripping with beads of sweat—"

"Ya, Dea!" Nova screeched, slapping her hands over her ears and sputtering out laughter while Taru gently slapped Raidea on the arm. She just laughed.

"Well, he saw me and dropped everything he was doing. Just stared at me. I thought showing up would be enough, but he expected me to talk? To admit why I had come?" She shook her head, a flush creeping up her cheeks. "Que verguenza!"

"But you told him," Taru guessed.

"I told him. I told him I had come to protect Tureene and the neighboring villages from the Borders as part of my Danrayen responsibilities."

"You didn't!" Nova gasped.

Raidea laughed. "I did. But I told him that while I was here, that I would give him a chance to convince me to stay."

Raidea looked at the two of them with a mischievous glint in her eye. "Which he began doing right away in the middle of that field. But given your response to my previous memories of that hot, sunny field and his bare body, I would guess you're not too interested in those details?"

Taruka threw a roll at her, and Nova tried to cover her friend's mouth with her hand, while they all laughed.

For a moment, it felt like before. Like when they were young, the five Daughters of Danray, happy and at peace in the temple.

But then Nova had caught Damika frowning at them from her place across the room, arms crossed and sipping from her cup alone, and all the hope that had been blossoming in her chest withered in the shadow of her glare.

Things were not the same, no matter how desperately she might wish that they were.

When Nova finally dragged herself up and into the kitchen, it was clear that hers was not the only headache from the excessive drinking of the night prior. Petra's father whipped out a tonic that smelled like rotting eggs and dirt ("and tasted even worse," according to the man), but once they were convinced to choke it down, it relieved most of their symptoms. Raidea had shown up early as promised and had made black corn tortillas, while Dante scrambled eggs and fried up some beans.

During breakfast, conversations ranged from farm life, to the logistics of their travels, to answering children's questions of, "What's beyond the end-all on the coast?"

"The vast and mighty ocean," Dante replied.

"Well, then what's after the ocean?"

"If you travel far enough, you reach the Western Isles," Petra explained around a mouthful of tortilla y frijol.

"...And after the Western Isles?"

It was loud, disorganized, chaotic, and Nova loved every second of it.

Between the happiness that seemed seeped within the very walls of the family farmhouse, and the fact that Raidea, Petra, and Taruka were all interacting with her that morning, Nova felt deliriously lighthearted. Even the fact that Damika had yet to meet her eye, or address her in anything other than animosity could not dampen her spirits.

As for Damika, she ate her breakfast, quietly, speaking to Petra and Taruka on occasion, and answering some of the questions from the children. But she did not seem any more keen to interact with the rest of the group than she had been the night prior.

When breakfast began to wind down, Damika stood abruptly and spoke. "Bueno, we thank you for your generosity and for allowing us to stay in your home. It is the nicest arrangements we have had in quite a long time," she addressed to Petra's father, inclining her head in respect.

"Pero I'm afraid we must get going if—"

"Not yet," Raidea interrupted, standing as well. The children seem to take this as a cue, as many of the older ones ran outside, clearly on a mission.

"Dami, ya sabes that we can't stay—"

"I know. I'm not asking you to stay for too long, but I promised the children," Raidea pressed.

"Promised them what?" Petra asked, confused.

Raidea grinned at her wolfishly, then whistled. At the sound, their nieces and nephews came clattering back indoors. Between them, they held a Danrayen blade, along with a wooden staff, drums, a wooden wind instrument, and a violin.

Everyone turned to Raidea in confusion.

Her eyes crinkled in the corners, her entire body radiating with mischief.

"I promised them a Dance of Danray."

CHAPTER 24

NOVA

I t took some convincing, on everyone's part. Taruka seemed like the only one who was as keen as Damika to try the dance.

Before Damika's ceremony and departure from the temple, the five of them had gotten rather good at the Dance of Danray. After Damika had left, however, it didn't seem right to continue practicing. They had no interest in recruiting a different, fifth member to their group, and four was not a large enough number to make the dance as fluid and beautiful and interesting as it should be.

Damika had been the one most ardently opposed to the "impractical, waste of time frivolity" as she had put it. Petra thought the whole thing was stupid. Nova was opposed, because she no longer felt part of their group. But ultimately Raidea's charm was as convincing as ever. As were the many pairs of small, beseeching eyes, and pleading *"por favores"* from adorably cute children.

When Churan had looked at Nova, full of interest and hope, Nova found she could not refuse. Hadn't she just encouraged him to take advantage of moments where he could act his age? He seemed so happy with the other children that she hesitated in dragging him away from the momentary break in fate, and destiny, and prophecies. They could at least delay long enough for a single dance.

Together they all made their way out past the long rows of crops and into a cleared out circular field in the midst of tall maíz stalks.

"We cleared it a few seasons ago," Dante explained. "For the wedding," he clarified, beaming at Raidea, who slipped her arm around his waist.

"After that, the children loved playing their games here, and we never replanted. We sometimes come and dance in the moonlight, or just lay out and see stars," Raidea interjected.

The way she looked at her husband made Nova pretty sure that they came out to the field to do more than just look at stars, but she certainly was not going to comment on it.

The women set up awkwardly. Damika removed most of her armor but kept her Espada clenched tightly in her fist. Taruka accepted the wooden staff that Petra's nephew offered her. Petra held her morning star at her side, not meeting anyone's eye. Nova selected two of her daggers, and hesitated.

No one made a move to start the circle. Even Raidea looked uncertainly from girl to girl, seemingly worried at the tense atmosphere.

With a sudden burst of fierce determination she had not been aware she was in possession of, Nova lifted her chin high and marched into the field, taking her place between Damika and Raidea as she always had.

She wasn't the shy, timid person she had been when they had first started practicing the dance. She had learned who she could be outside the shadows of the temple walls, without lies weighing down her heart. She found she was beginning to like the person she was becoming, and refused to defer back to her former self, even if that girl had more friends and lived a happier life at the time.

For a split second, Damika glanced at her in surprise, none of the hate Nova expected to see in her eyes was visible. But then Petra and

Rocha moved to take their places, and their gaze broke, shattering the spell. She and Raidea situated themselves, and the dance ring was formed.

Axchel, Rawl, Alric, and Churan set themselves up a few meters away from the circle, in Nova's direct line of sight. She would soon shift and lose them in the movement and focus that the dance required, but for the moment she was proud and pleased to have such fine men in her corner.

"Ten cuidado." Alric's voice was a little worried, but he gave her a determined nod.

"Have fun!" Rawl beamed at her in pride.

Churan bounced on his heels, betraying his age, which reinforced Nova's decision to accept the dance. It was good to see him happy.

"Is it fun? Why do they have weapons? Is it a dance or a battle? Can I learn?" Churan turned to Alric, wide-eyed. "Is there a *mage* dance? Where we do a battle dance but with magia?"

Nova saw Alric bend to explain the Dance of Danray to Churan, and she chuckled quietly to herself at the boy's excitement.

As for Axchel, he was staring at her with the same intense, unreadable expression that he had been giving her for the past few weeks. She didn't understand it, or perhaps she understood it all too well. It was not something that she felt strong enough to consider, especially not at that moment. So she did not meet his eye but adjusted the grip on her weapons and planted her feet, moving up into a defensive stance.

Once the other women were similarly situated, Raidea made a motion to Dante, who was standing with his father and the niños. At Dante's command, the children with the instruments began to play.

In many ways, it felt like the first time they had ever attempted the dance. At first, the music was slow, and their movements were clumsy, sputtering, and offbeat. There was no graceful fluidity of motion, no lyrical movement of body that could only exist in harmony. Their initiation was ugly and awkward, as if they were unsure how to rekindle that easy connection they had once shared.

But then, the music began to speed up, and their warrior instincts kicked in. Their movements were no longer jerky or halted; they were too well-versed in the language of battle to remain stiff and shy. The motions were deeply ingrained into both their muscles and their minds and came as natural to them as breathing.

As they began to spin, moving their way clockwise in the circle, each began attacking the other more earnestly. Nova swept her right arm in a slashing motion above her head, aiming toward Raidea's left bicep. Dea easily invaded the maneuver while circling her Danrayen blade behind her back and lunging toward Petra. Nova felt Damika attempting a similar move behind her, and blocked it with her smaller dagger.

The music grew faster.

Petra performed a particularly tricky maneuver where she circled her morning star above her head and flicked her wrist toward Taruka's midsection. The force of the blow would have pierced her love's skin and knocked her backward, but Taruka intercepted it with her staff, twisting the chain and tugging, which almost managed to knock Petra off-balance.

She whooped happily.

Raidea quickly angled her torso backward into a backbend, which allowed Nova's dagger to graze innocently above her flesh, before spinning and swinging her sword toward Petra once more.

One by one, they all began to smile. Satisfied little smirks grew on the faces of the women, each knowing how spectacular they were.

Nova felt powerful in that moment, and knew that the Danrayens felt it too. She knew these motions, this dance. It was instinctive; it was in her muscles and her heart and in her blood. It was in all of them, this physical demonstration of the bond and connectivity of their group. A bond that was once unshatterable.

She knew that they all felt it, and while the other four might have been born to be warriors, Nova, in that moment, was satisfied to know that at least in this she could hold her own against them. She was as much a part of the dance as they were, in the motions that they had practiced so much in the temple. In this circle, she was as much a member as any of them.

The music quickened even still.

She didn't know when the shift began, but at some point, their smiles began to drop. The movements, although still practiced and fluid, started taking on a more furious edge. Not between her and Raidea, or with Raidea and Petra, or Petra and Taruka.

But Nova felt Damika's energy from her left change, and her blocks to Damika's swings suddenly became more deliberate. She began putting more importance on defending herself from behind and attacking Raidea in her front, which she seemed to notice. Raidea risked a quick, curious glance her way, but what she saw behind Nova must have startled her, because her eyes went wide.

But they didn't halt the dance, they couldn't. It had gotten too fast, trying to end it now before the music stopped would have been too dangerous.

Nova struggled to keep up, to keep pace with the movement and the circle, but she was starting to feel nervous, prickling anxiety blossoming in her chest.

Surely Damika didn't mean to kill her right then and there, did she? Even if her old friend was capable of such a thing, it would have been against her mission, wouldn't it? Surely she needed to keep her alive, at least until they reached the temple. Or until she spoke with her superior.

Damika's blade nearly kissed her ribs and she swore, jerking her body away just in time. Sweat began accumulating at her crown and the nape of her neck, and she worried that some would drip into her eyes. She didn't have time for any distractions and certainly wouldn't be able to wipe it away while still keeping step with the dance.

Even so, Nova felt a fat droplet make its way down from the little hairs at her temple, and travel, slowly, rolling down to the arch of her left eyebrow. She was ready to give her head a little shake and hopefully dislodge the dangerous distraction, when suddenly the music stopped.

Nova acted on pure instinct. Instead of stopping her attack on Raidea to her right, she swung her entire body around to face her more immediate threat head on.

When she met Damika's gaze, she knew why Raidea had looked so shocked. Her old friend looked furious. Like something had possessed her body and discarded the woman that they all knew. Her eyes were cold and full of hatred.

They all stopped, motionless save for the heavy rising and falls of their chests as they all struggled for breath.

When Nova could finally think again, she realized that Damika's blade was at her neck.

But her daggers had made their way onto her flesh too, one underneath Damika's right rib cage, the other poised directly above her heart.

A loaded silence descended upon the field, and even the children who had been whooping and hollering in excitement were still. Even the youngest among them had seemed to pick up on the heavy tension in the air.

From the corner of her eye, Nova could see her boys, primed and ready, Rawl's bow cradled in his hands, Alric with pinpricks of red lighting zapping from his fingertips. Axchel had taken several steps forward, his hands clenched in fists at his sides.

Then, Raidea spoke.

"Why don't we give them some space? They have a lot to say to one another," she said, ushering the group past the empty field.

"But…" Petra protested, worry lacing her voice.

"We're *not* leaving Nova," Alric growled, and Axchel nodded, advancing another step.

"For dioses-sake, they're not going to kill each other!" Raidea snapped. "They just need a moment!"

The men still looked unsure.

Then Petra's father spoke. "Vamos, hombres, I always find the women to be much more knowledgeable than us in these sorts of things. If Raidea says they will be fine, then vamonos."

Damika's blade relaxed just a hair, and Nova pulled her blades away just as far. She heard Rawl give a loud sigh.

"Vamos mago," she heard him say. "Nova can take care of herself."

Axchel seemed the most hesitant, but even he eventually allowed the others to pull him back.

Slowly, they heard the sounds of the group leaving the area. As the footsteps receded, so did their weapons, until, finally, they were standing face-to-face, no longer on the verge of killing one another.

Nova wrenched herself away and backed up a few steps, not turning her back on Damika. Everything in her body, every single fiber of her being radiated with unwavering certainty that Damika would not actually harm her. But her brain refused to listen to her body.

They were too different, had changed too much, for Nova to trust blindly. She couldn't keep her faith in the woman who she once would have sworn would lay down her life for her own.

Damika stared at her unmoving for a moment, then angrily sheathed her sword. In turn, Nova put away her daggers.

In that moment, all of the hesitation, the crippling sorrow, the gut-churning guilt that had gripped her for the last few days evaporated in an anger so ardent, it burned away any emotion but rage.

"What is wrong with you?" she hissed at Damika, who looked stunned.

"What is wrong with *me*? How could you even ask that?"

"How can I not? We grew up together. We were friends. We were ..." she swallowed the last words, drawing in a sharp breath. Damika's eyebrows drew together above the bridge of her nose.

"You knew me better than anyone," Nova finally finished, her voice raspy with emotion. "Now you hunt me?"

"You're a traitor! You're the reason Andala is in danger, why the war rages on. How could you be so selfish—"

"Selfish? Everything I do, I do for Andala! For our people! I lied for ten years, lived in hiding, molded myself into the best warrior I could possibly be to end the war! And you call me selfish?"

"You can't really believe this will end the war! That this is right! Trusting a child, *a baby*, with the fate of our land over the monarchy who have trained every moment of their lives to rule!"

"They've been ruling for centuries and nothing improves! Nothing changes! Not for the people. They sit, fat and pretty, on their golden thrones while our people starve. Or are sold by flesh peddlers or have their blood spilled on foreign soil! Perhaps the Flowers are showing us another way!"

"Please, Nessa! You can't expect me to believe the Flowers really came up with this ridiculous prophecy!"

"You—you don't believe that the Flowers refused the Naming?" Nova was dumbfounded. She knew Damika disapproved of the Un-named Prince, but she had no idea that the Danrayen didn't even believe he was real. That the prophecy wasn't real.

"You think I made it up?" Nova asked.

"I don't know, Nessa." Damika admitted. "Maybe someone in-fluenced you in the palace. Insurgents have tried to overthrow the monarchy before, so perhaps you were their latest plot. Who could argue against the Name-Bearer, when they're the only ones who can speak to the Flowers? Who would oppose them?"

Rage mingled with regret. "I gave up my entire life because of the prophecy, because of what the Flowers told me, and you believe I fabricated the entire thing?" Nova questioned.

Damika shrugged her right shoulder so high it almost hit her ear. "The Flowers had never refused a Naming before."

Nova shook her head. "I'm not lying."

Damika scoffed, which made Nova even angrier.

"I know that I have lied, but I'm not lying about this! The Flowers refused the Naming. The Wizard believed me and smuggled me out of the palace. He contacted Adira—"

"Stop it, Phanessa," Damika warned, her face tight, her voice clipped in frustration.

"He contacted Adira," Nova repeated, stepping right up to Damika, her body vibrating in repressed ire mere inches away from her own. "And she agreed to allow me into the temple. So I could be trained."

"Adira wouldn't," Damika whispered, her voice desperate.

With those words, the anger dissipated from Nova's body, and all that was left was bone-weary exhaustion and sorrow.

"She believes in the Unnamed Prince," Nova insisted softly, but Damika just shook her head, her white curls bouncing with the movement.

They were very close, so close that Nova could see the faint outline of an old scar just underneath Damika's jaw, reaching from under her ear to just under her chin. She had the inexplicable urge to trace it with her fingers, to ask her how she had gotten it. She wanted to lay out in the middle of the field with the infuriating woman in front of her and hear what her life had been like all these years. She wanted to share her own stories with her and see the pride flash in her eyes when she told her about scaling the Borders, or battling monstros, or protecting the Padir children from bandits.

She wanted the cold Danrayen Warrior in front of her to melt away into the friend she had once known.

Damika's eyes also traveled the length of Nova's face, lingering on her cheekbones, which she knew would seem higher and more pronounced to her after having lost the baby fat of her youth. She avoided Nova's gaze but flickered over her hair, to the protection braid at her neck, then lingered over her lips before snapping away. Nova swallowed hard. Had she imagined it? Maybe seven years was a long time; they were not the same people they had once been.

"It's been a long time," Damika said quietly, voicing Nova's thoughts out loud. She could only nod, mutely. Before she could think of something to say, Damika's eyes hardened.

"A lot has changed. We don't really know each other anymore. I don't know that I ever knew you." Damika backed away a few steps, and the hope that had been lifting Nova's heart suddenly popped like a soap bubble.

Furious once more, Nova turned and began to walk away from both the field and Damika, unwilling to spend another second in her presence. Then just as abruptly, she stopped, her anger simmering into something else, something equally hot but tenuous and inexplicable. She swung around to meet Damika's eyes once more.

Damika was right, seven years was a long time, and they were not the people they once were. Nova had changed; she had grown. And though she may still not fully know who she was or who she was meant to become, she did know that she was stronger, braver, more self-assured than the scared girl hiding in the temple.

She may not fully know who she was yet, but she did know how she felt. And what she wanted.

With determined strides she stomped her way back to Damika, once again eliminating the space between them. Damika stood frozen, her face confused.

"You're right, I have changed. We both have," Nova told her. "But some things have not."

And with that declaration, Nova grabbed Damika by the waist, one hand gripping her behind her neck to pull her lips down to meet hers.

A soft tortured sound escaped from Damika's mouth before she grasped Nova's face between her rough palms, deepening the kiss.

It was nothing like their stolen moment at the temple gardens in their youths. There was no sweet, timid exploration, no soft, sweet caresses.

Their mouths were furious, their movements hard and rough, but Nova reveled in it. Damika tasted sweet, so sweet that when the first hint of salt reached her tongue she pulled back surprised.

Damika was crying. Shocked, Nova reached up one hand to wipe away the tears, but Damika grabbed her by the wrist, shaking her head.

"I missed you," Damika confessed.

Warmth flooded Nova's entire body.

"I missed you too," she replied softly, leaning in to capture her mouth again, but Damika held her at a distance.

"I don't know," she said. "I just don't know what to believe."

Just like that, all the warmth in Nova faded, doused like ice water spilling through her veins. She broke away from Damika's grasp.

"You don't believe me," Nova's voice nearly cracked, but she tightened her throat to get the words out unbroken.

Damika shrugged helplessly.

"I don't, I don't know. I don't know what to do. Maybe when we reach the temple and Adira..."

Nova stumbled backward. "You don't believe me, you *still* don't believe me," she repeated, emotion thickening her words.

Damika just looked at her, half desperation, half anger in her eyes.

Nova shook her head. "I thought you knew me better than this."

"I have no idea who you are!" Damika spat out with venom.

Nova recoiled as if she'd been slapped. The anger she thought she had buried reignited, but before she could say anything, a terrible, horrified scream pierced the morning air.

The two women shared a shocked look before turning and sprinting out of the fields together, not back toward the farmhouses but in the direction of Tureene.

CHAPTER 25

NOVA

They ran toward the sound, Nova positioning her blades at the ready once again. She knew, without looking, that Damika also had her sword drawn once more. The rustling of stalks and crunching of leaves underneath their thunderous feet was deafening, interrupted only by their quickened pants and the agonizingly terrified shrieks and screams coming from the direction of Tureene.

Together they ran west of Petra's family farm, toward the village itself. When they finally broke through the long, layered rows of produce and reached the rolling hills just shy of the town, Nova nearly faltered at the sight before them.

Monstros. The town was entirely overrun by monstros of the Night Wood.

Tureene consisted of mostly single-level homes with a few second-story businesses. People were fleeing into whatever building they could get to the fastest, and the adobe houses seemed to be faring better than the wooden ones. The creatures were scaling the wood, digging their talons in to rip off planks and panels with their hands and teeth.

Nova recognized a few of the beasts that she and her party had encountered in their journeys, the ugly, long-snouted wolf-looking beasts with hairless wrinkled skin and several rows of teeth. Two lay motionless on the ground a few feet from one another, clearly already having been dispatched, and she could see their friends battling another two not far from the corpses.

A few townspeople lay motionless near them, signs of monstro attacks on their lifeless bodies. But Nova did not have time to mourn for them. Because those demon beasts were not the only monstros in Tureene. Standing tall and hideous in the middle of the town's main courtyard square was a towering, horrendous Orcuyo.

Alric's fingers burned red as he hurled battle magia at the enormous creature, while Rawl's arrows pierced its thick leather flesh again, and again, and again, with seemingly no impact. The creature swatted at the arrows peppering its body like they were no more than the annoying stings of insects.

Petra and her brothers, Dante, and Adan, were both attacking one of the dog-like beasts as more townspeople fled in panic to their homes. Axchel was single-handedly battling another, bounding around it and striking it with as much force as he could muster. Meanwhile, Taruka attempted to land carefully aimed arrows at the monstros attacking the townspeople, while avoiding their intended victims.

Damika and Nova exchanged a quick look, and in wordless agreement sprinted down toward the fray. Instinctively she knew that Damika would run straight for the Orcuyo. With Rawl and Alric battling it on their own, they were only supported by their distance attackers, with the magia and the arrows, and they needed to add a closer, in-person fighter if they were going to take the creature down.

Nova, on the other hand, did not follow Damika but ran toward the closest beast to her, the one that Ax was fighting. Having had more practice with the creatures she had come to call "demon wolves" in her mind, she decided her best course of action was to help end them all as quickly as possible, so that all their fighters could converge on the

Orcuyo without the added distractions. They would need everyone if they were going to find a way to kill it.

When Nova got close enough to the demon wolf, she launched herself into the air and threw one of her daggers with all of her might, landing in the creature's right eye.

Axchel yelped and jumped away, the dagger having come dangerously close to grazing his arm as he attacked. The creature lurched back, and Ax was able to swing his sword underneath the thing's chin, plunging it through its throat, and up into its skull. The monstro collapsed, and Ax used the momentum of it falling to wrench his sword free once again. Once it was fully on the ground, Axchel grabbed the dagger out of the beast's eye and tossed it back to Nova, who caught it effortlessly in the air.

They didn't pause to celebrate their triumph. Nova ran to aid Petra and her brothers, Taruka still picking off the remaining ones that were now scaling the second-story homes. Ax ran toward her, and the creatures, to help.

Just as Nova reached Petra's family, Dante managed to deliver a deep cut in the demon's back leg. When it turned its torso around, snarling in rage, Petra used its distraction to her advantage, swinging her morning star up and down, crushing its head against the ground. It squirmed wildly, fighting against the weight of the spiked ball. From behind them Taruka ran up, shooting an arrow into its face, just as Adan brought down his staff, hard against the now dented skull, and with a sickening crunch the creature finally stopped struggling. Axchel joined them, panting.

"I think that was the last of them!" he called out.

Dante swiveled, searching the streets, his eyes tracking the team now battling the Orcuyo, then the surrounding areas.

"Raidea?" he questioned desperately.

"She ran home, with your father and the children!" Taruka told him, breathless from the battle. "She was going to get them to the farmhouse, where she could better protect them."

In an instant Dante turned and sprinted the way back to their home. Petra looked inclined to follow him, but then an inhuman roar bellowed out into the morning air, rattling the windows on the homes around them. The others were not having much luck battling the Orcuyo on their own.

Petra grabbed her other brother's shoulder. "Adan, go with Dante, make sure they're safe!" she yelled, and he immediately moved to comply. Then she, Nova, Taruka, and Axchel all turned and ran to join the fight.

The Orcuyo was tinged with red electricity, magical glyphs raising bubbling welts on its flesh. The magia poured freely out of Alric, his skin was slick with the sheen of sweat, his hair plastered down on his forehead. His arms, which were lifted out in front of him, were trembling. Taruka joined Rawl in shooting arrows at their enemy, but they seemed like pinpricks against his impossibly thick hide.

Nova threw a dagger as high as she could, aiming for his face, but it bounced off one of its long tusks, not even chipping the tooth. She held on to her other dagger, as she didn't have any more on her person. She hadn't been prepared for a battle, and only had the two that she had brought for the dance.

Stupid, she thought. It was a novice's mistake to be ill-prepared; she had been trained to believe that a warrior must be ready for battle at any time.

Nova and Petra inched closer, looking for any weak spot that they could find, an exposed tendon at the back of the creature's ankle, a vein or artery on its leg. But the thing moved surprisingly fast for something so big, and their blows did not seem to do much damage at all. The Orcuyo barely seemed to notice they were there and continued to move toward Alric, who seemed to be the worst source of its discomfort. Axchel had positioned himself behind the mage, supporting his weight and pulling him backward so that he could continue to attack the creature, but not trip and fall while retreating. As the creature took another step forward toward them both, Petra saw an opening and smashed her morning star against one of its exposed toes.

The Orcuyo roared and bent toward its foot on instinct, and that is when Damika swung into action.

She had been circling the creature and darting in close to slice quick, practiced cuts into any inch of exposed flesh that she could find. It hadn't appeared to be doing much damage, but as always, Damika seemed undeterred, leaping and spinning, taking any advantage given to her.

But when the creature bent toward its injured foot, she used it as her opportunity to inflict more direct damage. With her Espada gripped tightly in her right fist, she jumped onto the beast, scaling her way up his side, and then back, where its arms could not reach her. The Orcuyo began swinging its torso from side to side, trying to dislodge her, but she continued to climb, sometimes using her sword to stab into his muscles and use the hilt as a grip to pull herself up higher.

The rest of the group saw what she was attempting to accomplish and began redoubling their efforts to distract it as best they could, shooting arrows up toward its face, Nova and Petra attacking the same injured toe, over and over again, while jumping away from its kicks and scuffles.

Then, Damika was on its shoulders, and the Orcuyo reached up to grab at her. She just managed to duck its enormous hand, and with a loud, angry cry, she stabbed her Espada straight into the thing's neck, severing its carotid artery. The Orcuyo jerked so suddenly and aggressively that it knocked Damika off of its shoulders, and she pro-pelled toward the ground. A second later, the Orcuyo clawed the blade from its neck, which released a torrent of blood, and it swayed wildly on its feet. An inhuman groan bellowed from its mouth, and then it was falling too. The entire group scrambled away as fast as they could, Damika rolling sideways several times to keep herself from being crushed.

Its fall reverberated the windows and doors of the town even more violently than its shouts had, shaking the land like a small earthquake or volcanic eruption, and terrified screams once again pierced the air.

Then, it was silent.

For a moment no one spoke, no one moved. They all stood gasping in incredulity as they stared at the giant monstro at their feet. An Orcuyo was an impossible enemy, the thing of storybooks and legends. The type of creature that took down entire regiments. And yet, Dami-ka had managed to best it. They all turned to stare at the warrior, who finally stood. She looked terrible, some of the blood from the creature had managed to land on her, and the dust from the ground clung to the wetness in disgusting clumps. Even so, she looked as strong and powerful as ever, and Nova felt humbled to be in her presence.

She just took down an Orcuyo.

"Hurry," Petra called out, breaking their stupor. "Let's get back to the farmhouse; we don't know how many more of them there are."

Reminded that they still had loved ones in danger, the group sprang into action. Nova took a few steps toward Petra's family home before she realized that Alric was on the ground, panting heavily. Rawl was kneeling next to him, his hand on Alric's back as the mage clutched his Phoenixeye stone. The magia was slow to bleed off of his body, the red power clinging to him stubbornly.

Nova hesitated, not wanting to leave her friend so clearly incapacitated. He had just used more magia than she had ever seen him attempt before, and the toxicity of the effort would leave him vulnerable. Even after he purged the poison into the stone, he would be weakened and unprotected.

"Go!" Rawl told her, never taking his eyes off their friend. "I'll make sure he is all right. We'll meet up with you when he's ready."

Nova hesitated only a second longer, then nodded gratefully. She was worried for all her friends, of course, but her priority was making sure that Churan was safe.

She turned, and ran.

There was no one in the fields or outside of the houses, which Nova took to be a good sign. If Raidea managed to get everyone indoors before the attack, they would be much better protected. She did a quick scan of the surrounding area for any monstros, but didn't see any. They seemed to have clustered their attack in Tureene. Hopefully, none had made it out this far. When she was satisfied, she turned and headed toward the main farmhouse.

Nova knew something was wrong the second that she set foot inside. The air was thick and stale, apprehension and dread tasting like the bitter tang of steel on her tongue. She could hear crying from the back rooms, and her body tensed.

On her right, Damika was standing motionless, her back to her, staring into the kitchen. Her body was blocking whatever she was looking at that had her frozen.

Her eyes scanned the rest of the room and found Churan. His face was pale, and his eyes were wide with fear, but he was alive. He felt her gaze and turned to look at her. Nova almost took a step back. His eyes weren't wide with fear, they were filled with sorrow.

Nova was filled with cold panic. What couldn't she see?

Cautiously, adjusting the grip of her dagger in her hand, Nova inched forward and around Damika and looked into the room.

Her breath was knocked from her body, her vision blurred, and her body staggered.

In front of her was what had the room feeling so wrong, why it felt like there wasn't enough air. Why people were crying. Why Damika was motionless.

Raidea was lying on the kitchen table, hands clasped in front of her, resting on her stomach.

Raidea. Beautiful, funny, scandalous, vibrant Raidea.

Dead.

Nova's dagger slipped from her fingers and clattered against the floor.

Dante was kneeling at the head of the table, his hands buried in her hair, his forehead on top of hers, his tears streaming into her hair. Petra's face was buried against Taruka's shoulder, her shoulders shaking with sobs that Nova couldn't hear over the ringing in her ears. Taruka's face was streaked with her own tears, as she smoothed her hand over Petra's back again and again. Nova stood as motionless as Damika, her brain refusing to accept the sight in front of her.

Nova felt dizzy and weightless. She felt as if her head was full of clouds, of vapor, of gas. She was floating, detaching from her body and slipping away, far from the body on the kitchen table, away from the sobbing and the grief and the reality of death. Her body swayed, and Nova was sure that she was about to fall.

Then, a small body slid next to hers quietly. Churan. He slipped his small hand into Nova's. She gripped it tight, his presence helping to bring her back to her own body.

"She saved us, all of us," he said softly.

At his words, Nova instinctively pulled him closer to her. He leaned into her side.

"She grabbed all of us, the kids, and her and Petra's father."

"Where is —" Nova tried to get out, but Churan shook his head.

"A salta-sombras got him while we were running back here."

Nova squeezed her eyes shut.

Shadow jumpers. Creatures that dwell in shadows, only to reach out with murky black tentacles and suck unsuspecting people into the darkness with them. Once captured, no one was never seen again

"It almost grabbed Maria," Churan added, referring to one of Petra's younger nieces. "But he jumped and knocked her out of the way. It got him instead"

Nova felt hot tears rolling down her cheeks.

"Raidea didn't stop. She got us all here, but one of the monstros was outside. It looked like a puma, but without hair. And it walked on its back legs. It was terrible." He shuddered. "She distracted it and was fighting it. She made us come inside."

He swallowed hard.

"I looked from the window," Churan continued. "She was so strong. I've seen you all fight now, more than once, but I've never seen anyone like that. She wasn't going to let it take us. Not any of us."

His voice cracked, and Nova knelt to embrace him. He threw himself into her arms and wept openly.

"If I only knew how to use my magia! If I could only control it —"

"No," Nova interrupted him, pulling back to stare into his splotchy face. Again, she thought of how young he looked, and her already shattered heart broke further. She cupped her hands around his face, cheeks hot with tears, and made him look at her.

"This was not your fault," she told him sternly, letting her own tears flow, so that they could mourn together. She dropped her hands to his shoulders.

"Don't for a second think that way. It was the monstros. She would've died for any one of us, and I know she would be glad that all of you are safe."

Churan sniffled and rubbed beneath his eyes with the heels of his palms.

"She got it, in the end," he said, his voice hoarse. "She killed it. It's in the back near the barn. But it got her too. I didn't want to leave her lying there next to it."

"You brought her in?" Nova asked, surprised. "You put her on the table?"

Churan nodded.

"We did. All of us except the little ones," he answered.

Nova smoothed a hand over his head and stood up, turning toward the kitchen once more. She didn't want to look, but she made herself. Raidea was a warrior, had died a warrior's death, and deserved the respect of a warrior.

Damika had not moved, had not made a noise, had not cried. She stood rooted to the same spot, her eyes fixed on Raidea's face, as if she could resurrect her by sheer will alone.

Nova crossed to the table and looked down at her beautiful friend. Raidea had been so special to her; they shared a bond between them unlike the others. In the temple, Taruka and Petra had been the best of friends that anyone could ever ask for.

And Damika, well, Damika was Damika. She still wasn't sure what Damika was to her.

But Raidea? Raidea was her sister. How could she have lost her sister?

She placed a hand over Raidea's and bowed her head. She didn't pray, neither she nor Raidea had been particularly religious. And she would allow one of the other girls to perform the Danrayen rights. She was not a Danrayen, after all.

But she just stood there, holding her friend, and allowing herself a moment to mourn.

Chapter 26

Rawl

Back near Tureene, Alric's arm was swung around Rawl's shoulders, and together they were slowly making their way back toward the farmhouses. Alric's weight was heavy against Rawl as they staggered forward, Rawl doing his best to keep them both upright. The close proximity to the mage would have delighted him in any other moment, but he was too worried about the burning heat of his friend's body and his clear exhaustion to enjoy the feeling. Magia was still pouring freely from Alric's hands into his Phoenixeye stone, and the more that the man had to eject from his system, the more weak and sickly-looking he became.

"Are you sure you don't want to stop and rest, just for a few moments?" Rawl panted, struggling to hold up the sagging mage.

"We need to get to the others," Alric insisted. "There might be more of the Night Wood creatures."

Fear gripped Rawl by the throat, and he stopped moving. Alric grunted in disapproval.

"If there are more of them, you will not be using any more of your magia," Rawl told him. It was a statement, but there was a question hidden in his tone. Surely the mage knew that he was far too spent to continue using his magia, right?

Alric bristled.

"I will do whatever it takes to keep everyone safe," he retorted.

"Not if that means using any more magia, you can't! You don't have any more to give!" Rawl cried.

"Don't tell me what I can or cannot do," Alric replied, but his voice sounded deflated rather than angry.

"Fine," Rawl responded, shoving his arm off of his shoulders and stepping away as Alric swayed on his feet.

"Someone capable of taking out a Night Wood creature with magia alone should be able to walk by themselves, don't you think?"

Alric glared at him, but Rawl just crossed his arms.

"Go on, if you're so capable, you should be able to manage just fine on your own, right?" he taunted.

"Why are you so angry?" Alric asked him.

"I'm not angry!" Rawl cried desperately. "I am terrified!"

Grim determination set in the mage's face, his eyebrows cutting a hard crease down his brow. "I will not let anything hurt you," he promised.

"I'm not terrified for myself!" Rawl responded. "Look at yourself, mago! You can barely stand. You've done enough. And I won't take you any further if there is a risk that you will continue to hurt yourself."

"You're worried for me?" Alric asked him, sounding confused.

"What do you expect? You're my friend and you're being reckless." To his complete mortification, Rawl felt a single, hot tear course down his cheek. He batted it away, frustrated.

Alric stared at him, seemingly dumbfounded, then shuffled toward him. Rawl resisted the urge to rush forward, afraid the man would topple in his exhaustion. When the mage reached him, he lifted his trembling hand to brush the skin where his tear had just been.

"You really are worried about me," he said softly.

Overcome, Rawl gripped Alric's tunic in both hands and dropped his head down between them with a watery chuckle.

"Of course I am worried about you, mago ridiculo. I can't lose you."

He felt tentative arms wrap themselves around his shoulders, and Alric's forehead come to rest gently on the top of his head.

"You won't lose me," Alric promised softly.

There was nothing on Tierramadri that could have stopped Rawl from tilting his face up, grabbing the back of Alric's head, and pressing his lips against his.

If Rawl hadn't just watched the mage pour all the residual magia energy into his stone, he would have sworn it was still pulsing out of him, and igniting all the places that their bodies touched. He felt burning hot electricity where his chest was pressed against his; his hand felt like it was on fire on the back of the mage's head. And the lightning that coursed from their pressed lips felt powerful enough to set him ablaze.

With a jerk Alric pulled away from him, eyes wide, lips parted, a flush creeping over his cheeks.

Rawl swallowed, refusing to look away. They were both breathing hard. Rawl licked his lips, which were still tingling from the contact, and Alric's gaze dipped toward his mouth. In that moment, any hesitation seemed to melt off his body, replaced with a different type of tension. With a sound of surrender, the mage grasped the back of Rawl's neck, lowered his head, and kissed him back.

Their mouths met in hopeless submission, their kiss hard and desperate. But then, it softened, and slowed, and became so achingly sweet that a noise embarrassingly close to a whimper escaped the back of Rawl's throat. Alric's response was to tangle his long fingers into the hair on the nape of the archer's neck.

After a few moments they broke away, and Alric leaned his forehead against Rawl's.

"Oh," the mage finally said.

Rawl couldn't help but laugh. "Did you really not know?" he whispered, luxuriating in the feeling of being so close to him.

Alric pulled back, his face betraying both embarrassment and confusion. Rawl found it incredibly endearing.

"No," Alric admitted shakily. "I don't think I did."

"Are you..."

"I'm, I'm all right with it," the mage replied. "More than all right. I just didn't realize, or didn't let myself realize, what this was. I'm sorry, it's going to take a little while..."

"It's fine," Rawl said, placing his arm on his shoulder. "Take all the time you need."

Alric framed Rawl's face with his fingers, and he shivered at the contact. The mage scanned his face slowly, before meeting his eyes again. Then he leaned forward and placed a soft kiss on his mouth.

When he pulled away, Rawl could swear that he saw stars.

"We should get back, " Alric said, motioning toward Petra's family farmlands.

"Yes," Rawl agreed, shaking his head a little to clear the dazed, floating sensation his kiss had created.

Rawl turned, ready to offer his shoulders to the mage for support once more, when a crashing sound could be heard in the trees behind them. They both spun, quickly, as one of the demon-wolves from the Night Wood bounded out from behind the trees.

Rawl had already aimed his bow before it even broke the tree line, arrow after arrow hitting the thing's face and eyes. Then, an enormous red flash lit up the forest, and the creature was struck with a shattering of electric red magia. The monstro convulsed, as if being struck by lightning, and collapsed on the floor, dead.

Rawl swung around to admonish Alric for using his magia yet again, when he saw the look on the mage's face. He looked on the brink of collapse, the crimson power lighting up his veins from underneath his skin. Rawl watched in horror as the mage reached for his Phoenixeye, pouring the toxic remnants in a heavy torrent into the stone...

Which shattered right in his hands.

Nova was still attempting to console the distressed Churan while not completely falling apart herself, when she heard her name being called from outside the farmhouse. When she ran outdoors, Axchel and Damika following her, she saw Rawl with an unconscious Alric slung across his shoulder like an oversized flour sack.

"Por favor," Rawl called out desperately, sinking to his knees and allowing Alric to roll out of his grip.

The mage looked terrible. Deep maroon magia was undulating under his skin, moving through his veins like lava. His skin was periodically spitting showers of electric red sparks, singeing Rawl's flesh, but the man seemed either not to notice or care. He just held Alric's head in his lap and looked up at Nova, eyes pleading.

"Please," he repeated. "His stone, it broke. There was too much magia; he used too much," he rambled. "He doesn't have another, and he is sick with Mage Madness. He almost killed me before I was able to knock him out."

"Mage Madness?" Damika asked, unsheathing her sword. Instinctively, Nova threw herself between the warrior and her friends.

"Stay away from him," she hissed at Damika. Churan moved to stand with her, and after a moment, Axchel joined them.

"There is no cure for Mage Madness, Nessa," Damika told her. "He's a danger to us all, we need to eliminate him."

"Just stop!" Nova yelled at her, and then turned back to Rawl. "Are you sure?"

His eyes were wide and glassy, filled with both panic and sorrow. He didn't need to answer for her to know he was sure. Nova turned to Axchel.

"Cassalain," she said, her voice desperate. "*Axchel*. Please, you're a healer. There must be *something*."

Axchel looked tortured, but after a moment, shook his head. "I'm so sorry," he replied. "There is nothing once the magia is that deep into his system. He will try to kill us all."

Nova's eyes burned, but she didn't cry.

"No," Rawl said behind them. "No. I will not let him hurt us, but I will not let him die. I won't let any of you hurt him."

"Rawl," Axchel said softly, but Rawl was not listening.

"The Mage University," he said, looking up. "I have a sister, Filomila, in the Mage University. I could take him there."

"The Mage University doesn't have an answer for Mage Madness either!" Damika insisted. "Besides, how will you get him there? He'll kill you before you even reach the coast."

Rawl shook his head. "Please, Nova. I have to try."

Churan, who had finally stopped crying over Raidea, shed fresh new tears. Now he looked up at Nova, his expression broken, and so vulnerable it made her heart twist even harder in her chest.

"Please," Churan begged. "There has to be a way to save him."

Nova looked desperately at Axchel.

The Cassalain hesitated. "I have some potions and herbs from Ana and Patli's gardens," he said. "I could concoct something to keep Alric subdued. But the more the magia pollutes his system, the faster the doses will wear off," he warned them.

"Por favor," Rawl begged again. "Let me get him to Mila. Let us try."

Nova would do anything to see her friend well again. She nodded.

"All right, do it." Nova turned to Axchel. "Fetch the potions."

"This is so stupid!" Damika yelled. "You're putting them at more risk by allowing this," she told her.

Nova spun to glare at her. "What if it was Raidea?" she asked her. "If there was a chance to save her, no matter how small, wouldn't you at least try?"

Damika was silent, but after a moment, sheathed her sword. "You can't go with them," she told her.

Nova gritted her teeth. "I know," she responded.

She did know. She needed to protect Churan and get him to the Flowers. They couldn't travel with a volatile wizard in the grips of Mage Madness. It wouldn't be safe.

"I want to go with him!" Churan cried out, and Nova pulled him in for a hug.

"Lo se," she told him. "But we can't. Rawl will take care of him."

At that moment Axchel returned, followed by Taruka, who crossed to Damika. Nova could hear Dami quietly filling her in on the situation, but she ignored them. Instead she focused on Ax, who crossed over to Rawl with a small rucksack filled with bottles and herbs.

"I can't go with you," he told Rawl, glancing back at Nova and Churan. "I made an oath to protect the boy."

"I know," Rawl replied, his voice hollow. "But thank you for giving us a chance."

Axchel nodded. "I will show you how to make and administer the draft and how to increase the dosage when he starts burning it off."

"As soon as he does, I want you both out of here," Damika said to Rawl sternly. "There are civilians here, and children. We can't have you anywhere near us."

"There is a horse cart," Taruka called out. "The horse is old, but dependable. He belonged to Petra's father," she admitted, her voice cracking. "I'm sure he would want to help."

"Gracias," Rawl said, then grabbed the small bag of medicines.

"I'll ready him and the cart," Taruka replied, and headed toward the stables.

"Churan, go get their packs," Nova told the boy, who ran off to do as he was told.

When Taruka returned, pulling the horse by the lead, Nova helped Rawl load Alric to the back of it, covering him with an old, but clean, horse blanket. Her palms burned from where she was assaulted by the magia in the mage's skin, but she ignored it. Churan came running out with Rawl and Alric's packs, and his own across his thin shoulders.

"I am going with them," Churan insisted.

"No," Nova replied at the same time as Axchel and Damika. Rawl just shook his head. He smoothed the hair off of Alric's head, and then hopped off the cart to speak with Churan.

He crouched, getting eye-level with the boy. Churan's lower lip quivered, but he met the archer's gaze head on.

"I know you care about him," Rawl said. "I care about him too. And I will take the best care of him that I can. If there is any way to bring him back to us, I will find it," he promised.

"But you have other things to take care of," he reminded the boy. "You are special. Not because you are a child of prophecy. Not even because you are a sorcerer. But because you have been working toward peace even before you knew about those things. It is what you were born to do, and you can't give up now."

Churan shut his eyes tightly.

"Stay with Nova and Axchel. They'll protect you. We'll find you again when we can, all right?" Rawl told him.

Churan threw his arms around the archer's neck and gave him a big hug. After a moment, Rawl gently pulled him away.

"Take care of him," Churan told him, indicating toward the unconscious Alric.

"I will," Rawl replied solemnly.

He stopped to hug Nova and shake Axchel's hand before hopping on the cart and directing the horse toward the west.

CHAPTER 27
NOVA

The journey back to the temple was a solemn, sad affair.

As much as they all wanted to stay in Tureene, to mourn both privately and with family and friends, they knew that they could not. But every step away from Petra's family, and Raidea, felt like a betrayal.

It did not take much insisting for Petra to stay behind, while it was clear that she didn't enjoy being separated from Taruka, she seemed relieved to stay and spend some more time with her brothers. It was decided that she alone would remain in Tureene to perform the Danrayen last rights, and send their sister off to the realm of the dioses properly. And despite them not having their father's body in order to lay him to rest, they would celebrate his life as well, and hold a ceremony to make their farewells.

The rest of them continued on traveling to the Temple of Danray, and the tension among the group was an almost living, palpable thing. While their journey from Cassalan to Tureene had been full of hostile apprehension and suspicion, the new stress was a devastating, miserable strain.

Nova didn't know how to deal with her grief. While the priestesses of the Temple of Danray had tried to prepare them all for the inevitable loss that comes with war, Nova had never experienced the passing of a loved one. She didn't know what to do with the crushing pressure on her chest, or the tightness that made it hard for her to breathe. She didn't know if she wanted to cry or scream or just sleep, sleep and wake to find that it had been a mistake, just a terrible dream, and that Raidea was still with them.

She was also suddenly more afraid for her friends than she had ever been before. She worried for Petra, back in Tureene, with no other Danrayen support. They had dispatched of all the creatures from the Night Wood attack, but what if there were more? What if they returned?

She worried for Alric, who had overextended his magia, yet again, with disastrous results. She had known it was becoming a pattern for him, and she should have done more to stop him. Especially since she knew that the reason he continued to be placed in dangerous situations was because of her, and the prophecy.

And in regards to the prophecy, she worried for Churan. Young, sweet Churan, who had already seen so much, and experienced such horrors. That was not likely to end any time soon, they had quite the battle in store for them if they meant to continue on to the Andalan capital and palace, and return him to the Flowers of Prophecy. Her heart ached for him, just a boy who should be living a happy, innocent childhood.

Nova was even scared for Damika, who was the most powerful person that she had ever known. The woman had just killed an Orcuyo, and still she worried. As much as she seemed invincible, she was still only human, and Nova worried that she would be reckless with her safety for the benefit of others.

They were emotions that Nova had never had cause to feel before. Somewhere, deep down, she must have thought that they were exempt from the risks, that of course terrible things happened in war, but they couldn't possibly happen to them.

Not to her friends.

The rest of the group was dealing with their own grief. Taruka was sad and withdrawn, and quieter than usual, which was a difficult thing to accomplish. Churan was also very quiet, which was completely unlike the boy, and Nova worried that he was still blaming himself. He no longer had Alric to cling to or Rawl to try to liven the mood with songs or stories.

As for Axchel, he watched Nova and continued to care for her in his subtle, unassuming way. As before, her water skin was always full, her pack loaded and ready every morning. He encouraged her to eat when her appetite would have failed her, reminding her that she needed to conserve her energy for what was to come. Somehow, his sleeping mat ended up behind hers at night, keeping her nearest to the fire and him in the outer circle, closest to the road where enemies were more likely to approach.

Nova, to her surprise, found that she appreciated every gesture. She had never been coddled, never been cared for in such a manner. In the temple, whenever she was sick or injured or weary, there were at least half a dozen other sick, injured, or weary young women as well. Priestess Lanuaria, the temple healer, and her associates had little time to give each girl too much attention; she simply treated their ailments and sent them on their way. Nova would never have admitted her sadness or fatigue to her friends, not when she had tried so hard to prove herself to be brave and strong like the rest of them. But Axchel didn't expect her to be anything other than what, and who, she was. He knew that she was mourning, and while he didn't attempt to talk to her about it, he made her life easier in the little ways that he could, and she appreciated the effort. The first night that he had settled his bedroll behind Nova, she had felt the solid, steadfast energy of the man, and her body had naturally relaxed into it. He was far enough away for Nova not to feel like her space was being invaded, but close enough for her to feel protected. She had lain there for a long while, watching the low flickering, crackling flames of the fire that they no longer needed for warmth. They lit it just for cooking their meals, and light, then allowed it to die down as they relaxed for sleep. She watched until the flames consumed themselves, and her eyes swam with orange and gold and spots of black, before she blinked hard and looked away. Then, slowly, she turned on her mat to face Axchel.

Whether he had been conscious and watching her the entire time, or her movement had alerted him, she did not know, but he was awake. In the darkness, the fire's embers casting a low, humming glow, she examined his face. She didn't know what she was searching for, or if she was searching for anything, but she allowed herself to look at him. She examined his short, cropped hair that had been growing throughout their travels, his heavy brow that gave him the serious, fierce appearance, hiding the much sweeter nature of his soul. She looked at the heavy swatches of his eyebrows, framing his large dark eyes. She let herself travel the length of his broad nose and stop, for a moment, on the fullness of his lips. Ax remained still, watching her watch him. She found the slight dip in his chin before traveling his jawline back up to his temple, and meeting his eyes once more. Then, she reached her hand toward him, and without hesitating Ax met her fingers with his own, entwining them together in the space between their bodies. Only then did Nova close her eyes and sleep.

With Damika, they were able to take the main Andalan road, the long and wide path of well-trodden dirt that the Andalan soldiers used to travel to and from the northern battles. Their journey from the small border farm town in the North to the Temple of Danray—the same distance that had taken Nova and Alric more than a month to travel in reverse when they had first set out on their quest—took the group less than a week.

When they reached the outskirts of Pelgar, they could see smoke above the tree canopy. Not dancing ringlets of smoke from chimneys, but billowing pillars of smog that floated high on the horizon, making the air thick and hazy. The group looked at one another in horror, and most of them began quickly heading toward the city.

"Wait," Damika said, her body tense. "We can't jeopardize the mission any further. We should head straight to the temple."

Nova gaped at her. The Damika that she knew would never risk the safety of the citizens of Andala.

"People might be hurt down there!" she cried. "It could be another Night Wood attack!"

"Which is why we can't risk it! You are the mission. I am not going to risk you getting injured or escaping," Damika replied.

Anger ignited inside of Nova, a hot, burning, incredulous rage.

"If we were going to escape, we could have done that days ago," she hissed at Damika. "I have nothing to fear from going to the temple; High Priestess Adira is an ally. But we're not going to leave those people down there defenseless! I am not that person."

"So you're going to drag a boy, your so-called savior, the child of prophecy into danger? That's the sort of person you are?" Damika retorted.

That stalled her. Nova glanced at Churan, who was glaring at Damika.

"I can take care of myself," he shouted at her.

"I'll go," Taruka said. "I can figure out what happened, assess the damage, and direct people to go to the temple, if they haven't already done so. Which you know they likely have," she said to Damika. "The rest of you head to the temple."

Nova hesitated.

"They're right, that we can't go," Axchel reminded her softly. "We are both sworn to keep the boy safe, so we must stick together."

"Dami," Taruka insisted. "I won't be long; let me go."

Damika was quiet for a long moment. Nova knew she was debating the importance of her mission against the people of Pelgar, who could be injured or in danger. Finally, she nodded.

"Fine," she said. "Get to the temple as quickly as you are able."

Taruka reached out for Damika and drew her into a quick hug.

"Ten cuidado," Damika told her.

"You be careful too," she replied.

They watched for a moment as Taruka hurried down to the city, Nova's heart shattering further as yet again their group fractured, leading them on different paths.

Reaching the long golden steps leading to the Temple of Danray gave Nova a strange sensation. It had been her haven for so long, home to some of the happiest years of her life, but now, standing in front of the imposing building, she couldn't deny that she was no longer the person she was in her memories. Part of her was overwhelmed with relief to be back at the place she considered more of a home to her than she had ever had. But another part was sad to be standing there even more of an interloper than she had been as a child. Every insecurity that she had harbored in her youth came crashing back into her with full force, and the staggering sense that she was a liar and an imposter was made worse now that her former friends were aware of it as well.

Nova forced down her doubts and followed Damika up the steps, Axchel and Churan trailing her closely. When they reached the top, however, the enormous double doors would not open. Damika looked at Nova.

"Sealed," she said.

Nova's brows furrowed. If the doors were sealed, then Taruka had been right, something bad had happened in Pelgar, and it was likely that the townspeople had fled to the temple for refuge. It was now, essentially, a fortress.

Luckily, all Danrayen trainees were prepared for this possibility, and they knew the alternate way in.

They all circled the temple to the east until they came to the side that they were looking for. It was behind a particularly dense clump of towering trees, deliberately planted to obscure it from view. Even if they didn't, the wall face would look completely ordinary to anyone walking by. Only the Danrayens knew that some of the golden bricks had been strategically placed to create small ledges and fingerholds that only the most elite trained warriors could use to scale up.

When they reached it, Damika grimaced, looking between Nova and Axchel, then up the wall. Nova knew exactly what she was thinking.

"How many times do I have to remind you that we are not prisoners, and we're not trying to escape?" she demanded. "But if it worries you so much, I will climb it."

Damika looked dubious. "It's not an easy climb..."

Nova shoved her pack and sword at Axchel, bristling with anger. "I may not be a true Danrayen," she spat, "but I trained here just as you did. I can climb the dioses-damned wall!"

Nova backed up a few steps, then ran straight at the golden wall, bracing her left foot on a small protrusion, and using it to propel herself up, grabbing a barely perceptible ledge. Tucking her knees up, she managed to wedge her toes into another edge, where she could swing her body forward and up to grab on to the next hold.

Nova remembered practicing on the wall. Only advanced initiates far along enough in their training were told the secret of the scaling wall, and each had to be able to climb it in order to take their Trial. It had taken Nova several tries, but no more than it took most of the trainees, and she had experienced such a feeling of accomplishment when she managed it.

Damika, of course, had passed it on her first try.

Nova was getting to the most difficult part of the wall, where she needed to rely only on the pads of her fingers to pull herself up. She held her breath and from the corner of her eye could see Damika stiffen below her. Determined to prove her merit, Nova strained her burning muscles and managed to pull herself up, rolling onto a wider ledge that led to an inner tunnel. From the ground, the ledge wasn't even visible, the shape of the golden bricks were cut in a way that created an illusion of an impenetrable barrier.

She lay flat on her back for a few moments, catching her breath, before making her way through the tunnel and down to the main level. There she found the secret lever that pulled open a doorway, and with a rumbling grinding sound, it swung open to reveal the waiting party.

When Churan saw her face, he began clapping his hands hard. "Wow, that was so amazing! How did you learn to climb that? Was it hard? When you did it, it didn't look that hard, but after you made it I tried and I couldn't even get a few feet up! Your legs are longer than mine though. Do you think when I grow up a little that I could do it too? Will you teach me? I think it would be amazing to be able to climb a wall like that!"

Damika moved past Nova as Churan continued his breathless chatter and led them through the tunnels of the temple. The farther they walked the more it became apparent that there were many people in the temple, the buzz of conversation growing louder the closer they got. Soon they emerged near the inner buildings of the temple, in the center of them all were the training yards, which were completely overrun with tents and people. The entire space had been converted into a refugee encampment.

Nova could see some of the healing priestesses making rounds, followed by what appeared to be young Danrayen initiates checking on villagers with bandages or wounds. Some people were huddled in clusters, speaking to their families or neighbors, while other groups stood in a line waiting for the food that the temple cooks had set out in long tables.

Hesitantly they approached the large group, when suddenly a familiar face broke through the crowd.

"Mamá!" Damika called out, raising her arm in greeting. Mamá hurried over to them.

"Gracias a dios," she mumbled, sweeping Damika into a hug. Then she turned and did the same to Nova. She would have loved to melt into the woman's embrace, to take a moment to sit quietly with her and lay all her problems at her feet like she used to when she was young, but Mamá was wooden in her arms, and worry was carved deep into her round face.

"Mamá, que paso?" Damika asked. "What happened in Pelgar?"

"Night Wood attack in the village," Mamá answered. "There were so many of them, too many even for all the Danrayen Warriors. We sent everyone, even the older girls who had yet to pass their Trials. Everyone fought. It was terrible."

"Is there anything we can do?" Nova asked, momentarily forgetting why they were at the temple in the first place.

"No, there is something else you must do," she said, turning seriously to Damika. "The two of you must come with me. Your friends can stay here, get some food, and rest."

Damika stiffened at Mamá calling Axchel and Churan her 'friends,' but she did not argue. "Anything you need," she told her.

Churan and Axchel both looked at Nova for approval, and she nodded, placing a hand on Churan's shoulder.

"You'll be safe here," she promised the boy, hoping that that was true. She looked at Axchel. "Keep an eye on him."

The soldier nodded and ushered the boy toward the food, as Mamá began leading Nova and Damika away.

"Hurry," she told them, her voice as close to panic as Nova had ever heard her.

"Where are we going?" Damika asked. "What has happened?"

"It's Adira, she was hurt," Mamá answered. "Salta-Sombras."

Both Nova and Damika gasped.

"I don't know how she saw it; it was so fast. But it reached out to take one of the girls, and Adira cut its tentacle off before it could reach her. The arm evaporated, but the dark purple mist it left behind landed on Adira. It's been poisoning her blood ever since. There is nothing the healers can do, and she is running out of time."

"But, she'll be all right, won't she?" Nova asked.

Mamá did not answer.

Together they reached the building where the priestesses dwell, and made their way up a staircase to the High Priestess's chamber. Priestess Ianuaria was there, and she shook her head when she saw them.

"It won't be long now," she told them softly.

Nova and Damika approached the bed, and on it lay their High Priestess. Her dark brown skin was tinged in gray, and her already small frame had been made thinner from her illness. Where her body once boasted hard lines and strong muscles, she now looked little more than skin and bones. She looked much older than her forty-five years.

But the worst part of it all was the deep purple spiderweb markings on her flesh, tinged with a blue magia that traveled underneath her skin. It was clear that, just like the salta-sombras, her injuries were magical in nature.

"Priestess," Damika addressed her, bowing her head.

Adira managed a weak smile.

"My girls," she said softly. "You made it; I knew you would."

Nova was confused, as the priestess had no reason to believe that either of them were coming back to the temple, but she didn't comment on it.

"Is there nothing we can do?" she said instead.

Adira smiled kindly at her. "No, mija, my time is near."

"Adira, I'm so sorry," Damika said. "I know that this is a terrible time, but I need to know. It's important."

Adira's eyes flickered to Nova, then back to Damika, who swallowed.

"You know what my mission was, what Capitan Balam recruited me for," she continued.

"Yes," Adira answered. "To find the missing Name-Bearer."

Then, incredibly, she smiled, and looked at Nova. "It looks as if you have found her at last."

Damika sucked in a sharp breath.

"It's true then, you did know? You knew the entire time?"

"I knew," was Adira's only answer.

"But, why?" Damika asked, her voice pained.

Adira took a shuddering breath.

"I think it's time to tell you both a story."

CHAPTER 28
JESADIRANY

Jesa and Sofia were running.

They were east from the Andalan capital, in the more temperate forests near the volcan Andalango, as close to the border of the Night Wood forest as they dared. They had been able to stop in the last village for more than a week before Guerro's men had caught up to them, yet again.

Their warning had been fast and desperate, the women barely having time to throw their meager belongings into some packs and secure some food and water for their journey. The two had gotten increasingly better at packing up their lives and moving from location to location, but unfortunately they had caught a glimpse of some well-dressed gentlemen in black as they had made their exit, attracting attention and standing out from the more modest inhabitants of the town. They could not be sure whether or not the men had spotted them, but it wouldn't be long before their descriptions were recognized, and directions given to their last known location.

So they ran.

Jesa resented the heaviness of her distended stomach, and the added weight that kept her from moving as quickly as she desired, but the women had had cause enough to run throughout Jesa's pregnancy, and so she was still able to move her body more swiftly than most in her situation.

It was not lost on her that the added weight that hindered her running was in fact the very thing she was running to protect.

"How do they keep finding us?" Sofia asked as they traveled off path, doing their best to avoid thick, impenetrable foliage or dangerous, predator-inhabited areas.

"He had a bruja with limited sight when we were young," Jesa responded, annoyed that her voice sounded a lot more breathless than Sofia's did.

"You can't think she still lives! She was at least one hundred, even then!"

Jesa laughed, which sounded more like a wheeze. There were plenty of older women in the Danrayen Temple, so she would never laugh at a joke making fun of someone's age, but she couldn't deny that the bruja had been the characteristic old crone even when they were children. Now that she was older, she wondered if she hadn't chosen that look deliberately, to either instill more fear or respect from those around her.

Eventually the women felt secure enough to stop, catch their breath, and drink some water. Jesa sat on an overturned log, legs spread wide, her stomach bulging like a long egg in front of her. Absently, she rubbed it as they rested.

"Jesa," Sofia began.

"No," Jesa answered.

"I don't see why you won't consider asking the Danrayens for help. Surely we could seek refuge back at the temple."

"No, Sofia," Jesa repeated.

"But why not?"

"You know why not!" Jesa said, irritably. "Infants are not allowed at the temple. Even if they were, you know what the goddess said. I cannot raise her."

"So you give her to me, like we planned," Sofia insisted. "After you have given birth safely."

"No! I can't, Sofia," Jesa's voice was desperate now.

"So you prefer this? Running every few weeks, living out of our packs, afraid that you are not eating enough, that you are running too much, that Guerro's men wait for us in every town, every village, every city. When you could have your own room, your own bed, be somewhere safe?"

Jesa turned her head away.

"Please, just help me to understand why not," Sofia pleaded.

"*Because then they would know!*" Jesa burst out. "Everyone, all of them, the priestesses, the initiates, our friends. Everyone! The instructors, our trainers, everyone that I know and admire and care for. They would know that I had a child, and they would know that I chose to give her up."

Tears welled up behind Jesa's eyes, but she blinked them away.

"You would never judge anyone for that choice," Sofia said softly. "Do you believe that they would judge you for yours?"

"But it's not a choice, is it?" she demanded angrily. "Not *my* choice, in any case. It is the will of the goddess!"

Then, the anger in her deflated. "But that is not exactly true, is it? The goddess did give me a choice. The chance to be High Priestess. To be a part of ending the war. To help bring peace to the realm. But it has a price."

She looked down at the hand still above her stomach, her brown skin over the pale shirt, and clenched her fingers, watching the indentations crinkle the fabric.

"The price is never being able to be her mother."

She looked up at Sofia, tears finally escaping.

"I cannot stand the reminder, in every face, in every well-meaning remark, in all the questions that will arise later in life. I don't want there to be a mention of a pregnancy, or a baby, and have others look at me with curiosity or pity. I will never be High Priestess if I must live through that."

Jesa wiped her eyes with the back of her hands. "So you are right, I have made my choice, and now I am acting in the only way that I will be able to live with it."

Sofia didn't answer but sat next to her, wrapping a comforting arm around Jesa's shoulder.

Jesa let herself be comforted for as long as she could, before patting her friend's leg and moving to stand up.

Her first attempt was unsuccessful, and she rocked back onto the log with a huff.

Sofia laughed and sprang up, offering Jesa her arm. Grumbling, Jesa took it and was pulled to her feet.

About an hour later, the women found a small fishing cabin near a loud, bubbling river. Luckily for them it was undisturbed. Whether the fisherman who used it was only a seasonal fisher, or had passed, or was traveling to market to sell his catch they did not know, but they appreciated the warmth and security.

Especially when, later that evening, Jesa's water broke.

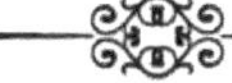

Sofia built up a fire in the chimney, dragging a thick pot over the flames to boil the water she had collected in the river.

"Sofia, the smoke," Jesa warned, panting. Her friend was soaked in sweat, propped up against the far cabin wall, claiming that she felt more comfortable there than the bed. So Sofia had stripped the sheets and was tearing them into long strips, ready to sanitize them in the hot water.

"Relajate," Sofia told her, working as fast as she could. "We need the water and to stay clean. Guerro's men can't move as fast as we can; they won't find us so soon."

Por favor, dioses, she thought. *Please don't let them find us so soon.*

Jesa groaned as another pang of labor pain worked through her. Sofia worked faster.

Leaving the water to boil, she crossed over to her friend and pulled her pack to her side.

"Mira," she said, lifting a bundle from the bottom of the bag. "I found this in that merchant town near the Mage University."

She opened the rough burlap cloth and inside lay the lightest, most delicate knitted blanket in a soft, rosy lilac. It felt as light as clouds over her fingertips, and she extended it to Jesa.

"For the baby," she told her with a smile.

Jesa looked at the blanket, her eyes full of both longing and pain. Sofia faltered for a moment, wondering if she had made a mistake. She just wanted the baby to feel that she was loved, and wanted, despite the uncertainty of her birth. It seemed like the kind of present that one would give on a child's birthing day, but she had never meant to make her friend sad.

But then Jesa reached out and touched the cloth, softly, lovingly, and smiled up at Sofia.

"It's perfect," she said. "So soft. Thank you, amiga."

Sofia beamed and moved back toward the fireplace, when a flicker from outside of the cabin windows caught her eye.

Torches.

Several torches.

Guerro's men had found them.

Sofia spun back toward Jesa and pulled two throwing knives and a long dagger from their weapons pouch. She pushed them into her friend's hands.

"They're here," she said, trying to sound confident. "I will head them off, stop them."

"Sofia," Jesa gasped frantically and tried to stand, only to hurl herself back down on the floor when another labor pain wracked her body.

Sofia held a hand down on her friend's shoulder.

"Stay here," she hissed. "Watch the door, but do not try to come after me."

She grabbed her sword and walked to the cabin entrance.

"They won't hurt you," she said, hoping desperately that her words were true. "Even if they get by me, they need you, and your child."

"Sofia," Jesa sobbed.

"I'll be back," Sofia promised, and walked outside.

There were three torch lights visible from across the stream, and Sofia guessed that there were at least two men per torch. They were approaching slowly, doubtless trying to sneak up on the women, but she was not going to give them the opportunity. She targeted the flame closest to her, just across a narrow point in the river and to the left. She took off running, with an exaggerated battle cry.

She reached the first man quickly, her unexpected approach making him fumble with his blade. She pierced him through the chest and then used her foot to kick him, hard, sliding his body off of her blade. She had been correct; he had been one of two people using the light of the flame, and she spun to face the man holding the torch.

He threw the flame at her, which Sofia blocked with her right forearm, burning her skin. It bounced away from her and onto the ground, lighting the grass around it on fire. Her block had positioned her sword arm wide, and she wasn't able to swing it back into place before the man pulled out his axe.

He swung it at her middle, and Sofia had to take a large leap backward, avoiding the fire that was quickly spreading. In the added light she could see two more men heading toward them. As she had hoped, her yell had attracted the men to her location, rather than the cabin. But there was still one torch unaccounted for, and Sofia could see the small ball of light in the distance attempting to cross the river toward the building.

She had to get to him, fast, before he reached Jesa.

Sofia was finally able to come into a defensive position and blocked a series of strikes from the man's axe before a second assailant joined him, brandishing a large mace with deadly looking spikes. Sofia let her years of training take over and acted on pure instinct, rolling into a practiced dive on the first man's right, forcing him to spin around to have a better angle with his dominant hand. Before he could, she swept her blade fast and low, severing the tendon in his ankle. He began to fall, and Sofia pushed off the ground to kick him with both of her feet, sending him flying into the man with the mace.

Furiously, he shoved his injured friend to the ground and raised his weapon, but it was too late, Sofia was already swinging her blade up into his stomach. He was dead before he hit the ground, pining the first assailant underneath him. By then, the mace man's partner had arrived, holding his torch high and viewing the scene in shocked disbelief. Sofia didn't let him recover, but sliced the man's neck. Then, she ran toward the cabin.

"Run, tell Lord Guerro!" she heard one of the men say, and she could see two others running back into the woods in the darkness.

Damn, she thought, but couldn't waste her time chasing after them. Instead she focused on the final remaining torch, dangerously close to the cabin. Before she could reach him, another one of Guerro's men leapt out from the dark, striking her hard across the face. Sofia's cheekbone exploded in pain, and she was knocked down to the ground. The man lifted her back up by her hair, a dagger glinting in the ever-increasing forest fire. Sofia screamed and struggled, but saw him grin before pulling back, ready to plunge the blade into her belly.

Then, just as the last man crossed inside the cabin, a guttural scream rang out in the night. Both Sofia and her captor turned to look at the entrance of the building as the man staggered backward from the doors, his hands clutching at a throwing knife deeply embedded in his throat.

Nice throw, Jesa, Sofia managed to think.

Without wasting another moment, Sofia used the distraction to kick the man holding her hard in the groin. The grip on her hair loosened as he gasped in pain, and Sofia grabbed his wrist with both of her hands, pulling his arm across his body and stabbing him under his ribcage with his own blade. He had a moment to look at her in shock before collapsing.

"Sofia!" an angry voice called out in the darkness, and Sofia jumped. It was not Jesa's voice. But how—

"Sofia!" the voice called out again, and she stumbled back to the man trapped by his dead companion. The one whose tendon she had cut.

When he noticed her, he laughed. "Yes, we know who you are," he spat at her. "Where do you think you can go where we won't find you?

Even now, Lord Guerro will hear of this. He'll know the child has been born. And then, there will be nowhere on Tierramadri where you can hide."

He laughed up at her, blood on his teeth, before Sofia ran him through.

It was a mercy, really. It was either her blade or the fire.

Her entire body aching, Sofia crossed the river once again, and took a moment to move the dead body away from the door. Then, she stumbled inside.

Jesa was still sitting against the wall, dagger in one hand, and the yellow blanket bundled in her arm. When she saw Sofia, she let her blade drop.

"Are we safe?" she asked Sofia, who nodded, still eying the blanket.

"Are you all right?"

Sofia nodded again, then crossed the room to crouch by her friend.

In her arms was the most perfect little girl she had ever seen. Her face was scrunched, her brown skin blotchy and still slick. She had a small tuft of hair on the crown of her head, which was plastered down. But she was beautiful.

"Oh," she said softly as she reached to touch her, but pulled away when she noticed the blood on her fingers.

Jesa's hands were also stained with blood, but it was blood that had come from life, not from death.

"Are they all dead?" Jesa asked.

"A few escaped. I'm so sorry, Jesa," Sofia answered, snapping out of her awe. "And there is a fire, even if the river stops it from spreading too far, the smoke ..." she trailed off, looking at the baby.

"Why are you sorry?" Jesa asked, her voice weak. "You saved us."

Sofia smiled sadly.

"I have killed half a dozen of their men, and they know my name and my face," she responded. "They know that I travel with you, and now they know the child has been born."

"They will hunt you now too," Jesa realized, forcing herself to sit up. "Oh Sofia, I am so sorry to have dragged you into this."

"You didn't; this was my decision," Sofia insisted. "But that means..." she trailed off.

"You can't raise her," Jesa realized, and Sofia's heart broke at the devastation in her voice.

"No."

Jesa let her head drop back against the headboard, tucking the perfect, tiny creature against her chest. The baby stirred, but did not cry again.

"Will you take her? Find a family for her? A good family?" Jesa asked her.

"Of course."

"And after, keep an eye on her, from afar? Protect her, if Guerro's men ever get close."

"I promise."

"When I am High Priestess, you will always be welcome in the Temple of Danray," Jesa said, looking her sister and friend in the eyes.

Sofia blinked, her mouth dropping open.

"You can't."

"I can and I will. The goddess will allow it. She will have to. Look what I am giving up for her."

Jesa didn't cry. Sofia was sure that Jesa realized her daughter would never remember her, but she could see her friend schooling her emotions so that their only moments together would not be spent in sorrow.

"What will you name her?" Sofia asked, but Jesa shook her head.

"No, I can't, I shouldn't. The family that takes her, they can name her."

"Jesa," Sofia said sternly, and Jesa looked up to look into her friend's solemn gaze. "You are allowed to name your daughter."

Jesa looked down at her child, her warm brown skin, the big doe eyes that blinked up at the world without fear. She ran her finger down her perfect little nose, stopping to marvel at the dip just above her lips.

"I will name her after my mother," she finally responded.

"I will name her Damika."

Chapter 29
Damika

Damika stumbled back from the bed, her knees buckling. It couldn't be, it was impossible.

All throughout Adira's story she had felt a tight knot within her stomach, which grew and strengthened in intensity the further the tale progressed. The familiarity of it, the parallels, the implications. She noticed, with new revelation, the strong slope of Adira's nose, so like her own, the tightly wound brown curls that mirrored the texture of her hair and the shape of her amber eyes.

And finally, she recalled her recurring dream, the small warrior who had saved her from the men in black, the one who had brought her to the temple. Suddenly, the face in her dream, which had always felt so familiar, sharpened with new clarity.

Damika looked up at Mamá, her eyes wild.

"Sofia?" she asked her, disbelieving.

Mamá met her eyes, and gave her a single, slow nod.

"And..." Damika trailed off, looking back toward the bed.

"Jesadirany," Nessa finished for her, her voice astonished. "Jes-Adira..."

Adira smiled weakly.

"When I returned to the temple, I no longer wished to be Jesa. I could not *be* Jesa. She was a different person. She was the girl who dreamt of a life outside of the temple. She was the young woman who loved Jose, and she was Damika's mother."

Adira looked back at Damika with such sorrow that the girl had to look away. She still couldn't fully process everything that had been revealed.

"So I dropped the Jesa and became Adira," the priestess continued, looking back at Nessa. "You of all people know the importance of names."

Damika saw Nessa nod in understanding.

But Damika did *not* understand. She didn't understand anything.

She looked back at Mamá, at Sofia, who felt safer to address than her moth— *Adira*.

"You rescued me, all those years ago," she said slowly.

Mamá nodded.

"I was always close by, watching when I could, living as near to the family we had found for you as possible. They knew the risks, though not exactly why there was risk. They believed that your mother gave you up in order to better hide you from an abusive father. It was not the truth, but close enough. They were happy to have you, niña," Mamá assured Damika, but guilt threatened to suffocate her. She had been the reason for their deaths.

"But even then I kept traveling to the neighboring villages and towns, befriending innkeepers, bribing soldiers, recruiting people, and listening for whispers. Anything that would help warn me if Guerro's men were getting close to you," Mamá continued.

"And when they found me, when they killed my par—" Again, Damika stole a glance at the High Priestess. "When they were killed, you brought me to the temple."

"I knew you would be safe behind these walls, just as your mother had been," Mamá said.

"And you," Damika made herself look at Adira. "You pretended not to know me?" she asked, her voice cracking. From the corner of her eye she saw Nessa reaching for her, but she jerked away. "You barely acknowledged me, treated me like any other initiate!" she yelled.

Damika continued. "Why didn't you say anything? *Why* didn't you tell me you were my mother?"

"I couldn't *be* your mother," Adira said weakly, her face contorted with pain. Whether it was physical or emotional, Damika could not tell, and found that she did not care. Not at that moment. She was even glad for it, a little. She should be in pain. She should feel even a fraction of what Damika was feeling.

The emotion shocked her.

Damika had never been comfortable crying in front of others, and rarely did so. She thought that if she started now it would be like a burst dam, that the tears would begin and never stop, draining her of everything she needed to remain upright.

Instead, she turned the unshed tears into rage.

"Because of the goddess? Because of yet another prophecy? Who are the dioses to play with our lives like this? To move us at their whim like ants on blades of grass? You should have told me, *I don't care what Danray said!*"

Nessa gasped, and Damika could guess why. She had never spoken about her goddess with anything but reverence and respect. She had dedicated her entire life to walking her path and being a warrior to her cause. To speak of her now with such anger in her voice surprised even herself.

With a frustrated, guttural yell, Damika stalked out of the room and into the hallway. She made it halfway down the corridor before collapsing on a bench, bending almost in half, with her face tucked between her knees. She pulled fast gulps of air into her mouth, her inhales sounding rough and ragged, her exhales sounding too close to sobs. Her heartbeat sped, and she felt dangerously close to losing control.

Instead, she focused on steadying her breathing. She made herself breath slower, slower, hold the breath in her chest for a moment before expelling. Again, slow, slow inhale, hold, even exhale. Beat by beat her heart rate slowed with her breaths, until she lulled into a trance.

Nothing mattered now but her breathing, *slow, slow, in ... hold, slow, slow, out*.

She allowed herself to grow numb, blissfully senseless to everything else around her. She wanted all the emotions that had sprung up at Adira's story purged from her system.

Damika wasn't surprised when Nessa sat beside her on the bench. Even now, at odds with one another, their connection drew them together. Apparently it was a connection that had begun even before they were born. Both children, affected by prophecies that changed the entire course of their lives.

"What gave them the right?" Damika asked, her voice hoarse from emotion.

Nessa didn't ask who she meant, which was good. Damika didn't *know* who she meant. Whether it was the Flowers, Adira, the Archwizard, or the dioses themselves, it didn't matter. The answer was the same. *No one* gave them the right, because they didn't *have* the right. It wasn't fair for their lives to have been so altered by the choices of those with more power than them. They should have had a choice, a say in their own path.

"Dami," Nessa said, tentatively reaching for her hand. Damika allowed her touch; she didn't have the strength to deny her then.

"I know you are angry, and confused," she continued softly, squeezing her fingers.

Dami didn't reply. She wanted to say that Nessa knew nothing of what this felt like, but she knew it wasn't true. Nessa had also lost her family and had been raised based on the words of a prophecy.

"But Adira is dying."

Damika was glad Nessa didn't try to call the High Priestess her mother. She didn't think she could handle that title at the moment.

"You have the rest of your life to be angry with her, or forgive her."

Damika looked sharply at her, and Nessa lifted her free hand in a peaceful gesture.

"Whatever you see fit," Nessa clarified. "But if you want answers, you don't have much time left."

With another squeeze of her fingers, Nessa stood and made her way back into the priestess's room.

Damika straightened and dug her palms into her eyes. She didn't want to go back in. She didn't want to face the truth of what her life had been.

But Nessa was right; she did want answers.

With one more deep breath, and a very long sigh, Damika stood up and walked back into the room. "All right," she said with as much confidence as she could muster.

"All right," she repeated, dragging a stool over to sit next to the bed on which Adira lay. "Your child was supposed to have an affinity, but I don't," she said, with a jerky shrug. "I have no affinity."

"My darling, you have one of the greatest affinities I have ever known," Adira answered her evenly.

"An affinity for what?" Damika asked, bewildered.

"For battle. You are not just the daughter of Danray, mija. You are her blade."

A cold chill rushed through her, and she looked up at Mamá for confirmation.

"You were the most talented initiate this temple has ever seen," Mamá said. "You are the youngest Danrayen to pass the Trial, and I believe that you would have been able to do so even earlier, had you so chosen," Adira admitted.

"No one moves like you, Dami; no one fights the way you do. You took down an entire Orcuyo, almost singlehandedly!" Nessa added.

"An affinity for battle?" Damika wondered. It seemed ridiculous.

"What better gift for Danray to give to her chosen?" Adira replied.

"But why?" Damika asked, suddenly desperate. "When I passed the Trial and was sent on the mission to find the Name-Bearer, why didn't you tell me the truth then?"

"Capitan Balam requested you specifically. He is a soldier of Andala. He was close with the king. He is a man of the capital. It is what they molded him to be. I could not trust him with the truth."

She remembered meeting the man before her celebration, when she had been in this very infirmary, recovering from her Trial. He had outlined the quest to her, stressed the importance of finding the Name-Bearer and bringing her to justice. Why having a traitor to the crown, running free and creating dissension in the realm, was so dangerous. How, with her help, they could protect the crown and the Andalan people from her lies.

"And me?" Damika demanded. "You couldn't trust me with the truth? Why wouldn't you tell me?"

"It was safer for you not to know," Adira replied sadly.

"We were friends! Nessa and I were friends, I loved—" she broke off. "I believed in you, I respected you. Had you told me, even as the High Priestess and not as your daughter, I would have believed in you." She looked at Nessa, desperately. "In both of you."

Damika looked back down at the bed and was shocked to see tears escaping Adira's eyes, sliding down her temples and into her curly hair.

"Perhaps it was a mistake," the priestess admitted. "One of so many I have made. I am so sorry."

Damika just shook her head, overwhelmed. "I need, I need to think," she stammered, moving to rise from the stool.

"Wait, mija," Mamá stopped her. "There is more you must hear."

"I cannot possibly hear anything more right now," Dami admitted.

"And yet you must," Adira replied solemnly. "For Lord Guerro has never stopped being a threat to us."

Damika sat back down. Of course. From the story the High Priestess just told, Guerro did not seem the type of man to simply give up.

"But he must be, what, seventy-five years old by now?" Nessa asked tentatively.

She was right. If he had been thirty years older than Adira, he would be an old man by now.

"And yet he looks and moves like a man no more than fifty," Mamá answered. "The magia of his brujas keeps him young."

"It seems that after the prophecy, he became obsessed with siring a powerful child," Adira added. "Even when he was hunting me, he was searching for alternative ways to get what he wanted. We think he has sired several children throughout the years, some more powerful than others. Sofia has discovered two that we know for certain to be his."

"How?" Nessa asked Mamá.

"When I returned to the temple, I never stopped searching, gathering information, and receiving reports. Over time, I have built a network of informants throughout Andala that could relay back important messages and information," she replied. "We knew he would never stop, so neither could we."

Dami looked up at Mamá. It was hard to believe that the sweet, motherly figure of her childhood had been a spy the entire time. The moments in her youth when Mamá had been absent, she had always assumed that she was traveling to other regions for new plants and herbs, or selling her wares in city markets. Perhaps she even had distant family that she visited from time to time.

Instead, it seemed that she had been weaving a complicated web, securing allies, and acquiring knowledge. Damika had always known that Mamá was much stronger than she appeared, but people underestimated her because of her stature and the sweetness she radiated. Which, she realized, would be the perfect misdirection for a spy.

Her High Priestess was her mother. The woman who had helped raise her was a spy. And her best friend was a traitor to the realm.

Was anything about her life real?

"So who are the two powerful children?" Damika finally asked. She refused to think of anything beyond the next step. She feared if she started unraveling the untruths of her life that she would unravel right with them.

"One escaped our notice until much later," Mamá admitted. "She was able to make her way into the very temple before we had discovered it, trying to get close to you, Damika."

"Kichka," Nessa gasped.

Damika frowned. The girl with magia, who had tormented Nessa all those years ago?

"She is Lord Guerro's daughter?" Damika asked.

Mamá nodded.

"At that time we didn't know, nor did we know that Guerro had found out about you, Damika. We still don't know how he did. But we believe that she was sent to get close to you, and felt that Phanessa was in the way of that."

Damika saw Nessa draw in on herself, as if reliving the memories of Kichka's abuse.

"The monstros that attacked Pelgar, and the temple, they were stained with blue magia," Mamá added.

Nova jerked. She had been a victim to a type of blue magia herself in her youth. Damika remembered the horrible, ugly spider web markings of attack magia on her flesh. But they couldn't think …

"You don't think Kichka summoned them?" she asked Mamá.

Sofia shook her head. "We believe that the monstros are leaving the Night Wood on their own, traveling farther than they ever have been, and lasting for far longer than they should be outside of the wood's protection. We don't know why. But the blue magia traces left on the ones that attacked us matched Kichka's magical signature. Somehow, she has learned to control them."

They were quiet for a long moment. Then Damika remembered something.

"And the second child?" she asked. "You said you knew of two?"

Mamá and Adira shared a glance.

"Zerlina," Mamá replied.

"Que?" Damika and Nessa exclaimed at the same time.

Zerlina was Queen Issalia's daughter, born a few years after the prince. Who her father was was a matter of great speculation around the realm, but the queen had never revealed who he was.

Before they could ask any more questions, Adira burst into a fit of violent coughing, her body curled on its side. When she pulled the handkerchief she had been holding away from her face, it was spattered with blood.

Without thinking, Damika reached for Adira's other hand and clasped it tightly within her own.

"Lo siento, mija," the priestess said.

Damika just shook her head. She couldn't say that she forgave her, not yet, but …

"You did what you thought was best," Damika replied.

Adira squeezed her hand weakly.

"There is one last thing I must ask of you. When I pass, you need to take over as High Priestess."

"Que?" Damika asked, pulling back in shock. "I can't be High Priestess, only a priestesses can ascend to High Priestess. And only Danrayen Riders can become priestesses. I am neither!"

"Do you think a title matters at this moment? For ordinary warriors, in ordinary times, perhaps. But nothing about this situation is ordinary. We are at war with far more than Cassalan right now. We need someone strong in command. There is none stronger than you."

Damika was shaking her head.

"But I can help, I can protect the people of Andala—"

"Are your Danrayen sisters not also the people of Andala? They need your protection and your guidance. They need your strength. You must take my place."

Damika squeezed her eyes shut.

"Please, at least, consider it," Adira pleaded. "Sofia will be here to help."

When it was clear that Damika was not going to respond, Adira turned her head to look at Nessa.

"I have something for you," she said, and Nessa got closer to kneel at the side of the bed next to Damika. She placed her hand over Adira's forearm, right above where Damika's hand had been. Adira nodded to Mamá.

Mamá reached into her pocket and pulled out a small wooden box, carved with flowers. Then she brought it to Nessa and opened the lid.

Nessa gasped, and her free hand flew to cover her mouth. Her eyes flickered from the box, to Adira, and then back to the box.

Inside was a scrap of the most beautiful fabric Damika had ever seen. It was a deep purple color, embroidered with several stunning flowers. And in the heart of each flower face was a gemstone.

Nessa reached for it, and the cloth seemed to slide across her fingers like air.

"A piece of my ceremonial dress," she breathed. "From the Naming Rite," she explained to Damika, then looked at Adira.

"You kept it?"

Adira took a rattling breath that made Damika wince. That didn't sound good.

"I wanted you to have a reminder of who you once were, so you can realize who you have become."

Nessa was crying.

"Thank you, Adira," she said. "Thank you for always making me feel welcome here. For making me feel like a true Danrayen, even if I never was one."

Adira smiled softly.

"My dear girl, who is to say we wouldn't have chosen you as a child, had the bees not chosen you as a Name-Bearer first? You are every bit as much as a Danrayen Warrior as your sisters are, and I am proud to call you one of ours."

Nessa gaped at her, her mouth hanging open, her tears suspended.

"Damika," Adira said, turning back to her. "I know I have no right to call myself your mother in birth. But as your High Priestess, I can call you my daughter in the path of Danray, at least. I have always, *always* been proud of you, and loved you in both."

And with that, High Priestess Jesadirany, daughter of, and mother to Damika, child of prophecy and leader of warrior women, returned to her goddess.

CHAPTER 30
NOVA

Nova stumbled out of the bedchamber, rocked to her core. There were so many things that she was struggling to understand. Adira had been Damika's mother. Mamá was a spy. Kichka was the daughter of a powerful and terrible man, who was also the father to princess Zerlina. Adira wanted Damika to become High Priestess.

Adira had said that she was just as worthy of being a Danrayen as anyone else.

Of all the new information, she knew that that wasn't the piece that she should be focused on. And yet, she couldn't stop thinking about it. All those years of guilt, and doubt, feeling like an imposter amongst her friends. Could it be true? Could she have been chosen as a true Danrayen, had her life, and fate, taken another path?

She walked without any real destination, roaming the halls and paths that she had grown up in. She passed the indoor classrooms and the kitchens and skirted along the sides of the center training fields, not wanting to be drawn into any conversations. She kept walking until she reached the Danrayen gardens, greeting it with the usual signal—raising a clenched fist high, then bringing it down to touch her thumb to her neck, where the goddess's arrows meet her enemy's flesh. She did the motion automatically, and for the first time did not feel any twinge of guilt in doing so. If she truly belonged there, if she could have been a Danrayen in another life, then perhaps she had the honor of addressing the goddess as one of her daughters.

Eventually, Nova ended up in the same small courtyard that she and Damika had been in on the night before she left the temple. Damika had told her about her secret mission and had sounded so certain about her path.

Then, she had kissed her.

Nova sat on the bench that the two of them had sat on that night, and drew up her knees.

Not long after, Damika entered the same courtyard, crossing to the bench and sitting next to her.

"I thought I'd find you here," Dami said.

"Why were you looking for me?" Nova asked, genuinely curious.

"I don't know," Damika admitted.

They settled into silence, both lost in their own thoughts. The garden was in full bloom, the scent of flowers heavy in the air. While that would usually have put Nova on edge, she was too shocked in the moment to resent their aroma. A light breeze rustled the plants, and the sun glimmered off of Danray's golden hair in the sky, creating sparkles of dancing light on the petals, grass blades, and stone floor.

After a while, Nova glanced at Damika. "Are you going to do it?" she asked her.

Nova didn't have to clarify what "it" was; Damika would know she was referring to Priestess Adira's final wish, that Damika take her place as High Priestess.

"I don't know," Damika responded. "I thought about it, before. I thought that after many, many years of being a Danrayen Warrior, and traveling the realm, doing good deeds and saving people, that eventually I would return and accept a position as a Danrayen Rider.

Then I would have new sorts of adventures, advise on the war, be in charge of special missions, and lead others."

She paused, rubbing a hand over her face.

"Then, when I was old, I'd be a priestess and help train the next generation of warriors. After, when I was really old, I'd become High Priestess."

She shrugged. "It was just silly fantasies, but I had thought of it. But only much, much later in life. I'm too young to be a High Priestess."

"Adira wasn't much older than you were when she became High Priestess," Nova reminded her.

"But now we know that Danray meant her for it. That she led her on that path."

"Perhaps she is leading you on this path too," Nova suggested.

"I am very tired of higher beings dictating the direction of our lives."

Nova didn't respond, because she could very much relate to that sentiment.

"I swore to dedicate my life in service to the goddess," Damika finally said.

"For what it's worth, I think that you would make a wonderful High Priestess."

She did, too. In fact, Nova couldn't think of anyone better suited to the position than her friend. She could inspire them, protect them, and lead them through the inevitable upcoming battle. Priestesses young and old would respect her, trust her, and defer to her leadership. And once it was all over, she would help shape the future generation of Danrayen Warriors.

Footsteps heading toward the courtyard had both of them looking up, and they saw Mamá approaching them. Her eyes were bloodshot and puffy from crying, her nose red and raw. Nova felt terrible for her. She herself had loved Priestess Adira, but Adira had been Sofia's best friend for decades. It was obvious that the two had shared an incredible bond and were true sisters. When Sofia reached them, Nova stood and greeted her with a hug.

"Lo siento, Mamá," she whispered to her.

Mamá patted her back and pulled away.

"I'm sorry too, mija, I know that you have been through so much." She looked at Damika. "Both of you."

Damika nodded but did not stand to embrace the older woman. Nova was sorry for it, but not surprised. She knew that it would take her some time to process everything that had been revealed to them and to overcome the betrayal that she must be feeling toward Adira and Mamá.

"There is much to say and much to prepare for," Mamá told them. "But first, there are two final things that you must know. Before her passing, Adira knew that the two of you would be coming to the temple."

Damika and Nova exchanged a look.

"Como?" Damika asked.

"No se," Mamá responded. "Maybe it was the salta-sombras magia poisoning her blood, maybe her proximity to death. Maybe the goddess visited her one last time. But she knew she was dying, and she knew you would come."

Mamá turned to Damika. "She asked me to give you this."

Mamá removed a sling from her back and placed it on the bench. When she opened it, there was a long item wrapped carefully in a bundle. Mamá parted the cloth, slowly and deliberately, until the most beautiful sword that Nova had ever seen was revealed.

She gasped.

"This is the sword that your father made for your mother," Sofia said.

Nova noticed that while Damika winced at the titles, she didn't correct Mamá.

"Adira wanted you to have it."

Nova half expected Damika to deny the gift, but the sword was such an incredible work of art, it was impossible to not want to touch it. Damika reached reverently for the hilt and drew the blade into the air. She and Nova sucked in a breath.

"It's perfectly balanced, like it was made just for me," Damika said in awe.

"It is special too," Mamá added. "A gift given from love to your mother, who gifted it from love to you. There is power in that."

Damika tensed, but nodded tersely, finding a leather sheath in the bundle and placing the sword away.

"Gracias," she told Mamá curtly. Then, Mamá turned to Nova.

"And before you came, Adira had the Inner Sanctum prepared for you. You are welcome to take the Trial of Danray at any time."

Nova recoiled. The Trial of Danray? It was one thing for Adira to tell her that she might have been chosen as a Danrayen Warrior had she not been recruited to be the Name-Bearer first, it was quite another to test that theory out in a trial that had killed people before!

Damika was staring at her, mouth parted in surprise. Then she said something to her, but Nova couldn't hear her over the ringing in her ears. She looked at the statue of Danray, where the sanctum was, and gazed at the hard, fierce lines of the goddess.

Then, she turned around, and ran the other way.

Nova could hear Damika chasing after her, but she didn't stop. She ran all the way to the edge of the gardens, which were a tightly clustered forest of trees before the temple boundary wall. Only when she had no further to run, did she stop. She could feel Damika behind her, but she didn't turn, only leaned her forehead against the rough trunk of a tree. She pressed against it so hard she was sure that the bark would leave wrinkled imprints on her flesh when she pulled away, but she didn't care. The dull pain was helping to ground her.

"You're going to do it, right?" Damika finally asked her.

Nova laughed ruefully, but didn't answer. She could hear Dami shift her weight.

"It is an immense privilege," she told her. "You should be honored they would allow you to, even though—"

Rage exploded within Nova. A white hot, burning ire that boiled her very blood. Every bitter resentment, every indignation, every word swallowed and emotion repressed bubbled up inside of her, erupting from her in a furious craze.

"Even though what?" Nova demanded, spinning around. "Even though I trained just as hard as the rest of you, if not harder? Even though I worked past the disadvantages of my age and the shortcomings of my prior life to carve my place here? Even though I excelled in tracking and hunting, and survival tactics, and passed all my classes and did *every single thing* that the rest of you did? *Now* I should feel grateful? *Honored*?"

"That's not what I meant," Damika replied.

"*Of course* it is. I should feel grateful, because even though I accomplished all of those things, I was *never* a true Danrayen. I was an imposter. A liar, right? That's what you called me. What you've been calling me. A traitor. So I should feel *honored*."

"Nessa," Dami started.

"*My name is not Nessa!*" she yelled. "It's not *Nova*, or *Rojya*, or the dioses-damned *Name-Bearer*. I don't have a name or a family or a life that is my own to live. And now, I should feel honored to be allowed a place somewhere that I spent ten years of my life convincing myself that I don't belong in."

"You do belong here. You are a true Danrayen."

Nova laughed mirthlessly.

"Now I am worthy of being your equal? Of being your friend? Now that your High Priestess confessed to her part in all of this? But not before, of course. Not when it was just my word. What weight does the word of a liar hold, right?"

"I was doing what I was trained for," Damika answered stiffly.

"So that makes it all right?" she raged.

"And you're right, you were trained for this too!" Damika said, ignoring her last question. "So you should take the Trial, not for anyone else but yourself."

Nova rolled her eyes and moved to walk away.

"As a Danrayen you can request our help!" Damika shouted, and Nova paused.

"You'll need help to get the boy to the capital. Now that we know what we're up against. If Lord Guerro is at the palace with Queen Issalia and his brujas, he poses a threat. We already know Kichka has the ability to control the Night Wood monstros. And who knows what insidious powers Princess Zerlina has, or how she has been corrupted."

Damika looked Nova straight in the eyes.

"If you pass the Trial, you can request the aid of your sisters, and they will provide it. Without it, you and Churan won't make it one hundred feet from the city, let alone the palace."

"What does it matter?" Nova replied, deflating.

"What does it matter?" Damika repeated, incredulously.

"Why should I care? Why even continue the quest? To serve a realm that stripped me of my family, my home, my very name? To further a monarchy that branded me a traitor? To protect the people that hunt me like a dog? Why should I help *any* of them?"

"Nessa—" Damika tried to say.

"No! Everyone is against me. Everything has been against me since I was a child. And none of it was my fault. None. I didn't ask to be born into my station; it was not my meddling that brought the bees to me. To be chosen as the Name-Bearer. And even when I submitted, when I bowed my head and accepted my role in the palace and—dioses—even *looked forward* to my days in court, I was still punished for things out of my control."

She sat down, hard, leaning her body against the trunk of a tree.

"People in power have moved me about like a piece on a table game. They've even turned my —"

She stopped, and averted her gaze, swallowing hard.

"They've even turned *you* against me."

She shut her eyes tightly, digging her thumbs into the sloping bones just above the bridge of her nose. Piercing slivers of pain shot behind her eyes, but she didn't move her fingers. Then, warm hands clasped over her hands, drawing them away from her face. Pinpricks of light danced in her vision, the result of having pressed down on her eyes too hard and squeezed her lids too tight. It cast flickering sparkles over Damika's face, which was now much much closer to hers. She met her gaze until the dancing light finally stopped.

"Lo siento," Damika said softly, and Nova frowned. She hadn't expected Damika to apologize. She didn't know what to say.

"I'm sorry that I didn't believe you. That I left and spent the last years of my life hunting you. I should have trusted you. I should have believed in you. But more than that, I'm sorry that you didn't feel safe enough to tell me the truth before all of this, when we were both here, in the temple."

Nova shook her head.

"That wasn't your fault, I didn't tell anyone. I couldn't."

Damika nodded. "I know," she said. "That took a lot of strength, which you have always had. I never doubted your merit. I always believed that you were meant to be here. Maybe that's why I was so shocked when I found out the truth, because I was always so sure about you. I'm sorry I made you believe otherwise."

Nova felt a tear slip from her eye, and she batted it away, irritably.

"What if it's not true, Dami?" she whispered. "What if Adira only said what she did out of kindness? To make a lost girl feel more included?"

"She would not have prepared the Trial for you if she didn't mean what she said."

"Then what if she was wrong? What if you're wrong? What if I was never meant to be a Danrayen?"

"You are a daughter of Danray. Take the Trial, not to prove it to me or anyone else. But so that you never have cause to doubt yourself again."

Damika stood and reached her hand down. Nova hesitated, then gripped her arm and allowed her to haul her up. They stood very close together, and the antagonism that she had come to expect in Damika's gaze had completely vanished, as if it had never been there at all. In front of her stood her childhood friend, and maybe more, looking a little older and a little sadder, but it was her.

"If I take the Trial," Nova started, "then you need to face your fears too. You need to at least consider becoming High Priestess."

Damika took a deep breath in, and released it with a low sigh. "You're right," she answered. "I will."

Together the two of them walked toward the statue of Danray. When they arrived, some of the priestesses were sitting in vigil, and Priestess Ianuaria was there with a basket of medical supplies. A small shudder shook Nova's body, remembering the last time she had seen that basket, on the day of Raidea's Trial.

Mamá was there too, and she had gathered Axchel and Churan to join her.

"You were confident that I was going to accept," she told her.

Mamá smiled.

"I know my girls," she answered, and pulled her in for a hug. "I knew that you would find your way home."

When Mamá released her, she turned to Ax and Churan.

"You both understand what this is?"

They both nodded solemnly.

"I wouldn't take the risk if it wasn't important," she assured them, looking at Axchel.

"I know," he answered simply.

Churan threw his arms around Nova's middle. "Buena suerte," he said, wishing her luck.

Nova smiled and gave him a good squeeze. "Gracias," she replied.

"We'll be right here when you return," Axchel told her.

And then, to her complete shock, he bent his head and placed a soft, chaste kiss on her lips.

She lifted her hand to her mouth, and her eyes darted to Damika, whose lips were pressed into a thin line. "You can do this," was the only thing she said.

As ready as she could be, Nova turned to Mamá once again. "Should I begin my meditation?" she asked her, but Mamá shook her head.

"I'm afraid we don't have time for you to prepare in that manner, mija. But I know you will be just fine."

Nerves coursing through her entire body, Nova removed two of her long daggers from her belt and turned to the large altar doors. As she walked toward them, two priestesses grasped a handle each, pulling them open for her.

With a deep breath, Nova walked into the inner sanctum, and began the Trial of Danray.

To be continued.

Flowers of Prophecy Will Return
The Daughter of Danray
2024

Name Meanings and Pronunciation Guide
In order of appearance

Jesadirany: *Jes-ah-dee-rah-nee* "the gift of strength, nobility, and power"

Alonzo: *Ah-lon-zow* "noble" / "ready for battle"

Danray: *Dan-ray* Goddess; of battle and transition

Sofia: *So-fee-ah* "wisdom"

Nova: *No-vah* "New"

Rawl: *Rah-ool* "Wise wolf"

Alric: *All-rik* "Regal ruler"

Axchel: *Ahk-shell* "Man of Peace"

Lionel: *Lee-oh-nell* "Little Lion"

Fernanda: Fehr-nan-dah "Adventurer"

Taruka: *Tah-roo-kah* "Doe"

Tz'ola: *Ts-oh-la* Goddess; of the sun

Rojya: *Row-hyah* Animal; fox-like creature with red fur

Vago: *Vah-go* "Lazy"

Perdita: *Pehr-dee-tah* "Lost"

Damika: *Dah-me-kah* "Open-spirited"

Balam: *Bah-lam* "Jaguar"

Petra: *Peh-trah* "Stone, rock"

Fernando: *Fehr-nahn-doh* "Adventurer"

Paolo: *Pa-oh-low* "Small"

Carlos: *Car-lows* "Free man"

Ana: *Ah-nah* "Favored grace"

Peruda: *Peh-roo-dah* Goddess; of love

Raidea: *Ray-dee-ah* "Wise goddess"

Eduardo: *Ed-war-doe* "Wealthy guard"

Daniel: *Dan-yel* "God is my judge"

Jose: *Hoe-zay* "One who pardons"

Alcor: *All-core* "The forgotten one"

Patli: *Paht-lee* "Medicine" / "Healing"

Enrique: *En-ree-ke* "Home Ruler"

Huallpa: *Hwall-pah* "Warmth of the sun"

Frederico: *Freh-deh-ree-ko* "Peaceful ruler"

Zerlina: *Sehr-lee-nah* "Beautiful Dawn"

Churan: *Choo-rahn* "Savior"

Sarakshi: *Sah-rak-shee* "Good sight"

Atuq: *Ah-took* "Cunning like the fox"

Kunaq: *Koo-nak* "He who advises, counselor"

Kallpa: *Kall-pah* "With force"

Lucia: *Loo-see-ah* "Light"

Dante: *Dahn-tey* Steadfast, Enduring

Adan: **Ah-dan** "Earth"

Iskay: *Is-kay* "Second child"

Chusku: *Choos-koo* "Fourth child"

Maria: *Mah-ree-ah* "Beloved"

Filomila: *Fee-low-mee-lah* "Knowledge, Researcher"

Ianuaria: *Ee-oon-our-ree-ah* "Healer"

Kichka: *Keech-kah* "Thorn"

Acknowledgments

I'm not going to lie ...

Writing this book was HARD!

Everyone warned me that it would be, that second books are impossibly challenging, that it would be a struggle. I heard the phrases "sophomore slump" and "second book syndrome" but I thought; I know the story! I know what needs to happen next! I'm sure it'll be fine.

Oh, how naive I was!

HUGE thanks to everyone that read The Name-Bearer and took a moment to reach out to me to tell me how much you enjoyed it, and how exciting you were to read The Follower of Flowers. I can't stress enough how much that encouragement and support kept me writing, even when I thought my brain would melt and dribble out of my ears and my eyes would burn if I stared at the computer screen for another second.

Too much?

Once again I want to extend my endless gratitude to my amazing friend Cody Von Ruden, beta reader extraordinaire. You have a way of always knowing what it is that I am trying to accomplish, and find a way to get me there. You are constantly challenging me to deliver more than I think I can, and I am becoming a better writer because of you.

Thanks for always taking the time to reread a chapter, hop on a call, or leave me a slightly unhinged google doc comment!

An enormous thank you to my friend and fellow author Michael LaBorn, who was kind enough to not only beta read for me, but spend hours on the phone discussing changes, edits and ideas. You encourage me to work harder, do better, and do more, not only for me, but for our communities, and I am so grateful to call you a friend.

Thank you to my editor My'Kayle who made me aware of how many times I use the phrase "swallowed hard." He swallowed hard. She swallowed hard. We swallowed hard. I hear it now, thanks!

Mami y Papi - gracias again! Your continued support in my chosen career is the most encouraging thing in my life. I can't believe you didn't try to warn me off when I decided to quit my day job and pursue this full time! I love being a full-time author, and as scary as that can be sometimes, it's a lot less scary knowing I have you both in my corner. Gracias.

And to everyone who got to the end of this book, I appreciate your support more than I could ever say.

Thank you.